Quest of Eight Part Four: The Race to Virkio

Richard Reda

Quest of Eight Part Four: The Race to Virkio

Richard Reda

The Quest of Eight
Part Four: The Race to Virkio

Quest of Eight Part Four: The Race to Virkio

Richard Reda

The Quest of Eight
Part Four: The Race to Virkio

By
Richard Reda

Quest of Eight Part Four: The Race to Virkio

Richard Reda

This book is dedicated to our first eight Grandchildren

Summer
Lochen
Solveig
Sean
Natalie
Stella
Quinn
Liam

With a special thanks to my wife for her support and her editing and to Melanie Simon for her editing. And a special thanks to Quinn for the names of many of the characters.

Quest of Eight Part Four: The Race to Virkio

Richard Reda

Quest of Eight Part Four: The Race to Virkio

Richard Reda

Quest of Eight Part Four: The Race to Virkio

Richard Reda

The Quest of Eight Part Four: The Race to Virkio

Chapter one

When the mining operation that the Rebbercands had forced the Trepans to undertake was disrupted by the release of the Scyllas, B'nair had immediately run into a nearby side tunnel to hide. He watched in horror as the complete project that had been his idea came to a crashing end. As chaos reigned down, he could see that the attack from the Scyllas was being supplemented by forces of some kind of underground rebellion. He caught glimpses of spells being cast and shots being fired from a slingshot. He was determined not to let whoever was behind all this get away with it – at least not unscathed. He ran through the tunnel in an effort to work his way to the source of that unexpected intervention.

As he crept through the twists and turns of the underground channels, he heard a sound of someone or something moving behind him. He stopped and turned. He then moved cautiously in the direction of the sound. He had seen the damage inflicted by the Scyllas and didn't relish the thought of running into one of them. On the other hand, if the noises were coming from an escaped Trepan, or whoever had helped them revolt, then he intended that they pay dearly for their actions. Then the sound stopped.

He held his whip loosely in his hand and as quietly as possible stepped forward. He was inching his way along a narrow path, careful not to make a sound that would give away his presence. He was certain that whatever he was following had no safe place to go. Maybe it had run into a dead end and was trapped. If it came charging back towards him, he wanted to be as ready as he could. As the darkness dissipated, he could see that the source of the noise was a small forest creature hunched down, trying to hide.

"Well, look what I found," B'nair said in a low voice. "I'll bet you're a Dozor."

He grinned and let out a low rumbling chuckle that was anything but humorous. He was glad the sound hadn't come from a Scylla. He recognized the figure as a forest creature. This was going to be much easier – and much more satisfying, he thought to himself.

"I like Dozors," he said, in a taunting voice. "I usually can't eat one all by myself, though. But in your case I'll make an exception."

As he took a step forward, the forest creature shifted his position for only a second and fired at him with his slingshot. Then he ducked back in his hiding place. B'nair saw the stone coming. He immediately flicked his whip and struck it in mid-flight. At least he's making a fight of this, B'nair thought. That will make destroying him all the sweeter.

"You'll have to do better than that," he goaded the Dozor.

B'nair was pelted with two successive stones quickly fired from the slingshot. He cracked his whip and brushed both shots aside in a single motion. He had to admit the little guy was fast and accurate. It would be wise not to underestimate him, he thought. What he lacks in size he makes up for in courage.

Two more shots came his way as the forest creature turned and scurried down the path, picking up more stones and taking more shots as he fled. Very few of them even came close to B'nair. He cracked his whip and it snapped within inches of the Dozor's head, as he seemed to stop at a fork in the path and to debate about which way to go. The crack of the whip helped him decide to go to the right. B'nair knew where that path led. He had been through these tunnels extensively over the last several months. He was leading the forest creature right into a trap.

B'nair followed behind him and watched as his small foe scooted across a very narrow bridge and slipped on the slick stone, nearly falling. The bridge was only inches wide and smooth as glass. As the forest creature regained his balance, he looked down. Past the shimmering milky colored bridge was a fissure so deep the bottom couldn't be seen, but the heat flowing up from the river of lava far below was unmistakable. The Dozor carefully made his way across the bridge and followed the narrow ledge as it curved around to the right. And there it ended. He was up against a solid wall with no other avenue of escape.

B'nair could see the panic on his face as he spun around and started to run back to the bridge only to stop suddenly when he found B'nair standing in the center, looking directly across the circular expanse that separated them. B'nair shifted his eyes between the narrow bridge and his target. He wished the bridge was a little wider, but he'd be off of it soon enough.

"Suppertime," B'nair said with that same rumbling chuckle.

He was inching sideways. His movement and his weight caused some of the ground at one end of the bridge to shift. He spread his arms to maintain his balance. He could feel that the bridge was starting to give way. He knew he had to get off quickly. As he looked down to make sure of his footing, the forest creature took advantage of this momentary distraction and fired a stone with all his strength. The stabbing sensation in B'nair's right eye brought his attention back to the small enemy firing at him. He reached up with his free hand to cover the eye. Blood poured through his fingers. He'd played games long enough. It was time to bring this to an end.

"I'll eat you slowly just for that," growled B'nair threateningly as he continued to side step along the bridge.

13

More ground shifted and debris slid down the side of the cliff to the abyss below. This time two quick shots struck B'nair's knee. It felt like his knee was on fire. He had mistakenly assumed the forest creature would have given up by now. The stinging sensation in his knee traveled up his leg. When he bent down reflexively to grab it, he threw his balance off and started slipping. His arms were flailing and he stood upright to regain his balance on the shifting bridge, but he overcompensated. It looked like he was about to fall when the Dozor stood up and shouted, "That's for what you did to my people."

As B'nair continued to flail his arms his feet began slipping more and more. They were starting to slide on the slick surface of the bridge. He knew he was falling. Just before he toppled over he snapped his whip in the forest creature's direction, wrapping the end tightly around his narrow ankle. Unable to regain his balance, B'nair dropped off the bridge and down towards the bubbling lava deep in the darkness below. The whip drew taught and yanked the Dozor off the ledge. He flew at the bridge and caught it in his arms. The whip tightened around his ankle with B'nair's weight pulling on the other end.

B'nair was prepared to splash into the river of lava below. It was a fitting death for a warrior, especially since he would be taking one of his enemies with him. He looked up at the small creature holding on to the thin expanse of stone with both his arms. He wondered how long the little person could hang there, keeping the two of them suspended. His thoughts were distracted when he heard another voice.

"Hold on, Sean. I'll get you," shouted a giant who was running towards the bridge.

Not to be robbed, B'nair yanked on the whip. He tried to yank the forest creature's grip loose. The forest creature wrapped his arms more tightly around the narrow bridge and was holding on with all his strength. B'nair watched from the other end of the whip as he hung

14

several feet below. When it looked like the Dozor was losing strength and releasing his grasp, the giant landed with a grunt, slid along the narrow overpass and caught the Dozor's arm, just as his strength gave out.

They hung there, the two of them suspended over the chasm. The giant sprawled and straddling the thin stone bridge holding on to the Dozor's arm, with the whip still wrapped around his ankle and B'nair dangling at the other end looking up in surprise. Then B'nair thought it would be an even better end if he took two of them with him instead of just the one. The ground around the far end of the bridge gave way some more, and it was apparent that it would not hold for much longer. B'nair started to swing to increase the pressure, twisting the whip with his weight. He was intent on pulling two enemies with him into the abyss. The giant started to wiggle backwards off the bridge, but only managed to dislodge it even more. At the same time his grip on the forest creature was starting to weaken.

Just when B'nair was certain neither the forest creature nor the giant could hold on much longer, he heard another noise in the distance. It was footsteps running towards them.

"Careful," he heard the giant shout. "There's a tiny bridge that's holding all of us and it's about to give."

B'nair wasn't sure whom he was shouting to, but he was almost overjoyed at the thought of taking a third with him. He pulled himself up on the handle of the whip, twisting it around his fist. He could feel the bridge move slightly and some of the dirt and stone near the loosening edge dropped passed him into the lava below. Then he heard something whiz through the air a few feet over his head and saw the flash of a blade as it sliced through the whip, cutting it cleanly. In an instant B'nair dropped into the abyss, robbed of even the slightest of victories. As he was plummeting downward, he heard the ground over his head shift more significantly. A smile crept over his face as he heard the bridge slide away from the edge and drop down after him. The last thing he heard was "I wish I was home," followed by a boom that echoed off the sides of the chasm and a flash of blue light.

The force of the shock wave threw him against the cavern wall. He scraped and slid along the wall, scrabbling for a handhold as sharp edges cut into his skin. He seemed to fall forever, but in reality he landed a few short seconds later with a crash on a ledge that jutted out from the side. The landing was bone crushing and the heat was intense. He wasn't sure how he got turned around, but he was flat on his stomach. His head and his right arm hung over the edge of the shelf. His hair singed and his skin began to burn. The leather armor he wore absorbed the heat from the lava below and was baking him alive.

He tried to move, but it felt as if his legs no longer worked. He pushed himself up with his left hand. His right hung limply, dangling over the rising heat. He managed to slide back enough to slow the burning he felt on his head and face, but his strength gave out and he fell back to the ground. It was difficult to breathe. His ribs were throbbing and it felt like he was sucking boiling syrup into his lungs. He had no sensation in his right arm and was unaware that his hand was severely burned. He was in agony. His eyes clouded over with pain and his vision blurred. He was sure his end was near.

He felt something grab his legs and pull. The sharp pain rejuvenated his senses. He kicked out with his legs and rolled over. The heat had filled his eyes with tears. He could only see vague shapes reaching for him. He felt hands on his legs again, and he tried to lift his head up, but the stabbing sensation in his back and neck nearly made him black out. He had no more strength to fight, and could only allow himself to be pulled. The little light that existed in the fissure disappeared and he was in total darkness. As he was moved, his head scraped against the floor of the cave through which he was being pulled. The charred skin was ripping off, and in spite of the excruciating pain, he was too weak to lift his head. At this point he no longer cared.

"If you're going to kill me, do it now," he mumbled.

His voice came out in a dry crack. He had breathed in so much heated air that his throat was burned nearly as badly as his skin. His attempt at speech failed him and he began to cough and wheeze. He was sure he was choking, as the spasms wracked his body. He could feel several hands at different places on his body and he could hear low rumbling voices interspersed with grunting sounds. He wasn't sure, but he believed he had been lifted off the ground. He also believed that the heat was decreasing, but only slightly.

He could barely notice any of this, though. He had drifted in and out of a state of semi-consciousness. His armor had trapped heat inside and his skin was burning. He had been dragged by his legs along an uneven dirt path. If they hadn't been broken by his fall, he felt certain that they were broken now. He was awake enough to feel the pain, but not clear-headed enough to be aware of what was going on. He had been dragged, and then carried, and then the moving stopped – or maybe he had blacked out. He couldn't recall. Now he felt himself being lifted and then lowered not altogether gently onto a wooden floor. The floor was moving, he thought. Why would it be moving?

The wooden floor shifted and bounced. He heard a creaking sound. He was on some kind of cart, he reasoned. His head rocked from side to side. The raw and bleeding skin scraped against the rough wood every time the cart moved, sending jolts of pain into his skull. He could take no more. Gathering all his strength, he lifted his head up as high as he could. He didn't bother to look at his surroundings. He wasn't interested. Instead, he slammed his head back down against the cart, knocking himself unconscious; finally relieving his pain, if only momentarily.

------------------ *** ------------------

"Is he alive," a voice asked.

Quest of Eight Part Four: The Race to Virkio

Richard Reda

"Of course he's alive," another answered. "You can hear him breathing, can't you?"

"Yes, but will he live?"

"That's up to him."

"I don't think he's going to live. Look at him. Saving him was a waste of time. Even if he lives, what good will he be?"

The sounds of the voices were barely more than a buzzing noise to B'nair. They were enough, though, to bring him out of the darkness. As his mind struggled to awaken, the torment his body had been through was also awakened. His mouth, throat and lungs were on fire. Every breath was like swallowing sand.

"Water," he managed to croak.

"Here," one of the voices answered. "I'm going to lift your head a bit, but it's going to be painful."

He was right. The pain was searing.

"Sip it slowly," the voice told him. "Not too much."

The water was warm, but it soothed his mouth. His throat, however, rebelled as the muscles contracted to swallow. He choked and coughed. Pain shot through his body. Eventually, the coughing subsided and he fell back into the blackness of sleep.

Several days went by in the same manner. He would slowly awaken, ask for water, and then pass out from the pain caused by the choking. In spite of this, his benefactors maintained their vigilance, tending to his broken bones and his burned flesh, and gradually getting more fluids into his system. Finally, one day, he was able to drink without choking and he was able to remain conscious. He could tell that his head was bandaged. His eyes were covered and he could feel something like bandages on his face. He flexed his arms. The right one was still numb, but the left one seemed fine, although sore. He moved his legs and discovered that one was in a splint. He flexed his back and stomach, learning that aside from being stiff and sore, there seemed to be no injuries there.

"Where am I?" he finally asked.

"You're safe," his caretaker answered.

"That's not what I asked," he rasped.

"No. It's not," the voice responded. "You're in a cave. Does that tell you anything?"

"No. It tells me nothing. I've been in caves for the last several months. One cave is like any other."

"Well, then, it seems that where you are really doesn't matter, does it?"

"Who are you?" B'nair asked.

"That's a better question. My name is Ercon. I am the leader of the hobgoblins. And for the time being, I'm the one who is caring for you."

"Why?"

"I'm not sure, to tell you the truth. At least not yet, but we can come back to that when you're feeling a little better."

"And when will that be?" B'nair asked after thinking for a few seconds about the last comment.

Quest of Eight Part Four: The Race to Virkio

Richard Reda

"That's hard to say," said Ercon. "A lot happened to you and we don't have much in the way of potions or medicines, I'm sorry to say. Of course, I could take you to a healer – an alchemist or an enchantress, perhaps, but I don't think you'd get the kind of care you really need."

B'nair wheezed a slight chuckle at that.

"No. I don't expect I would. What happened to me?"

"None of us understands what caused your fall, but fall you most certainly did. You dropped into one of the chasms over the lava field. Something pushed you against the wall, which was fortunate. You appeared to have slid down the wall and landed on the lip of a tunnel, which was both fortunate and not so fortunate. It was fortunate since it kept you from falling into the lava, but you broke your leg in the fall – that would probably be in the not so fortunate category. You also fell in such a way that your head and right arm hung over the ledge: again, not so fortunate. Your leg seems to be healing all right, but the burns are another matter. What exactly were you doing that put you in such jeopardy?"

B'nair was cautious about what information he was willing to reveal. Since his eyes were covered and he couldn't see whom he was talking to, he was reluctant to believe what he was being told and, therefore, reluctant to share anything that might be used against him.

"I was exploring."

Ercon waited for B'nair to expand upon this. The silence lingered for several seconds. When he realized no further explanation was going to be provided, Ercon filled the void.

"Exploring," he repeated. "It seems you might want to consider another line of interest. This one doesn't appear to agree with you. For now, get some rest. We'll discuss this further when you have recovered a little more."

B'nair could hear his visitor walk away, but he was suspicious enough to believe that he probably wasn't alone. It didn't matter, though. He knew he was in no condition to go anywhere. He reached up with his left hand and touched the bandages that covered his face and head. He pressed gently on the left side and felt no pain. He had a different result when he touched the right side of his face. The tenderness extended from the center of his forehead to just behind his ear, and from the top of his head to a line extending from his nose to the bottom of his ear. That must have been where his head hung over the ledge, he thought.

He could feel nothing with his right hand. Running his left hand down his arm from the shoulder, he discovered a burning sensation beginning at the elbow and ending at his wrist. He could feel the burned skin with his left hand but he couldn't feel the pressure on it from his left hand. It was difficult to determine the extent of the damage through the thick bandages. The hand was still there. That much he could tell. But he couldn't understand why he didn't feel anything.

Another week went by. Ercon met with him every day; sometimes several times a day. B'nair remained vague about the reasons for his presence in the underground tunnels, in spite of Ercon's comments about the Trepans and how the hobgoblins normally kept away and hidden from them.

"Don't misunderstand," he was quick to explain. "We don't fear them. But they have some powerful friends, and we've learned it's better to be discrete about our activities."

B'nair wanted desperately to know to whom Ercon was referring when he mentioned the powerful friends. He wanted to know who had aided in the Trepans' rebellion; who had brought his operation to a grinding halt; who had done this to him. He knew about the Dozor and the giant that had rescued him, but he had no idea who the other

21

one was – the one that cut the whip. Were there others? Finally, his curiosity won out.

"Who are you talking about? Who are these powerful friends?"

"The same ones who cast the Rebbercands out of their homeland and made them nomads."
"What?" B'nair hadn't expected this response. He had been so fixated on the Trepan rebellion, that he hadn't considered anything beyond the most recent incidents. "What are you talking about?"

"The history of your people. The history of my people. Do you think what happened a few short weeks ago was an accident? Do you believe we don't know who you are and what you were doing? Do you think we're stupid?"

B'nair could hear Ercon stand up and start to walk out of the room. His last comment had been shouted in anger. B'nair tried to lift himself up. He was only able to roll over onto his side.

"Wait," he called to Ercon.

The sudden exertion was more than he was able to handle. He had twisted his leg, aggravating the break. His shouted call had put more pressure on his still healing throat. He began to cough and choke. Exhausted, he rolled onto his back, trying to control his breathing and waiting for the pain to subside.

"Please wait," he managed to say, not knowing if Ercon was still there to hear him.

"I'm still here," Ercon answered.

B'nair could tell from the sound of his voice that he was on the other side of the room. He waited a few seconds until his breathing returned to normal and he could gather his thoughts.

"No. I don't think you're stupid," he said. "We…I am suspicious by nature. Among my people that's not considered a character flaw. It's a necessity. I can't help what I am, and I make no apologies for it. You and your people saved my life and have cared for me. I am not ungrateful, but I only have your word on who <u>you</u> are and what <u>you're</u> doing down here. It is not in my nature to trust what I can't see."

Ercon considered this before answering.

"I take your point."

He took a few steps closer to B'nair.

"Perhaps I've been too impatient. You should be able to remove the bandages from your head tomorrow. Let's allow that to take place, and then we can consider where to go from there. You're right. It will be better when we can look each other in the eye."

Without waiting for a response, Ercon turned and left the room, and left B'nair to his thoughts. He had always considered himself a decisive individual, but he didn't feel that way now. He was beginning to realize what an impediment his physical limitations had become. He was also beginning to realize how much he was at the mercy of his caretaker. It wouldn't do to alienate this person or whomever this person was with. He had no reason to distrust Ercon, but still, he felt more like a prisoner than a patient. If he had been asked, though, he would be unable to explain why he had this feeling.

He thought about the last weeks. During much of it he was unconscious or semi-conscious. He had no recollection of who fed him, cleaned him or tended his injuries. More recently he had assumed that there was someone in the room with him. He doubted that Ercon would perform those tasks. That made him wonder if he was alone at this precise moment.

"Is anyone there?" he asked. "Can I have some water?"

The fact that no one answered didn't mean no one was there. As he had said to Ercon, he was suspicious by nature. Those suspicions had served him well in the past. He decided to try something different. He stretched out his left arm and felt along his side. He was on some kind of low bed or pallet. He rolled over onto his left side and carefully slid his right leg around, at the same time pushing with his left hand and moving up to a sitting position. The effort nearly wore him out, but he heard no sign of anyone coming to stop or help him.

He was too low to the ground to stand up. He couldn't move his right leg or situate himself to rise. He scooted off the pallet onto the floor and then rolled over onto his stomach. He curled his left leg under him and tried to push himself up to his hands and knees with his left hand. He was off balance and not strong enough to compensate. He fell towards his right and reflexively stuck out his right arm to stop his fall. Without any feeling in his right hand, he couldn't tell when it made contact with the floor and it wasn't ready to support him. He crashed down on his right side, twisting his right leg in the process. Try as he might, he couldn't keep himself from screaming out in pain. He heard footsteps running into the room. He couldn't tell if the sound came from one or more people. If someone had been in the room with him, he was very well disciplined.

"What are you doing?" shouted Ercon. "Where do you think you're going?"

"Water," gasped B'nair, gritting his teeth through the pain. "I only wanted some water."

"Of course," answered Ercon. "I should have thought of that."

His words were apologetic, but B'nair didn't sense that in his voice. Ercon managed to move B'nair back onto the pallet, and got some water for him.

"I'll make sure someone is here with you until you can care for yourself."

B'nair considered the pain was worth it. Whether he was being spied upon or not, he had forced Ercon's hand. In a few minutes, he heard another person enter the room. Whoever it was sat on the floor a few feet away from the pallet.

"If you need anything," Ercon announced, without introducing the attendant, "you need only ask. Someone will be here to get it for you."
When he heard Ercon leave the room, B'nair turned his head slightly towards where he assumed his nursemaid was sitting.

"What's your name?" he asked.

"Camin," came the response.

B'nair couldn't tell if the voice was masculine or feminine, not that he cared either way. Judging from the sound, he had guessed right about the person sitting on the floor and being on the opposite side of the room.
"So, Camin. Where are we exactly?"

"In a cave."

B'nair started to smile. "Ah. A man of few words. I like that. You _are_ a man, aren't you?"

Camin uttered an indistinct grunt, not really responding either way. B'nair only continued to chuckle. After a while, he drifted off to sleep. He had been recalling Ercon's words that tomorrow the bandages over his eyes would be removed. His last thoughts were that since he couldn't see light or dark, he wouldn't really know when tomorrow was. It felt like he had just fallen asleep when he heard a voice.

Quest of Eight Part Four: The Race to Virkio

Richard Reda

"Are you ready?" it asked.

B'nair struggled to clear his head. He wasn't sure he recognized the voice.

"Ready for what?" he asked. "Who are you?"

"I'm your healer, Rebbercand. I'm the one who set your leg, bandaged your burns and cleaned up after you. I understand you tried to undo all my hard work yesterday by trying to crawl out of bed. That's not my idea of an expression of gratitude. Now are you ready?"

"I don't know," B'nair answered, clearly confused. "Ready for what?"

"To get the bandages off your head," the healer answered gruffly. "What else? Are you ready for anything else? I don't think so."

B'nair never had anyone speak to him in this manner. He wasn't sure how to react. He felt a pair of hands reach under his arms and move him to a sitting position.

"Let's get you upright first," the healer said. "Be careful of that leg."

The hands gently moved his broken leg around. This was much easier and less painful than his attempt to sit up yesterday had been. He heard another person approach.

"Do you think the burns have healed?" the person asked. B'nair recognized Ercon's voice.

"The poultice has been on for over two weeks. The skin will still be tender, and there will be a lot of scar tissue, but right now it needs air. So, for the third time, Rebbercand; are you ready?"

"My name is B'nair," he said with more confidence than he felt. "And yes, I'm ready. Let's get this over with."

"Very well," the voice answered. "Here. Drink this first."

"What is it," B'nair asked as he felt a cup being placed in his left hand.

"It's tea. It will help you relax while we tear away the bandages."

"I don't need tea, and I don't need to relax."

"If you flinch or move at all, you're liable to pull away from the poultice at the wrong time. If you do that, then the skin may tear. If that happens, we'll have to wrap you in another poultice, to seal the break, but in doing so, it will cause the other parts of your skin to necrotize. Do you know what that means? No? I didn't think so. It means the skin will rot. But it will be rotting under a poultice, so I won't be able to see how fast that's happening or to what extent. It could cause an infection that could seep into your brain. Now, drink the tea or don't. It makes no difference to me."

B'nair thought for only a second, and then he drank the entire cup.

"Keep your eyes closed until I tell you," the healer ordered. "The poultice is designed to heal burned skin. It's not meant to get into your eyes."

B'nair could hear a knife cutting into the edge of the bandage material. The healer cut the covering away from one ear, over the top and down to the other ear. Then he cut it from front to back. Starting with the back pieces, he gently pealed them away and wiped off any seepage from the wounds or excess salve that had not dried. He had been right about the skin being tender. To B'nair it felt like he was using a wire brush on open cuts.

Once the first section had been removed, the healer started on the second section. B'nair was becoming impatient; it was taking so long. With the second section finally removed, the entire back of his head was uncovered. He reached his left hand back to feel. At the sound of the healer's voice, he stopped in midair.

"Be careful," warned the healer. "The skin is still healing. It won't take much to tear it open, but you can go ahead and feel it. You won't ever be growing hair again – at least not there."

B'nair hesitated a moment, then slowly placed his hand on the back of his head. Though sensitive to the touch, his skin felt leathery and rough. The bristly hair that had covered it was gone completely. In its place was a network of scars. He pulled his hand down and told the healer to keep going. The next section was the right side of his face. The healer was especially careful in pealing the poultice away from the ear. When it was cleared, he blotted at the skin, cleaning it off.

"Can I open that eye?" asked B'nair.

The healer wavered before answering.

"It's already open. I'm afraid that eye was lost."

A wave of despair swept over B'nair. That was immediately followed by a sense of panic.

"What about the other one?" he asked. "Was that lost, too?"

"I don't think so," answered the healer. "It wasn't burned like the right one, although there was some damage to the retina. We'll find out soon enough."

The healer worked as quickly as he could, but the wait was excruciating for B'nair. This last section of his head had suffered the least amount of damage. When the poultice had been removed and the remnants cleaned away, he opened his eye. The cave was dark and the figures before him were little more than shadows.

"You were right, healer," he said. "This one is not lost, but I can barely see anything."

"No, it's not," the healer responded. "But it's still damaged. You will be very sensitive to light. Do you understand me? You must not expose it to full daylight; otherwise you could further damage it. Anything lighter than that and you'll lose your vision completely. We have reduced the light in here as much as we can. Camin will gradually increase it at my direction, but only gradually. You must not rush. Am I clear?"

"Yes. I understand. What about my arm and leg?"

"We can unwrap the arm now, if you like. The leg, however, needs to remain in a splint for another month."

"Yes. Please remove the bandages from my arm."

B'nair watched as the healer slowly removed the dressing from his arm. The room was lit by a candle off to his side. He saw the healer nod towards the darkness and another candle appeared. At first the increased light was too much for him and he squinted and turned his head away. Slowly he adapted to it and could see the healer's hands at work. The hair covering those hands was very similar to the hair on B'nair's arms – at least to what he had before it was burned off. The skin, though, appeared to be grey. At first he thought that the lack of color might be due to the low light. Without being aware, a third candle had been added to the room and B'nair could clearly see the grey skin color.

The healer's hands where long and thin. B'nair's were short and stubby, with thick fingers. When the healer asked Ercon to hold B'nair's arm steady, he saw a pair of hands that looked more like his, but with the same grey color as the healer's. His attention was diverted to his own arm as the poultice was cut away.

Quest of Eight Part Four: The Race to Virkio

Richard Reda

His forearm was devoid of hair and the skin looked like what he imagined his head looked like. It was covered with a network of scars and welts. The skin color darkened towards his wrist. When all the coverings had been removed, he saw immediately why he could feel nothing. His hand, his fingers and his thumb were black and charred. He held them close to his face to get a better look. He tried flexing them, but nothing happened.

"What happened?" he asked, too shocked to react.

"The burning was too extensive," answered the healer. "The heat from the lava bed was too intense. The radiation crystallized the tissue, turning it to carbonized stone. I'm sorry, but there was nothing we could do."

The reality of his situation was slowly sinking in. He stared with his one salvaged eye at the hardened, misshapen object at the end of his arm. He lowered his arm and, leaning slightly forward, tapped it against the stone floor. He felt nothing, but could hear the echo of stone on stone.

"Be careful," warned the healer. "The connecting bone and muscle are still weak. You could break your hand off completely."

"And what difference would that make," shouted B'nair. "This...this... thing is no more use to me than a stump would be!"

He tried to rise, but his broken leg wouldn't cooperate. He flailed his arm in frustration, seemingly ready to smash it into the floor when he was overcome with an intense feeling of fatigue. He tried to shake it off, assuming he was reacting to the trauma of having the bandages removed and of discovering the damage to his hand. He felt overwhelmed by exhaustion, and then it struck him.

"That wasn't tea, was it?"

"No," admitted the healer. "I lied. I thought you might react this way. It was a strong sedative. You're going to fall asleep now. When you wake up we can discuss some exercises you can do to strengthen your leg and we'll discuss what to do about your arm. I'll be back when the potion wears off."

"The arm is useless," B'nair slurred. "Might as well cut it off."

"We'll see," said the healer, but B'nair was already unconscious and didn't hear him. "We'll see."

B'nair slept fitfully the rest of the day, into the night and until the next morning. He was awakened by a gentle shaking. He opened his one good eye and struggled to focus in the dim light.

"Camin," he heard the healer say. "Bring the light closer."

As the room gradually brightened, B'nair watched as the shadows took shape and the images became clearer. There were three of them. The one holding the candle was obviously Camin. He knew one of the others was the healer, by his voice. He assumed the third was Ercon. He stared at them in stunned silence. Despite some individual differences, they all looked similar.

They were about the same height he was, but not as heavy. Still, they were shaped much the same - like a barrel: rounded and thicker in the middle. Atop each of their lean, but rounded bodies was a large head with bristling hair. He almost reached up to feel his own missing hair, the similarity was so close. Their eyes were larger than his, but close set on either side of a large round upturned snout and a wide mouth with two large fangs rising up from a lower jaw nearly to the outside edges of their snout. Where his fangs were straight, theirs tended to curl somewhat outward. Their arms were large and muscular and ended in long, thin fingers.

Aside from some minimal distinctions and the overall grey and wrinkled appearance of their skin, they looked uncomfortably like him.

"What trick is this?" he demanded. "Who are you people?"

"Hello, cousin," answered Ercon with a wide grin.

Chapter two

B'nair could only stare at the three of them in silence. At first he wasn't sure he had heard Ercon correctly. Did he call him cousin? Did he use that term on purpose, or did he mean nothing by it? What was he talking about? Who were these people? The room suddenly felt like it was closing in on him. The events that had recently unfolded – his damaged hand, his lost eye, the burns, and now this – were flooding over him. He struggled to get to his feet only to find himself restrained. He jerked his arms in an attempt to free himself. His legs were bound to the pallet, as were his arms and his chest.

"What have you done?" he bellowed. "Why have you restrained me? Release me this instant! Let me out of here!"

"Calm yourself," said the healer in a low voice. "You will come to no harm. Think about it. If we wanted to hurt you, we would have done so already."

"Then why have you tied me down?" he shot back. "Do you view me as a threat, even with these injuries?"

"For your own safety," answered Ercon. "We are not unmindful of the disturbing news you received yesterday – the loss of your eye; the damage to your hand. You found yourself in a strange place, surrounded by strangers. It was clear that you were distraught. We wanted to ensure that you did nothing drastic."

B'nair gave one more pull against the restraints and then accepted his fate. He dropped his head back down to the pallet and relaxed. His mind was racing, trying to find a way to escape, and trying to understand what was happening.

"You called me cousin," he finally said, turning to look back at Ercon. "Is that a term you use for anyone, or am I special?"

"I did," he responded. "And, no. I do not use that term casually. I called you cousin, because we are."

"I thought you said you were a hobgoblin. I'm a Rebbercand. I've never seen your kind before. How is it that you believe we are cousins?"

"I am a hobgoblin. That's correct. Admittedly, our parents were not directly related, but we have the same ancestors. I suppose it may be a stretch to consider us to be actual cousins; however, we share a common origin."

"How is it then that I don't know anything about this? How do you explain the fact that none of this has ever been mentioned in any Rebbercand lore?"

"I don't know what you've been told or not been told. And I don't know what you've chosen to ignore or forget. Tell me this, though. Do you know of an ancient Enchantress named Meri Hocto? Or of her accomplice – an Alchemist?"

"No," he answered. "I don't know that name, and I know nothing of an Alchemist. Neither is familiar to me."

"What about two powerful sorcerers who were long ago cursed and exiled, or a stone that is the key to their imprisonment?"

"I've told you, I..." B'nair was on the verge of denying any knowledge of the sorcerers or the stone, when something stopped him.

"Ah, you do know something. What is it? Have you heard something about the sorcerers? Or the stone. It's one or the other. I can see it in your face," Ercon said.

"I...I'm not sure," answered B'nair. He was struggling to recall. "I'm trying to remember what it was."

"It's the stone, isn't it?" Ercon tried to encourage him. "I saw the flicker of recognition when I mentioned the stone."

"Yes, there was something about a stone, but there was more," B'nair replied.

He debated for a moment about revealing anything. He didn't know what importance this information held for his captor. Or if this person was just that: his captor. Or was he a savior? He wasn't sure if what little bit he could recall meant anything at all. He decided to reveal it and see how it was used.

"It was something my brother once said," he finally continued. "I dismissed it at the time as foolishness. He was insistent about following the direction of some stone he had found. He said that he

35

could feel the stone pulling him to search for some undefined power. He argued with me constantly about it."

"Does he still have the stone?" asked Ercon.

"I'm sure he does," B'nair answered. "He never let it out of his possession. He never even showed it to me. He only spoke of it."
"And where is he now? Where is the stone?"

"I have no idea," said B'nair. "I had ordered him to oversee the construction of a monument, but he argued with me. He said we were wasting our time memorializing the past. I gave him a menial assignment because of his insubordination. He was away from the mining operation when it all collapsed. I don't know where he is now. In fact, I don't even know where I am now or when 'now' is."

"You're in the caverns of the hobgoblins," explained the healer, "about ten miles from where you were mining with the Trepans. And you have been in our care for almost three weeks. There is no sign above of any Rebbercands. After the collapse of the mine and the attack on the settlement, they all seem to have disappeared."

"From what we could tell, you had not been in that settlement long. Where would they likely go next?" Ercon asked.

"I don't know," B'nair answered. "We never know where we're going when we move our villages. They could be anyplace."

"Maybe we can send out search parties and find them," the healer said in a low voice to Ercon. "They can't have gone too far in three weeks."

Ercon turned to the healer and said, "No. They are not confined to traveling by land or by any distance. They travel until they decide not to. We could send out a hundred search parties and may never find them. I think we must return our attention to Virkio. If we can break through the last tower and obtain that stone, it should lead us to the others; including the one the Rebbercand's brother has."

B'nair listened intently, and then interrupted what had become a private conversation between Ercon and the healer.

"You'll never find them unless they want to be found. We are able to move quickly and cover great distances," B'nair said; and then diverting their attention asked, "What is this 'Virkio' you mentioned?" Ercon thought a minute before answering. The hobgoblins had followed the movements of the Rebbercands for centuries. He wasn't as sure as B'nair was that they would remain hidden for long, but he also knew that much time could be wasted locating them again. He considered the person before him. He knew his patient was a powerful leader of the Rebbercands, and that the hobgoblins were rooted in the same family tree with them. But he also knew that B'nair had nearly died; that he was far from being recovered and may never fully recover. How much use would he be to them? Could he be the leader they had been looking for? He considered the rage that B'nair had demonstrated when he discovered he had been restrained. There is still a fire within him, thought Ercon. He is still a leader.

"It is the fortress of the Alchemist," Ercon finally said, deciding to gamble on B'nair's future with the hobgoblins.

"The Alchemist – again. Who is this Alchemist? I don't understand any of this."

B'nair was realizing that there was much of his own history that he didn't know. He was also beginning to regret not having paid closer attention to his brother's diatribes. Maybe he knew more than B'nair had given him credit for. He had much to learn. He wondered if this hobgoblin would be the one to provide the explanations, and, if he was, would the hobgoblin trust him enough to do so? B'nair had not yet accepted the claim that they were long lost cousins. That was about to change.

Quest of Eight Part Four: The Race to Virkio

Richard Reda

"Let me begin at the beginning," explained Ercon; and he began to describe the series of events that happened so long ago, and set the course on which they found themselves today.

He took B'nair back to the citadel of the Enchantress, Meri Hocto. He explained what he knew about life in the Rebbercand village where Meri had inserted herself. He shared what little he knew about the sorcerers Ena Ray and Tebaga. As with similar tales, his version was not completely accurate, but it was close enough that the deviations from reality were unimportant.

He couldn't tell much about Tebaga, other than that he was a student, as was Ena Ray. At some point in their development, Ena Ray had become the leader of a group of Rebbercands who were overseen by a person named Grewt. How and why they were in pursuit of a mystical pendant was still uncertain, but what was known was that Ena Ray had discovered it. When he had secured it, he was confronted and attacked by the witch, Meri Hocto. Grewt had been there to witness their battle.

The witch had railed at Ena Ray, accusing him of betrayal. In a fit of rage she struck him with a lightning bolt. The bolt tore him apart and sent his spirit into exile in some far off prison. As the bolt struck Ena Ray, it shattered the pendant into several pieces. One of those pieces grazed Grewt, cutting into his forehead before glancing off and disappearing. The piece that struck him splintered and imbedded a tiny sliver in the gash. The remnant that broke off was about an inch long and thinner than a needle. It split from the larger fragment, striking Grewt's head and burrowing into the bone of his skull. Recovering quickly, but in an attempt too late to save the sorcerer, Grewt fired his crossbow at the witch, striking her in the back.

Seeing that his blow wasn't fatal, and that she was only wounded, he reached behind him to pick up the weapon of a fallen comrade – a large double-bladed axe. He stepped forward in quick long strides, the axe raised to finish off the witch when she cast her final spell.

"I banish you and your kind to the underworld. Your image shall be cast to reflect your souls," she gasped with her dying breath.

In a flash of green light, Grewt and the rest of Ena Ray's followers were turned into gargoyles and driven deep underground. But as the witch cast her spell, Grewt reacted by holding the axe up to defend himself. The axe didn't deflect the spell, but diverted some of its power, absorbing the brunt of the curse. The witch's spell blasted against the blade of the axe, sending a surge of energy down through the haft, sealing the axe to Grewt's hand.

In the blink of an eye, he was no longer in the Sanctorum of the Enchantress; he was no longer anywhere recognizable. He found himself in a warren of underground tunnels and caverns with hundreds of other displaced and transformed Rebbercands – the remains of the army of Ena Ray. He knew nothing of what had happened to the followers of Tebaga or to the rest of the Rebbercands in the village.

To add to his astonishment, the axe he had randomly picked up to finish off the witch was fused to his hand. Nothing he could do would release if from his grip. He tried everything imaginable short of cutting off his own hand, but nothing could separate it from his grip. It remained as a part of him until his death, at which time, that part of the spell on him was broken and the axe simply fell away.

Many of the followers of Ena Ray who were transformed into gargoyles remained living underground from generation to generation. For centuries they lived in the same caves and corridors to which they had been originally banished, with no direction or leadership and with no effort at making any changes. Not long ago, however, some unknown force descended upon them. They marshaled their forces in an effort to break the spell on Ena Ray and on them. No one person directed or led them. They seemed to be guided by some unseen power, only to be thwarted by a group of unknown adversaries – undoubtedly accomplices of the witch and the Alchemist.

Quest of Eight Part Four: The Race to Virkio

Richard Reda

Grewt, however, followed a different path. As the laceration on his head slowly healed, the particle left behind by the piece of the stone that struck him became more solidly imbedded. The stone has its own power. The sliver submerged beneath his skin and bone drove Grewt to find the other scattered pieces. He left the underground and found a small enclave of Rebbercands – some of the villagers who had been displaced. In spite of his altered appearance, they accepted him. His descendants became the present day hobgoblins.

In the years he lived with the Rebbercands he quickly rose to leadership. When he first found them, they were wandering – lost and frightened. They had not been among the followers of either of the two sorcerers who had been exiled by the witch. But they had been made to suffer from the same spell. The fact that an axe was welded to his hand made him a rather formidable figure. And since there was a void in their leadership, he quickly took advantage of the opportunity and assumed that role.

This lasted for several years. During this time, the pull of the fragment that had taken root beneath his skin became stronger and stronger. He began to have inexplicable and uncontrollable urges to search for the lost pieces of the pendant. He led his small band of cast out Rebbercands from one location to another. There seemed to be no pattern or logic to his travels. Many times he and his band encountered significant hostilities. Many of his followers were injured or lost in battles that could have been avoided. Grewt's obsession was blind to the dangers into which he all too often wandered. His role as leader faltered and began to come into question.

No one in his tribe of nomads had ever seen this stone; they knew nothing about the pendant or the witch or the two exiled sorcerers. For years they had listened to Grewt's claims and had followed him wherever he led them. Eventually, fewer and fewer believed him, and his leadership was challenged. By now, though, he no longer cared about leading the community. He only cared about finding the stone. He lapsed out of the leadership and that role was quickly filled by someone else. Grewt continued to be obsessed with finding the stone, but no one paid attention to him any longer.

One afternoon, when the wanderers had established another temporary home along the shores of the Veridian Ocean south of a huge mountain range, he was searching for clues as he always did. On this day, though, the fixation was stronger than it ever had been before. He knew he was close. He was hacking his way through the forest, several miles from the encampment when a blur of red swarmed around him. He had no idea what was happening. He heard a buzzing sound and felt like he was being stung by hundreds of insects. He ran blindly through the woods, trying to escape.

He swung his axe in the air, not sure if he was making contact with anything and not sure where he was going. He splashed across a stream and ran up the embankment. The stinging continued to follow him. He broke through a small clearing in the trees and tripped over a large root. Crashing to the ground, he slid through the low-lying grass. He was exhausted from his run and the stings were aggravating his skin. He was feeling a bit light-headed. He pushed himself up and crawled on his hands and knees past the clearing and into the woods on the other side.

The sun was filtering through the leaves and his eye was attracted to something reflecting the light. His initial thought was to disregard it, but when it flickered again, the particle of the stone long buried under the skin against his skull sent shock waves through his body. He struggled to his feet and staggered forward. For a second or two, he lost sight of the reflection and he started running. Sweat began pouring down his body; his head was swimming. He didn't understand what was wrong – what was happening to him. His forehead began to throb. His legs wobbled as he began to topple forward. Just as he dropped to the ground, the sunlight hit the object again and the light flashed. It was only a few yards in front of him.

Quest of Eight Part Four: The Race to Virkio

Richard Reda

He couldn't find any strength in his legs. He couldn't get his feet under him. He was pulling himself across the ground, his eyes fixated on the sparkling object ahead of him. Then he saw it. It was an oddly shaped stone – round on one side and nearly triangular. The two other edges were rough and broken. It was a reddish-brown in color, but the color seemed to shift as if reflecting clouds. He couldn't tell why, but he was certain this was one of the stones from the witch's pendant.

And then it seemed like the sky opened up. Light flooded the forest. It was followed by a rumble and the appearance of a figure standing between him and the stone. It was not very tall, but it was thin and covered in white. It had long white hair that blended into the clothing it wore.

"I've been looking for you," the figure said as it bent over and picked up the stone.

"No!" shouted Grewt. "It's mine."

The figure turned around and looked at him. He was holding the stone in his hand.

"You're the Alchemist," declared Grewt.

He had no idea how he knew this. He had never seen the Alchemist before, but he had heard about the wars the Alchemist and the Enchantress had been engaged in with the Kelpies. As this thought went through his mind, he realized that was not true. He had never heard about these wars – and he had never heard the witch referred to as the Enchantress. He knew nothing about Kelpies. In fact he had never heard of them before. Where were these thoughts coming from? They had to be coming from the stranger – the Alchemist.

"And you are a Rebbercand. In fact, you are the Rebbercand who shot the Enchantress," answered the Alchemist.

Quest of Eight Part Four: The Race to Virkio

Richard Reda

Grewt pulled himself forward, his eyes fixated on the stone held in the Alchemist's hand. He was dragging his body along; his legs useless for some reason he couldn't understand.

"Give me that," he demanded. "That stone is mine."

The Alchemist looked at the stone in his hand and then turned his gaze back to the creature crawling towards him. He knew others might know of the stone and the power it contained. He would have to keep this one well protected. In the meantime, he had to deal with the immediate situation.

"No," he responded. "It does not belong to you. It never belonged to you. Not any part of it, no matter how small."

He stretched out his free hand towards the Rebbercand, turned it palm upward and jerked it back towards his body. The sliver of the stone imbedded in Grewt's head shifted, pulling itself free to join the larger piece in the Alchemist's hand. The remnant slowly cut through the bone that had grown over it and the scar tissue of the skin. Once free, it shot across the expanse between Grewt and the Alchemist and attached itself to the piece in his hand.

Grewt cried out in pain. He stopped crawling. His left hand flew up to the re-opened wound on his head, too late to stop the splinter of the stone that had become part of him. Blood poured out of the cut, through his fingers and down his face. But before it left him, the power of the stone had opened a channel between him and the Alchemist. He knew where and how the stranger intended to hide and guard the piece that had been stolen from him.

"You and your kind were also cursed to live beneath the ground, as I recall," added the Alchemist. "Somehow you have managed to slither back to the surface. That, too, comes to an end here and now."

Quest of Eight Part Four: The Race to Virkio

Richard Reda

With another wave of his hand and a flash of light, Grewt disappeared. He found himself with the rest of his enclave deep in a cave beneath the ground. However, as the spell had been cast, Grewt had raised the hand that held the axe. It couldn't stop the spell, but it managed to deflect it – to diminish its power. His community would continue to live underground, but they were able to return to the surface in times of darkness and for short periods of time during the daylight.

Grewt's former obsession with finding the pieces of stone now became even more all-consuming. He had been robbed and cheated, he believed. But at least now he knew where to look. The site of his confrontation with the Alchemist was not far from where the stone was now hidden. A few days journey farther north brought him and a few of his followers to the base of a mountain range. Through the clouds they could see a fortress towering above them. It rose nearly a thousand feet into the air. For the next several years – until the day he died – Grewt tried to breach the fortress, but without success. It was impregnable. The Alchemist had shrouded it in spells and counter-spells.

By the time Grewt died, he had become more than a pariah among his community. He was a joke: the strange looking creature with an axe fused to his hand, who ranted about some magic stone and an Alchemist no one else had ever seen. Only his sons still believed in him, but even their faith had been severely shaken over the years. On the day Grewt passed from this life, the axe, that had been part of him for so many years, fell from his grip to the ground.

When it did, the younger son reached for it without thinking. He had intended to place it back in his father's hand to join him in his final resting place. As his fingers grasped the haft, a strange sensation crept up his arm and into his shoulder. When he tried to put the axe in his father's hand, he found he could not release it. The older brother became angered, assuming his brother was mocking their departed father.

"Return it to him," the older brother demanded. "Stop making more of a mockery of him than he did to himself."

The younger brother insisted he was unable to release the axe, which only further angered the older son.

"You should not have taken it," he shouted. "By rights it should be mine. I'm the first-born. I'm the one who should have it."

They began to argue. Eventually, the younger brother threatened the older one with the axe itself. In retaliation, the older brother pulled a long dagger from his belt and in one quick motion, cut off the hand holding the axe. The hand and the axe fell to the floor, but the hand was still clutching the axe handle. The older brother reached down and tried to pry the hand loose, but was unable to do so. Though detached, the hand's owner was still alive.

Enraged, the older brother rose, spun around and drove the dagger into his brother's heart, killing him instantly. He turned back to the axe and saw the severed hand uncurl its fingers and release the axe. He hesitated only a moment and then picked up the weapon. He felt the same surge flow up his arm into his shoulder. He tried to put the axe down, but it was now secured to his arm, and would remain that way until his death.

Something about possessing the axe caused the son to renew his belief in the tales his father had told of an Alchemist and a powerful stone. He took up the father's quest and attempted to find the secret to the tower. He only failed. On one occasion, though, when he was at the base of the fortress, the clouds that shrouded it cleared away. The sight that opened up to him at first defeated him, but then offered a different solution. He discovered that there was more than the one tower he, his brother and his father had, for years, attempted to enter. There were five; each one taller than the one before it.

Quest of Eight Part Four: The Race to Virkio

Richard Reda

His first reaction had been to give in to the apparent futility. He returned to the community, depressed and overcome. More than two years went by before another approach came to him. The leaders of his small tribe, like all Rebbercands, felt forced to move. They had spent too much time in this location. However, unlike the others from whom they had been separated, they needed to remain underground. So, rather than return to the surface and relocate, they began to dig.

They tunneled several miles to the northwest and came upon a cavern with an underground stream. They called this place home until the urge to move struck them again. It was the tunneling to a new location that gave the son the idea. For as long as he could remember, he, and whomever else he could enlist, had been trying to get to the tower by a frontal assault. He believed that by digging under it, he could bypass the protective spells. He began the tunneling immediately.

The task was simpler in the planning than it was in the execution. The tower was built on rock and granite. The digging was arduous and time consuming. The son was an old man by the time the tunnel reached the foundation of the first tower, and they were more than a mile beneath the surface, when they began to dig upward into the fortress itself. They finally managed to break through, but several perished in the traps and mazes that filled the fortress. Further, the stone was not there. The digging continued.

Centuries passed. The axe was handed down from one generation to the next. Sometimes the passing was natural, but too often it was the result of greed and envy. Many of the owners held it for very short periods of time, as the younger son had. Eventually, as the hobgoblins evolved out of the original gargoyles and Rebbercands, the leaders determined that the axe should not be possessed by anyone until a chosen one made his presence known. Until then, the axe was enshrined, and served as a symbol of what had been stolen from them: the power and the glory of the past.

"A very interesting story," said B'nair when Ercon had finished. "But I don't see the point. You obviously still don't have this stone, or even know if it exists, do you? And all that stuff about the axe seems like a bunch of mumbo jumbo superstition."

"It's more than a story," replied Ercon. "It's the history of our people. The stone exists. We are certain of that, and we are certain it rests hidden and protected in the fifth tower."

"Then why haven't you claimed this prize? Haven't your tunnels dug through to the last tower?"

"It's taken almost two thousand years. We've tunneled all the way to the end of the fortress, but we can't break through. Even more than a mile beneath the surface, it's built on a foundation of iron that is impenetrable. We can get into the fourth tower, but we can't get past the spells to cross to the last one."

B'nair thought about this for a minute, and then turned his attention to the stone itself.
"What do you hope to attain once you possess this stone?"

"The pieces of the stone seek each other. Possessing one will lead the owner to the other pieces. The stone was part of a pendant that was the source of the witch's power. It enhanced it – magnified it in some way."

"And what good will it do you? Or me, for that matter? Rebbercands have no mystical powers. Even if we possessed this stone, we don't have the abilities of your witch. Nothing will be enhanced."

"That's true," replied Ercon. "You don't have any special powers, but it is believed that the stone can confer them. Even if it can't, though, it enables visions."

"Visions?" B'nair asked, laughter creeping into his voice. "Visions? What good are visions? Unless they can give me back my eye, what will visions do?"

"They might allow you to see beyond your limitations and your self-pity," Ercon shot back.

"This from the one of us with two good eyes," countered B'nair.

Ercon ignored the retort, and continued. "The stone will also lead us to the exiled sorcerers. They were banished by the witch and the Alchemist, and have been imprisoned ever since. They have the abilities that can be expanded by the stone."

"The sorcerers that the witch claimed betrayed her?" asked B'nair.

"No," answered Ercon. "Not them, but the ones who rose up against the Alchemist. The Kelpies."

"And what exactly is a Kelpie?"

"They are the most powerful of sorcerers. It was the Kelpies that fought the Alchemist and the witch. The witch used the power of the stone and the treachery of the Alchemist to defeat the Kelpies."

"Maybe we should join forces with the Alchemist and the witch," B'nair taunted Ercon. "If the two of them managed to defeat these two sorcerers and a bunch of Kelpies, it seems to me the real power is with them."

"The power was with the stone," insisted Ercon.

"I see," said B'nair. "Tell me. How will this trinket help us?"

"We need it to find and release the Kelpies," answered Ercon. "If the stone is ours, the power will be with us."

"With the Kelpies, you mean," corrected B'nair. "I still don't understand. If we find these Kelpies – these powerful sorcerers – and we release them from whatever prisons they are held in; what's in it for us?"

"Haven't you ever wondered why your people must move their homes every several years? Haven't you ever wondered why your people are viewed as outcasts by every other society? Haven't you ever wondered why you seem to have no sense of purpose? All that was taken from us by the witch when she cursed us. She and the Alchemist wanted all that for themselves. When the Kelpies fought against them, they were singled out, cursed and exiled. There has been no sign of the witch since she cast her spell. That leaves only the Alchemist to stand in the way of our taking back what was once ours. We – the hobgoblins and the Rebbercands – can't do that by ourselves. We need the Kelpies. The only way we can find and restore the Kelpies is with the sorcerers."

B'nair gave careful thought to Ercon's words. Even as a leader in the Rebbercands, he had always felt something was missing. His victories felt shallow and purposeless. Could this be the source? Could Ercon be offering something that would change all that? He was still not fully convinced.

"Here," said Ercon, after a length of silence had passed between them. "I brought you something."

He walked back to the entryway to the room and came back with a long stick-like object.

"What is it?" asked B'nair when Ercon handed it to him.

"It's a crutch. It will allow you to walk while your leg heals. It's about time you were able to leave this room. Place it under your left arm and put your weight on it as you walk."

He helped B'nair to his feet and positioned the crutch for him. He guided him as he took a few tentative steps around the small room until he was able to manage on his own. Ercon led him down a long hallway. This was the first time in several weeks that he had been anywhere in the underground village other than his own recovery room. He was shocked by how many people he saw.

"How many live here?" he asked.

"We number more than two thousand," answered Ercon. "As you can see, we've become very adept at digging."

"I see. This is as impressive as the tunnels of the Trepans."

"We learned a lot from them," Ercon informed him. "We also manage to keep distant from them. Our relationship is not one of allies, and they greatly outnumber us."

The tunnels were larger than what he had experienced when he had overseen the mining with the Trepans. There were torches at regular intervals along the walls, providing subdued lighting throughout. Periodically there were large openings as well as intersections and side tunnels.

"How long have your people been here?" B'nair asked as he hobbled slowly through the corridor.

"Longer than your people have stayed at any one location," Ercon answered. "We seem to have less urgent of a need to move. I'm not sure why."

"How do you know the frequency of our moves?"

"We have followed your civilization for centuries. We knew we had a common heritage, but both of our peoples are suspicious and apprehensive of others. We were reluctant to make contact. Your unexpected arrival has provided an opportunity to change that."

B'nair laughed. "You think I'm the 'chosen one'?"

"I don't know," Ercon answered. "Perhaps you can tell us."

B'nair stopped and turned towards Ercon to see if he was being mocked. The expression on Ercon's face told him he wasn't, and he continued his awkward hopping motion forward. They walked for a few more minutes until they reached an alcove off to the left of the main corridor. When they turned into it B'nair could see that it was relatively small – barely ten feet in diameter. At the far side against the wall was a rough-cut block of wood. Wedged into the wood was a large double-headed axe. B'nair was at a loss for something to say for a few seconds. Ercon allowed the silence to continue unbroken.

"So, I assume this is the fabled axe," B'nair finally said.

"You assume correctly," answered Ercon.

"And it's just here out in plain sight for anyone to take?"

"It's not as if we wouldn't know who took it," replied Ercon. "Besides, we all know the ramifications of placing our hands on it. For more than five hundred years, no one has relished the thought of holding that in their hands for the rest of their life. There's not a real likelihood that someone will steal it."

"I suppose you're right."
B'nair stared at it for some time, and then hobbled closer to it. He studied the blade and the handle closely, careful not to get too close. He felt a tingling in his right hand. He looked down at his charred fingers, still black and rock-like – unmoving. He dismissed the sensation as a phantom feeling. After a while he turned around and looked back at Ercon.

"I appreciate the history lesson, but I'm not your man," he said. "However, you <u>have</u> piqued my curiosity about that stone and the fortress."

"One step at a time," replied Ercon.

B'nair wasn't sure if Ercon was talking about his recovery process or about being convinced he was the chosen one. He elected not to pursue it for the time being and staggered back to the main hall. Ercon showed him other areas of the compound before returning him to his room. The next day he showed up with the healer and another person.

"This is Nodar," Ercon said. "He's going to help you rebuild your strength; especially in your leg."

"You will still need to be careful and avoid putting too much weight on it," advised the healer. "But the muscles need to be worked, otherwise they will wither."

For the next three weeks Nodar spent most of each day working with B'nair, forcing him to exercise until he could take it no longer. Nodar not only forced him to rehabilitate his leg, but to rebuild the strength in his right arm. The lifeless hand and wrist made this more difficult than normal, but B'nair refused to show any signs of weakness, in spite of the pain. In the evenings Ercon met with him to fill him in on the tunnels that had been dug under the Alchemist's fortress and the spells they had encountered. They discussed various approaches to the fifth tower, discarding them one by one.

By now, B'nair was able to walk without the use of the crutch, and Nodar was no longer needed to push him in his recovery. His walk was still an awkward shuffle, but it was unassisted. Something else had changed in him. He began to feel a kinship with the hobgoblins – deeper than he felt with his own people at times. He wondered if he was simply caught up in Ercon's dedication to reaching the stone, or if it was more than that.

Ercon had provided him with leather armor, similar to what he had worn before, and yet distinctly different. He had been fitted with a patch to cover the dead eye, but nothing changed the black stone that began in the middle of his right forearm and ended in the black stone fingers. Although, he was even coming to terms with that.

One evening Ercon had been describing what he knew about the fifth tower and the bridge that connected it to the fourth tower. They had gotten that far twice before, losing several men along the way.

"The Alchemist is very clever," acknowledged Ercon. "The spells he has cast change of their own accord. If we learn how to get past them one time, they'll change the next time we approach."

"And you're sure you can't get into the fifth tower from below?"

"Very sure. The others are shells around halls and rooms and stairways to the top. The only way to avoid going up the inside of them is to cross the bridges that run from the top of one to the top of the next. But that way is just as dangerous as going up the inside. We've been able to bypass the first three towers by going underground to the fourth one. There we must go up through the interior to the bridge to the fifth tower. The fifth tower is unlike the others. It is built on a foundation of iron and the interior is solid ice."

"Then melt it," suggested B'nair.

"We've tried that. It's possessed. The hotter the fire, the colder and harder the ice becomes. Picks and axes don't even make a mark on it. Believe me. We've tried everything."

He then described the bridge from tower four to tower five. He told B'nair that with enough men, he was certain he could lead a party back to the bridge, but he was at a loss once there as to how to cross it.

"And if that's not enough," he added. "A dragon guards the fifth tower."

"What kind of dragon? Scyllas?" asked B'nair, recalling the devastation wreaked by the Scyllas on the Rebbercands.

"Worse that Scyllas," Ercon answered. "They prey on Scyllas."

B'nair thought in silence for several minutes. Then he asked Ercon to show him the room with the axe. Ercon led the way, with B'nair shuffling behind him, dragging his still damaged leg. When they arrived, B'nair hesitated at the entrance, and then slowly stepped up to the axe. He studied it much as he had the first time he saw it. Once more he felt a tingling in his dead right hand. He looked at the lifeless fingers and then back at the axe. Slowly he reached forward. As his hand got closer and closer to the handle, his fingers still did not move but the tingling persisted.

He stood there motionless for several seconds before finally sliding the handle into the opening between his thumb and his curled fingers. The fingers slowly began to close around the haft. As they did an electrical charge began to grow, crawling up his arm to his shoulder. He still had no feeling in his hand, but he watched as it closed on its own around the handle. There was no visible sign that the weapon had fused to him, but he knew that it had. With one powerful jerk, he pulled the blade from the wood and turned to Ercon.

"Let's find that stone," he announced.

Chapter three

Liam had carefully maneuvered the *Wedgamaroon* up through the shaft of the dormant volcano, out past the tiny island, and over the ocean. The sail filled with the wind and pulled the unusual craft. The twin rotors that moved by way of a series of gears and pulleys connected to a pedaling mechanism gave the ship a certain degree of stability, but not enough to keep the vehicle from swaying from left to right. No matter how he shifted the direction of the sail, he couldn't control the irregular motion. For most of them the movement was making them mildly nauseous. For Summer the movement was more like an earthquake. She took her chances by flying just behind Liam's shoulder. However, this had been going on now for nearly an hour and she was getting tired.

"I could use some help here," Liam finally called out to anyone who would listen. "Can one of you cast a spell or something?"
Natalie and Solveig looked back at Liam, then to each other and just shook their heads.

"I can give him light and some thunder, and maybe a few other things, but I can't make this boat, ship, or whatever it is, go straight," muttered Solveig.

"I could put a bubble around it, but then we'd drop like a rock," said Natalie, who then leaned as far over the side as she could and threw up.

Sean was holding on with both hands and both feet, staring wide-eyed at the vast body of water several hundred feet below them. It wasn't the altitude that bothered him. It was the thought of dropping into the sea with no land in sight that was raising his anxiety level.

Quinn was hanging over the front and seemed to be completely unphased by the erratic swinging back and forth. Lochen staggered back and sat next to Liam. He tried to put on a brave face, but it was turning an unattractive shade of green. Stella inched her way to the back as well, stepping carefully on the boards that were patched together to make a floor. She took one look at Lochen, then reached into the folds of her cloak and pulled out a small vial. She removed the stopper and waved it under her nose to make sure she had selected the right potion.

"Here," she said as she handed the small bottle to Lochen. "Put a few drops on your tongue – just a few! Let them get absorbed slowly. You should feel better in a minute or two."

"You are a savior," he said, taking the bottle.

He held it over his opened mouth and slowly turned it to pour the contents. He was holding it too far away, and the first drops splattered on his nose and into his eyes. He lowered his hand and his head, wiped his face off and tried again. This time he was more successful.

"Thank you," he said to Stella, handing the vial back to her. "That potion won't affect my vision will it?"

"Your vision? No, it shouldn't. It's for nausea, unless, of course you poured it in your...did you pour it in your eyes?" she asked.

"Well, not on purpose, I assure you," he answered.

He was afraid to ask anything further and directed his attention – and hers, he hoped – to Liam.

"I'm assuming you were not asking for help with anyone's gastric distress, were you?"

"No, although if you could fix that, it would be great. I need help keeping this thing from wobbling back and forth. I should have thought to install a rudder. I thought since we weren't going into the water that it wouldn't be necessary. I guess I was wrong."

"That kind of magic is not in my bag of tricks," answered Stella. "Let me see what I can do to keep the seasickness to a minimum." She got up and went to tend to Natalie.

"I'm not sure I can help you either," Lochen told him after Stella left. "I'm not sure I ever learned a spell to control a flying machine. There aren't a lot of references to such conveyances in the materials I've read. I can increase the wind in the sails, if you think that will help."

"It's not the speed or lack of speed that's causing this," Liam told him. "I think it's the pull of the oars in the wheels that's doing it. They're turning in the same direction, which is pulling us one way, and the wind in the sails is pulling us in the opposite direction. I would have thought they'd cancel each other out, but instead they're working against one another."

"I'm not sure that's what's happening," said Lochen, studying the movement of the wheels and the oars compared to the wind in the sail. "It would seem to me that the two rotors, even though going in the same direction, are offering some semblance of balance. But I could be wrong. What do you think would happen if we dismantled the gears to one of the wheels? Would that help?"

"Your guess is as good as mine," said Liam. "It's not like there's a guide that came with this ship. We could end up worse off."

"Or not, correct?" asked Lochen.

"I suppose. The problem is that I don't want to cut the ropes that connect the pedals to the gears that control the rotors. Untying them is going to take time, which means that we won't be lifted into the air. This craft was made to fly, not to float. I mean, it's made out of wood, mostly, so those parts will float, but it won't float like a boat. It'll float like a bunch of broken boat parts."

"If you can gain more altitude, how much would you need in order to do what you have to do with the ropes?"

Liam just looked at him.

"Ah, yes," said Lochen. "You've no way of telling. No operator's guide. You already said that. I suppose the only way we can know is to try. I always enjoy a good experiment."

Liam looked at him a bit apprehensively. Jumping right ahead, Lochen turned to Summer and asked if, when ready, could she cover the craft with faerie dust. She said she'd give it all she had. Lochen then took over the pedaling from Liam, who hesitated for a second, and then, deciding there was a chance Lochen was right, climbed beneath the floorboards to the drive mechanisms. There was no hull below him – just a series of long shafts, which held the frame together and supported the gears. He positioned his feet so that he was facing the nearest sets of ropes, cogs and other related components.

"OK," he shouted. "Summer, start sprinkling, and Lochen, pedal as hard as you can."

In a few minutes the craft had gained as much altitude as it could. With no land in sight, it was difficult to tell exactly how high they were. When Lochen felt they had reached their maximum altitude he shouted to Liam and then stopped pedaling. Liam immediately began to untie the connection to the rotor in the back of the ship.

"What's happening?" shouted Sean. "The water...it's getting closer. We're falling. Stop the falling. Start pedaling again. We're going down."

"This will only last a minute or two," Lochen shouted back. "We're trying to stabilize the ship. Fear not. We won't let you crash into the sea. At least I hope not," he added under his breath.

The *Wedgamaroon* hovered in the air for a second or two after the rotors stopped moving, and then began to drop – quickly. The sudden change in altitude only aggravated the motion sickness felt by Natalie. She bent over the side again, but immediately pulled her head back when she saw the ocean rushing up at her at an alarming rate. Quinn, on the other hand was cheering.

"Oh, wow!" he screamed. "What a rush! This is great. We could have been doing this all along."

Summer watched as the ship dropped away from her and reached out just in time to grab the hood on Lochen's cloak to keep from being left behind. The dropping continued and got faster and faster as the time ticked by.

Quest of Eight Part Four: The Race to Virkio

Richard Reda

"I'm sure you're working as diligently as possible," Lochen shouted to Liam. "But we're approaching the sea at an alarming rate. I'm quite certain that landing in the water at this speed would have devastating consequences, not only on your flying machine, but on us, as well."

"Done," he shouted back. "Start pedaling."

Lochen kicked into high gear and pushed with all his might. The ropes grabbed and the front shaft began to turn. The rotor caught the air, and the descent began to slow. The drop finally ended about twenty feet above the water, and the *Wedgamaroon* began to lift back up. Summer flew from front to back and then back to front, boosting the ship's elevation with a generous dose of faerie dust, and everyone cheered as they started to climb.

Their elation was short-lived. With only one rotor, the ship slowly began to spin in a circle. The sail had little if any affect on the spiraling motion. The swirling gradually increased, matching the turn of the large wheel and the oars.

"That's not it," shouted Lochen.

"No," answered Liam. "I think you were right about the two of them having a stabilizing effect. What now?"

"Put it back," shouted Sean. "Otherwise more of us are going to start barfing. It won't be a pretty sight. Trust me."

"Get us as high as you can," said Liam. "I'll have everything ready whenever you are."

Lochen pedaled and Summer sprinkled, but they couldn't get the craft as high as they did the first time. With only one rotor, the task was twice as difficult. When Liam saw that they were not going any higher, he called to Lochen to stop pedaling.

"We're not high enough," he gasped. "You won't have enough time to re-secure the other rotor."

"If we don't do it now, you're going to tire and we'll lose what altitude we've gained. Have Quinn take over. Once I've attached the other rotor, fresh legs will certainly help in keeping us from crashing."

"Point well taken," answered Lochen. "Quinn."

"I heard," replied Quinn.

"As soon as the wheel stops come back here and be ready to pedal."

"Let's do this," shouted Liam.

Lochen stopped pedaling. The ship hung in the air a second and began to drop again. The spinning, however, continued. Quinn stood up, but had to crouch over to avoid running into the oars jutting out from the wheel around the front mast. Sean, who had been on his hands and knees on the floor, scooted to one side to get out of Quinn's way. Unfortunately, Quinn expected him to move in the other direction. He stopped his foot from coming down on top of Sean, but at the cost of maintaining his balance.

He lurched to the side where Solveig and Natalie were perched. Solveig saw him coming and pushed herself out of the way. Natalie was leaning over the side, once again emptying the contents of her stomach into the sea. Quinn reached out to grab the center mast to keep himself from falling over the side. The spiraling of the ship shifted his weight, which was supported on one foot, and he pivoted sideways, colliding with Natalie. She was already almost halfway over the side. The bump from Quinn did the rest. Solveig watched in horror as all this unfolded almost as if it were in slow motion. Just as Natalie flew out of the ship, over the side and downward towards the ocean, the sudden shift of weight caused the ship to lean radically in the same direction. It was enough for Quinn to keep hold of the mast with one hand and reach out with the other to grab Natalie's ankle before she disappeared from sight.

"Hey," shouted Liam, who had slid away from the cogs on which he was working when the ship lurched to the side. "What's happening up there?"

He was standing nearly sideways, with his feet planted against the poles that served as the wall. He was outstretched trying to maneuver one of the ropes over one of the gears, both of which now appeared at different angles than they had mere seconds before.

Quinn pulled Natalie back on board and jumped to the opposite side, returning the boat to a more upright position, although it was still making circles. He staggered to the back and plopped down on the seat vacated by Lochen. Fortunately, Liam had the rope in his hand and looped in the right direction, ready to attach to the cog when the ship righted. The shift threw him back towards the gears, and in a diving motion, he made the final connection. As he released the rope and landed face down on the network of rods, he was face-to-face with the sea that was rushing up to meet them.

"Now," he shouted. "Go now. Fast. Faster."

Quinn started pedaling and the rotors started turning. The craft started lifting, but not without splashing into the water. Liam got drenched, but the *Wedgamaroon* survived the contact and began to climb back into the air. He climbed back on deck and sat on the floor towards the back, next to Quinn. Lochen came over to sit next to him and Summer floated down to sit between them. Natalie seemed to be over her latest bout of vomiting and was sitting on the floor on the other side of Quinn. Solveig and Sean sat across from them, completing the circle.

"I guess you were right about needing both rotors. We were lucky that time," Liam said to Lochen.

"It was only a theory," Lochen answered. "You were able to prove it. Now we know."

"Next time, let's try to do these experiments when it's a little safer," said Solveig.

"I'd prefer it if we didn't have a next time," said Sean.

"But we need to do something," pleaded Natalie. "I'm sorry, but I can't deal with this swaying back and forth."

"You don't need to apologize," said Liam. "You're right. We have to fix this problem. We still have a long way to go, and the constant shifting of weight is wearing on the construction of the ship. The frame is only tied together with old rope. There's no telling how long it will last. We need to control the motion better and make the frame more stable."

"I think you're right about needing a rudder," said Lochen, "or perhaps another wheel, extended towards the back and moving perpendicular to the others. I once saw a toy that was comprised of a wheel in a globe-like frame. The wheel was spun with a string. Once the spinning began, it was very difficult to twist or turn the globe. The person who invented it called it a gyroscope. At the time I thought it was merely an interesting plaything, but of little practical use. I see I may have been mistaken."

"That sounds... fascinating," said Liam. "But I don't see the connection."

"The force of that spinning wheel was so strong it was able to maintain a constant orientation in spite of contradictory forces."

"Of course," said Liam, staring at him in complete confusion.

"I'm certain that such an addition to the back of our craft will be beneficial."

"Wonderful," said Solveig, who joined the conversation. "Can you whip one of those things up?"

"Even if your idea would work," said Liam, "we don't have any spare parts. I have nothing to construct anything like that."

"What if we made our way back to Nohkmar Cambin?" offered Solveig. "We might find what we need there."

"NO!" shouted Summer, Liam, Lochen, Quinn, and Sean in unison.

"That's probably not the best option," Lochen clarified. "The reception some of us had when we were last there was a bit less than hospitable."

"It's going to be dark soon," said Liam. "And we're still not in sight of land. We're going to have to endure this at least until morning. Sorry Natalie."

Natalie lifted her head up from over the side. Her pallor was shifting back and forth from green to grey and had a waxy look to it. She was much too sick to respond, and only nodded her head before dropping it back downward.

"Try heading slightly to the north," said Quinn. "I've seen a few birds flying overhead. They seem to be going in that direction. There's probably an island or something that way."

"But if we're going home," said Summer, "won't it be faster to keep going east?"

"We need to go north," announced Stella. "We need to find the other missing pieces of this pendant."

She reached up to touch the two parts that had merged themselves together and rested in her headband. She didn't need to see, but she could tell that their color was shifting and the flashes of light from the centerpiece were more pronounced.

"I'm not sure what all those images I saw on the walls of the cave meant, but I think something important is happening or is about to happen. I don't know how to explain it, but I have this overwhelming sense of urgency. We have to go north. We have to find that castle or whatever those towers were –or are."

No one objected or commented, so Liam made a slight course adjustment, although the view remained exactly the same. Once the suns set and darkness filled the sky, the others volunteered to take over the pedaling responsibilities and Lochen, who needed no sleep, kept the helmsman company through the night. As dawn broke over the horizon, Quinn's observations turned out to be correct. There was a small string of islands off towards the northeast.

Liam lowered the ship and slowly flew over the southernmost islands. Most of these were little more than dots on the ocean's surface. They seemed to be coral masses, and not at all suitable for making a landing. The chain of atolls stretched for several miles.   Larger ones were interspersed among a number of smaller ones, but none of them presented anything but sand and rock.

Finally, some trees began to appear on the northern horizon. Then came the hills on which the trees were growing. At last they had found an island large enough to support vegetation and a long sandy beach. Liam eased the craft down and came to a stop. Natalie was the first to jump off and was immediately followed by the others.

"Summer, can you make a reconnaissance flight?" Lochen asked. "See if you can find a source of fresh water. Be careful, though. Keep an eye on the birds. The ones we've seen appear to be rather benign, but don't take any chances. Solveig and Natalie, can you try to find something edible? Stay close to the shore, just in case, and stay together. The walking and the fresh air will do much to improve Natalie's seasickness. Liam, what do you need to make the modifications we discussed?"

"Well, the easy stuff will be a long pole – probably from a sapling – and some vines. The hard part will be a wheel of some kind."

"Sean and Quinn, please find us a sturdy sapling about – what would you estimate, Liam? About fifteen to twenty feet long?"

"That should be about right. Make sure it's not too thin. It shouldn't bend."

"And how are we supposed to cut it down?" asked Sean. "Do you expect us to use our teeth?"

"Find the item first," answered Lochen. "We'll discuss procurement later."

"What about the wheel?" asked Liam. "Even if they find the other things, without a rotor like the ones we have, the rest of it will be useless."

"Actually," answered Lochen. "That may prove the easiest to find. Look around. All the islands we passed are comprised of rocks and reefs. There is no other land in sight – and there's no warning for ships passing in the night of the danger these islands present. I would venture a guess that more than one vessel has come upon these islands in the dark and have not survived the encounter. Stella, would you be so kind as to search the surrounding ocean floor for any wreckage? I image a ship's wheel will be about the right size."

With no further instructions, they all went off on their assigned tasks. Once they had all gone their different ways, Lochen sat down in the sand, closed his eyes and relaxed. Liam was standing next to him at a loss as to what to do.

"So what do we do in the mean time?" he asked after a minute or two of   silence.

"Nothing," answered Lochen. "That's the beauty of delegation. We sent the others to do all the work and we can sit back and enjoy the breeze, the warm sun and the solitude."

"Yeah, but…"

Liam looked from Lochen to the shoreline where Solveig and Natalie had run, then to the wooded area where Sean and Quinn were in search of a pole. He turned to look where Stella had splashed into the water and disappeared, and then up to the sky where Summer was no longer visible.

"But…shouldn't we…I mean…"

Lochen opened one eye and glanced up at Liam, who was clearly confused.

"Rest while you can. I'm sure the days ahead will provide us little time to do so."

Liam looked around one more time, and then seemed to concede and sat in the sand next to Lochen.

In the meantime, Summer was soaring above the treetops, glad for the opportunity to spread her wings. The sky was clear and there was a gentle warm breeze. She gained some altitude and then floated and glided in circles and figure eights, throwing in a loop-the-loop every once in a while. She didn't mind being asked to find water, but thought it would be much easier if the rest of them could drink salt water, as she could.

Quest of Eight Part Four: The Race to Virkio

Richard Reda

She kept a watch out for predatory birds, but Lochen was right. All she saw were some gulls and terns, which didn't seem at all interested in faeries. After a few minutes, she found a stream flowing from the top of the highest part of the island. She followed the stream to its source – a small lake in a natural crater. The water looked cool and clear. She zoomed in for a closer examination, and then headed back to report her findings.

Solveig and Natalie walked to the far side of the shore and began following the line of vegetation northward paralleling the coast. At first Natalie struggled to keep up, even though Solveig was setting a fairly slow pace. Finally, just as Lochen had predicted, the fresh air and the walk eased away her nausea. The color in her face returned to normal and she began to feel much better. She still had a bad taste in her mouth from all the retching she had done.

As they walked along the shore, she looked closely at the variety of plants that were present. Finally she saw what she was looking for – a spearmint bush. She plucked a leaf, sniffed it to make sure, and then popped it in her mouth. The mint flavor quickly spread and she felt even better.
"I hope you know what you're chewing on," said Solveig. "Some of us have had some pretty strange reactions to certain plants."

"This smells and tastes like spearmint," answered Natalie. "Unless it's been hexed by some mystic who somehow got lost on this particular island, I think it's safe."

"OK," said Solveig, "but if you start howling at the moon, don't say I didn't warn you."

In a few minutes, they came upon a field of bushes filled with berries. There were large blueberries, juicy red raspberries, plump blackberries, and some very tempting peach colored berries. As they started gathering them, they couldn't resist eating a few. They were familiar with all but the peach colored berries; and even though they picked these, too, they tried to keep them separate from the others until they could find out if anyone knew what they were.

Natalie tore off a part of her clothing to form a small sack to hold the fruit she picked, and Solveig was stuffing the ones she picked into the deep pockets of her robe. They'd each pick a handful and toss one into their sack or pocket and the next handful into their mouths.

"These taste incredible," murmured Solveig as the juice exploded across her taste buds.

"I hadn't realized how hungry I was," said Natalie as she packed an entire handful into her mouth.

Before long, they were both eating everything they were picking.

"I feel like such a pig," said Solveig.

Juice was running down her chin as she shoveled one handful of berries into her mouth after another. Natalie was busy doing the same thing and paused for only a second. She turned and looked directly at Solveig.

"Oink," said Natalie and she started laughing while stuffing more berries into her mouth.

"Double oink," said Solveig, joining in the laughter.

They both began laughing uncontrollably until Solveig looked down at the cluster of berries in her hand and then at the bush from which she had been picking them. They were all peach colored.

"Oh, oh," she said between spasms of laughter.

"How can you say, 'oh, oh' and still be laughing? "Oh, oh' means something bad has happened; not something funny."

Solveig immediately stopped laughing. The sudden change in her demeanor made Natalie stop as well.

"I ate some of the peach colored berries," she said. "Or at least I think I did. Is that why I was laughing so hard? Is what happened to Quinn happening to me?"

There was a note of anxiety in her voice.

"Are you sure?" asked Natalie. "Open your mouth. Let me see."

Solveig did as she was asked and Natalie leaned forward to peer inside. She looked at Solveig's tongue, the roof of her mouth and at her teeth.

"I don't see anything peach colored. Maybe you didn't eat them."

"But I couldn't stop laughing," Solveig whined, clearly on the verge of tears.

"But you did stop laughing." Natalie pointed out. "You're not laughing now. Quinn couldn't stop no matter what he did; remember? I'm sure you're all right. Just the same, we should probably get back to the others. We can ask if any of them know what these are."
While Solveig and Natalie were gathering berries, Sean and Quinn were making their way deeper into the wooded area of the island. They were well out of sight of the beach, searching for a thin but sturdy tree and some suitable vines. They had found the vines first, and had coiled several feet over Quinn's shoulder. He was unaware that the vine was very slowly, but very surely, constricting and tightening in on itself.

In the meantime, he was marveling at all the trees, pointing to one after another and suggesting that this one and then the next was exactly what they were looking for. Sean on the other hand had his slingshot at the ready and was more focused on what remained unseen – any other form of life.

"Slow down and stop making so much noise," Sean complained to Quinn.

"Why? What are you worried about? There's no one around."

"We just can't see them, that's all," responded Sean.

"Maybe that's because they're not there. Hey look! There's another one that we could probably use."

"Are you for real? That one's more than a foot thick and almost thirty feet high. Besides, how are we going to be able to cut it down?"

"OK – maybe that one's not so good. Hey! What about that one over there?" shouted Quinn as he ran off in another direction.

"Not so loud," Sean whisper shouted.

He was looking to his right and left and then behind him as he tried to run quietly after Quinn. He heard a noise to his right and pulled the slingshot back, ready to fire. As he spun his head in the direction of the sound, he tripped. The slingshot fired, the stone ricocheting off one tree after another, whizzing by Quinn's nose in the process, and Sean let out a scream.
"Wow," said Quinn. "Is that your idea of being quiet, or were you trying to scare off anything within a hundred miles?"

He turned to look back in the direction from where Sean's scream had come. Sean had disappeared from view. Quinn's first reaction was that Sean was playing a trick on him, but it was immediately replaced by a sense of panic.

Quest of Eight Part Four: The Race to Virkio

Richard Reda

"OK, Sean," he said in a squeaky whisper. "I promise. I'll be quiet. This is not a time to play games. Please come out."

"I'm not hiding," muttered Sean as he pushed himself up through the shrubbery to his hands and knees. "I fell. I tripped over this..."

He looked down and saw a fallen tree trunk. It was about six inches in diameter and about fifteen feet long. The root system at one end was truncated and there were no limbs to speak of.

"Hey," shouted Quinn. "You found one. Good job. Let's take it back to Liam and Lochen.

He bent down, picked it up and headed back to the shore. Sean slowly got to his feet and took one more look around, wondering what the sound had been that had distracted him in the first place.

As soon as Stella dove into the water, she could see in an instant that Lochen's assumptions about the chain of islands had been correct. They were the tops of a long and very high range of underwater mountains formed by centuries of coral and rock build up. They were also a death trap for unsuspecting ships in the night. She could see the wreckage of dozens of them strewn along the ocean floor in the space immediately below her.

This should be easier than I thought, she said to herself. She dropped her head and began to kick. Taking long full strokes, she reached the rubble in a few seconds. She headed for the closest ship first. It was an ancient wooden galley of some kind. This one had been down under the water for a long time. As soon as she touched the side of the wheelhouse, the rotted wood crumbled in her hands. This one won't do, she thought, and she quickly moved to the next one.

As she swam out of the first ship and along its side to the next one, she noticed a lot of damage to the side of the galley. That's odd, she thought. If it ran into the coral, wouldn't the damage be more towards the front? She didn't give it much thought as she came upon the second ship. This one was a merchant ship. She made her way back to the ship's wheel only to discover that it was cracked in half. She assumed this had happened when the wreckage from other ships or some similar debris landed on it, although there was no sign of any such debris.

She made her way to the next ship. When she swam around the bow, along the side and up towards the tiller, she saw that the sides of this ship had been crushed much the same as the first ship. This isn't damage from running into coral, she thought. This was done by something else. She quickly swam up against the side of the ship and pressed her back against the hull. She looked as far as she could see in every direction. For the first time, she noticed there were no signs of any fish or other sea creatures in the area.

This is not good, she thought. She looked over her shoulder at the destruction of the hull. Whatever did this was very big and very strong. She looked around once more, and then eased her way to the ship's wheel. It had broken off its mount, but was otherwise in good condition. She picked it up and began to swim back the way she had come, staying as close as she could to the ship's deck before heading for the surface. As he passed over the open cargo hold, she thought she detected some motion.

She immediately stopped and tucked the wheel under one arm, freeing the other in case she needed to cast some kind of spell. She backed away from the open hatch, but kept it in her sights. There was enough sunlight from above that shafts of light filtered into the hold. Maybe that's what I saw, she thought, but was not fully convinced. Just as she kicked to the surface, she saw movement again. This time she was certain. This time it was a large circle of black. She had never seen anything so dark, so devoid of life. And then it was gone.

She nearly dropped the wheel as she kicked and pulled with all her might. She broke the surface a few seconds later and swam as quickly as she could towards the shore. Even after she was back with the others she didn't feel entirely safe, but she kept her fears to herself for the time being.

Solveig and Natalie were the first to return, having run all the way back. They displayed the berries they found and asked about the peach colored ones.

"I've never seen anything like them," said Liam. "But that may be a good thing, since nearly everything I normally see is poisonous."

"I'm not familiar with them either," said Lochen. "Are you certain you ate some?"

"Not really," admitted Solveig. "I'm ashamed to say I was in a feeding frenzy before I noticed they were in my hand. Natalie said she couldn't see any in my mouth, but that doesn't mean anything."

"Do you feel any differently?" Lochen asked.

"I don't think so."

"You're probably all right, but it might be best to set them aside just in case. You've gathered enough of the other berries. Let me know immediately if you feel strange. Once Stella returns we can ask her, too."

The words were no sooner out of his mouth than Stella waded ashore with the wheel under her arm.

"Excellent," said Lochen. "Now all we need are some vines and the drive shaft. By the way, can you look at these berries Solveig found? Can you tell if they're safe to eat?"
Stella gave them a quick glance and said, "I don't recall seeing this kind before. I'd suggest we not eat them, to be on the safe side."

74

Her encounter with the unknown beneath the water had distracted her. She failed to recognize the rare and unusual berry that Solveig had, in fact, eaten. By now, though, it would not matter.

Sean and Quinn returned almost at the same time as Summer. Summer reported where the stream and the small lake were and offered to lead the others back to it. Lochen instructed everyone to follow her and to drink their fill, since it could be a long time before they found fresh water again. Quinn said he wasn't thirsty, and Liam wanted to get to work on the modifications to the ship. The others expressed a desire to get moving as quickly as possible, so Lochen didn't pursue the matter.

The wheel that Stella had found was still connected to its original base, which made it easier to attach to the shaft that Quinn and Sean had discovered. Liam made a few adjustments to the cogs and gears beneath the pedal mechanism while Lochen secured the shaft through the back end of the ship. When they were done, the *Wedgamaroon* looked like it had a long tail with a pinwheel on the end.

"Let's give it a try," said Liam with more confidence than the others felt. "Climb aboard everybody."

Natalie took a deep breath and got on, followed by the others. Summer once more provided a generous dose of faerie dust to aid in the lift off. In a few seconds the craft lifted into the air. Quinn lowered the sail to catch the strong breeze and the ship shot forward. Natalie was poised near the edge in case she needed to empty her stomach of the berries she had eaten, and the others waited expectantly. To everyone's surprise, and Natalie's relief, the ship was steady as a rock.

"Oh, man," shouted Liam. "It worked. I can't believe it."

"Of course it worked," said Lochen. "It's simply the principle of conservation of angular momentum – just as I had thought."

75

"Well why didn't you say so from the start," piped up Sean. "I could have told you it was a conversation with antelope monuments."

Chapter four

They flew northward for several days, making landings whenever any amount of land appeared. Twice they turned eastward to find the shore in order to gather food supplies and find fresh water, but once they were airborne again, they returned to their original course. The daily routine varied little. All but Summer took turns relieving Liam at pedaling, and most often she was flying farther ahead to scout out potential landing opportunities. Too often they flew through the night with little rest.

Solveig had forgotten about the peach colored berries. In fact, she was no longer sure she had even eaten them. And Stella, if asked, wouldn't have recalled Solveig showing them to her. And even if she could, it was too late to do anything about them. The tiny seeds in these berries had not passed through Solveig's system as the other berries had. Instead, they had incubated and now, nearly a week later, they began to germinate. As they did, they reacted with her body's chemistry and sent false messages through her nervous system. The toxins in the seeds were carried to her brain.

All the while this was happening, she felt no different than before, either physically or mentally. But the poison was causing slow, but steady short circuits in her neocortex, distorting the transmissions to her frontal lobe and her occipital lobe. The result was a deterioration of her ability to reason, to control her impulses, and in the visual images that passed from her eyes to her mind.

Had she eaten the entire handful of berries at the time she discovered what she was doing, the damage would have occurred much more quickly and would have been fatal. It was purely by chance, and her good fortune, that she had eaten only two. Those two, however, were enough to have a significant impact.

As evening was approaching, Liam decided to steer the ship eastward towards land once more. They had been flying for more than two days straight and needed to put down on the ground. A rainstorm was approaching from the west. It didn't look too serious, but he wanted to be safe. The sky had started clouding over and the wind had picked up. As the wind increased, so did their speed. There was no way for him to slow down the speed of the ship unless he reduced the size of the sail. However, the sail also provided the ability to steer the ship, so he wanted to get on the ground before they gained so much speed they wouldn't be able to land.

He spotted some tall trees on the horizon and set his course in that direction. Since he had already spotted land, Summer didn't need to fly off to scout ahead, and she was comfortably seated in the nose of the ship, napping. Natalie and Stella were on the left side, where they could see faint indications of land of some kind far to the north. The air had gotten considerably colder in the last few days, and Stella was hoping that the fortress they were seeking wasn't too much further off.

Quinn and Sean were on the right side of the ship. Quinn was leaning over the edge, watching the water below, and Sean was on the floor, avoiding the water as much as he could. Lochen was just then being relieved of the pedaling by Liam, and the two of them were discussing some minor repairs that needed to be done when they made landfall. Solveig was sitting on the transom at the back.

She was watching the sea behind them when she looked at the tail rotor and the intertwined vines that connected it to the gears underneath the pedals. Something looked odd, but she wasn't sure what it was. At first things looked blurred. She was certain the tail rotor was wobbling. She rubbed her eyes and looked again. It seemed to be moving even more. She then changed her position. She turned around to look at the mechanism straight on and saw that the wheel that served as the tail rotor was coming loose.

"Hey," she yelled. "That wheel in the back is coming off. We need to get down...to drop...I mean to land or we're going to crash."

Lochen spun around and moved next to her to examine it. He looked where she was pointing, but could see nothing wrong with it.

"It's fine," he told her. "The vines all look intact, and the wheel is sound. What did you think you saw?"

"I don't think I saw anything. I know what I saw, and no, it's not fine," she insisted. "It's...it's...what's the word I'm looking for?"

"Turning?" asked Lochen

"Don't be silly," she snapped at him, frustrated at him and at her inability to express herself. "It's a wheel. It's not supposed to turn."

Quest of Eight Part Four: The Race to Virkio

Richard Reda

Lochen looked at her for a moment. He attempted to feel her forehead, and she just pushed his hand away. He then asked Stella to come over. He explained what Solveig had just said. She looked at the wheel and then to Solveig.

"I believe you saw something. Can you tell me, what exactly did you see?" she asked, after watching her for a few seconds.

"It was...I thought it was covered with – no – the pokers, the pokies, the...the...those things in the middle"

"The spokes?" Lochen offered.

"That's what I said," she snapped again.

She turned back to the wheel and could see nothing wrong with it. When she turned back to Lochen and Stella, she could see they thought she was crazy. I'm not crazy, she said to herself. Before either of them could do or say anything, and in an attempt to diffuse the situation, Solveig just laughed.

"I'm sorry," she said; although Lochen could tell she didn't really mean it. "I must be tired. It's nothing. Really."

Maybe I am just tired, she thought to herself. Stella went back to where she had been with Natalie, and Lochen sat down, but kept his eye on Solveig. Solveig sat back down. But the more she thought about what she had seen, and what wasn't there now, the more she became concerned. She started wringing her hands. What's wrong with them, she asked herself. Can't they see this whole boat is falling apart? No. It's not a boat. What is it? It's a macaroon. No. That's what it's called.

She was staring at her hands as she held them in her lap. She was unaware of how much closer they had come to land, and didn't see the trees that were climbing higher and higher on the horizon until

Quest of Eight Part Four: The Race to Virkio

Richard Reda

Liam began to lower the ship's altitude. When she felt the change in altitude and looked up, what she saw wasn't the trees Liam had used as a focal point. Instead of trees moving in the increasing breeze, she saw giant snakes – thirty and forty feet tall – standing on their tails, shaking their heads back and forth.

What is he doing, she thought in a panic. Doesn't he see those snails? No. That's not right. They're not snails. They're...they're...they're snakes. That's it. They're snakes. Can't he see them? She jerked her head from the trees to Liam and back again, waiting for him to take evasive actions.

"Look out," she finally shouted, standing once again and reaching out to touch his shoulder. "You're going to run into them."

"I see them. Don't worry. We have plenty of room."

How could he be so casual about this, she wondered. Isn't he taking this seriously? Is he crazy? They were getting much too close. Those snails – no, not snails – snakes – those snakes were going to strike. She couldn't trust Lewis – no that wasn't his name. I know his name. It's...it's...what is it?

By now Liam had maneuvered the *Wedgamaroon* about two hundred yards from the line of tall, narrow trees. He could see large nests in the tops of the trees. Lochen saw them too and started to move closer to him.

"I see them," he told Lochen.

He had spotted several nests of Blue Falcons, though they were barely visible. He turned the ship to the left to avoid coming any closer. At the same moment, Solveig had reached the limit of her tolerance. She was certain the giant snakes were poised to strike. In her mind Liam has steered them within mere feet of the dangerous reptiles, rather than the two hundred yards that actually separated the ship from the trees. She clapped her hands and sent a bolt of lightning at the treetop nearest to them.

"What are you doing?" shouted Liam when he saw the blast strike the treetop and shatter the nest.

"Solveig," shouted Lochen. "They were unaware of our presence. They weren't going to attack. What have you done?"
The sudden shouting aroused everyone on the ship. The destruction of the nest aroused the Blue Falcons in the nearby nests. The noise and confusion on the ship attracted the Falcons, who turned their attention in that direction. To make matters worse, Solveig was sending more explosions in the direction of the Falcons. Within seconds, chaos reigned. Solveig was trying to send more blasts of lightning, but they were going off in every direction; Lochen was trying to restrain her; Liam was trying to steer the ship into the more densely wooded parts of the land to evade the Falcons.

Very quickly the Falcons were overhead, dive bombing the ship, nipping at the large rotors and the sail, and clawing at the sides of the ship with their talons. They were too close to the rotors for Stella or Lochen to cast spells on them or to protect the craft. They made contact with a few of the predatory birds when they dropped down to strike at the side of the craft, but there were too many of them. Some of the birds struck the rotors, rocking the ship and causing it to drop several feet closer to the ground in sudden and unexpected bursts. The rotors that were making it impossible for anyone to cast effective spells were also keeping the Falcons from clawing or nipping anyone.

Solveig, who had freed herself from Lochen's grip was standing at the back of the ship, sending blasts of lightning out to imaginary targets. Most of them crashed into trees, sending limbs and branches flying into the air, only to rain down on the Falcons or the *Wedgamaroon*. Instead of scaring them off, her efforts were only enraging them further.

The wind from the approaching storm had increased, and when Liam turned the ship towards the forest in order to escape the Falcons, the sail was now taking the wind in full force. The *Wedgamaroon* was rocketing through the woods. The Falcons were struck by flying branches and a few of them crashed into the rotors, shaking the ship. It was dropping too fast, and Liam was quickly losing control.

As the ship careened into the forest, limbs from standing trees swept by at a blinding speed. It was still nearly sixty feet in the air, but dropping steadily. Summer was on the floor with Sean. Sean knew Summer would be an easy target and a quick snack for the predators and was firing his slingshot at any that came close. Quinn had reached up and pulled Stella and Natalie down and was covering them with his body.

Lochen was trying to shield Liam so he could steer the ship, and Solveig was standing in the back in a corner, still sending blasts of lightning towards threats that existed only in her mind. Until the branch of a large evergreen ripped across the side of the ship, over the top of Liam's head and hit her squarely in the back.

She was swept off the craft in the blink of an eye and collided into branch after branch as she dropped to the ground. She was battered and bruised, and had the wind knocked out of her, but otherwise she was miraculously unharmed. She lurched to her feet and looked up to the darkening sky. She could see a number of Falcons circling above her. In her mind, they had spotted her and were redirecting their attack.

"They're looking for me," she gasped. "I have to save the others."

She began running deeper into the forest. Her attention was divided between the obstacles in her path and the threat from above. She tripped several times over tree roots and rocks and staggered to her feet as fast as she could. Then the rain started. The forest got darker and darker; her footing got slicker and slicker. She ran to the right and then to the left in no particular pattern and with no particular direction. She slid and fell and crashed to the ground. She began climbing up a long hill covered with thick brush and undergrowth. The trees were so close together she could no longer see the sky, but the rain managed to seep through the canopy of leaves and pine needles, soaking everything.

When she crested the hill, the ground dropped out from beneath her. She fell flat on her face and slid down the other side nearly forty feet before coming to a stop in a stream. She dragged herself to her feet again and looked around. The black limbs of hundreds of trees against the dark grey sky appeared to her as hundreds of Rebbercands hunting for her. Where did they come from, she asked herself in a panic. She stumbled through the stream, kicking up sprays of water trying to find the quickest way out.

The raindrops pelted the trees and leaves, drowning out nearly all other sounds – except for the sounds in Solveig's imagination. She heard her name echo through the woods. She heard the thunder of the hooves of wild animals chasing her. She heard screams from animals trapped by predators. She heard the grunts and roars of the Rebbercands. She ran blindly, pushing herself forward, in and out of the trees that seemed to be moving closer and closer together. They were so thick the sky was no longer visible. It was as if night had descended. For all she knew, it had. Her worst nightmares had come alive.

She was gasping in air, soaked to the skin, cold and shivering. She stopped running and leaned against a tree. She had her hands on her knees with her head lowered, trying to catch her breath. She had no idea where she was or how to find the others. She waited as patiently as she could and listened with all her wits. All she could hear now was the rain as it seeped through the treetops and struck the carpet of leaves on the ground. That and her heaving breath. Exhaustion had nearly taken over. And then she heard the growl.

Quest of Eight Part Four: The Race to Virkio

Richard Reda

At first she couldn't tell where it was coming from. She straightened up and slowly poked her head around the tree she was pressed against. Her eyes adjusted to the dim light and she could make out a form. There – about fifteen feet from her – in the middle of that form were a pair of burning red eyes. They slowly inched forward. In a few seconds, the form and the eyes broke through the blackness and into enough light for her to see the owner. It was a jackal. Where had it come from, she wondered. How long had it been following her?

She had seen these creatures before. When she had, they had been no bigger than a medium-sized dog. This one was more than twice that size. Its teeth glistened in the dim light. They were long and looked very sharp. The jaws were enormous. She gathered her courage and slowly crept around the tree to face it, ready to blast it with a bolt of lightning. Then she heard another growl.

This one was on the opposite side. She had been facing right in its direction before she turned to spot the first one. How could she have missed it, she wondered. It had been right in front of her. She chastised herself for being so inattentive. This second one was closer to her than the first. She knew she would have to act fast if she was going to blast two of them. Then she heard the third one.

This one was between the other two. They had her surrounded, she realized. She pressed her back against the tree and inched carefully all the way around it, looking for an escape route. As she was completing the circle, she spotted four more. There was an entire pack that had been hunting her. Each one was larger than the previous one. She had never seen jackals so big. What did these things eat, she asked herself, and then realized it was people like her, who got lost in these woods.

She looked for the weakest part of the circle. There was a small opening between two of them that led her deeper into the forest. She had no choice. Before they got any closer, she blasted a flash of lightning in that direction and then made a run for it, following as closely behind the explosion of light as she could. She dodged past snapping jaws on both sides, and ran, slipping and stumbling, dodging in between the trees. She could hear their barks and growls getting closer, and she was too afraid to look behind her.

She tripped over a root and slid through the rain and mud, springing back up to her feet, only to fall again. She was scrambling on her hands and knees, certain the jackals were about to pounce on her when she fell flat. Her strength was gone. She had resigned herself to the inevitable and prepared for teeth to sink into her flesh. When nothing happened, she slowly opened her eyes, still not daring to look over her shoulder.

She was staring at the ground right beneath her. Slowly she raised her head. Immediately in front of her she saw a pair of feet. They were human feet. They were also bare. The skin on the tops was like parchment – dry and cracked. The nails were thick and yellow with age, and broken. The soles were leathery, calloused and blackened. Solveig had never seen feet that looked so old and worn.

Her eyes moved upward, taking in a figure of a woman in an old gray robe that was dirty and threadbare. It was torn in places and soaked from the rain. Two gnarled hands appeared from large, baggy sleeves. The hands were little more than flesh and bone, white and smooth with age, with large blue veins prominent. The fingers were long and thin; the nails, like the nails on the toes, were yellow and broken.

When Solveig shifted her gaze to the figure's head, she saw long white hair, as wispy as cobwebs, wet and plastered to the head of an old woman – older than anyone she had ever known. Long spidery strands of her snow-white hair trailed down over her shoulders, front and back, nearly to her waist. The skin on her face was pale and nearly translucent, lined with tiny blue veins. She had a long narrow nose that matched her long thin chin. Her cheeks were sunken deeply, making her face look skeletal. Above her nose there were no eyes to be seen. The vision made Solveig gasp. The old woman was not only blind; her eyelids had been sealed over the empty sockets.

"Stop that, right now," she said in a voice that rasped with age.

Solveig thought the old woman was talking to her and was about to apologize for her shock, until she heard the jackals stop growling. She twisted her head to look behind her and saw the pack turning this way and that in confusion. And then one-by-one, they each sat down or stretched out on their bellies, whimpering. They looked as docile as kittens.

"Are you a Kelpie?" the old woman asked, still staring straight ahead.

Solveig still wasn't sure whom the woman was talking to or if the woman even knew she was on the ground in front of her. She also didn't know if the jackals remained a threat. She was afraid to move or make a sound.
"Probably not," said the old woman. "Get up, child. You're just getting wetter by lying in the mud. It's not like I don't know you're there."

Solveig slowly got to her feet, glancing back and forth between the old woman and the jackals, which suddenly seemed much smaller than they had before, although no less menacing. Why had she thought they were so big, she wondered. It must have been her fear. The crone reached for her and she flinched, unsure of the woman's intentions.

"I'm not going to hurt you, child. There are plenty of others who are waiting to do that. Come with me. We need to get you out of this rain and get something warm into you."

The old woman turned around and walked deeper into the woods. Solveig hesitated for only a second.

"What do you mean, there are plenty of others waiting to hurt me?" she called after the woman.

When no answer came, she decided she would take her chances with this strange person rather than stay behind with the jackals. She had to run to catch up. The woman had quickly gotten ahead and Solveig nearly lost sight of her in the dense woods. Once she was closer, she slowed down and stayed what she felt was a safe distance behind. She followed the woman for several hundred yards until they came to the opening near the base of a large, dead tree. The old woman climbed down the opening and disappeared from sight. Solveig stood at the edge and looked into the hole, seeing very little.

"I've run out of engraved invitations," the old woman called from under the tree. "So if that's what you're waiting for, you're going to be disappointed."

Solveig looked around once more, and then cautiously stepped down into the hole. She felt her way along with her feet and with her arms outstretched. Her right hand touched old, rotten roots and dirt, and every once in a while something slimy or something that moved, but her left hand felt only air. There were no steps. The ground seemed solid, though, and slanted downward. She slid her feet along, searching for any drop off or holes until her head was finally lower than the bottom of the dead tree.

The area inside was larger than Solveig expected. The roots had been cleared away, either cut off or rotted and broken, to form a ceiling of sorts. There were still large shoots all around the opening that served as the walls, and which dug deeply into the ground. The floor was packed earth, but there were woven reeds that served as rugs scattered all around.

In one curved corner was a pile of stones shaped into an odd-looking fireplace. The stones were stacked up to and through the ceiling to serve as a chimney for the fire, which was lit and burning in the hearth. There was a small pot hanging from a rod over the fire, but no smell rose from whatever was cooking. Extended along the back part of the cave was a series of shelves made from an assortment of twigs and branches laced together with reeds and vines. On the shelves were dozens of canisters.

Some of the canisters were glass – discarded bottles, lanterns, and bowls - anything that could serve as a container. Others were more like boxes. Inside the ones that were see-through, Solveig could make out various powders, leaves and roots. One of the boxes moved periodically. She didn't want to know what was in that one.

Solveig crept further into the improvised hut and could see a small table. There were two large candles on the surface that illuminated the inside. The tabletop was made from an old sign for a pub or an inn that most likely no longer existed. The legs were all different sizes and thicknesses, pulled together from junk piles or trash heaps. On either side of the table were two sections of tree trunks, which served as stools.

"Sit down, sit down," insisted the old woman. "I'm not going to bite you. Not enough teeth for that."
She turned towards Solveig and pulled her lips out with her fingers, displaying her gums. She jutted her face forward to display five widely separated, crooked, and nearly black teeth. She then turned back to the fireplace and removed the pot that had been extended over it. She put the pot on the table and then took two items off one of the lower shelves. One was the bottom half of a broken bottle and the other was an odd looking bowl with rough edges. The jagged breaks on the bottle had been worn down and were nearly smooth. The bowl was not exactly round, having a somewhat flat bottom and was a whitish-gray color.

"Glass or skull?" asked the old woman.

"What?" asked Solveig, uncertain about what she had said.

"Glass or skull?" repeated the woman with no further explanation.

"Glass, I guess," answered Solveig.

She was still puzzled about what she was being asked, but decided that the thought of a skull was enough incentive for her to indicate glass – whatever the reason. The old woman pushed the broken bottle across the table towards Solveig and moved the bowl closer to her side. She then poured the liquid from the pot into each.

"I don't get many visitors, but the ones I do always want the glass. I suppose the idea of drinking out of a skull puts some people off."

Solveig's eyes darted to the bowl. Then she recognized it as the top of the skull of something or someone, and immediately stood up.

"That's a skull!" she shouted, pointing at it.

"I know," said the old woman. "I just said that. Don't worry. It's no one you know. At least I think it's no one you know. Are you a Kelpie?"

"A what?"
"I asked you that already, didn't I? Here," she said, changing the subject. "Have some tea. It will take the chill off."

"Does that skull belong to a Kelpie...did it belong to a Kelpie?" asked Solveig.

The old woman was silent for a few seconds as if pondering the question. Realizing that no answer was coming, Solveig slowly returned to her seat and looked at the liquid in the glass, and then more closely at the glass itself. She looked up at the old woman again, debating about drinking whatever it was she had been given. The crone lifted the skull to her lips and took a loud sip, and then smacked her lips.

"Ah," she said. "Nothing like a good cup of tea to warm the bones."

Solveig reluctantly lifted the glass, looking for a clean spot or at least the cleanest spot on the edge and took a sip. It was the worst thing she had ever tasted. She was glad the old woman couldn't see the face she made.

"Uh...It's...very interesting," said Solveig, trying to cover up her cough. "I don't think I've ever tasted this particular brand before."

"Of course not," said the old woman. "I blend it myself. From things I find in the forest."

Solveig wasn't sure if the old woman was serious or trying to shock her. In spite of how bad it tasted, Solveig had to admit it was warming her up. She wondered if maybe the first taste was just a shock and that a second one wouldn't be so bad. She took another sip. No. It was worse the second time. She started to cough again.

"What a terrible hostess I am," said the old woman. "You must still be soaked."

She stood up and walked over to the other side of the small room to a chest Solveig hadn't seen before. The woman opened the lid and felt around, finally pulling a large cloak out. She brought it over and handed it to Solveig. She seemed to be moving slower than she had been earlier. Or maybe, Solveig thought, it's just my imagination.

"Here," she said. "Put this on."

"Oh, I couldn't" said Solveig, wondering what kind of insects or vermin had made their homes in the fabric.

"Nonsense," said the woman. "You're one of them, aren't you? You'll need it before much longer."

"One of who?" asked Solveig as she took the offered cloak.

She was surprised when she touched it. It was soft. She held it up and could see that it was in excellent condition. It was a deep purple color – almost black, but seemed to shimmer in the candlelight. It was nearly circular in shape, with an opening for the head and one for each arm, much like a poncho. She could see that there were deep pockets on both the inside and the outside. She gave a slight tug on the material and could tell that it was very strong.

She put the cloak over her head and stuck her arms through the opening. It fit perfectly, as if it had been made just for her. She immediately began to feel warmer. She was admiring the garment as she took another sip of the tea. She failed to notice that the glass had been refilled, and she also failed to notice that the woman had not answered her question.

"Are you going to Virkio?" the woman asked.

Her words seemed slightly slurred and she seemed to be slumping forward just a bit. The changes were so slight, that Solveig didn't notice them at first.

"Where?" responded Solveig. "I don't know where that is."

"What, not where."
"What?" asked Solveig.

"Yes," answered the woman.

"No, I meant what did you mean when you said 'what, not where?'"

"Virkio," said the woman. "The fortress of the Alchemist. Are you going there?"

Solveig took another sip of the tea in order to give herself time to think. She didn't think she could trust this person, in spite of being rescued from the jackals and being sheltered. She was also curious as to why this tea tasted worse each time she took a sip, and why she felt compelled to keep drinking it.

"I don't know what you mean. I simply got lost in the woods."

"But you're one of them. I know it. You must be seeking the Alchemist. You're not a Kelpie, are you?"

"One of whom? And who or what are these Kelpies you keep asking about?" she asked as she took another sip of tea.

"No. You're not a Kelpie. You must find the Kelpies. You must find the stone. Beware of the dragon's breath when you go to Virkio."

The old woman seemed to be growing agitated. At the same time she appeared to be less and less aware of Solveig's presence. She rocked back and forth. Solveig was getting more and more confused. She didn't know if this woman was harmless, crazy, or a threat. She decided she should try to remain as calm as she could and try to have a normal conversation. She took another sip of the tea.

"So," she said. "How long have you lived here?"

"You need to make haste; you and your friends. Others are making their way to Virkio."

"My friends?" asked Solveig.

She was worried now that her friends may be in peril. How did this blind woman know about her friends? Why, now all of a sudden, did she have to make haste, and who were these others? She drank more of the tea. Good grief this stuff tasted horrible, she thought. The old woman rocked back and forth some more. Then she slowly stood up

93

only to drop back down again. She seemed exhausted. She reached one hand forward and grasped Solveig's arm. It was almost as if she was noticing Solveig for the first time.

"You are in danger. Others are making their way to Virkio," she repeated. "I see blood – dragon's blood. Beware the dragon's blood."

"I thought you said to beware of the dragon's breath. Now you are telling me to beware of the dragon's blood. Which is it? I don't think dragons really even exist. Are you trying to scare me?"

Solveig pulled her arm free and took another gulp of the tea. She was finding it difficult to have a normal conversation with this person. She was coming to the conclusion that she was definitely crazy. She was also coming to the conclusion that nothing would make this tea taste any better, but she took another drink.

"Find the stone," the old woman suddenly shouted, as if she had been startled from a deep sleep. "Find the stone. Stop the others before it's too late. Find the Kelpies. Keep them hidden. Beware of the dragon's blood."

"You're not making any sense at all, I hope you understand," answered Solveig, a bit indignantly and slightly frightened. "And there's no need to shout. I'm sitting right across from you. I can hear you perfectly. It might be helpful if we start at the beginning. My name is Solveig. What's yours?"

"No time!" shouted the old woman as she reached across the table and grabbed both of Solveig's arms. "You must go to Virkio. And then on from there. Another will show the way. More of the stone is missing. Others are looking for the pieces. The powers will be released. Find the Kelpies and keep them hidden."

"Really!" said Solveig, once more pulling her arms free. "You are becoming quite rude. I thought I was a guest in your..." She looked around the cave. "Your...home?"

She looked down into her glass, certain that she had finished drinking the vile tasting tea. The glass was nearly full. That's impossible, she thought. She took a large, long gulp and put the glass back down. She watched as the level of tea rose to the top all by itself. Her first reaction was amazement. How neat, she thought. It fills itself as if by magic. She was still smiling as she stared into the glass, ignoring the rambling of the old woman when it finally sunk in.

"Magic!" she nearly shouted.

She jerked her gaze from the glass to the old woman sitting across from her. The woman had stopped talking and turned her head towards Solveig. They stared at each other in silence for a few seconds. Solveig looked at the empty eye sockets. She knew the woman was blind, but something told her that in spite of this, the woman was clearly looking at her. Either that or she had fallen asleep. It was almost impossible to tell.

"You've given me a potion," she said in an accusing voice. "What have you done to me? What will this potion do?"

"Virkio," gasped the woman, not answering the question. "Find the stone. Hide the Kelpies. Beware the dragon's blood. Beware the dragon's breath, but do not fear the dragon."

"I don't understand what you're babbling about," shouted Solveig. "I want to know what you've given me. What is this potion going to do?"

The old woman only continued to ramble. It was clearly an effort for her to speak. She was babbling about Virkio, some stone, the Kelpies and dragons. It was like she was growing older and more senile right

95

Quest of Eight Part Four: The Race to Virkio

Richard Reda

before Solveig's eyes. She couldn't tell if this was really happening or if it was the result of the potion she had been given. She repeated her questions to the old woman, only to get the same incomprehensible gibberish back.

Solveig's frustration was escalating rapidly. When she asked once again what the potion was going to do to her and got the same nonsensical response, her control evaporated. She raised the glass and flung the tea in the woman's face. It had no reaction. She kept repeating the same things nonstop, as if nothing had happened. However, when Solveig threw the tea, the candle light on the table revealed something more.

Her hands had been in shadows the entire time she had been drinking the potion and conversing with the old woman. When she raised the glass to fling the contents the candlelight revealed a change.

"My hand is blue," Solveig said in a stunned voice.

My hand is blue!" she repeated, expecting some kind of reaction from the old woman.

She looked more closely at the hand that threw the tea and moved it closer to the candle light to make sure it wasn't her imagination. It was blue. Not a light blue or even a sky blue. It was a deep royal blue. She reached to pull the sleeve of the cloak back and saw that her other hand was the same color blue.

Not believing what she was seeing, she pulled back the sleeves on both her arms and saw that the color ran up as far as she could see. She twisted around on her seat and lifted the ends of her clothing to look at her legs. They were blue.

"You turned me blue," she said in disbelief. "I can't believe you turned me blue. Why would you do that?"

She seriously expected to get an answer. Instead, the old woman continued to stare blankly ahead and repeat the same thing. The excitement or agitation – whatever it had been – was gone from her voice. She was gasping with every word. It was evident that merely speaking was an effort.

"You must hurry, before it's too late. You must get to Virkio. Find the stone. Find all of the stone. Stop the release. Hide the Kelpies."

Solveig stood up and grabbed the old woman by her shoulders. She pulled her to her feet and shook her.

"Answer me!" she demanded. "Why did you do this to me? What does it mean?"

The old woman stopped her rambling. Her head hung down; her limp hair hung on either side of her face. She had looked ancient when Solveig first met her, but somehow, now she looked even older. Through the ragged and dirty clothing she wore, Solveig could feel her bones. It was as if she was holding a skeleton, the woman was so thin. The skin on the woman's face appeared to shrivel almost imperceptibly. Solveig knew she would get no answers – at least no answers she would be able to understand.

She lowered the woman to her seat, took one last look around the hut and climbed to the exit. The rain had stopped and the jackals were nowhere to be seen. She took her best guess as to which way she had come and began to run in an attempt to find her friends. She was too far away to hear the final words from the old woman. They were spoken in a voice barely above a whisper as she slumped back in her chair, her breath wheezing in a death rattle.

"Please hurry. The others are making for Virkio. They must be stopped. Beware the dragon's blood and the dragon's breath, but have no fear of the dragon. She will understand you and you will be safe."

97

Chapter five

At the instant Solveig was swept off the ship, Liam was moving levers and gears, and pedaling frantically, trying to regain some altitude, but with little success. The Blue Falcons were keeping up the attack on the rotors and had started shredding the sail. Several of the oars in the large wheels had broken, the parts flung in every direction. The constant siege by the Falcons was pushing the ship down, keeping it in the treetops.

The ship was careening off one tree after another. The passengers were being bounced from side to side. Most of them were huddled on the floor. Lochen was crouched behind Liam, trying to protect him and cast a spell whenever he saw the opportunity, but most of them were reflected or diverted by the spinning rotors.

Quest of Eight Part Four: The Race to Virkio

Richard Reda

In an effort to get away from the birds, Liam had steered the battered ship into a dense copse of pine trees, pulling on the sail lines as hard as he could. The branches were thick with needles and provided a good shelter from the attacking Falcons. The downside was that the branches were whipping along the sides of the *Wedgamaroon*, crashing into everything: the sail, the rotors, and the shafts that held them. No part of the ship was made to withstand such a beating and it started to break apart.

The speed it had gained from the approaching storm was driving it with an incredible force. The ship began vibrating violently, shaking its connections loose. The first thing to go was the front rotor. A large branch got caught in the spokes as the craft shot past, and the wheel was ripped from the mast and flung into the air. With half the lifting capability gone, the ship dropped nearly twenty feet in a few seconds.

Everyone on board was thrown into the air and then landed hard back on the deck or their seats. Lochen was pitched backwards, and nearly fell over. He instinctively reached out and grabbed the back of Liam's shirt, pulling him up and away from the controls. The ship spun wildly to the left and then back to the right as it crashed into one tree and then another. It was also leaning towards the front, since only the rear rotor was providing any lift at all.

A few seconds after the front rotor was lost, the sail and the mast that held it were ripped out. However, that didn't do much to slow the craft down. By now it was almost propelling itself. It wasn't much longer – only seconds – before the second rotor was damaged. Another large branch struck the support shaft just below the midpoint, cracking it, but not separating it. The weight of the wheel on the top was too much.

The shaft bent in half with the wheel swinging in a downward arc. It crashed like a hammer into the side of the ship, knocking Sean and Summer into Quinn. Quinn had been covering Stella and Natalie, and was positioned a little higher. It was high enough to push him out of the ship and into the nearest tree.

He slid across a branch and slammed up against the main trunk. Reflexively, he grabbed the trunk with both arms and kept from falling. When he stopped moving and opened his eyes, he saw that he was almost thirty feet above the ground. He turned in the direction of the ship from which he had just been tossed to see it crash to the ground about two hundred yards deeper into the woods.

Almost immediately after Quinn departed from the craft, the wheel still hanging to the remainder of the mast got caught on another branch, and jerked the ship to the left. It spun almost half way around the tree, pulling free of the wheel and the top portion of the shaft and continued to careen and drop through the woods.

Liam searched for a soft landing, although by now he had lost complete control. There was no way to land the ship or even slow it down. They were all at the mercy of chance. Lochen began casting spells, trying to bend the trees out of the way to minimize the battering. Stella joined him, and for the most part they were able to reduce the number and the impact of the collisions.

"Brace yourselves," shouted Liam. "We're going to hit the ground pretty hard."

Everyone held tightly, either to each other or to one of the benches or a piece of the frame. After what seemed like an eternity, the *Wedgamaroon* bounced across the forest floor and came to a stop. One rotor mast was broken in half; the other rotor and the mast that held the sail were gone completely. The bow of the ship and the port side were damaged beyond repair – the frame had cracked and splintered.

Sean had curled up in the front with Summer tucked in beside him, covered and safe. He, however, had not been so lucky. His back was covered with several pieces of broken parts. As they had splintered, the jagged points had dug into his skin. He looked like a porcupine and was bleeding quite heavily. Stella immediately cast a spell to reduce the pain and told him not to touch anything.

She jumped out of the wreckage and went in search of some leaves and herbs. She found what she needed in only a few minutes and created a salve, which sealed the cuts. She then ministered to Natalie, who was fortunate enough to only have received some bruises. They all took inventory of one another and determined that no one was seriously injured. That was when they discovered that Quinn and Solveig were missing.

"They can't be too far away," offered Liam. "They probably fell out when we made that sharp turn a couple of hundred yards back."

"Then we need to search for them," said Lochen, a bit anxiously. "We should probably stay together, but if some of you are too injured to move, I will go on my own. They may be hurt and need our assistance."

"Hold on a minute," said Liam. "You're right. We shouldn't separate. We don't know where we are or what – or who – is in these woods with us. We already know there are nests of Blue Falcons nearby. We don't need to get anyone else injured or lost."

While they were having this discussion, the rain began to fall. It wasn't a heavy rain, and most of it was deflected by the enormous canopy of trees. At the same time, Quinn was negotiating his way down from his perch. He wasn't comfortable being so high in the air, and was hugging the trunk tightly. He stretched his foot out and down as far as he could while not releasing his grip any more than he had to. He inched his way down, slipping periodically on the branches as they got wet from the rain and tightening his grasp when he did so, scraping his chest and chin against the bark. Eventually, he managed to climb down from the tree, only falling twice, but not doing anything more than give himself a couple of minor cuts, a few bruises and a large bump on his head.

He had no difficulty finding the others. He knew exactly where they were. Some of Liam's path finding skill must be rubbing off on me, he thought to himself. In a few seconds he could hear their voices over the splattering of the raindrops on the awning of leaves and branches.

"Is everyone all right?" he shouted as soon as they were in sight, greatly relieved to no longer be by himself in such a strange place.

All heads turned in his direction. Their debate about either staying put or going in search of their lost partners was interrupted by Quinn's voice.

"See?" said Liam. "They've already found us."

Quinn was lumbering through the woods, happy to see his friends and even happier to be back on the ground. He even bounced a little as he walked along. As he came closer, the others were looking behind him for a sign of Solveig.

"Solveig's not with you?" asked Lochen. "Have you seen her?" he continued, not waiting for an answer to the first question.

"No," answered Quinn. "She's not with me. I thought she was with you guys. I sort of got ejected. I didn't see anyone else getting off. Actually, I had my head down, so I didn't see much of anything. And then I got thrown into this really tall tree. I mean I was pretty far up and I don't like..."

"We have to find her," interrupted Lochen.

He started walking back the way Quinn had come, not waiting for anyone else, or even looking to see if they were following him.

"Lochen!" shouted Liam. "Wait. You don't even know where she is. How do you intend to find her?"

"We can't just do nothing. She could be injured. She could be in danger. In this rain, she could get even more lost than she is right now," he answered, turning back but not retracing his steps and not stopping.

"I didn't say we should do nothing," said Liam, trying to keep things calm. "We need to have a plan. We need to be smart about this. Otherwise we could all get lost."

Lochen finally stopped walking. He turned back towards the woods, hoping for some sign of where she might be. Seeing nothing, he tried to think logically, and then reluctantly walked back to the others.

"I suppose you're right. What do you have in mind?"

"Uh...well...I don't really have anything specific in mind," Liam said, caught off guard. "But we should all discuss whatever options there are and agree to the best approach," he quickly added.

"You have no plan? Then why have you stopped me? I don't intend to debate the situation," Lochen answered a bit gruffly. "The more time we waste blathering the more time we lose in finding her. If you all want to converse, feel free. I will venture out on my own. When I find her, we'll catch up with the rest of you. You needn't wait for either of us."

"That's not what anyone wants to do," interjected Summer, irritated that he would think so.

She flew up and got directly in Lochen's face. Hovering inches from his nose, she wagged her finger at him. As she fluttered her wings, tiny droplets of rain flew off in every direction. Some of them splattered on Lochen's nose.

"Now you just listen to me! She's our friend, too! We all want to find her as much as you do, but Liam's right. We need to be smart about this. We don't know where we are. We don't know where she is or even when she got separated from us. If you go off on your own, we will lose two of our friends. We can't let that happen. You're both too important to us. You know, you're being pretty stupid for a smart guy!"

Lochen jerked his head up at her last remark. Then he looked back over his shoulder into the woods as the last bits of defiance drained from him. He slumped his shoulders and turned back towards Summer and the others.

"I'm sorry. You're right. It's just that she's my sister and I've always felt responsible for her. Right now I feel like I'm letting her down and I'm powerless to do anything about it. I'm worried about her."

"We'll find her," declared Sean. "No matter what it takes or how long it takes."

"Look," said Liam. "It will be dark soon. We need to get some rest, and the stuff Stella made to heal Sean's cuts needs some time to work. Let's make camp here for the night and figure out the best way to begin a search at first light. Quinn and I will go through the wreckage and see if there's anything useful we can salvage. Can some of the others look around for something to eat? Just don't go too far."

Natalie offered to forage and told Lochen to come with her. She said it would keep his mind occupied and make the waiting a little bit more bearable. Stella ordered Sean to stay put while the poultice she had made sealed his wounds, even though he argued that he felt fine. She and Summer found some dry dead wood and started a fire.

In less than an hour, everyone was back at the camp. They each returned without any mishaps. Natalie and Lochen had found some fruit trees and brought back enough to satisfy everyone. Liam reported that there was nothing left of the sail that was usable, but he had managed to retrieve several lengths of rope and a few stakes from the ship's frame that hadn't been shattered in the crash.

"I have no idea what any of this can be used for, but I've always found it handy to have some rope. I thought we could sharpen the ends of the stakes. We may need to have weapons of some kind – more than just Sean's slingshot and my blades. I hope we won't have to use them, but I'd rather be safe than sorry."

"We can use them to make a lean-to," said Sean. "And we can cover it with some of these fallen branches, to keep us out of the rain. If we face it towards the fire, we should be warm through the night. I can feel the temperature already dropping."

"Maybe we should set up a guard rotation," suggested Quinn. "These woods are kind of spooky. Have you noticed? There's no sounds – no insects or animals; nothing."

"A guard rotation sounds like an excellent idea" said Lochen. "You all get some sleep. I will take the first watch. In fact, I can take all the watches. I don't need the rest and it will give me time to formulate a proper plan."

By the time the lean-to was constructed and everyone curled up around the fire, night had completely settled in over the forest. The canopy of trees blocked out the sky and the woods were so dense that the small encampment was surrounded in a blanket of total darkness. The storm had passed and the rain had stopped. However, no stars could be seen, and there was no moon in the sky. Even if there had been, it would have been blocked by the trees and the few lingering rain clouds.

Quinn had been right. There were no sounds other than the crackling of the fire. Lochen waved his hand and the flames rose a little higher. They also changed to a greenish hue, but would burn with a steady consistency throughout the night. He moved a few feet away from the fire to a point where he could watch over everyone and have a clear view in the event they had visitors during the night.

As the dawn approached, Lochen returned to his place near the campfire and waited as everyone awoke. He was anxious to get started, but restrained himself as the others woke up and had a breakfast of nuts and fruit. Once they were ready, Liam asked him if he had given some thought to how they should conduct their search.

"Yes," he answered, more than ready to begin. "Actually, I have. During the night I made some calculations, which, of course were hindered somewhat by the diminished visibility. However, before my vision was totally obscured, I was able to calculate the direction our craft took on its final trajectory. I made some assumptions about the wind speed as it was impacted by the friction caused by the ship intersecting with the trees, as well as the moderating azimuth caused by several other factors..."

"Say it in words, genius!" interrupted Sean, clearly frustrated by Lochen's dissertation.

"Uh...well...I thought I was," said Lochen somewhat puzzled. "Saying it with words. I mean what else would I be saying it...Yes. Of course. Well, then..."

He stood up and pointed behind them.

"We came from that direction, about four hundred yards back, where we made the sudden course change. I propose that we start there. If Solveig had been ejected subsequent to that, Quinn would likely have seen her. Although I have often found him less than observant, I doubt he would have missed seeing her, had she been along that route."

"I'm observant," countered Quinn. "I just don't pay some stuff a lot of attention."

"All right," said Sean. "That's where we start. Where do we go from there?"

"I will need to see the exact angle of our approach prior to the point where we were anchored temporarily by one of the rotors. That will tell me the route along which Solveig separated from us."

"What good will that do?" asked Natalie.

"Solveig was on the starboard side of the ship. I have to assume she either fell or was knocked off somewhere between the point of the attack by the Blue Falcons and the sudden change of course when the rotor was lodged in a tree and twisted us around. Being on that side of the ship, it is most likely that she fell in that direction and probably rolled or slid away from that line – to the right, rather than to the left. Well, to the right when we were coming in this direction. Now it would be to our left."

"That makes sense," said Summer. "I can try to scout the tree tops and branches for some sign of where she might have fallen."

Lochen smiled at her, relieved that he had been talked out of marching off the previous night by himself. He turned his gaze to the others, who were equally ready to set off in search of their lost partner.

"That would be very helpful," he said. "Shall we begin?"

- - - - - - - - - - - - - - - - - *** - - - - - - - - - - - - - - - - -

By the time Solveig emerged from the old woman's cottage under the tree, the rain had slowed down considerably. It was still overcast, but light enough to see. It wouldn't be long before nightfall descended, though, and she had no idea of which way to go. She moved cautiously, keeping a watch for the pack of jackals that had chased her into the woods. They were nowhere to be seen.

I don't know if that's a good thing or a bad thing, she thought. It was difficult to see through the treetops to the sky above and to determine which way the suns might have set. Making her best guess, she started walking towards what she believed was west. Nothing looked familiar but she decided she couldn't simply sit still and hope her friends would find her. She would need to take care of herself.

She tried to recall what had happened, but her memory of the events was foggy and evaporating quickly. She remembered being attacked by Blue Falcons, but couldn't imagine why. After that, everything was a blur. She was in the ship, and then she wasn't. How that happened was a puzzlement. She couldn't fathom the possibility that her friends would leave her voluntarily. Had something happened to them, she wondered.

She tried to find something ahead of her in the distance to focus on to make sure she kept on track, but the daylight was rapidly disappearing. After a while she was passing trees, clumps and rocks she was certain she had passed before. She was convinced that she was now only walking in circles. She knew she needed to stop and make camp for the night, and get a fresh start in the morning.

She walked a little further, trying to find a clearing large enough that she could safely start a fire. The trees in this section of the forest were much different than the pines she had stumbled through and that surrounded the hut of the old woman. She didn't remember when that change had occurred. Solveig was worried that she was becoming even more lost than she was when she first started – if that was even possible.

The surrounding trees were very large and unlike all the others. It was apparent that they were also very old and as far as she could tell, they seemed to be located only in this area. Their trunks were very wide, and were twisted and gnarled. Branches turned in odd directions, intertwining with one another. In some places they blocked any openings that existed between them.

She also noticed that the shape of the bark, especially where branches had been cut or broken off, looked almost like faces. They were severely distorted, but in a few of them, she could clearly see what looked very much like closed eyes and mouths open in expressions of agony.

"This is too weird for words," she said out loud to no one in particular.

She looked closely at one of the shapes. It looked like a large knot in the side of a twisted trunk. The bark was thick and rough, but she was sure she could see two smaller knots – one slightly higher than the other – that could pass for eyes. There was a protrusion of bark that ran between them that looked like a large and broken nose. Underneath it was a large gouge cut into the trunk, shaped like a wide inverted "U" with one side drooping lower in the same manner as the off-set eyes.

She looked to the next tree and saw another face. This one almost looked like it was gazing skyward, pleading for something. As she turned around, she saw several more. They all looked like they were in such pain, that she was beginning to feel depressed herself.

She told herself she was imagining things and to get a grip. She looked around and realized she was in just the right kind of clearing she had been looking for. The branches were high enough above that any fire she lit wouldn't run the risk of spreading throughout the forest. In spite of the imagined faces in the surrounding trees, she thought this was as good a place as any to camp for the night.

She found some dried twigs – not an easy task after the rainfall. They had apparently fallen off the surrounding trees, since they had the same twisted shape and the same unusual bark. Near the base of the trees, in between the extensive root system, she found some brush that was dry enough to light. With a clap of her hands and a flash of lightning, she ignited the brush and started the fire.

The temperature had dropped significantly. She and the others had traveled north for quite some time, so the climate was naturally cooler. Deep in the shade of the forest and soon after nightfall, though, the cold was setting in. She could see her breath and knew it would get even colder as the night progressed.

"This cloak is a lot warmer than I expected it to be," she said. "I'm talking to myself – out loud. I must be really starting to lose it."

She held her hands out to warm them by the fire. They were still blue. I didn't imagine that, she said – this time silently to herself. She realized that in spite of the temperature, she wasn't cold, and in spite of not having eaten for quite some time, she wasn't hungry. And even more unusual, in spite of being completely lost and alone, she wasn't frightened. Until she heard a voice.
"Are you one of them?" asked a voice from behind her.

She jumped up and spun around; her arm was poised to throw a bolt of lightning. The voice had been little more than a whisper, but in the dead silence that surrounded her, it seemed as loud as a scream.

"Who's there?" she shouted with more bravado than she felt.

"It might be a Kelpie," whispered another voice.

Solveig jumped at the sound of the second voice. She realized that by standing so close to the fire, she was in plain sight of whoever had called out. She stepped sideways, moving away from the firelight until she considered that she might be moving towards the voice instead of away from it. She spun around, looking in every direction. She pressed her back against one of the nearby trees.

110

"We can do you no harm," another voice called out, somewhat muffled.

"Who's there?" she shouted again, spinning around.

That voice had come from right behind her. Where were these people? And I don't believe for a minute that they can do me no harm, she thought. If that was true, then why didn't they show themselves? She was jerking left and right, trying to make sure no one snuck up behind her, and trying to see where that last voice had come from.

She rubbed her hands together and generated a small orb of light. Holding it in one hand she thrust it forward like a lantern to light up the forest. Shadows jumped back and forth as she swung her arm, but nothing appeared.

"It's not a Kelpie," whispered the first voice. "Besides, what more harm could they do to us?"

"I know it's not a Kelpie," said the third voice. "That's why I told it we could do it no harm."

"I'm not an 'it,'" Solveig shouted. "I'm a she. Now show yourselves. Come out where I can see you," she demanded, although she was as much afraid of seeing something as she was of not seeing something.

"We can't," came an answer.

Solveig jumped and screamed. The voice was right behind her. She spun around, her heart hammering in her chest, and backed away. She nearly tripped over the campfire trying to put some distance between herself and the sound. Side stepping the fire, she stumbled to her knees and dropped the orb. The light extinguished as it rolled from her hand. She scrambled to her feet and began rubbing her hands together again, while searching for the source of the voice.

Quest of Eight Part Four: The Race to Virkio

Richard Reda

"I'm a powerful sorceress," she stammered. "If you don't show yourself immediately, I will turn you into a...a...I don't know, but it will be something horrible."

"You're not a sorceress," said a voice right next to her, "but you are one of them."

Trying to control her panic, she slowly turned towards the sound, but didn't move away from it. It was so close, that she realized it could only come from one place – the tree. She generated another orb of light and held it in the palm of her hand. Raising it slowly, she brought it up to a gnarled shape in the trunk of the tree.

"I'm one of who?" she asked, focusing on the face in the tree, but hoping deep down that it didn't answer.

The bark on the tree began to move. Two knots opened up to reveal a pair of eyes, filled with pain and suffering. The distorted gash several inches lower twisted as it formed words. She fought her urge to run away, but kept quickly glancing around and over her shoulder to make sure this wasn't some kind of trap.
"One of them," the face answered. "One of the ones searching for the pendant of the Enchantress. One of the ones to open the portal."

In spite of watching the face take shape, she was almost praying that she had been imagining what was happening. When the face spoke, she quickly backed away and tripped over a stone, falling flat on her back. This time she held on tightly to the orb. Staring up at the face, which now had opened its eyes, she tried to overcome her shock and find her voice.

"I...I...I don't know what you're talking about," she stammered. "Who are you?"

"We are the sole survivors of the village of Kalayaan," said another voice.

112

Solveig jumped up to her feet and spun around towards the sound. Seeing nothing but darkness, she pushed the light in that direction. A few feet away in the bole of another tree, another face was slowly moving – slowly coming alive.

"I've never heard of that village," she said.

I'm really losing it, she thought. First I was talking to myself; now I'm talking to trees. What a stupid thing to say – I've never heard of that village – she said to herself. Although, what else would you say to a talking tree? Strangely enough, she didn't feel as frightened as she did when she first heard the voices.

"It has been dead for over two thousand years," said a voice from yet another of the faces in the trees.

She stepped back to the campfire and waved her hand across it and tossed the orb into the center. The flames grew higher, throwing out enough light to brighten the entire clearing. Solveig looked around and saw faces in more than half a dozen of the trees. Each one was slightly different, but each one had the same expression of pain and despair.
"I don't understand," she said. "Was this a village of trees? I've never heard of a village of trees."

"No," said a different voice. "We are people. We were people. We stood against the Kelpies. This was our reward."

"That old woman mentioned Kelpies. I don't know who or what they are. None of this makes any sense."

"The Kelpies," explained the first figure, "were ancient sorcerers. They became too powerful and turned to evil. Only two had the courage to fight them – the Alchemist and an Enchantress. But they were outnumbered. It was just the two of them against all the Kelpies."

113

"There was a lot of in-fighting," voiced another face. "Some of the Kelpies destroyed one another, but, still, the odds did not favor the Alchemist and the Enchantress."

"The two of them had to plot and make their moves when they could separate the Kelpies from one another."

By now nearly a dozen voices had joined in the telling of the story. Solveig was captivated as much by the mysterious faces in the sides of the trees as she was by the tale they were describing. She sat on a rock on the side of the clearing so she could see most of the speakers at one time.

"While the wars raged on, the Kelpies were ruthless. They couldn't find the sanctuary of either the Alchemist or the Enchantress. They plagued villages from ocean to ocean, terrorizing the people of the world."

"The Alchemist did his best to protect us, but he couldn't save everyone. Our village was one of the one's he couldn't help in time."

"The Kelpie Rovek descended on us. What he did was unspeakable. We lost everyone – our families; our friends; our homes."

"We were the village leaders. We were powerless to stop him or to convince him that we knew nothing. We think he knew that even if we could have helped him, we wouldn't. That probably enraged him even further. When he had destroyed everyone else and still didn't have the answers he was seeking, he sealed us inside these trees."

"We were unable to move, to see, or to speak. We would age within the trees themselves, at the same pace, making our lives stretch out for thousands of years, with no relief."

"When the Alchemist and the Enchantress discovered what had happened, they tried everything they knew to break the spells. The only thing they could do was allow us to speak and see, but even that is limited only to the night."

"They knew then that they needed to destroy the Kelpies."

"They combined their powers and cast spells on them one at a time, entombing them and hiding them. They knew that the spells would not last forever."

"Even with the power of the stone. That was what the Kelpies were really after."

"All the while, the Enchantress was schooling two others to help in the battle. But that went terribly wrong."

"They betrayed her."

"The stone was shattered."

"And the Enchantress was lost to us."

"Over the centuries, the Alchemist has come to us whenever he can. With each visit, he tries again to break the spell, but he hasn't been able to do so. He says if the stone is discovered, he may find the key. We have come to accept our fate."

"We know that we will remain as we are until the tree which we have become completes its own life cycle. Only then will we be at peace."

They were all silent for several minutes. Solveig was stunned. She knew of the Alchemist and had heard about some Enchantress from Stella. She guessed that the stone they were talking about might be the one that Stella now wore. It clearly had magical powers, even though it was evident that parts of it were missing. She wondered if she should tell them about it.

By now she could see light beginning to break through the thick treetops. The first sun was close to rising. She hadn't slept at all, but oddly, she didn't feel tired. She looked from one face to the next. Their eyes were so sad, that she could feel their pain.

"You said I was one of them; that I was one of the ones searching for the pendant of the Enchantress."

"Yes," answered the voice that had spoken to her first. "When the pendant was shattered, the pieces dispersed to distant places. They have never been found, and are still separate. In order for the stone's power to be resurrected, the pieces must be found and united."

At those words, she was certain that the triskelion that Summer had worn and the stone that had been taken from the Rebbercand were parts of the Enchantress' pendant. She had seen those two pieces seal themselves together. She was also certain that at least two more pieces existed, which fit on either side of the remaining leg of the triskelion.

The old woman had insisted that she find the stone. At least that part of her ranting made sense now. But that was about all that did. Solveig still didn't know what or where Virkio was, and what it had to do with anything. She still didn't know how the Kelpies fit in to all this, especially if the Alchemist and the Enchantress put spells on them and hid them. What was she supposed to do?

And who are these others that are trying to get there? Are these others good guys or bad guys? Probably bad guys, she thought. And then there was something about a portal. What was that all about? There were more questions now than answers.

Solveig was momentarily distracted by a soft creaking sound. She looked behind her and couldn't see where it was coming from. She stood up and took a few steps into the forest. Her first thought was

116

that someone was trying to sneak up on her. Was it these "others" the old woman had mentioned?

Then she heard it again. It wasn't coming from behind her. It was right next to her. She looked at the nearest tree and saw that the face that had been speaking only moments before was closing down. The eyes were shut. The mouth stopped moving. The features blended back into the bark on the side of the trunk.

She turned the other way towards one of the other faces. It, too, had faded back to the image it had been earlier. She ran around the clearing looking at each of the faces. One by one they were returning to lifelessness. She ran back to the tree from where the first voice had come.

"What's happening?" she demanded. "Why did they stop talking? Why have they gone back the way they were?"

"The dawn is coming," answered the first voice in little more than a whisper. "We will not be able to speak again until a month has past."

"Wait," she objected. "What do you mean 'we'? Is this happening to you, too? It is. I can see it. You said you came to life at night. That means I can talk to you again tonight, once the suns have gone down."

"No. We are able to return only in the darkest of dark. The moon will begin to grow again before nightfall. We will be silent until the next night of the new moon, when the night is fully black."

"A new moon?" she cried out. "I can't wait that long. You can't leave, yet. I have more questions."

"You must get to Virkio," said the face, its voice fading quickly as its features withdrew and blended back into the tree.

117

Quest of Eight Part Four: The Race to Virkio

Richard Reda

"I don't know what that is," Solveig wailed. "Wait, you can't go, yet. What am I supposed to do?"

She was pounding on the tree trunk. She reached up to try to force the eyelids to remain open, but she was powerless to stop them. She pulled at the gash that formed the lips, but couldn't stop it from closing.

"Get to Virkio before the others," murmured the voice. "They are racing there now. Find the stone. Find the portal."

"What portal? Where is the stone? Where is Virkio?" she shouted.

It was too late. The last voice from the last face had returned to its dormant state. She had slumped to the ground, still pounding her fists against the trunk of the tree, but with no effect. Eventually, she gave up and looked around. The clearing looked exactly as it had when she first found it.

Even with the sun breaking over the distant horizon, it was still quite dark this deep in the woods. However, there were shafts of light poking through the few openings, sending rays of sun from the sky down to the forest floor. At least Solveig now knew which way was east.

She knew there was nothing she could do to bring the village elders back to life, and that she couldn't stay until a month had passed. She needed to find her friends. Maybe they could help figure some of this out.

She looked at her hands. They were still blue. She pulled back her sleeves, and her arms were the same shade. She closed one eye and peered down at the little bit of her nose that she could see. It was blue.

"Oh, poop," she said out loud. "I was hoping all that was a dream."

Richard Reda

She waved her hand and the campfire was doused. Then she looked for an opening through the copse of trees that would take her towards the west. The clearing appeared to be completely surrounded by the ancient trees.

"How did I ever get in here in the first place," she said out loud, not really expecting an answer, although by now she wouldn't have been completely shocked if one had been forthcoming.

She had to wriggle through some branches and some dense foliage. After several minutes, she was away from the clearing and the village elders. She started climbing a slight incline, keeping an eye out for those jackals. The lack of any sounds whatsoever was a bit unsettling. She slowed her pace and listened intently.

She knew she had been in a panic yesterday, and that she was wandering aimlessly, but none of what she was seeing now looked the least bit familiar. The trees were giving way to long, intertwining vines and hanging moss. She was certain she hadn't encountered anything like this before.

She tried to encircle the clearing, but only ran into denser and denser undergrowth, which made it impossible to continue. This was obviously not the way she had come the night before. She turned back the way she had come, only to find the woods had closed up behind her. Now she was really beginning to worry.

Chapter six

Jochen led the party along the path their ship had taken on the final leg of its journey. Their going was slow. At ground level, they were encountering large roots, several saplings and an extensive network of vines. The approach they had taken coming into the forest had been nearly sixty feet higher or more. As much of an obstacle course that journey had been was nothing compared to what they were navigating now.

After almost two hours, they reached the point where the rotor had gotten caught in the tree and radically changed their course. The day before, they had covered this same distance in a matter of minutes. They knew they were in the right place. The back rotor was still stuck in the branches high above them. Quinn pointed out the spot, almost sixty feet away, where he had been ejected and flung into a tree.

"Summer," said Lochen. "If you would be so kind, please fly up above the damage and see if you can determine the precise direction from which we came. Be careful, though. The Blue Falcons may still be in the area."

She fluttered upwards and was quickly out of sight. Once she passed the dangling wheel, she was close to the tops of the trees. She kept close to the branches and the leaves and wormed her way through them to the highest point.

When they had been evading the Falcons, it seemed like it had taken only seconds to reach this forest. Now it was plain to see, they must have been flying for several minutes. The range of trees stretched off into the distance for more than a mile. She looked around and didn't see any predators.

Taking a deep breath, she gave a strong push and flew straight upward. She was more than thirty feet above the treetops before she could see the ocean and the shore on the other side of the forest. Instead of being happy, she was demoralized. Solveig could be anywhere along that expanse. This was worse than she first thought.

She dropped back down into the woods and flew in and out of the branches, back to the others. The first face she saw was Lochen's. He was looking at her expectantly, and must have detected the feelings of discouragement that were written on her face.

"What's wrong?" he asked. "Did you see her? Is she hurt?"

"No," Summer answered quickly. "I didn't see her."

"Then what's wrong?" he persisted.

"Nothing's wrong," she protested. "It's just that we're further from the ocean than I had thought. That's all. It's going to take longer to find her."

"Then we need to get started," interjected Sean. "Where should we begin?"

"How far away is the ocean?" Lochen asked, ignoring Sean's attempt to remain positive.

"I don't know," answered Summer, trying to be evasive. "I'm not really good at guessing distances. After all, things look much bigger to me than they do to you."

"Guess," demanded Lochen.

"At least a mile," she mumbled. "Probably close to two."

"I see," said Lochen.

It was clear he was mentally calculating the possible search area. He turned back from Summer and looked off into the woods. The impossibility of their successfully finding Solveig was beginning to become a reality to him. Quinn was the first to break the silence.

"Can't you do some kind of spell or something?" he asked. "Or maybe you can connect with her, you know, mental like?"

He turned to Liam and asked, "You can find stuff without a map or anything. Can't you just lead us to her?"

"It doesn't work that way," answered Liam. "I can find places. I can't find people."

"Well, we have to do something," he said, his voice rising.

"The problem is," Lochen finally said, "that, assuming she can walk, we will in all likelihood miss her as we search. You saw how long it took us to get to this point. There is nothing different in the forest ahead that will make our traveling any faster."

"We can't give up," said Sean.

"I have no intention of giving up," answered Lochen. "I just need to think. If there was a way we could narrow down the point where she left the ship, that would be ideal."

"Maybe I can help with that," said Stella. "I'm not making any promises, you understand. But if I can get a vision of where it might have happened, maybe we could find that spot and start searching there."

"But there's no Sanctorum anywhere near here," said Natalie. "How are you going to conjure a vision?"

"I'm going to try something else," she answered. "I don't know if it will work, but it's worth a try. I'm going to see if I can recreate the events through the eyes of each of us and piece things together."

"Good luck," said Sean. "My eyes were closed most of the time."

"But not all of the time," said Stella. "Every little bit will help. Lochen, let me start with you. You were closest to her most of the time, and I think your visions will be the strongest."

"Whatever you need," he said.

Stella sat down on a log and motioned for him to sit next to her. When he did, she held one of his hands in hers and with her other hand held the stone from her headband, which she had removed and was now holding.

"Concentrate on what you remember beginning with the attack by the Blue Falcons. You don't have to actually try to recount what happened. I just want your memories to begin there."

He nodded in understanding, and his recollections began to take shape. Through his eyes, Stella could see the birds attacking the ship, the ship dropping into the treetops, and the branches flying by. She caught images of Solveig in the corner of Lochen's eyesight. She was flashing bolts of lightning in every direction, but not at anything in particular. She watched the entire event to the point where Quinn flew off the ship. By then it was evident that Solveig was no longer on board. When she was done with Lochen, she asked Liam to sit next to her.

"Did you see her?" asked Lochen. "Do you know where she fell off?"

"Not yet," Stella answered. "Give it time. And remember. I don't know if this is really going to work."

She held Liam's hand in hers and once again rubbed the stone from the headband. She could feel a tremendous amount of tension in his grip. She could sense his feelings of responsibility for the safety of them all. Through his eyes, she could not see Solveig, but instead she concentrated on the surroundings. She could see when the flashing of the lightning that Solveig was generating suddenly stopped. She saw a large branch sweep past at almost the same instant.

She released his hand and waited for the tension to leave her. Then she asked for Quinn's hand. She saw his eyes dart from the Blue Falcons to both Natalie and herself. She watched as he threw himself on top of the two of them, and then everything went black. It was apparent he had shut his eyes. She was almost ready to end her connection with him when the visions returned. She could see him looking up at the sky, and then she had the sensation of weightlessness. His vision was fixed on a tree that was rapidly coming closer. She realized this was the moment he had been thrown off the ship and onto the tree.

She had similar visions with Summer and Natalie. Both of them had been grabbed and pulled to the deck of the ship and covered almost

124

from the start. Their view had been blocked by Sean and Quinn. They had no view of Solveig at all during the entire event. Stella was concerned that she didn't have much information with which to narrow their search. Sean had already told everyone that he hadn't seen anything at all of Solveig, so she didn't hold out much hope that seeing through his eyes would help.

"You don't have enough, do you?" asked Lochen, reading the look on Stella's face as she asked Sean to sit next to her.

"I'm not going to answer that. I haven't given up, yet," she answered.

"You don't have to answer," he said, dejection filling his voice. "You already have."

"Just wait," she pleaded.

She took Sean's hand and began to see what he saw. He had been watching the horizon, glad to be over land instead of water. Then suddenly he was looking up at the Blue Falcons as they reacted to the flashing lightning. He scanned the tree line, wondering where it had come from. He saw the Falcons racing to the ship and start snapping and clawing. He saw Summer flitting in and out, trying to avoid the Falcons, and trying to avoid being blown away from the ship and the limited protection of the large rotors overhead. She could see him shooting his slingshot at the predators, striking most of them.

Then he reached out and plucked Summer out of the air, inches from the razor sharp talons of one of the Falcons. As he dropped to the deck, she could see him glance towards Liam. On the edge of his field of vision, she saw Solveig's feet. Sean looked up and could see the Falcons striking the rotors. The oars began to break. Pieces began to fly in every direction. Sean ducked his head down and closed his eyes.

In the split second before he shut out the vision, in the blur of motion, Stella caught a glimpse of Liam and the space next to him and slightly behind, where Solveig had been standing. She wasn't there.

"Start again," she told Sean. "Start your recollection from the moment you grabbed Summer."

He did as she requested, concentrating hard on that precise moment, not even actually recalling the events. He let his mind run as Stella re-examined the vision. There was Liam, and then there was the space where Solveig had been only moments before.
"I think I know where to start," she announced.

"Where?" shouted Lochen, excitedly. "Let's get there. Please. Let's hurry."

"I don't have a precise location," Stella cautioned. "And it's only a starting point. We need to go back along the direction we were taking from the ocean. We need to find where the oars from the rotor first started to break off. That's our starting point."

They were at the point where their course had been unexpectedly altered by the rotor anchoring itself into a tree. The damaged branches above them provided an obvious indication of the course they had followed from the sea over the land. Summer flew above the treetops to lead their excursion, looking for signs where the damage first began.

This wasn't as easy as they all thought it would be. There were bits and pieces of debris all along the way. In addition to pieces of the sail and broken, splintered oars, wheels and masts, there were damaged tree limbs and branches. The trail of wreckage seemed to go on forever. What made it worse was that coming in they had been near the top of the forest. Now, except for Summer, they were all trying to negotiate the forest floor.

Quest of Eight Part Four: The Race to Virkio

Richard Reda

The trunks of these enormously high trees were enormously wide. The roots were often as high as walls. They all had to climb and crawl, and double back as they worked their way through the maze of woods.

"This is taking far too long," complained Lochen. "There must be a better way. What if we divided up? With two or even three teams we could cover more ground."

"I don't think that's a good idea," countered Natalie. "We still don't know our starting point."

"I know you're anxious to make progress," offered Stella. "But we need to stay together."

"You're right. You're right. I know, but I'm having difficulty trying to be patient," Lochen said.

His anxiety was increasing rapidly the longer their search took, and the more taxing the obstacles they faced. In his haste he had already slipped or tripped so many times, his shins were black and blue with bruises. He had cut his hands and arms on rocks and branches in several places, but wouldn't stop to have them tended to.

His impatience finally bubbled over when Liam announced that they would have to stop for the night. Summer had still not been able to find the point where the ship had first begun to fall apart, and darkness was falling.

"No!" argued Lochen. "We can generate light. We have to continue."

"And generating that light will announce our presence to anything and everything in this forest," Liam argued back.

"I'll find the spot tomorrow," said Summer, pleading with him. "I promise. I'll fly out ahead of everyone."

"No," Sean interjected. "You can't go off by yourself, especially not so close to the nests of all those Blue Falcons."

"I have to," said Summer. "Lochen's right. We need to move faster. Solveig could be hurt or in danger. I'll be careful. I have to do this!"

None of them got much sleep that night. They were all too worried and on edge. And if that wasn't enough, for the first time, they heard sounds coming from the woods. Twigs snapped, leaves rustled, and in the distance – but not enough in the distance to suit any of them – they could hear growls. Lochen had cast a protective spell around their encampment. It wasn't very strong, and wouldn't really stop anything, but it would slow down an intruder long enough to alert them. As it turned out, the spell was not needed – or it was in some way detected by whatever was out there and sufficient to deter them. At the first signs of light in the sky, Summer was off and flying along the tops of the forest again.

The others continued to make their way on the ground. After several minutes, the trees started to thin out and the walking became easier. Large openings between the trees began to appear. Not long afterwards, Summer returned.

"I found it," she shouted. "At least I think I did. There are still some trees with broken branches, but I finally stopped seeing bits and pieces of our ship. I went back and forth a few times to make sure."

"How far away?" asked Lochen.

"And there's more," she added, smiling broadly, and not answering his question. "I think I found a piece of the clothing Solveig was wearing."

She had expected this information to be received more positively than it was. She saw Lochen's face cloud over, and realized what else this could mean.

"It was just a little piece," she rushed to say. "A small tear – a scrap. I didn't see any blood or anything."

"How far away?" Lochen asked again.

"Not far," she answered.

"Once we know where she landed, I can track her from there," said Sean. "Don't worry. We'll find her."

Not far took nearly an hour to reach, walking through the forest. When they arrived, Summer pointed out the scrap of clothing. Lochen was trying to calculate how far she could have been flung, estimating the speed of the *Wedgamaroon*, the angle of her direction and the altitude at the time. Sean ignored him and began looking at the ground, walking back and forth in a widening arc. Finally, he saw something.

"Over here, everyone," he shouted. "Look at how the ground here seems to dip."

"It's just a long, narrow hollow in the ground," said Quinn. "What's so special about it?"

"It's more than a hollow," answered Sean. "Look at how it's deeper at the end closest to where Summer found that piece of clothing. It's smooth and the same width the whole length until it ends over there. That's not natural. This is where she landed and slid. I'm sure of it."

Without waiting for the others, he began to follow the trail that, for the most part, was only evident to him. Along the way he picked up more pieces of cloth and found indications of where she had fallen or stumbled. The others followed along, watching him and at the same time keeping an eye on their surroundings.

Quest of Eight Part Four: The Race to Virkio

Richard Reda

When they came upon a stream – the one she had fallen in – the trail seemed to disappear. Sean asked the others to stay put while he walked in the water up one way and back the other.

"I can't tell if she crossed to the other side or went back the way she came," he told them. "I don't want all of you tramping around messing up any tracks I can find."

They waited patiently while Sean examined every inch of both sides of the stream. The rainfall had washed away much of the trail he had been following. After a few minutes – it seemed much longer to Lochen – he found something, and he was off again. A little while later, he spotted other footprints.

"Hold on," he whispered to everyone.

He got on his hands and knees and studied the prints closely. Then he moved back to the impressions left by Solveig. Finally he stood up and looked around.

"This looks like a footprint from a jackal," he told them. "But it's much bigger than any I've ever seen before."

He made a wide circle, stopping every once in a while.

"There were several of them. They had her surrounded."

"Solveig," shouted Lochen. "Solveig. Can you hear us?"

"Save your breath," Sean told Lochen. "These tracks are a couple of days old, and it doesn't look like they attacked her, although it sure looks like she ran away from them. Let's keep going."

They continued further into the forest following Sean's lead. Eventually, the tracks of the jackals seemed simply to disappear. There were tracks from Solveig that led in and out of a large hole in the base of a tree. Sean armed his slingshot and carefully poked his head into the hole.

"There's nothing in there. I mean there's stuff in there," he said. "It looks like someone lived in there, but no one's there now."

He backed out of the opening and picked up the trail again. The others stayed close behind him.

- - - - - - - - - - - - - - - - - ******* - - - - - - - - - - - - - - - - -

Solveig had wandered in the forest an entire day. She tried to keep on heading west, but in the denser parts of the woods that was often difficult. Ever since she had been knocked off the *Wedgamaroon*, she had been unnerved by the lack of sound. Lately, though, she had begun hearing things: twigs cracking and leaves rustling, and every once in a while she was sure she could hear a low growl.

Trying to remain as silent as possible she slowed her progress considerably. It was also exhausting. Between creeping along, trying to stay on track and looking around every tree and at every shadow, her nerves were on edge. She was afraid to eat any of the berries or other fruit she came upon, unsure whether it was safe or not. All she could think about were those dreadful peach colored berries.

By the time night fell, and she was still alone, she began to think she was never going to find her friends again. She was hungry and cold. She was sore from all the climbing over roots and around trees, slipping and falling, scraping her knees and legs, and cutting her hands. On top of all that, she was dead tired.

I've had it, she said to herself. She was nowhere recognizable, the suns were setting, the temperature was dropping, and she was too tired to go any further. She looked around for a potential place to stay for the night. She huddled next to a tree where the ground was covered in leaves and grass, and pulled the cloak the old woman had given her over her head – both for warmth and to hide.

Within seconds she fell into a deep and dreamless sleep. It felt like she had just drifted off when a snapping sound brought her immediately awake. She stayed as still as she could, listening intently for another sound. She slowly and quietly pulled her head through the top of the cloak. All around her was nothing but black.

At first she thought her eyes were still closed. When she was sure they were open, she raised her hand and slowly moved it back and forth in front of her. As close as her hand was, she couldn't see it.

At least I can't see that it's still blue, she thought. I suppose that's one good thing. She thought about generating some light, but then worried that all this would do would be to pinpoint her location. She lowered her hand, pulled it back under the cloak, and pulled the cloak back over her head.

She told herself that doing this didn't make her invisible, but she didn't care. If I can't see what's going to eat me, she thought, I won't know it's happening. Within seconds she was again in a deep sleep. This time, though, she began to dream.

In her dream she was someplace that was very cold, although she didn't feel cold at all. She could see her breath, even in the darkness. Except it wasn't completely dark. She looked up and saw the sky filled with millions of stars. It was beautiful. Lochen would love this, she said to herself.

"I do love it," he answered. He was standing right next to her.

"Where did you come from?" she asked him.

"I've never left you," he replied.

"No," she said. "I was alone in the woods."

"Only in your mind. I've been with you all the time."

"You're not making any sense," she told him.

"Beware of the dragon's breath."

"What are you talking about?" she asked. "That's what the old woman said."

"Beware of the dragon's blood."

"Stop it, Lochen. You're scaring me."

"Who did this to my child? What have you done?"

"What child? What are you talking about, Lochen?"

"I am Uzradzi, Guardian of Virkio. You have killed my child and now you will pay for your crime."

"No," Solveig shouted. "We didn't do this. It wasn't us..."
She jerked her head up and it popped through the top of the cloak. She had been dreaming. The first sun had just risen, dappling the forest with rays of light. Dust particles floated through them, sparkling as they moved. There was a layer of frost all around, covering everything with a thin white layer.

"What a nightmare," she mumbled out loud as she pulled her hands and arms out from under the cloak to push herself up. "And I'm still blue. It just doesn't get any better than this, does it?"

Her sarcasm was lost on the trees. She stood up and arched her back, stretching out the kinks and her tired muscles. She looked up through the leaves and could see where the sun was. Taking direction from that, she turned in the opposite direction and continued moving westward, hopefully towards the ocean.

In another part of the forest, Lochen had spent another night fully awake, trying unsuccessfully to think of anything but the dangers his sister might have encountered. Even before the sun broke over the horizon, he was standing over the others, perched like a vulture, waiting for them to awaken so they could continue their search.

One by one, they were startled as they opened their eyes to see his expectant face immediately above them. Each time he apologized for frightening them, but he persisted all the same until they were all up and ready to begin again.

"Are we any closer," he asked Sean for the hundredth time.

"I don't know," Sean answered for the hundredth time. "I can't tell how old the tracks are – only the direction they lead. Remember?"

"I'm sorry. I'm sorry," he said. "I know you've already told me that. I thought that by now we'd have found her. It seems we have to be close, don't we?"

"Lochen," said Natalie. "I don't want you to lose hope, but if she's moving, which she seems to be doing, she could still be as far away from us as she was from the beginning."

"At least she seems to be moving to the west," said Liam. "If she stays on this course, she's going to reach the ocean. By then we should be able to see her, if we don't catch up to her sooner."

"But she must be all right," said Lochen. "If she's moving, she must be all right."

No one wanted to tell him that she might still be injured, even if she was moving. They didn't have to. They could see in his eyes that he was as aware of this as they were. And they knew this was why he was so insistent about continuing their search.

In the meantime, Solveig was in fact on the move again. She had been moving since first light, and hadn't stopped once. She tried to keep the direction of the suns in view, as hard as that often was, in order to keep her on a steady westerly course. In trying to do that, though, she often wasn't paying enough attention to where she was walking. She tripped repeatedly over tree roots, fallen branches, rocks and unexpected changes in the level of the ground.

She had fallen into more than one stream and was soaked, dirty, bruised and tired. She was also becoming more and more panicked. She was certain that by now she would have either seen something that looked familiar, or would have some indication that the ocean was near. Neither was happening.

She eventually came to a section of the forest where the trees opened up and there were larger areas in which to walk and larger patches of sky above. She took this opportunity to quicken her pace, hoping to cover more ground in a shorter time. She was staring above, once more getting a fix on the direction of the suns when her foot caught in a long thin tendril of a honeysuckle vine.

Without even looking down when the vine tangled itself around her shin, she merely gave it a sharp pull to free her foot. Instead of freeing it, though, the sudden movement tripped the snare. The vine tightened around her lower leg and the sapling to which the other end was attached, snapped upward, yanking Solveig with it.

Before she knew what had happened, she was dangling several feet in the air, suspended by her left leg, hanging upside-down. She bent her body almost in half so that she could see what had tied itself to her ankle, but could hold this position only for a second or two. Her head dropped back down, causing her to sway back and forth, and spin in circles.

Quest of Eight Part Four: The Race to Virkio

Richard Reda

The forest twirled around her as she tried in vain to steady herself. She was getting dizzy. Every movement she made to reach up towards her leg and to try to free herself, resulted in more bouncing up and down and only increased the twirling motion.

"Help," she yelled, even though she was sure no one was anywhere near to hear her.

All she could see was a sea of green and black as the trees around her raced past her field of vision. She was moving so fast that nothing was in focus. She closed her eyes, but that didn't help. Her stomach felt like it was doing handsprings. All she could think was that she hoped she wouldn't throw up – or would that be throw down, she asked herself.

"Help," she yelled again.

Her voice echoed off the trees and bounced back to her from several directions. Or maybe it was only one – the one she kept spinning past. Oh, she thought, all the blood is rushing to my head and it's giving me a headache.

"Someone, please. HELP!"

In the midst of the blur of green that spun in circles around her, she spotted something red. She didn't recall seeing it on any of her other spins. As she completed another revolution, she tried to get a better view of whatever it was.

It appeared to be some kind of red cloud. It was moving in and out of the trees and coming towards her. It was not only getting closer, it was getting much larger. Then she heard the buzzing.

"Help," she screamed as loud as she could.

As she continued to twirl, the blur of red grew larger and closer. She was jerking her shoulders now to force her body to turn in the direction of the approaching image. Her efforts were unnecessary. The blur of red began to encircle her and the buzzing got louder.

Trying to focus on what the large red blob was, she didn't notice that, whatever it was, it was wrapping her in strands of honeysuckle vines. The haze of red moved in closer to tie the vines tighter around her arms and legs. It was then that she could see they were faeries.

No, she said to herself, not faeries. They were much smaller and they were all red. They were pixies, she realized. Their voices were so highly pitched that she couldn't understand what they were saying. All she heard was an incessant buzzing.

"Wait," she yelled. "Please. I'm not here to hurt you. I'm actually quite friendly."

The swarm kept circling her, pulling the vines around behind them, wrapping her up like a cocoon.

"That's not really necessary," she protested. "I'm clearly not going anywhere. Please. You don't have to tie me up. If I've done something wrong, I'm sorry. Just tell me what it is."

The high-pitched whining sound only increased, as their circle got smaller and smaller, and the vines got tighter and tighter.
"Please stop," she pleaded. "You're tying me too tightly. I...can't...breathe. You're...squeezing...the...air...out...of...me."

In a matter of seconds, her legs were tied tightly together and her arms were wrapped close to her sides. Her hair hung down towards the ground as her body continued to swirl and the vines hugged her more and more. As if the vines weren't enough, the pixies began shooting tiny arrows at her.

Quest of Eight Part Four: The Race to Virkio

Richard Reda

"Stop," she yelled again, expending all her breath with the single word.

The arrows continued. Fortunately, none were aimed at her face. They landed with little effect in the cloak in which she was covered. They were tipped with a particularly strong venom which the pixies used to paralyze their victims. Whatever magic the old woman had transferred to the cloak caused the arrows to simply bounce off.

"Help," she yelled with one more breath, as loud as she could.

In another part of the forest, her friends were still following her trail, moving painfully slowly, as far as Lochen was concerned. Sean's view was glued to the ground, looking for footprints or other clues to tell him which way Solveig had gone. He was searching as fast as he could, but he too, felt it was not fast enough.

"Did you hear that?" asked Lochen.

He stopped walking and jerked his head up. His eyes scanned the forest looking for some indication of where the sound had come from and who had made it. The others stopped and looked first at him and then in the direction he was staring.

"Hear what?" asked Summer, who had flown over to him and then moved ahead several yards, searching for whatever it was that had alerted Lochen.

"A voice," he said. "It came from that direction."
He pointed slightly to the left of where they had been headed. He took a few steps in that direction, hoping for another sound.

"There it is again," he shouted, and began running off by himself.

"Wait," shouted Liam.

When he didn't, the others all ran after him. He was a few yards in front of everyone else, except for Summer, who was flying right over his shoulder, trying to get his attention.

"Not so fast," she said. "Wait for the others. You don't even know what you heard. What if you're running into a trap?"

Lochen was running faster than she had ever seen him move. His arms were flying, as he tried to swipe branches out of his way. He was jumping over fallen trunks and dodging in and out of trees and limbs. Summer was having a hard time keeping up with him, trying to avoid branches swinging back at her.

"It's Solveig," he answered, not heeding her caution. "I know it is!"

He stumbled and immediately righted himself, without breaking his stride.

"How do you know this?" Summer persisted, trying to get him to stop and listen to reason.

"She's yelling for help," answered Lochen. "We have to get to her."

"But I didn't hear anything," Summer argued. "How do you know it's her? And besides, if it IS her, and she's yelling for help, don't you think we should..."

And then she heard the voice. It was Solveig, and she was yelling for help. She spun around to go back to get the others, but they were all running behind the two of them. In fact, Quinn was running very fast, and quickly catching up. He was only steps behind and it didn't seem like he planned to slow down. Summer watched him as he got closer and closer and then dove at Lochen.

"Oh, my!" she said, startled as Quinn flew past her and tackled Lochen.

"Hold on, Lochen" Quinn said as he brought Lochen down to the ground. "We need to save her, but we don't want to run into a trap."

"That's exactly what I told him," said Summer.

The others arrived right behind Quinn just as he was letting Lochen up. They came up so fast that they all collided into one another and on top of Quinn and Lochen. As they were peeling off they all heard another muffled cry for help and looked up to see an object hanging from a vine about twenty feet in front of them.

It was almost completely wrapped in honeysuckle. It had stopped swinging and spinning. Aside from the cocoon of vines wound around the body, all that could be seen was long red hair dangling towards the ground. Lochen pushed everyone off of him, stood up and marched towards the clearing.

"Solveig," he called out.

The swarm of red pixies stopped swirling around Solveig and turned toward the sound. In that instant Lochen could see what they were and that they had been firing hundreds of arrows at their captive. They started heading towards Lochen, bows primed with their lethal darts.

Lochen was deaf to the calls of his friends behind him. All he saw was Solveig hanging helplessly and being attacked by the pixies. The cloud of red was coming directly towards him.

"Leave her alone!" he shouted.

As he marched to meet the pixies head on, he moved his hand back and forth in front of his body and then thrust his arm forward. A wave of energy shot out in a widening circle of rippling blue light. As the wave met the advancing swarm it engulfed the pixies, completely disintegrating them. All that could be heard above the hum of the wave was a sizzling, crackling sound as the pixies evaporated.

"Cut her down," he shouted as he stood immediately beneath her.

Liam quickly pulled a blade from his belt and threw it with perfect accuracy, slicing through the vine from which Solveig was hanging. She dropped right into Lochen's arms. He stood her upright so he could pull the vines from around her body. When she was free, he hugged her tightly in his arms.

"I thought we'd lost you," he said into her ear, his voice choking.

He then held her by her arms and moved her back to look into her face. She wobbled slightly on unsteady feet, as her eyes fluttered open.

"You're safe now," he told her. "You're all right. You're...you're...you're blue!"

Chapter seven

Several miles to the north and west, another group was making its way through the forest – more specifically: underneath the forest. B'nair had mended quickly, but was still not fully recovered. He and his hobgoblin followers had moved quickly through the underground caverns from their starting point of several days ago. Along the way, Ercon answered more of B'nair's questions about the Alchemist and the towers at Virkio.

Much of his knowledge was from lore handed down over the generations that descended from Grewt. Consequently, much of it was skewed, but the basic information was correct. In the battles that thwarted the uprising of the Kelpies, a powerful stone, at the time in the possession of an Enchantress, was destroyed. The pieces were scattered to the far corners of the world. Some had been found, but the finders knew nothing of the powers of the individual pieces or of the stone as a whole.

Most who found the pieces thought they were merely interesting and colorful trinkets. Grewt had known better and had spent his life in search of them. The one he found was stolen from him by the Alchemist – one of the people who had put down the Kelpie rebellion. Knowing that others were looking for the stone, the Alchemist hid the piece he stole from Grewt. He not only hid it, he cast several spells on the hiding place. The spells were designed to discourage any seekers from pursuing their search.

The hobgoblins had found the hiding place. It was in one of the towers at Virkio. Virkio was the Alchemist's fortress. It was comprised of five towers, each one higher and more difficult to reach. The complex was located in the mountains, far to the north and west.

Over the centuries, the hobgoblins had made several attempts to breach the spells, but had been unsuccessful. Many had been lost in these efforts and never seen or heard from again. They simply disappeared. After several attempts, one of their leaders had the idea of tunneling under the towers.

This was easier said than done. The towers were built on a mountain of granite and ice. But they persisted. Generations of hobgoblins had dedicated themselves to digging the tunnel. And they succeeded – to a point. They were able to extend the tunnel to the base of the fourth tower, but could go no further.

The protections cast on the fifth tower were too powerful, even deep into the ground. That meant the search parties would have to enter the fourth tower and climb to the top to the only access point that led to the fifth and final tower. They would have to somehow bypass the spells.

The problem was that the spells continually changed. Teams had crawled into the fourth tower and had managed to bypass the first spell, but had fallen victim to the second or third spell. Teams that followed them were unable to use the information learned by their predecessors. The spells they encountered were different. They fell victim to new and different traps.

"Then how do you expect our effort to be any different?" B'nair asked Ercon.

"We have not learned how to combat the specific spells," he answered. "But we have learned what types of things to beware of. We have also learned not to separate, but to make very short advances. With a force as large as we have now assembled, we expect to be victorious."

B'nair wasn't as sure of being successful as Ercon apparently was. But he was a different person now than he had been before. His brush with death in the lava had given him a new perspective. He no longer had any concern for his own well being. If their mission resulted in the end of his life, so be it. Death no longer concerned him. He looked at Ercon and smiled. The scar tissue on the side of his face made the smile more of a sneer.

"I'm sure we will," he said, although he wasn't convinced he believed it.

He could tell without being informed when the tunnels through which they had been traveling reached the point at which they were below the first tower of the fortress. The black earthen walls changed to rock. The rock was golden in color, although B'nair wondered if the color was only a reflection of the light from the torches the others were carrying.

He stopped and reached out to touch the stone with his gloved hand. He instantly pulled it back when he heard a hissing sound. He had expected the noise to be the result of the glove's material burning. When he looked at his palm, he saw crystals of ice. The wave of extreme cold penetrated the glove and began to dig into the flesh of his hand.

He shook his hand violently, trying to shake off the glove. With his other hand locked permanently around the handle of the axe, he couldn't pull the glove off. He was about to tear it away from his hand with his teeth, but was stopped by Ercon.

"I wouldn't do that, if I were you," he said.

He reached over with his own gloved hand. He took B'nair's hand and pulled the glove off, immediately dropping it to the ground. It was still making the hissing sound as the frost continued to penetrate the material. In a few seconds it curled up and hardened. B'nair poked it with his foot and the glove shattered into hundreds of pieces.

"Almost anything that comes in contact with that stone freezes solid in a matter of seconds," Ercon told him. "We lost several men digging through this rock. We also went through a lot of hammers, picks, and chisels. Once it's chipped away it's harmless, but it isn't easy chipping it away."

B'nair struck at the rock with his axe. The blade vibrated harshly in his hand, but remained otherwise unaffected by the stone. It did, however, break a small piece off. It flew up into the air and then dropped to the ground. B'nair reached for it, hesitated only a moment, wondering if Ercon was telling the truth or not, and then picked it up. It was still cold to the touch, but not dangerously so.

He moved closer to one of the torches and looked more closely at the shard. The golden color he had initially seen was not a reflection of the torches. He could see the color shimmer in the piece in his hand. He felt the edge and noticed it was as sharp as glass.

As if reading his thoughts, Ercon said, "Once we were able to break larger pieces from the walls, we used them as tools. They were much more effective than the ones we had been using before. Especially since they never seemed to get dull."

Anticipating B'nair's next question, Ercon went on, "However, once we took those tools out of this cave, they crumbled like sand."

B'nair tossed the scrap away and looked at the cave through which they were traveling. He considered the size of the opening that had been carved and realized it must have taken centuries to cut through all of this. The cold from the stone filled the passageway. A few steps into this part of the tunnel, the temperature dropped dramatically.

"We need to move quickly through here," Ercon told him. "It can get cold enough to freeze us all. What happened to your glove can happen to each of us. And be sure not to touch the walls. That will be instantly fatal."

"How long does this last?" asked B'nair.

"As far as we can tell, it extends from one side of the first tower to the other side – slightly more than three hundred feet."

"What happens then?"

"Then we have a short break before we're under the second tower. There are bridges that connect one tower to another. Those don't seem to have spells cast on them, so the area between the towers is safe."

There were about forty men with them, walking in pairs to reduce the length of their procession and the amount of time exposed to the extreme cold. They were well-trained, it appeared to B'nair. They stayed as close to one another as possible, keeping a good distance between themselves and the walls. They moved quickly and quietly, with Ercon and B'nair following closely behind. B'nair wondered why Ercon hadn't brought more men with them, but didn't ask. Instead, he studied everything and tried to reason it out for himself.

"How do you know about the bridges?" asked B'nair.

146

"For centuries our ancestors tried to break through the spells on the surface. Each time they tried they learned more, but not enough to get past the third tower. We've seen the first two bridges. The spells that block the way to them always change, but the bridges remained the same. At least the first two did. We can only assume the others remained the same, as well, but we don't know for sure."

Ercon was turning out to be much smarter than B'nair had first believed him to be. He was an effective leader. B'nair wondered if he would become a problem later on, and decided he would have to watch him closely.

The cold was becoming increasingly uncomfortable. B'nair had gotten used to seeing his breath. He wasn't expecting it when the moisture in his breath crystallized and dropped to the ground in a fine icy powder. Frost had formed on his clothing, in spite of the heat being generated by his body. He could feel the cloth and leather becoming stiffer, making it more difficult to walk.

The metal in the head of his axe was like ice, and the cold traveled down the wooden handle into his hand and up his arm. His feet felt like blocks of ice and the cold was creeping up his legs. The air was so cold it burned when he breathed in. The only parts of his face that were unaffected by the frigid temperature were the areas that were dead and covered with scars.

He knew they must be near the end of this section, but doubted they would survive if they had to turn around and run back to the beginning. He looked behind to see that no one was following and realized how vulnerable they all were. Any slow down or obstacles ahead of them could strand many of them in this frozen passage. It dawned on him at that moment why Ercon had limited the size of his force to forty men. There was just enough room between the towers for a crew of this size. Any more would potentially clog up the passage, exposing some of the members to certain death.

Quest of Eight Part Four: The Race to Virkio

Richard Reda

He looked up and could see the line ahead of him begin to slow. As it did, each pair moved as close as it could to the one in front of it. His first reaction was that he had been led into a trap. What treachery is this, he thought. Then he understood. The front of the line had reached the end point between the first and second towers. It was standing poised at the beginning of the second area of spells.

"Why have they stopped?" he asked.

"They are covering themselves with water," explained Ercon. "From the canteens they brought," he added as he pointed to the ones he had insisted B'nair carry on his belt.

"In this cold?" he asked.

"It is uncomfortable at first," Ercon admitted. "But the next tower is one of fire – something I am sure you would prefer to avoid."

B'nair reflexively glanced at his burned hand and arm, and then back at Ercon.

"They also need time to prepare themselves mentally. What they are about to see – what you are about to see – will appear to be impossible to pass through. It is an illusion. The heat is real – that you must understand; but you cannot trust your eyes."

As the line began to move forward, B'nair watched those immediately before him. One pair at a time poured the water from their canteens over their heads and splashed their bodies. They then dropped the canteens and began to walk quickly through the shadows into the next section of the tunnel. Unlike their passage under the frozen tower, where they all moved as a single unit, this time the pairs waited a few seconds until the pair before them had disappeared. Then they entered.

"Why do they delay?" B'nair asked.

"They need to know the two before them are well ahead. As I said, what you see is only an illusion. You cannot trust your eyes."

When their turn came, Ercon motioned for B'nair to wait until the darkness ahead swallowed the pair before them. When they were no longer visible, he poured the water over his head and B'nair did the same.

"Stay close to me, but be careful not to jostle me," Ercon instructed. "I have no wish to depart this life today."
They stepped forward through the darkness. For several steps, B'nair noticed nothing different. The air in the interim passage had been a comfortable change from the arctic air under the first tower. But soon he could feel the heat. It reminded him uncomfortably of his condition when Ercon first found him. The dead nerves in his face and hands started to itch. Then he saw the fire.

The walls on either side of the tunnel seemed to burst into flames, reaching across the ceiling and joining together. He felt like he was walking through an oven. Then it began to get hotter. The flames became solid, looking more like molten steel – turning from a bright yellow to an even brighter white. Heat waves distorted the air in front of him. The floor appeared to move, wavering in ripples.

Although he had no fear of death, B'nair was afraid of burning. His all too recent experience in the lava fields was beginning to undermine his will. He faltered slightly until Ercon pressed his hand against B'nair's back. Silently, he moved them on.

A few yards later B'nair saw bodies being burned within the walls. They were in anguish, as they slowly melted – consumed by the blast. As he got closer to them, he recognized the men. They were the pair that had entered this section immediately before him. He faltered a second time, certain that he was about to meet the same fate.

"It is an illusion," shouted Ercon. "It's a part of the spell. The images of those who went before you are captured in the walls of magma. It is not them. Remember what I said. You cannot trust what you see."

He gave B'nair another push as they passed the images.

"How can you be certain?" B'nair asked. "You cautioned me not to jostle you. How do you know they didn't push each other into the walls?"

"See for yourself," Ercon answered.

He pointed ahead. A few yards further, the flames ended. The rest of the force had passed through and was waiting for those that followed. Immediately in front of him, B'nair could see the pair that he was certain had fallen victim to the walls of the furnace.

Their clothing was smoldering, as was his, and they were covered with sweat, but otherwise appeared unharmed. B'nair wondered how many before him had tried to save comrades thought to be in peril, only to land there themselves. Whoever this Alchemist was, he was very clever and very devious. If I ever meet him, thought B'nair, I will be sure to hand him his head.

The line continued forward to the section of tunnel under the third tower. As they approached, Ercon asked B'nair if he could swim.

"Will I need to?" he asked in response.

"No, but you will need to be able to hold your breath. This next section will require that. It will appear open and filled with air, and, in fact, it is. You will see no difference between the air in that section and the air in the tunnel leading up to it. However, once we cross under the third tower, the air will change.

"It will be thick, like water. It will be impossible to breathe, like water. If you try, you will drown, but no water will ever appear in your lungs. We will have to take a deep breath and make our way quickly, but carefully to the other end."

"Why can't we run?" B'nair asked,

"Have you ever tried to run while holding your breath? You can't go as far as you think you can. That will be more critical in this passage, since this tower is wider than the ones before.   We also have to be careful not to run into the walls."

"Why?" asked B'nair. "Would we be in danger of getting wet?" he added with a note of sarcasm.

"The walls will look like water. If we fall against them, we will be sucked into a whirlpool and disappear. Getting wet will be the least of your worries."

In a manner similar to how they passed through the tunnel of fire, the pairs allowed for sufficient space to develop between them and the pair that preceded them. When they were ready, they filled their lungs to capacity and immediately set off. When their turn arrived, B'nair and Ercon did the same.

They walked swiftly and steadily forward. The pair in front of them was visible not far ahead. Several seconds elapsed and B'nair's lungs were beginning to burn. He couldn't tell how much further they had to go. He watched the team in front of him for some indication that the end was near, when they suddenly appeared to encounter something on the path. One of them stepped over a body lying in the path, but the other attempted to reach for it. The first one continued walking forward, but the other attempted to aid a fallen comrade.

The fallen hobgoblin was drowning. He couldn't make it to the end and had tried to take a breath. His lungs filled with invisible water and there was nowhere for him to go to save himself. The one from the pair in front of B'nair acted out of reflex and reached to pull his comrade up, only to lose his balance.

He swung his arms to keep from falling. One arm splashed into the wall of water behind him and he was instantly sucked in. He was visible on the surface for mere seconds and then disappeared from sight. Ercon and B'nair stepped quickly over the fallen body and hastened forward. As they passed the spot where the other had vanished, B'nair looked but saw no sign of him.

By the time they reached the end of this section of the tunnel, B'nair was struggling to keep the stale breath in his lungs. His chest was heaving and he was getting light headed. He staggered the last several steps and when they finally stopped, he bent over with his hands on his knees, gasping for air. His appreciation for the Alchemist's treachery was increasing steadily.
"What manner of hell do we face next?" he asked once his breathing returned to normal.

"Wind," answered Ercon. "Ferocious wind. We will stop, however, before we reach the end of the tunnel. At that point we will be directly below the fourth tower. Our miners dug beyond that, but couldn't penetrate far enough under the fifth tower, and had to stop."

"Why don't I think that will make this journey any easier?"

"Because your instincts are correct. It isn't any easier," Ercon explained. "We are likely to lose the first pair who enters that section of tunnel. The winds change direction at random. Unlike the other passages, here we need to press against one of the walls. The problem is, we don't know which one until we have entered. The first to go through may choose wrong. If that happens, they will be lost to us."

"That will be four men that will have been sacrificed," B'nair observed.

"Seven," corrected Ercon. "Two were lost in the fire tunnel. By the time we reached that point, there was nothing left of them to be seen. And one more was lost in the water tunnel. This is nothing compared to what we have lost in creating these tunnels, or before in our attacks directly on the towers."

Fortune was with them, however, and the first pair to enter the tunnel of wind chose correctly. They pressed their bodies against the right wall. The first gust of wind pushed them harder against it. Almost immediately another gust of monumental force nearly lifted them in the air, trying to push them against the ceiling.

They locked arms to increase their weight and, as the next pair entered, their arms were locked with the first pair. This continued as the line crept forward step by step. Each new pair to enter the tunnel linked their arms to those before them. Each man pressed his back against the wall with all the strength in his legs, fighting the sudden and unexpected shifts in the wind.

Even with the strength and stability of the other men, B'nair could feel the power of the wind as it buffeted him from all directions. He watched as Ercon showed him how to side-step along the wall. His right arm was linked with the man in front of him, his axe held tightly to his chest. His left arm was linked with Ercon, who was last in line.

B'nair hoped that whoever was leading this line knew when to stop and what to do when that time came. He was also glad that they would not be traversing the entire tunnel. The wind was banging his head against the wall. He wasn't sure how much more he could withstand.

"When the leader gets to the center, we will all be pulled down the line." Ercon shouted over the roaring wind. "Don't fight it. Let yourself be pulled. We will all be sucked up into the center of the lowest part of tower four. Once that happens, stand perfectly still until I can assess the surroundings and understand the nature of the spell."

153

B'nair nodded his understanding, although he was convinced he didn't understand much of this at all. He tightened his grip on the men on either side of him and continued to inch his way along. Then he felt a sudden pull on his right. His first instinct was to resist, but he recalled Ercon's instruction, and, against his better judgment, he relaxed and let himself be yanked down the tunnel and up through an opening in the ceiling, into the fourth tower.

The wind swirled around him, twisting him as his feet left the ground. He was pulled through the air into a field of total darkness. As suddenly as it had all started, it was over. He felt himself still linked arm in arm, standing on a stone floor. The opening from the tunnel had sealed completely.

He realized he had shut his eyes some time after he had been pulled up from the ground. He opened them to see his feet planted firmly on stone. He shifted his gaze to his surroundings, moving along the floor, which seemed to be made of large squares of stone, curving upward to the walls.
There were odd-looking beams along the floor that led to pillars against the walls. He also noticed lamps on the tops of long chains that stood up at various places along the beams. There were no windows in the room, but there were sconces on the walls. They were upside-down. Then he realized the entire room was upside-down.

"What kind of place is this?" B'nair asked.

Ercon ordered everyone to stay calm and to stay where they were. He walked around the group that had clustered together, making sure everyone who had made it this far had come through whatever portal brought them inside the tower. Satisfied that everyone was accounted for, he took two men with him and began to expand his search of the room.

Although he hadn't included B'nair in his search, B'nair included himself and stayed close by. They walked the circumference of the hall, careful not to touch anything. Ercon and B'nair were in the lead with the other two men following behind. The room was circular and had no furnishings. The floor, which was now above them, was made up of the same large square stones as the ceiling on which they were standing, as were the walls.

There were eight beams that met in the center of the ceiling and led to eight large wooden pillars that extended to the floor. At the center point of each beam was a lamp hung from a long chain. The lamps were all lit, as were the sconces in the walls. The flames all pointed to the ceiling, in spite of the fact that the ceiling was under their feet.

The room was perfectly symmetrical and perfectly normal, except that it was all upside-down. At opposite sides of the room were two openings. Neither opening had doors. They were both large square openings. In one was a stone stairway that led up – which was now down. In the other was an identical stone stairway that led down – which was now up.

"Which one would you choose?" Ercon said to B'nair.

He studied them both. Since they needed to get to the top of the tower, it made sense to him that, in spite of the upside-down nature of the room, they still had to go up.

"That one," he said, pointing the stairway that, from their perspective, went upward.

Ercon motioned to one of the two men that had been accompanying them, directing him to step onto the stairway B'nair had selected. He walked up to the opening, hesitated for a second, looking back at his leader, and then stepped into the passage, placing one foot on the first step. Nothing happened. Then he placed his other foot on the step, moving completely into the opening.

He immediately fell upward, the same as if he had stepped off a cliff. The shock and disorientation choked off his voice, but he soon found it. His scream echoed into oblivion.

"It appears that in order to go up to the top of the tower," said Ercon, "That we must take the stairway going down."

B'nair had a momentary feeling of guilt for having chosen the wrong opening and costing someone his life, but the feeling passed quickly. He watched as Ercon led the remainder of the men through the opening and down the stairway.

They traveled on a dimly lit and winding staircase, as it appeared to curve along the tower walls. There were small openings on the sides at regular intervals, but Ercon ignored them. Eventually, the staircase emptied out into another room. This one was right side up.

Although there was no indication that the tower was narrowing as they climbed the stairs, this room was smaller than the one from which they had started. This room, though, had four openings in the walls at equal distances. Ercon and B'nair walked the circumference of this room, as they had the previous one. Through one opening they could see nothing, but they could hear what sounded like rain falling and water rushing. Through the second they could see a long hall. At the end of the hall they could see a reflection of light coming from an undetermined source. They could also hear a strong breeze beating against the walls.

The third opening was equally dark, but the heat coming from it told them both what they could expect in that passage. Similarly, the fourth brimmed with frost and cold.

"What do you think, this time?" Ercon asked B'nair.

"Since everything seems to be opposite of what is expected, it would appear that the right choice would be the entryway that resembles the passage under the third tower. That would be back the way we came, but nothing here is as it seems. The openings of fire and ice were not connected to this tower. I believe them to be merely diversions."

"I agree – in part. If things were normal, the passage that sounds like the wind would be the correct choice. But in this tower, all appears to be in reverse. Considering that, then, going back the way we came – through the water passage - would seem to be the path we should take. But should we choose the reverse because that's what we think we should choose? Shouldn't that choice also be reversed?"

"How can anyone know? This could go on indefinitely," argued B'nair.

"But then maybe we are expected to dismiss the other two openings – fire and ice as you referred to them – when one of those might be the correct choice.

B'nair was growing frustrated with all these riddles, all these tricks, and all this treachery. He motioned to the group of men waiting behind them.

"Send another sacrificial lamb," he suggested. "Send four. One is sure to survive."

"Let's send one at a time," replied Ercon. "Why waste three when our first choice might prove correct?"

He motioned to the group for one of the men to come over. He then pointed to the passage that sounded like the wind.

"I believe this to be the correct one," he said.

"No! Wait," B'nair shouted just before the man stepped into the hallway. "They're all the correct choice."

"How can they all be correct?" asked Ercon. "They lead in four different directions."

"Yes, but why would only one be correct? You said yourself that the spells always change."

"Yes," answered Ercon. "Which is why any one of these passages could be correct, and that could change the next time anyone comes this way."

"But the Alchemist would know that an intruder would eventually choose the right one, even if only by chance. If we enter only one it will be the wrong one – no matter which we choose. It makes sense, then, that we must enter all of them – at the same time."

Ercon considered B'nair's suggestion. If he was wrong, they could lose three quarters of their team. With what would be left, they wouldn't be able to reach the fifth tower. Their mission would be a failure. He also considered that no one rose through the ranks of the Rebbercands, as B'nair had, by being stupid or by taking foolish chances. He decided to trust B'nair's judgment.

"I hope you're right, Rebbercand. We are all dead if you're not."

He divided the rest of the men into four groups and then turned to B'nair.

"You and I will have to separate for this journey," he said. "It will increase our chances in the event you are wrong. Which passage would you like?"

B'nair looked at his choices. The one that gave him the most fear was fire. He could feel the scars on his face and upper body tingling, even though he knew the skin beneath them was dead. He looked at his blackened hand, clenched forever around the handle of his axe.

"I'll take the passage of fire," he declared, committed to conquering his fears.

"So be it," responded Ercon, and he moved to the line that was facing the passage of wind.

He turned back to the other three lines and ordered them to proceed. Without hesitation, they all marched forward into their respective halls and disappeared from the central room. Each team was immediately confronted with complete darkness and a total absence of sound. The man in front of each line blindly continued to walk with the hand of the man behind him on his shoulder. That was the only way they didn't lose one another.

The air was so heavy in the passage that no light at all penetrated and any sound died immediately. Even the sound of their own footsteps faded before it could reach their ears. Each line's leader held his arms outstretched, hoping not to be impaled on some unseen projectile and hoping that the floor beneath him didn't suddenly disappear.

After what seemed like an eternity, the lines each encountered a nearly blinding flash of green light and an ear piercing crack of thunder. When the flash dissipated they all found themselves on the roof of tower four in a gale-force wind and sub-zero temperatures. The four lines were at equal angles to one another, facing the center of the tower roof.

The roof itself was flat with a wall around the outer edge. The floor on which they stood was the same large square block pattern as the rest of the tower. It was smooth and slick with moisture that was quickly becoming a layer of ice in the freezing wind. There were battlement cut-outs every several feet. One of the men at the end of one of the lines let his curiosity overcome him. He stepped over to the nearest battlement and looked out over the edge of the tower. He could see the first three towers clustered below and behind him. They seemed to curve in parallel to the shape of the mountains over which they were built.

He could see a bridge running from the roof of tower three to some place above the center level of tower four. He leaned over the edge to get a better look and saw the ground was nearly two thousand feet below him. At that moment the wind gusted brutally, spinning him off balance. Before he could catch himself, he was swept over the side and was hurtling down to the rocks below. No one even noticed he was gone.

Ercon looked at B'nair, glad to see that he had been right and then assembled the men in a tight cluster in the center of the roof. He surveyed their surroundings, and saw the fifth tower shrouded in the mist and clouds, the top barely visible. He carefully made his way to the edge and could see a long narrow bridge connecting tower four to tower five.

B'nair joined him. He leaned against the battlement, carefully planting his feet and reached out to touch the bridge. It was barely a foot wide and extended nearly thirty feet upward through the clouds. Neither the end of the bridge nor the top of tower five were visible.

"The surface of the bridge is solid ice," he said. "We will never be able to cross that, even if there was no wind."

"We not only can," said Ercon. "We will."

He turned to the waiting men and muttered a few commands. His voice was lost to B'nair in the wind, but the men heard the instructions. They all moved to the edge where the bridge left tower four. One of the men climbed over the battlement and crawled out onto the bridge. He lay flat on his stomach with his arms and legs wrapped around the narrow span. Tied to his belt was a length of rope. The other end of the rope had been tied to the nearest battlement.

160

As soon as he was secure, a second man began to climb out, pushing the first one forward. The second man lay on his stomach and clutched the bridge with his arms and legs, as the first one had. But the second man rested his head on the first man's butt.

Then a third man climbed out. He followed the steps the second one had taken, pushing them further out onto the bridge. One by one the remaining men kept pushing the men before them up the expanse and out of sight. They were creating a bridge of hobgoblins that covered the icy expanse, sliding one after the other ahead.

Not long after the first man disappeared in the clouds, the rope was elevated and pulled taut. Five men still remained with Ercon and B'nair.

"It's good that we didn't lose more men," said Ercon. "The last few yards would have been difficult."

"What are we supposed to do now?" asked B'nair.

Without answering, Ercon motioned to the remaining five men. One by one they climbed out onto the bridge, holding onto the rope and walking on the bodies of their comrades over the span to tower five. Ercon turned to B'nair and extended his hand towards the rope, offering him to go next and then brought up the rear.

As B'nair carefully stepped across the backs of the men on the bridge, he wrapped his one free arm around the rope, using it for balance rather than pulling himself along. The wind was whipping him and he could feel bits of ice in the air as it stung his face. More than once he lost his balance and if it hadn't been for the rope, he would have been blown into the abyss below.

"It might have been better to have spent another decade or two trying to dig through and come up from below this tower, as you did the others," he shouted over the wind to Ercon.

Quest of Eight Part Four: The Race to Virkio

Richard Reda

"Actually, we did," he shouted back. "The problem is that the tower itself is solid. There is no way in or out other than across this bridge."

B'nair wasn't happy to learn he would have to come back this same way. He hoped that none of the men on whom he was walking got blown off. He didn't want to think about having to cross this bridge on a footing of ice. He never had a fear of heights, but when he looked down through the patches of clouds, he could barely see the jagged mountainside below.

Tower four was nearly two thousand feet above the ground, and tower five was even higher. The terrain over which these towers were built was not merely mountainous; it was filled with splintered rocks and needle sharp spires. One misstep and he would be impaled or slashed to pieces.

The cold in the second passage and the wind in the fourth passage had combined forces out here. What made it worse were the sounds made as the wind screamed through the cracks and fissures in the stone. It was as if the souls of the damned were howling for mercy.

He looked once more at the scene below him. Something unusual caught his eye. He saw something fluttering near one of the spikes of stone. Below whatever it was, the stone was streaked with red. He stopped momentarily to try to see it more clearly. When he did, he felt Ercon's free hand on his shoulder.

Instinctively he flinched, thinking that he was being pushed off. Instead, Ercon bent his head close so that B'nair could hear more clearly.

"He's one of ours. Apparently he didn't hold on as tightly as he should have. I suggest we move more quickly. It won't get any safer standing out here."

It was then that B'nair recognized the item fluttering. It was what remained of one of the men who had climbed out immediately before him. The man was skewered on the spire and the remains of his body were flapping in the gusts of wind.

For some reason he couldn't fathom, this enraged him. All the instability of his life; the constant movement with no permanent home; the destruction of his mining operation; his near death in the lava fields; his long and painful rehabilitation; the dangers faced in this expedition – all because of the Alchemist.

He failed to consider the circumstances that led to those conditions, or to accept any responsibility for his own actions. He had spent his life blaming others for his lot and now was no exception. His fury exploded. He began to pull himself with his free hand. He was so determined to get off the bridge that he was yanking the rope as he went. Ercon had to stop and hold on with both hands.

B'nair broke through the cloud cover, reached the end of the bridge, and climbed over the battlement. He was breathing heavily from both the exertion and his anger at the Alchemist. When he got his feet on the floor of tower five, he saw that the few men who had crossed before him were pressed against the nearest wall, all huddled together.

He was nudged aside as Ercon climbed off the bridge to join him. He was still looking at the men when he heard Ercon gasp. He turned his head back to see the expression on Ercon's face. It was one of shock. He was reaching back for the rope and appeared to be trying to climb backwards over the wall and out onto the bridge.

What's he doing, B'nair wondered. He turned to look at what had caused such a bizarre reaction. He stepped forward, peering through the darkness and the mist that shrouded the flat expanse of the top of the final tower. Through the clouds he saw two brilliant green glints of light, about ten feet in the air. They were moving slowly out of the darkness and through the clouds. Behind the two sparkling lights appeared the head of a dragon, quickly followed by the rest of the beast.

Chapter eight

ochen was still holding Solveig by her arms. His gaze had shifted from her eyes to the rest of her face. From there he looked down at her hands, and then pushed back the sleeves of her cloak to examine her arms. He was still studying her, and the others were gathering around the two of them. They were looking back and forth between Solveig and the burst of energy that was still burning off and electrifying the last of the pixies as it did.

"You're blue," he kept repeating. "You're blue!"

"Really?" she asked, relieved at being found, but quickly tiring of Lochen's repeated announcements about her being blue. "I hadn't noticed."

"How could you not notice?" he asked, bewildered. "You only had to see...oh, of course. You know you're blue. How did this happen? Are you all right?"

"Where have you been?" asked Summer.

"What happened to you?" asked Sean.

"Are you all right?" asked Natalie.

Solveig freed herself from Lochen's grip and raised her arms, signaling for everyone to quiet down. She took a deep breath, in part to give herself time to collect her thoughts, and in part to keep her voice from cracking. It didn't work.

"I must have...fallen off the ship," she started.

She was having difficulty speaking. She was overwhelmed with emotion. Like Lochen, she thought she had been lost to them. In spite of her determination, deep down she had believed she would never see them again. The events of the last few days were finally sinking in. Her knees started to buckle and she had to sit down. Everyone rushed to help her, running into each other and nearly stepping on her.

"I'm fine," she managed to say. "Really. I'm just worn out and more than a little confused. I know I must have fallen off the ship, but I don't really remember that happening. I remember being alone and walking through the woods. I'm not sure how long I was wandering or where I was exactly, but I ran into a pack of jackals and that was when I got more lost than I was before."

Lochen, Quinn and Sean exchanged looks, recalling their own encounter with a pack of jackals. At least they had the benefit of a wolf to come to their aid.

"Then I ran into the strangest person. She was scary, but friendly at the same time. I know that doesn't make any sense. She is really old, and blind, and she lives in this cave under a tree. She gave me tea and then started rambling about some place called Virkio and a dragon and Kelpies. None of it made any sense."

"We saw a place like that," said Sean.

"She gave you tea?" Stella interrupted. "What did it taste like?"

"It was horrible," answered Solveig. "But I couldn't stop drinking it. And the glass it was in − I think it kept filling up all by itself. At least it seemed like it did. Oh, and she gave me this cloak."

Stella reached out to feel the fabric of the cloak.

"It's enchanted," she said. "That's why none of the Pixie arrows penetrated it, which was lucky for you. Tell me more about this tea."

"There's nothing more to tell," said Solveig. "She said she made it from things she found in the forest, but she didn't say what."

"Was it bitter tasting?" Stella persisted.

"Yes. In fact, it tasted worse with each sip, but I couldn't stop drinking it."

"That's probably what turned you blue," said Stella.

"Can you reverse it?" asked Lochen.

"No," she answered. "I don't know what the tea was made of, or if the color is only a side effect of some other kind of spell. How do you feel otherwise?"

"I feel fine," said Solveig. "I'm tired and sore, but considering the last couple of days, I feel pretty good."

"Sean," asked Liam. "Do you think you could follow Solveig's tracks back to that tree cave?"

"Sure," he answered. "I'm certain it was the one I saw before. Why?"
"If we can find this old woman, maybe we can find out what she gave to Solveig and then maybe Stella can fix something to change her back."

"What?" asked Solveig. "You don't like my shade of blue?"

"It clashes with your red hair," answered Liam.

"I should be able to pick up her trail from right here and work backwards," said Sean. "But it may take us longer to backtrack than it did for her to get here. She was probably running at least for part of the time. We're going to be moving a lot slower."

"If we can find a clearing," Solveig offered, "it shouldn't be too far from here. There are some talking trees – oh, no. Never mind. They won't be able to talk again for another month."

Everyone turned to look at her, wondering if she was joking with them.

"Talking trees?" asked Quinn, with a nervous smile on his face. "What did they have to say?"

Solveig filled them in on what she had learned from the survivors of the village of Kalayaan. She told them about the wars among the Kelpies, the intervention of the Alchemist and some Enchantress, and the destruction of the stone.

"This stone," said Stella, as she removed her headband.

"It must be," said Solveig.

"I've known it has special power. I've felt it," said Stella. "I never knew the source, though, or its significance. That explains why I've had the strong sensation to go north. One of the pieces must be in that direction. Maybe that's what or where Virkio is."

"I don't know," said Solveig. "The Kalayaans turned back into trees before I could get enough answers."

"Perhaps the old woman who took you in can answer some of those questions," said Lochen. "She obviously knows much more than she told you. At the time you didn't know the right questions to ask."

"And maybe she can get rid of all that blue," said Quinn. "I mean, unless you like being blue. It doesn't look all that bad – once you get used to it."

"Whatever we decide to do," interjected Liam, "We need to decide quickly. At this time of year, and this far north, the days are getting shorter. We need to either find this old woman, or get back on course to wherever we are going."

No one wanted to make the decision until Solveig said she'd like to look normal again, if that was all right with them. They quickly agreed and Sean took the lead, picking up the trail that Solveig had travelled. In a few hours, as it was getting close to twilight, they found the clearing with the copse of misshapen trees.

In the waning light, the gnarls and broken limbs looked less like faces than Solveig recalled. At first she wasn't sure it was the same place, until Liam pointed out the remnants of her campfire. Solveig went over to the tree that had first spoken to her. She felt the bark and the twists and gouges in the trunk where the face had been. Had she been dreaming, she wondered. Had it all been a figment of her imagination?

"They were real," she said. "Honest. I wasn't imagining things."

"No one said you were," replied Lochen. "But you were in a state of agitation, you had been acting strangely before you fell off the ship; and who knows what was in the tea or potion – whatever it was – that the old woman gave you."

"Why don't we make camp here," said Liam.
"NO!" shouted Solveig. "Any place but here,"

"But maybe they'll come back to life if we camp here," said Summer.

"Besides," said Quinn. "This place is spooky enough. Do we really want to try to find someplace less spooky – in the dark?"

Solveig reluctantly agreed. She stayed awake the entire night with Lochen who had her repeat several times everything that had happened to her and everything she could recall that had been told to her. After the fifth time, she told him she had had enough. She stretched out by the campfire to rest for a minute and fell instantly asleep.

It had taken a little longer for her to wear herself out than Lochen had expected, but he was relieved when it finally happened. He let her and all the others sleep for several more hours – even after the dawn. It gave him some time to try to make sense of what she had told him, and he enjoyed the peace and quiet.

The next morning Sean led them off again. By midday he had discovered the large tree with the opening at the base of the trunk where Solveig said the old woman lived. It was the same one he had found earlier. Liam had suggested they approach cautiously, but Solveig ignored him.

"If she was going to harm me," she said. "She could have done that the last time. Besides, what can she do to me? Turn me green?"

"Could she really do that?" asked Quinn, as he took a couple of wary steps backwards.

"Sure," said Solveig, and then seeing the worried look on his face, quickly added, "No. I don't know. You'll be fine."

She turned to the opening and abruptly climbed down. The others followed closely behind. In seconds they were all crowded inside the tiny cottage. Everything was as Solveig had described – except there was no sign of the old woman. The glass she had drunk from was on the odd looking table across from the skull the old woman had used.

Everything was exactly the way it had been at the moment Solveig left. The only change was that the stool on which she sat when Solveig was with her was covered in dust.

"She couldn't have gone far," said Solveig. "She was blind after all."

"But if she knew this forest well," said Liam. "She could be anywhere.

Stella was studying the objects in the containers on the wall at the back of the cottage. Summer was hovering near the entryway, not at all comfortable with entering the room. Quinn was right behind her, having declined the offer to go in. He was leaning against the roots peering into the opening.

Sean was looking at the chest from which the old woman had taken the cloak she had given Solveig, and Natalie was looking at the objects on the far wall. Lochen had bent over and was looking closely at the stool the old woman had used. He reached out and felt the dust, taking a pinch between his finger and thumb. Then he sniffed it. After a few seconds, he stood bolt upright.

"I don't think she went anywhere," he announced. "I think this dust is her."

Quest of Eight Part Four: The Race to Virkio

Richard Reda

"What are you talking about?" demanded Solveig. "I may have been imagining the talking trees, but she was real, and she wasn't made of dust. I saw her; I talked to her; I felt her grab my arm; she was here."

"And you said she told you of the Alchemist and the Kelpie wars, isn't that correct?" asked Lochen; he was recalling all that Solveig had told him the night before. "She said that Virkio was the fortress of the Alchemist; she talked about the stone being shattered and that pieces were hidden. That all happened about two thousand years ago."

"What are you saying?" asked Natalie. "That this woman was two thousand years old?"

"Yes," said Lochen. "I believe she was. She seemed to know who Solveig was and that she was with friends, in spite of the fact that Solveig never mentioned us and we were nowhere near her at the time. She knew we were searching for something, even though none of us knows what we're searching for. She talked about the stone – some powerful stone that had been shattered. It's obviously the same stone as the parts in Stella's headband."

"But why did she turn to dust?" asked Summer, who was starting to back out of the cottage. "Who does that?"

"I don't know," said Lochen. "It may be that her purpose was to deliver a message to Solveig and once that was done, that purpose was served and she ceased to be. It's just a theory."

"I vote that we get out of here and get back to – and I can't believe I'm saying this – the ocean," said Sean.

"I agree," said Liam. "We're too vulnerable here. There's too much we don't understand."

No one needed to be convinced. They all exited the cottage and Liam took the lead, heading for the most direct route to the shore. Along the way they passed the stream Solveig had fallen in and the place where she first encountered the jackals. Both locations were unfamiliar to her and went by without comment. In a few hours they could hear the sound of the waves crashing on the sand, and a few minutes later they arrived at the Viridean Ocean.

There was still a lot of daylight and they all agreed to follow the coast north until it was time to settle in for the night. Summer and Quinn found enough driftwood to build a roaring fire while Natalie and Stella went diving for clams, mussels and other sea food tidbits. Sean and Liam found enough branches to make a lean-to. Although the sky was clear, the air was getting colder and colder as they moved further north.

In the morning there was a thin layer of frost on the ground and they were all glad for the cover of the lean-to. They spent the next several days hiking over constantly changing terrain. They talked about where they were going and why, piecing together images Stella had seen in earlier visions with the information Solveig had imparted to her from the two mysterious sources – the faces in the trees and the old woman.

They concluded that they were headed for the fortress of the Alchemist – a place called Virkio. They assumed that at least one part of the stone pendant worn by an ancient Enchantress was being held in the fortress. This piece was probably like the one that had been taken from the Rebbercand in the volcano and that merged with the triskelion that Stella now wore.

The stone was the object of a search by some unidentified others who were also trying to get to Virkio. Somewhere in all this were some people called Kelpies, but no one knew where they fit in exactly.

By the end of a week, they had left the forest far behind and had started a long and increasingly steep climb uphill. The coast had given way to cliffs of sheer rock that rose higher and higher. Summer usually flew out ahead of the rest of the group to search for the best passageways. More recently, however, her travels had been more upward than forward, and the options had become fewer and fewer. Still there had been no sign of a fortress of any kind.

No one questioned whether or not they were going in the right direction. Everyone could feel that they were, even without the power that was pulsating in the stone Stella wore. No one complained about the hazards as they increased, climbing up rock that was first moss-covered, and now, more often than not, ice-covered.

The weather had been cooperating, but by now the temperature seldom rose above freezing, even at the height of the day. The nights were nearly arctic. Quinn felt right at home, and Solveig was well protected in her mysterious cloak. The others, however, were beginning to suffer. Firewood was getting harder to find. Even with Solveig's ability to cause things to burst into flame, without something flammable, this skill was useless.

Lochen was able to heat up a rock, but the spell didn't last long and the rock threw out little heat. Sean suggested that he blast "a bunch of them" and then they would each have something warm to sleep with. That seemed to be sufficient for the nights, but the rocks were too much to carry during the day.

Almost another week went by when Summer was once again scouting ahead. She struggled against the wind, staying as close to the mountain side as she could. She flew up the next series of crags and over the top when she saw the towers. The sight took her breath away. She immediately turned around as soared back to the group.

"I found it," she said breathlessly. "It's over the next mountaintop. I mean it's not exactly over the next mountaintop, but you can see it – them – there are more than one – three; maybe four. It's hard to tell. They go up into the clouds."

Everyone was eager to see the object of their search. They clambered up the rocks, pulling each other up and over the ledges and outcroppings. When they reached the crest, they stopped because of the wind. One by one they poked their heads over the top and saw their first glimpse of Virkio.

The first tower jutted out and stretched up towards the sky, as if it were perched on one of the several surrounding peaks. It was the same color as the stone of the mountain – a deep, flat, lifeless gray, almost black. Even in the sunlight, nothing reflected in the stone. It had no windows and rose steadily upward to a flat top, battlements circling it like a crown.

To the right of the tower was a bridge that connected it to the nearest mountain range. But there was no opening in the tower where the bridge led. They would have one more passage to negotiate to get to the bridge. From there they would have to find a way inside.

All they could see of the second tower was the top part of it, with battlements similar to the first one. The rest was hidden behind the mountain and the towers that seemed to surround it. It was the same color as the first tower, and was almost impossible to see. It looked more like a shadow of the one in front than a separate tower. From where they were, they could see no access to this structure. Like the first, there were no windows.

The third tower rose even higher and followed the line of the mountain further out. It stood to the left, behind and above the first tower. Like the first two towers, it seemed to stand independent of the mountain, an extension of one of the several surrounding spires. This one seemed to have more of a bluish cast to it, separating it more clearly from the other two.

The fourth one was higher still, and, like the second tower, was mostly hidden from view by the others as the line of towers rose in an "S"

175

pattern. What they couldn't see was the fifth and final tower, standing to the back of the four, its top hidden by the clouds.

"Oh, poop," Natalie whispered. "Those are really high."

"We certainly have our work cut out for us," said Lochen. "It might be wise to continue to the next range – the one that appears to connect to the towers – and make camp there for the night. We can tackle the towers with a fresh start in the morning."

They all agreed and climbed over the crest of the ridge, and down the other side. They were stopped on a ledge while Summer looked for a safe way down into the valley between the peaks. After several minutes, she returned.

"I couldn't find any good way across," she reported. "Maybe if we go back and try to go around..."

"No," said Stella. "We have to keep going forward. We need to get to those towers."

"What's the rush?" asked Sean. "It's not like they're going anywhere. It'll probably only take a day or two to go around."

"No," echoed Solveig. "I can feel it, too. Someone or something else is trying to get to that stone. We need to hurry. We've wasted too much time because of me."

"Nonsense," said Natalie. "Searching for you was never a waste of time."

"Maybe not, but the fact that you had to search for me didn't help."

"That's all irrelevant," interjected Lochen. "Besides, if you hadn't taken that little side trip, we wouldn't know what we do about the

Alchemist and the stone. Stella, tell me what you're feeling now. Why is it more urgent that we get there?"

"I can't describe it. I just feel it. I've had this strong pull ever since we left that volcano. The closer we've gotten to the fortress, the stronger that pull has become. I'd have us travel in the dark if I thought we could get there sooner – and safer."

"I feel the same way," said Solveig. "I feel...impatient is the only way I can describe it. The old woman and the faces in the trees said the same thing – that we had to get to Virkio; we had to get the stone; that others were searching for it."

"Who?" asked Liam. "Who else is searching for it?"

"I don't know," Stella and Solveig said almost in unison.

"I don't know," repeated Solveig. "I only know that we're not the only ones going after that stone."

"I feel that if we don't get there first," added Stella. "That something terrible – something evil – will happen."

"That's good enough for me," said Sean. "Liam, give me your rope."

Liam took the coil of rope he had recovered from the damaged ship and had worn over his shoulder. He passed it to Sean.

"What do you have in mind?" he asked.

Sean looped part of the rope around a large rock. He tied the end around his waist and passed the rest of the rope to Quinn.

"Lower me down. I'll secure the rope to something down below and then the rest of you climb down. Once we're all at the bottom, we can untie it and pull it in. On the other side, if we can't find a good way up, Summer can fly one end up, tie it off and we can climb up."

Quinn took the rope and pulled it taut. Sean scrambled over the ledge and told Quinn to start lowering him. A few seconds later Quinn could feel the tension in the rope relax and he lowered the remainder down the face of the cliff.

Liam went next to help Sean hold the line secure, and the others followed, one by one, with Quinn coming last. Summer had flown down to wait with the others, although the wind was getting stronger and flying was becoming difficult. She hoped that, if she had to fly the rope up the other side, she wouldn't get blown away.

Once everyone was in the narrow section between peaks Sean untied his end of the rope and pulled the rest up around the rock at the top and back down to him.

"Easy," he said. "Now let's do the same on the other side."

Summer flew up the face of the cliff on the opposite side of the crease and was disheartened when she had to report that there was little in the way of steps, handholds, or anything else conducive to an easy climb. Sean handed her the end of the rope.

"OK, now just fly it up to the top and see if you can tie it off on something."

The rope was almost an inch thick. In his hands it was easily carried and tied. In her hands it was nearly a third of her size. It was like asking her to carry a log and tie it in a knot.

"I'm not sure I can carry that thing," she said. "I'll never be able to tie it in a knot. Can't one of you put a spell on it and make it float up there by itself?"

178

"It really doesn't work that way," said Lochen. "At least give it a try. Even if you can't tie it off, maybe you can wrap it around something."

She took the end of the rope from Sean's hand and the weight dragged her down to the ground. She sprinkled some faerie dust on it to lighten it and hugged the end in both hands. This time she jumped up and flapped her wings with all her might. She was moving upward, her face just inches from the cliff.

This isn't as bad as I thought it would be, she thought. She struggled harder, trying to move faster. She was pretty proud of herself until she noticed that no one was saying anything. She thought they would at least be offering cheers of encouragement.

She looked downward over her shoulder, expecting to see their heads below, looking up in expectant silence. Instead, she found herself looking at their feet. She had risen less than two feet. And worse – she wasn't even carrying the full weight of the rope. Sean still had most of it looped in his hand.

"I believe you were correct in your initial estimation," Lochen announced. "There must be another alternative."

They studied the face of the cliff for several minutes and eventually all came to the same conclusion. There was no way for Summer to get the rope to the top and without the rope, there was no way any of them could get up there.

"As much as I hate to say this," said Liam, "But I think we're going to have to go back the way we came and find a way around this peak."

Even Stella and Solveig had to admit this seemed to be the only choice. When they all turned back to the precipice from which they had descended, they realized there was no way up that side, either.

"Oh, poop," said Quinn. "This isn't good, is it? How are we going to get out? In either direction?"

They were all silent for a few minutes while they came to terms with their situation. They were trapped. What had at first looked like a crease between the crests was more like a funnel and they were at the bottom.

"All right," said Sean. "I got us into this, and I'll get us out of it. This isn't any harder than climbing that mountain to your castle," he said to Solveig.

He tied one end of the rope around his waist and began to climb up the rock.

"Wait," said Lochen. "I may be able to help you get a start."

He snapped his hand forward and a blast of energy struck the face of the stone. He had expected the shock wave to break at least a small chip into the cliff, large enough for Sean to get a footing. However, nothing happened.

"That's odd," said Lochen. "Let me try once again – with a little more force."

He wound up like he was throwing a spear and flung his arm at the cliff. A larger bolt of energy crashed into the cliff. The light flashed and a loud crack echoed up the mountainside, but the only evidence of his effort was a slight scorch mark where the blast had hit.

"I don't understand," Lochen said, perplexed. "That should have bore a rather large hole into the rock."

"Don't worry about it," said Sean. "I'll make do with what's already there."

"But nothing's there," said Quinn. "Do you have suckers on your feet?"

"I'll find something," he said as he turned back to the wall and began to climb.

"Let me help get you started," offered Quinn.

He pressed his back against the wall and laced his fingers together. Sean stepped into Quinn's hands and was lifted up onto his shoulders. Now he only had about forty more feet to go. He studied the cliff for a few seconds, looking for the best approach, before he finally started climbing.

He found tiny fissures at various places. In some cases small plants had taken root and he used these as a toehold. Ridges traversed the cliff, cut into the stone over centuries by the wind, rain, and ice. He was able to get the tips of his fingers into these and pull himself up.

Summer flew right next to him, spotting whatever openings, cuts, handholds and footholds she could spot, recalling how he had climbed up the side of the mountain to Solveig's castle. Except that climb offered more cracks and outcroppings, and it hadn't been as cold. She was having a hard time the higher they went. The wind was getting stronger.

It was also starting to get dark. With the darkness came condensation. The rock was getting slick with moisture; that is, where it wasn't freezing and turning into ice. Summer flew up a few feet and saw a narrow crack in the rock. She glided back down to let him know.

He had stopped to catch his breath. That was when she realized that the air had grown thinner. She hadn't realized how high they had climbed until now. The exertion was taking its toll. Sean was panting as if he had run for several miles instead of climbed several feet.

Quest of Eight Part Four: The Race to Virkio

Richard Reda

She flew back down to where the others were watching. By now he was nearly twenty feet above them, and was only about half way up.

"Stella," she pleaded. "Do you have something to give him to increase his stamina?"

"No," she answered.

She recalled the containers of herbs and potions in the old woman's cottage, and regretted not taking some of them. She had decided against it at the time, since she couldn't be positive what any of them were. If Lochen was right about the old woman being two thousand years old, she was glad she hadn't taken anything. Most potions changed over time. Not only did their potency change, but what they were intended to do could change as well.

If she had taken something to increase Sean's stamina, depending on how old the potion or herb was, it could do something completely different. Like turn him blue, she thought with a sudden surprise.

"No," she repeated. "I'm afraid he's on his own."

Summer flew back up to offer encouragement and to continue scouting for him. As she caught up to him, she saw blood on some of the rock. She looked up and saw that he had cut his foot. A sharp edge of a rock had sliced across the tip of two of his toes.

"You're bleeding," she said to him when she was next to his ear.
"Oh, don't tell me that," he whined. "I hate the sight of blood, especially if it's mine. It's a good thing I can't see it."

"I can see it," she continued. "You've got a really bad cut on your..."

"Don't!" he shouted. "Stop. I don't want to know."

Summer backed away from the rebuke, and continued flying upward. Almost at the same time as he said these words, his left hand slid across another jagged piece of rock, which sliced through the skin. Blood began to flow from his fingers.

"Your hand!" Summer gasped when she saw the blood.

Sean jerked his head towards her and glared at her. She turned her head at the sudden motion, pulling her eyes from the red seeping down his arm. She was only a few inches from his face and could practically feel his piercing stare.

"What about my hand?" he asked through a tightly clenched jaw.

"It's…nothing," she squeaked. "It's a really nice hand. I'm going to fly up higher, now, and see if I can find some more places you can put your nice hand."

"Good idea," he mumbled as he watched her float upward.

He bit down to fight against the pain in his hand and foot and continued to climb. The wind was pushing in between the face of the cliff and his body, driving him away from what little there was to grasp. Between the wind, the water, the ice on the rocks and the blood seeping from his cuts, it was getting harder to hold on.

Summer tried sprinkling faerie dust on him to help lighten his weight, but the wind just blew it away before it could have any effect. To make things worse, the sky was getting darker. Not only was night falling, but dark clouds were rolling in. Sean wasn't sure which he feared more – rain or snow.

He didn't have to wait long to find out. It started snowing. The small chinks in the cliff were getting fewer and farther apart. At one point he was nearly spread-eagle, with his feet placed as wide as he thought he could stretch. He was concentrating so hard, that he had forgotten Summer was with him, until her voice startled him.

Quest of Eight Part Four: The Race to Virkio

Richard Reda

"You're almost there!" she shouted.

The sudden noise made him flinch, and he slid down about three feet.

"Don't <u>do</u> that!" he shouted up to her.

"Sorry," she murmured. "I just thought you'd want to know how close you are...or were."

In spite of being startled, he was glad to know he was close. He had been wrong. This was much more difficult than scaling the mountain that led to Solveig's castle. After several more excruciating minutes, he reached a plateau and scrambled over the edge.

"Is it all right to cheer now?" Summer whispered.

"Yes," Sean gasped.

He looked around for some place to tie the end of the rope, but could find nothing suitable.

"Go back down," he told Summer, "and have Stella climb up first. She's the lightest one. I'm going to have to hold this end until she gets up here. Then have Natalie, Solveig, Liam, Lochen and Quinn. In that order! It's going to take all of us to pull Quinn up."

Summer did as instructed and one by one the others scaled the precipice to the gap in the mountains to join Sean. By the time they were all up, they were snugly situated in a narrow groove between two peaks. Liam was coiling the rope and looped it across his body. Lochen took a few tentative steps further into the crevice. The path ahead took a number of twists, and the other end was, for the present time, obscured.

He came back to the others and suggested that, since they were somewhat sheltered from the wind, it would be wise to make camp where they were. Solveig generated a small fireball that provided enough heat, contained as it was in the folds of the narrow rift in which they were huddled.

Between Lochen and Stella, they were able to close the cuts in Sean's hands and feet. As exhausted as they all were, they were too excited to sleep, or at least to sleep soundly. Some of them drifted in and out, while the others talked.

Dawn came slowly, barely breaking through the dark clouds. It had snowed during the night and everyone who slept was covered in a light white blanket. There was nothing to eat, so once they were all awake, there was nothing to keep them from venturing forth. They wound their way back and forth along the twisting path to the end of the narrow gorge.

At the end, they came upon a long, wide stone bridge. The bridge spanned a chasm between the peaks through which they had come and a tower that rose high above them. From this angle, they could barely see tower two and the others were all hidden from view.

"It looks even scarier up close," said Quinn.

No one disagreed. The top of the tower was well below the clouds, but the color of the stone almost blended in to the darkness of the sky. The drab, dark gray at the base seemed to get drabber and darker, almost to black, the nearer the top. There was nothing at all inviting about the tower.

The bridge seemed solid enough, although no one was eager to cross it. Summer, floating in the air in the midst of the group, was caught by a sudden gust of wind and blown across the width of the bridge, out over the chasm. When she looked down, she gasped. The others, alerted by the sound, crowded to the edge of the gorge in the space where it met the bridge.

"Oh, poop," said Natalie. "We're really high up."

Below them were dozens of pinnacles, jagged and pointed, like bristles on a porcupine. Tower one rose up from among them, carved from the same stone. Quinn reached out and grabbed Summer, pulling her back into the group. The others looked from the rocks below to the tower and back.

"This is it," said Stella. "This is Virkio."

Chapter nine

B'nair saw the two burning coals staring at him as the head in which they sat lowered through the mist. Beneath the eyes of green was the rest of the dragon's face, including its massive jaw, filled with razor sharp teeth and two very large fangs. The dragon was a pale blue in color and towered above them.

Long tendrils trailed from its face, flowing like tentacles towards the back of its head. Its front legs were thick and ended in large, pointed talons. There were two rows of horn-like bristles that ran down its back to a long, thick tail. On the top of the tail were five large spikes that could smash or pierce stone, as the dragon desired. The hind legs were much larger than the forelegs and very muscular.

187

The dragon did not rush them as B'nair had expected. Nor did it breathe fire on them. B'nair hesitated, waiting to see what the dragon was going to do when Ercon came over the battlement and bumped into him. The unexpected bump pushed B'nair forward towards the dragon.

He reacted reflexively, springing like a cat, raising his axe to defend himself. The sudden and aggressive movement startled the dragon, which snapped at the disturbance. One of the men who had crossed onto the tower roof first had moved surreptitiously to the side. He took the opportunity while the dragon's head was turned towards B'nair, and stepped closer. He pulled a large dagger from his belt and hurled it at the beast. The blade clanged as it struck the scales that covered the dragon's flesh, and bounced harmlessly to the stone floor.

The dragon took the motion for what it was – an act of hostility and a threat. It took a quick step forward, once more snapping its enormous jaws. The single bite cut the man in half. The lower half of his torso wavered a few seconds before it dropped lifelessly to the ground. The other half remained in the dragon's jaws until one of its tentacles pulled it from its mouth and flung it over the side of the parapet.

While everyone else cowered against the wall, too frozen with panic to make any real attempt to escape, B'nair's anger was immediately refueled. All the resentment that had been sparked in him as he crossed the bridge boiled over. The fact that he and the hobgoblins were invading the Alchemist's fortress to steal a stone was lost on him. All he could understand were the defeats he and his people had suffered at the hands of this unseen magician.

His adrenalin pumping, B'nair let loose a blood curdling scream and charged the dragon. The dragon saw the Rebbercand coming at it, but responded too slowly. It made a lunge at its attacker, but missed. B'nair ducked under the dragon's snapping jaw as he ran towards it. As the dragon's head dropped downward to bite at B'nair, the

188

Rebbercand spun around, swinging his axe in a backhanded motion, upward.

The blade sliced through the protective scales in one swift movement. B'nair completed the spinning motion, his momentum carrying him past the dragon's side. He regained his balance and prepared himself for the dragon's countermove. It had all happened so quickly and smoothly, he was certain his blow had missed, and was ready to attack again, depending on which way the dragon moved. He looked back at the beast, fully expecting to see it turn its head and try to finish him off.

Instead, the dragon's head fell as if in slow motion, from its body. The head dropped to the stone floor and rolled a few feet forward, coming to a stop not far from Ercon. Ercon and those around him quickly stepped back as far as they could, expecting the severed head to bite at them.

The dragon's body, not yet realizing that it was dead, swung its headless neck upward where it hung motionless. When no more signals were sent from the dragon's brain, the motion of the large neck pulled the body sideways where it slumped to its right side in a heap, and the neck crashed down to the floor, more than fifteen feet away from the others who were too stunned to move.

B'nair had expected to see blood gushing from the severed carcass, but instead of the blood he anticipated, a thick silver fluid seeped out into a small glistening pool, and then stopped. B'nair sidestepped the puddle of liquid and walked over to the head. In a final act of defiance, he stomped on the dragon's jaw, breaking one of the two large fangs off, sending it spinning across the floor. He bent over and picked up the head by one of the tentacles that extended from the side of its mouth, and hurled it over the side of the battlement into the abyss below.

He turned to Ercon and the others, his breath coming hard. He noticed for the first time that it had started to snow. In spite of the cold, he felt a rush of heat course through his body. He could see everything around him in vivid clarity. He could feel the individual snowflakes as they landed on parts of his face. He could feel the wind. He could see the mist moving slowly around the top of the tower. He could even hear the heartbeats of every one of the men who stood there watching him.

"Where's the stone?" he demanded hoarsely. "It must be here, somewhere. Find it and bring it to me."

Ercon realized their roles had suddenly changed. He was no longer the leader guiding the Rebbercand towards recovering the power of the Enchantress' pendant. B'nair was now the undisputed leader. He saw B'nair looking directly at him. He bowed his head slightly to the new leader and then turned to the others.

"Spread out and search," he shouted to them. "But be careful. That beast may not have been alone."

They all fanned out and started to examine every inch of the tower roof. One of them, heedless of where he was walking, stepped into the pool of the dragon's silver blood. As his foot came into contact with the fluid, he slipped slightly. Regaining his balance, his other foot stepped into the silver. Over the sound of the wind, he heard a crackling noise. It was coming from immediately below him. He looked down at his feet in the blood of the dragon. By then it was already too late. His feet instantly froze and the frost quickly shot up his legs to his torso, then to his other limbs and finally to his head.

Within seconds he was frozen solid, even before he could let out a sound. Statue-like, he stood there motionless until a shift in the direction of the wind toppled him over. As soon as he hit the stone floor, he shattered into thousands of pieces. The pieces spread out across the floor, rolling like marbles. When they stopped, they suddenly changed direction, moving back on their own back to be absorbed into the silver puddle of dragon blood. All the others had heard the crackling sound as the unfortunate one's body turned to ice, and they watched in shock as he fell to the floor and broke apart.

"Watch what you touch," was the only caution Ercon could utter.

After that, they did. They carefully walked along the outer edge of the tower. At almost each battlement was a large urn. In each urn was a strange substance that appeared white in the center and then became a glowing pale blue and finally a darker blue at the outer rim. There seemed to be a faint mist rising from the surface. Recalling what had happened only a few minutes before to one of their comrades, no one dared to smell or touch the substance, and merely continued the search.

Towards the far side of the tower, one of the men discovered a small chest. It appeared to be made of wood. The wood was red with cream-colored veins. It was almost two feet square and glistened in the dim light.

The one who found it called to B'nair. This was not lost on Ercon. It was another sign of the transition of leadership. B'nair had been called, not him. They all walked more quickly to the chest, careful of where they were stepping.

The man who found it tried to pull it from the wall, more into the open. There were no signs that it was secured to the side of the battlement, but he was unable to budge it. He looked for a clasp or lock, but none could be found. He reached underneath the carved feet at the corners and tried unsuccessfully to lift it. Impatient, B'nair ordered him to move away.

He swung his axe, cleaving the chest in two. As the box broke open, the fragments began to sizzle and dissolve. In seconds it evaporated to nothing. In its place was a clear cube, nearly a foot square. The cube appeared to be solid ice, although no one had the resolve to touch it and find out. Suspended in the center of the cube was a small triangular shaped stone, reddish brown in color.

B'nair poked the cube with his toe. Nothing happened to the cube or his toe. He reached down to touch it, but recalled the effect the dragon's blood had. Wasting no more time, B'nair once more swung his axe, bringing it down over the center of the cube.

The blade of the axe stuck in the cube, cracking it, but not cutting through it. B'nair's first reaction was that he had released a spell similar to the one that had frozen the other man. A wave of panic flashed over him and was immediately replaced by an even greater flash of rage.

He raised the axe with both hands, with the cube still stuck on the end of the blade and brought it down with all his might. The cube split in half with a resounding clap of thunder, and then, like the chest in which it had been held, it disappeared. The stone skittered across the floor, towards the pool of dragon's blood.

Everyone watched in horror as the stone spun around, flipped once and came to a stop inches from the silver puddle. B'nair realized he had been holding his breath. He released it slowly and then walked calmly over to the stone. He looked down at it for a second before bending down to pick it up.

He hesitated for a second, wondering what other disasters or curses would be let loose when he touched it. It was too late to turn back now, he considered, and there was no other way to retrieve the stone. Steeling his resolve, he placed his fingers around the gem and scooped it up into his hand. Nothing happened. As he slowly straightened up he closed his hand over the stone, pressing it into his palm.

At first he thought it was just a piece of broken rock. Then he could feel a surge flow from the stone through his hand and up his arm. In that instant he knew that someone else was searching for it, that this person was not alone, and that the person was near. He also had an image flash in his mind. It was a location. He didn't recognize this place. He was certain he had never been there before.

After a few seconds, he raised his head, looking around the rooftop of tower five as he tried to contemplate the importance of this image. Then he looked skyward and saw that the snowfall had increased. Large flakes were pouring out of the sky and accumulating on the floor. It was difficult enough to cross the bridge of ice. Waiting would only make it harder.

He shifted his gaze to the tower top, scanning the battlements, the body of the dragon, and the men watching him. He studied their faces, looked back at the stone in his hand, and then once more at the tower.

"We must go," he said, over his shoulder. "We have what we came for, and we've spent enough time here."

No one needed any further encouragement. They immediately assembled at the bridge and the rope guideline. One by one they climbed over the battlement and, holding on to the rope, walked across the bridge of bodies, most of whom were oblivious to what had transpired on top of the tower. They held the rope tightly, moving as quickly as they dared.

When only B'nair and Ercon were left, Ercon motioned for B'nair to go first, but B'nair declined and motioned for Ercon to proceed. The shift in leadership was now complete. Ercon looked into B'nair's one good eye, and B'nair returned the stare. No words were exchanged, but Ercon nodded his acceptance and climbed over the battlement. He moved across the bridge and didn't look back. B'nair swung his axe and arm over the rope and, holding the stone tightly in his other hand, strode confidently across the bodies. He was the image of a conquering invader, surveying the damage he had done in making his conquest.

Quest of Eight Part Four: The Race to Virkio

Richard Reda

When he reached the end of the bridge and set foot on the roof of the fourth tower, the man closest to the end of the rope stood up to untie it, and then resumed his position. Reversing their order, one after the other, they backed off the bridge as the line of men before them slid backwards to the starting point, pulling the rope with them.

In a matter of minutes they were all back on the roof of tower four. The openings through which they had originally arrived, had all disappeared. B'nair thought for a minute about what trick the Alchemist had set for anyone trying to return. The wind had picked up strength and was rapidly and unexpectedly changing directions, blowing them from one side of the roof to the other. It was as if the wind was trying to push them over the side.

B'nair moved carefully towards the center of the large circular top of the tower. When he was almost dead center, his foot felt a softness that was not evident to the naked eye, and not to be expected of solid stone.

"The portal is here," he announced, pointing to the center of the floor. "We must lock arms and allow ourselves to be drawn in."

The others started moving forward. Before they could begin to prepare themselves to step into the portal, B'nair turned to Ercon.

"Leave half of your men behind," he ordered. "Others who are searching for this stone are close by. Have your men hide against the battlements. The snow will soon cover them. They are not to alert these others to their presence until they are able to ensure that none of them leave these towers alive. Is that clear?"

"Yes," he answered. "Of course."

He turned to choose the men who would remain behind, but stopped. He considered his question, and then turned back to B'nair. He leaned close to speak in a low voice, so no one else could hear.

"How will they get back?" he asked. "As you know, the spells change constantly. Once we go through this portal, it will no longer be here for them to use, and there will be no one to guide them."

B'nair looked directly into Ercon's eyes, not immediately responding. He had considered this when he made the decision to leave a part of the team behind.

"They will discover either another exit or not," he finally answered, barely more than whispering in Ercon's ear. "If you feel there is a need for them to be guided, you are more than welcome to stay with them and assume that responsibility."

Ercon pulled away from B'nair and looked at him in surprise.

"N...n...no," he stammered.

"I thought not," answered B'nair. "Now make it happen."

Without any further discussion, Ercon signaled to half the remaining men. He conveyed B'nair's instructions, telling them to crouch down against the wall until the snow covered them from view. He told them there were others close behind, and they were to destroy them to ensure the safety of the others. Once that was done, they were to follow.

He didn't allow for any discussion, immediately turning and grasping the arm of the last man in line ready to step into the escape portal. Taking the lead, B'nair quickly stepped forward and disappeared into the stone floor, pulling the line of men down after him, leaving the rest to consider their fate.

After a few seconds, one of them realized the implications of having been left and stepped to the center of the floor. He was determined not to be sacrificed. In defiance of Ercon's direction, he moved to step where they had and to follow them. Let those who wanted to, stay behind and fight some unknown enemy.

It had returned to solid stone. He looked around and saw that the portals through which they had arrived were also gone. If there was a way off this tower, it was not evident to any of them. At first he was filled with rage. But he and the others soon resigned themselves to their fate. They moved lethargically to places opposite the bridge to tower five, and squatted down against the wall. They wrapped their arms around their bodies, trying to keep warm and silently waited as the snow fell harder and the drifts began to bury them.

They had started with forty men – forty-two with Ercon and B'nair. Now there were fewer than thirty and fourteen of them remained in wait for some unknown intruder, assuming these intruders ever made it past the spells. The fourteen men huddled in the snow knew they had been sentenced to doom.

As they sat, silently considering their fate, their comrades had dropped through the stone roof into the tower itself. They landed in a heap, almost on top of one another, in a narrow hallway. They slowly got to their feet and looked around.

There was a dim light coming from somewhere above, or maybe below. They couldn't tell. The walls of the hall were about eight feet high, and made of either glass or mirrors, as was the floor and ceiling. Panels of mirrors lined the walls, floor and ceiling, interspersed with panels of glass. The hall wound in a haphazard manner with sudden stops and sharp turns.

The initial reaction of each of them was to step away from each other for fear of breaking through the floor. B'nair commanded them to stop, reminding them that they needed to stay close together. He pointed out that if the floor was so weak that it couldn't hold them, it would have broken when they landed.

He looked in the two directions the passage led, and arbitrarily chose one. At first the way was easy to follow; but soon the passage narrowed even further and the labyrinth of reflections grew more complicated. B'nair was leading the way, moving slowly and cautiously. He had given Ercon the task of securing the back end of the line. Then the path came to a dead end. He stopped a few feet from the end, facing a mirror and his own image. He stood there looking at himself, trying to determine if there was some other trick to be solved. His anger mounting, he turned around.

There wasn't enough room for him to squeeze past everyone and resume the lead. He shouted to Ercon, who was now in front, and told him to carefully retrace his steps to where they had started. It was apparent they had chosen the wrong direction at the start, and would have to go the other way.

As they traveled, he paid closer attention to the walls on either side. Most of them were mirrors, merely reflecting the images of him and the hobgoblins shuffling through the maze. The periodic intervals where the mirrors were replaced by panes of glass seemed to be in no specific pattern. When he passed one of the glass panels, all he could see on the other side were more mirrors and more reflections of him and the others.

Ercon was no more successful than B'nair. Within minutes, he, too, had come to a dead end, facing a mirror similar to the one B'nair had encountered. He shouted back to B'nair to report what he had found. Thinking he had missed a cut off of some kind, B'nair turned the line around again and led them back down the passage. He looked carefully for a sign of another path, but found none.

Once more they faced the same dead end. Once more the line reversed. B'nair called to Ercon and told him to look for hidden passages. As he walked along, he pushed on each mirror and each panel of glass. None of them moved. Ercon was unable to find any intersections or side passages.

Quest of Eight Part Four: The Race to Virkio

Richard Reda

On the return trip, B'nair thought the direction of the passage had changed. He couldn't be positive, though. He concentrated on when the glass panels appeared and on the number of right and left turns. When he reached the same dead end, he was convinced that the passage had changed. Now, instead of facing a mirror, he was looking through glass. Beyond the glass was another maze of glass and mirrors and angled reflections of him and his men.

He raised his axe, prepared to smash the panel, but then thought better of it. He turned once more and ordered Ercon to lead them back the way they had come. The tension was having its effect on more than just him. He began to hear grumblings from some of the men in the middle of the line. The grumblings worsened when Ercon again arrived at a dead end.

"What do you see?" shouted B'nair.

The front of the line had wound around one of the many sharp turns. B'nair's line of sight was limited. He couldn't see Ercon, and guessed by the groans from further on that the passage was still blocked.

"Myself," answered Ercon.

"Are you facing a mirror or a reflection through a plate?"

"It is a mirror," answered Ercon. "The same as before.

"Turn around," B'nair ordered. "This time count the panes of glass and note where they are."

The line turned around and headed back the way they came. Once again B'nair was convinced the path had changed. The number of turns he had counted the last time had increased and there were more panels of glass. He also determined that the passage was getting longer, even though it still only went in one direction.

Quest of Eight Part Four: The Race to Virkio

Richard Reda

Before they reached B'nair's end of the maze, one of the men in the middle of the line, out of fear and frustration, kicked at one of the glass panels. The large pane cracked. Everyone stopped. B'nair could not see what was happening, but sensed a change. The stone in his hand felt different. He could feel a slight tingle – something between a vibration and an electrical charge.

"What's happened?" he shouted, hearing the sound, but unable to see its source.

Before anyone could answer, the cracked pane of glass exploded into hundreds of pieces. The opening created by the broken glass led to another path, identical to the one they had all been passing back and forth on. It was lined with more glass and mirrors.

"What's happened?" B'nair shouted again.

"Another path has been discovered," answered one of the men close to the opening.

A sense of foreboding flooded B'nair's mind. Something was terribly wrong. That way only led to danger.

"Do not enter," he shouted.

Before he could be stopped, the man who broke the panel stepped through, thinking it led to a way out. As soon as he stepped through, the panel reappeared, replaced by another glass. Seeing himself separated from the others, the man turned back and beat on the plate. His shouts could not penetrate the pane. His comrades watched as he pounded the glass in an eerie silence.

When the pounding seemed to have no effect, he kicked at it in the same manner as he had the first time. Now, however, his kick merely bounced off the plate. Panic filled his eyes. He screamed for help, kicking and pounding the glass. Nothing of this could be heard on the other side – it could only be seen.

B'nair pushed passed the line of men until he reached the image at which all who were nearby were staring. He was at first taken aback by the sight and the lack of sound. He pressed his hand against the glass, and was unable to feel the vibrations of the man's pounding and kicking. It was as if the glass were made of steel or stone.

B'nair looked closely at the edges of the panel, looking for a seam or some other way to open it. As he did so, he noticed the reflections deep on the other side begin to blur. His attention was drawn from the glass to a growing mist that was taking shape behind the lost hobgoblin.

The mist became a cloud, dark and ominous. Reflexively, B'nair and those around him stepped back. The narrow passageway gave them little room to distance themselves from the approaching cloud.

Seeing their reaction, the isolated man turned around to see what had caused their show of fear. Instantly he turned back to his comrades and resumed pounding and kicking. He was screaming for them to help, but nothing could be heard.

B'nair debated only a second and then raised his axe. He knew that breaking the barrier could release whatever was on the other side, but these were his men now, and he couldn't stand by watching one of them in danger. He swung down as hard as he could. The axe struck the plate without leaving so much as a mark.

B'nair swung again, and then once more, but to no avail. A fourth strike was pointless. By that time the cloud had enveloped the man on the other side, and he was gone. As quickly as it had appeared, the cloud, or the mist – whatever it was – was gone.

Quest of Eight Part Four: The Race to Virkio

Richard Reda

They had to get out of this tower, thought B'nair. And quickly. He resumed the lead and when he once again reached the end of the passage, he was confronted with his own image. A mirror now replaced the glass that had been there the last time they had come this way.

He was about to turn once more when something about the reflected image caught his attention. He turned back and looked more closely. It was not a reflection. In the mirror image, his axe should have been on the right. It was on the left. He raised his left hand. The image on the other side did exactly the same thing, but the hand was on the right, instead of on the left.

It's as if I'm facing a live person who looks exactly like me, he thought. He stepped closer to the panel. He raised his axe, but instead of smashing it down, he tapped it lightly against the pane. The image rippled like the surface of a pool of water. He stepped back quickly, anticipating some other threat. None came.

He looked behind him at the expectant faces and then turned back to the panel. Looking beyond the images in the front, he could see an exact replica of all that was behind him, but in the reverse of what it should be if this were merely a mirror. Boldly, he stepped forward into the plate.

His foot went through, and he hesitated for only an instant. He moved completely through to the other side. He was out of the maze and on the landing of a giant circular staircase. He looked behind him and could see the others waiting. He started to step back through to them but stopped, wondering if in doing so, the passage would be lost.

"Follow me," he shouted, not sure they would hear him.

For a few seconds, he was certain they hadn't, until one by one they each took tentative steps into the mirror panel and onto the landing.

When Ercon stepped across, B'nair turned towards the staircase and began the descent.

The steps were the same stone as the tower walls. They extended from the walls, circling downward. A dim light from an undetermined source from above provided only enough illumination to see the steps. The center around which they circled was as black as night. The air in the tower was dead. The sounds of their footsteps on the stone steps were absorbed in the darkness.

For more than thirty minutes they climbed down the steps. When they finally stopped to rest, B'nair looked up towards the tower ceiling, expecting to see the maze of glass and mirrors above him. All he saw was the flat circle of the ceiling. It seemed no further away than it had been when they started.

He started the group down again, cutting their break short. For twenty more minutes he moved down the staircase, shifting his gaze from the steps to the ceiling trying to gauge their progress. Nothing seemed to change. He stopped again, looking at the stairs, the wall and the ceiling.

"What is it?" asked Ercon. "Do you sense some danger?"

"I can sense nothing," replied B'nair. "That's the problem. There's no change in the air, no change in the light, and no apparent change in our progress. Look below. It is pitch black. Then why has the light from above not changed at all?"

He raised his axe and struck it against the wall, cutting a small mark into the stone.
"Keep walking," he ordered.

He kept one eye on the step nearest the mark on the wall as he resumed his descent. Walking carefully, with his arm against the wall to keep his balance, he stared at the step as it faded away. When the staircase had made a complete circle, and was immediately under the step where he had cut the stone, he looked at the wall next to him. The mark was there.

"We haven't moved at all," he shouted, incredulously.

"That's not possible," declared Ercon. "We've been advancing for nearly an hour. We must be close to the bottom."

"Look for yourself," answered B'nair, pointing to the mark he had cut into the wall.

He looked to the ceiling once more and then into the darkness below. He moved to the interior edge of the staircase and peered down into the abyss. He turned to the man nearest him.

"That dagger at your belt," he said. "Toss it into the center."

The hobgoblin did as he was ordered. He removed the dagger from its scabbard, stepped to the edge of the staircase and dropped it. No sound of it striking the bottom of the tower returned.

"I don't understand," said Ercon. "There must be something below us. We came up through a portal in the floor of the tower."

"We came up in a gust of wind," B'nair reminded him. "What if there is no floor?"

"How are we to get back?" asked the man whose dagger had been lost to the black opening.

B'nair looked at him, and then opened the hand that held the piece of stone he still clutched. He looked from the stone to the opening and then back to the man.

"The same way we came in," he answered. "Hold the arm of the man next to you."

When he saw that they had all linked arms, he stepped off the edge of the staircase. Anticipating the fear of the others, he held tightly to the arm of the man he was next to, keeping him from pulling free as he immediately dropped downward. Like dominoes, the line toppled in after him.

In spite of all he knew of the Alchemist's spells, and all the efforts of those who went before him, and as much as he wanted to trust in the wisdom of his new leader, Ercon could not make such a leap of faith. At the last minute, he jerked his arm free as the last man disappeared into the void.

He ran down the steps, hoping they had all been wrong. Once he completed the circle of the staircase, his eyes were riveted on the cut in the wall from B'nair's axe. He ran down further only to find the same mark in the same spot on the wall. He changed direction, trying to get back to the maze. The mark again appeared when he came full circle. He ran up another flight with the same result.

"NO!" he shouted into the emptiness. "What a fool I've been."

In desperation, he moved to the center, and stood on the edge of the steps. He stared down into the hole.

"B'nair!" he shouted.

No echo returned. His voice fell flat and died in the darkness.

"B'nair! Please! Help me!"
Nothing answered him. Knowing he had waited too long, he stepped off the staircase anyway, and began to drop. The blackness devoured him, sending him to oblivion.

Quest of Eight Part Four: The Race to Virkio

Richard Reda

No sooner had B'nair and the others made their jump, than they landed in the tunnel deep under the fourth tower. The wind was still fierce. B'nair hit first, falling to the ground. The others tumbled down after him, skittering and sliding across the tunnel floor. Some slid into the solid wall, while others slid into the wall of wind.

They all held each other tightly, and as some of them began to get sucked into the wind and lifted from the ground, those on more solid ground pulled hard and fought to hold on. B'nair squeezed the stone in his free hand and concentrated his strength. He pulled himself to his feet and pressed himself against the safe wall.

The man next to him gradually did the same, pulling the one next to him to a safer position. One by one they each struggled against the hurricane force winds and rescued their comrades. B'nair took a minute to take stock of the remainder of the force and noted that Ercon was not with them.

"The fool," he said, his voice lost in the wind. "I will miss his counsel."

Once they were all secured and standing against the wall, the wind stopped. The sudden change was almost as unsettling as the wind had been. Uncertain if this was one more trick of the Alchemist, they moved cautiously along the wall back the way they had originally entered.

Section by section they moved through the tunnel. Each time they expected to encounter the same or some changed spell, but each time there was nothing. B'nair wondered if this was because the stone was in his possession or if it was merely because the reason for the spells no longer existed. He didn't really care.

When they passed beneath the first tower and were finally clear of it, B'nair asked if there was a way to the surface. He had grown tired of traveling underground. There was, and he was led to a long narrow shaft. A pair of ropes rose through the shaft out of sight to the top.

"Are we supposed to climb up?" he asked.

"No," answered one of the men.

He untied one of the ropes from a block to which it was attached and a distant rumbling noise began. In a few seconds a platform appeared. It was only large enough to hold three or four of them. B'nair went first and three others squeezed on. One of them untied the other rope and secured it to a winch on the platform and began to wind it.

They slowly rose through the shaft and in a few minutes arrived inside a small cave. They got off the platform and sent it back down for the others. B'nair stepped out of the cave and found himself in a clearing on the edge of a mountain range. Once everyone had been hoisted from the tunnels, he turned to the one who had led them all to the lift.

"What's your name," he asked.

"Budala," he answered.

"Do you know where we are, Budala?"

"Yes, I believe I do,"

"Do you know how to get back home?"

"Yes."

B'nair opened his hand to reveal the stone. He pressed it hard against Budala's forehead and concentrated on an image that had flashed into his mind the moment he picked up the stone from the floor of tower five.

"Do you have an image in your mind?" he asked Budala.

"Yes, I do," he answered.

"Can you find this place?"

Budala thought for a minute before answering. At first he was puzzled. How would he know where this place was? He had never been there before. He wasn't even sure what it was, not to mention where it was. Then a dawning came over him and he began to smile.

"Yes," he answered, surprised at the knowledge. "I can."

"Good," smiled B'nair. "That is where I will be going with the rest of these men. You will go back and assemble another team. Fifty should do. Make sure they are well armed and well trained. Once they are ready, bring them to this place. Is that clear?"

"Yes," he answered. "It is."

"Go now," he instructed. "Stop for nothing. Do not sleep or rest until you get home. Do you understand?"

"Yes, my leader."

Satisfied that Budala would comply, and pleased with the way he had been addressed, he turned to the others and motioned them to follow. Although he didn't know that there was only one more piece of the stone that was still hidden, he knew where this one was. He began the long journey to capture it.

In the meantime, the fourteen men who had remained on the top of tower four were now completely covered in snow, and well hidden from view. Each one of them was certain they had been left behind for no good reason, and expected to die at their posts.

The wind was howling around them. The cold that had chilled them to the bone earlier was somewhat abated by the layer of snow that now covered them. A sudden change in the sound of the wind caused one of them to open his eyes. The coating that hid him from view broke slightly and small particles crumbled away.

The amount that was disturbed by his movement was minimal, and did nothing to reveal his presence. However, it was enough for him to see what had caused the change in the sound of the wind. It was another one of the Alchemist's spells. The spell had deposited new visitors on the roof of tower four.

There were seven of them. What an odd collection, thought the hobgoblin as he remained motionless and studied his target. They didn't look like soldiers. And he was wrong. There weren't seven. There were eight. One of them was a faerie.

Chapter ten

They were all huddled around one another, staring across the stone bridge at the tower that loomed in front of them. No one was ready to take the first step. The gust of wind that had blown Summer over the side of one of the low walls that ran along the bridge had not abated. Lochen had reached out and grabbed her before she got too far away. The sudden movement towards the edge made all of them gasp.

"I wasn't in any d...d...danger," Summer stammered as Lochen pulled her back towards the rest of them. "But thanks just the same."

"I didn't think you were," he answered. "I was a little worried, though. Just because you can fly doesn't mean this wind won't smash you against the rocks. And you're welcome."

"So," said Quinn. "Are we supposed to cross this thing, or what?"

"It's just a bridge," said Sean, taking the first step forward. "At least there isn't any water around."

"Don't get too far ahead," said Natalie. "We don't know what kind of spells are on the bridge or the tower. We should probably stay close together."

They walked in a tight cluster, almost like they were tied together. Summer crawled up Lochen's arm and nestled herself in his hood.

"I hope you don't mind," she said as she climbed over his shoulder, wrapped her wings in close and buried herself in the folds.

"Not at all," he answered, hardly paying any attention. "It might be safer for you there. At least until we cross the bridge."

It was about a hundred feet long. The wind whipped about their heads, but the footing seemed safe. None of them got too close to either side, staying as close to the center as they could, taking a few small steps and then stopping, before moving forward again. After several minutes, they reached the tower.

The bridge ended on a small landing. To the right, a stone staircase wound around and up the outside of the tower. To the left the bridge's wall had broken away and opened to several narrow steel beams that poked out of the tower wall. The beams were about three or four inches wide and protruded about a foot and a half to two feet from the wall. They rose in a manner similar to the steps on the opposite side, winding up and around the left side of the tower.

Natalie took a cautious step towards the beams and looked out past the edge of the bridge. The spire of rock which formed the foundation of the tower dropped more than a thousand feet downward into a mass of crags and peaks.

"Oh, my," she managed to whisper, her throat tightening. "I vote we take the steps."

"You won't get any argument from me," said Solveig, who had been peeking at the view from over Natalie's shoulder.

"Stay close to the tower wall," said Liam, who took the first steps up. "There's no handle or rail or anything. The steps are open and go up pretty steeply."

Without any words, they held each other's hands, pressed their backs against the wall and climbed sideways up the steps. As they rose higher and higher, the other towers came into view, each one stretching further upward than the one before. A few seconds later and several steps higher, the other towers disappeared from view.

As they rounded towards the side of the tower from which they started, Liam could see another bridge ahead of them. When they made a full circle, they arrived at another landing at the end of a bridge identical to the one they crossed from the gap in the mountains.

"Hey," shouted Quinn. "That wasn't so bad, and look! There's another bridge, exactly like the first one."

"That is the first one," said Stella.

"What are you talking about?" asked Sean. "How could we cross a bridge, climb up a stairway and end up in the same place?"

"We're not in the same place as where we started up the stairway," answered Lochen, who had turned around to see what was behind them. "We're at the same place we started before we crossed the bridge."

They all turned back to see the mountain gap from which they had exited. The bridge they had crossed a few minutes ago was again stretched before them, crossing over to the first tower.
"What kind of trick is this?" complained Sean, as he strutted across the bridge. This time he moved more quickly and with a sense of indignation.

He was more than halfway across before any of the others realized what he had done. They all scrambled to catch up to him. Quinn reached out and pulled him back before he could start climbing up the steps.

"Don't get carried away, Sean," he said. "No need to rush up there only to end up in the same place again."

"OK," answered Sean. "But what are we supposed to do? There isn't any other way up. Are we supposed to sit here until something happens?"

No one answered him. They all looked around at the mountain peaks, the towers, the stairway and the bridge they had now crossed twice. Lochen was studying the staircase and Stella was looking at the bridge. Finally, after a few minutes of silence, Summer spoke up.

"Look," she said. "The wind has died down. I can probably fly up the staircase – I'll keep close to the tower wall so I won't get blown away. I can see what happens and where I end up once I make a complete circle."

She unwrapped herself from the folds of Lochen's hood and was about to fly towards the stairway.

Quest of Eight Part Four: The Race to Virkio

Richard Reda

"NO!" shouted Lochen and Stella at the same time.

"Each of the towers is..." started Lochen, talking excitedly.

"The most obvious way isn't..." interrupted Stella.

"If we get separated..." interjected Lochen.

"And to avoid that, we have to..." continued Stella.
"Otherwise none of us will..." said Lochen.

"So we have to take the..." said Stella.

"STOP!" shouted Summer. "Do you realize that between the two of you, neither has completed a sentence?"

They stopped talking and looked at Summer. They seemed to be thinking the same thing as they turned to face one another.

"Of course," said Lochen. "It's just that..."

"The spells cast by the Alchemist..." inserted Stella.

"It apparently dawned on both of us..." interrupted Lochen.

"It made sense that..." continued Stella.

"STOP!" shouted Summer once more. "You're doing it again. What's the deal?"

"Sorry," they both mumbled, then looked at each other, neither one speaking.

"Go ahead," Lochen finally said. "You explain."

"No," said Stella. "That's all right; you can tell them."

"Please," said Lochen, "Continue."

"Oh, for crying out loud," Solveig finally interjected. "What's with you two?"

She stepped forward and pointed right in Lochen's face.

"You," she ordered. "Explain. And keep it brief!"

"OK; yes," Lochen answered. "We know that these towers belong to the Alchemist, although 'belong' may not be the right term. It's not clear if he actually built them or that he ever lived here. However, we have reason to believe that a piece of the stone that was broken off from the original pendant is secured somewhere in one of these towers."

"Brief, I said," cut in Solveig. "This isn't brief."

"Whatever the origin, the Alchemist has hidden a piece of the stone in these towers and has protected it by a spell or a series of interlocking or overlapping spells," he said, rushing his words together. "The long and the short of it is that we must think like the Alchemist. The most obvious path is most certainly not the right path."

"And I happened to think," interrupted Stella, "that to make his spells even more protective, they would probably change at random. That way, even if someone got past the first one, anyone following wouldn't be able to go the same way or get past the spell in the same manner."

"That was why we were opposed to the idea of Summer going ahead of us," Lochen continued. "In all likelihood, she would be separated from us for quite some time – maybe even forever."

"We could climb this stairway a hundred times," said Stella. "And each time we'd end up someplace different – or maybe not, but in any case, we wouldn't get inside the tower."

"Then how do we get inside the tower?" asked Quinn, certain he wasn't going to like the answer.

"Do we even need to get inside?" asked Natalie. "There's another bridge from the top of this one to the next tower. Can't we make our way up there to cross?"

"Why do we need to get to the next tower?" asked Liam. "How do we know the stone isn't in the first one? If this Alchemist was such a tricky guy, maybe he hid the stone here, thinking that anyone looking for it would believe it was hidden in the last tower."

"No," answered Stella. "The missing piece is in the last tower. I can feel it."

"We may not need to go inside," said Lochen, answering Natalie's question. "We won't know, though until we have gone as far as we can go with the first one. We need to find the way past the spells and see where we're taken."

"But if we don't go up this staircase, where do we go?" asked Quinn, still certain he wasn't going to like the answer. "There aren't any doorways in the wall."

"I'm afraid we have to go the way that would be least appealing," explained Lochen.

Everyone turned around to look at the broken section of the wall near the end of the bridge that opened to the metal beams along the side of the tower.

"Wonderful," mumbled Quinn.

"No problem," declared Sean. "This will be easier than climbing out of that gap in the mountains."

He stepped forward and leaned out over the edge of the bridge. The first metal beam was about two feet higher than the bridge and a little more than two feet away. He hung his toes over the broken stones of the bridge, looked down only once, and then let himself fall forward. Liam and Quinn made a grab for him, but Lochen blocked their way.

Before anyone could react, Sean stuck out his arms and grasped the beam. He pulled himself up, placing one foot on the beam, and then reached up to the next one to pull himself the rest of the way. It was like climbing a ladder. Step by step he began to move upward.

"Summer," said Lochen. "It might be best for you to resume your position in my hood. Stella, if you would go next, followed by Liam, then Natalie, then me, then Solveig and finally by Quinn, we should be able to watch out for each other."

One after the other, they followed Sean's lead, leaning out over the edge, letting themselves fall forward onto the lowest metal bar, with Quinn bringing up the rear.

"Try not to get too far ahead, Sean," cautioned Stella.

They inched their way up as the beams rose at an increasingly steeper angle. As they wound around to the opposite side, the stone staircase they had taken earlier was nowhere to be seen. Instead, the metal bars continued upward. By the time they had completed one full revolution of the tower, it was evident that they had chosen the correct path. The bridge below them was growing smaller.

By the time they were completing a second lap of the tower, Sean began to notice that the bars were getting shorter, protruding less and less from the tower wall.

"Hey, everyone," he shouted down. "We're running out of steps."

"Can you see if they disappear completely?" asked Stella.

"Not yet," he answered. "But it won't be long."

He also began to notice they were spaced further and further apart. He was beginning to have to stretch to reach the next ones. Soon they were too far apart for Stella to reach, and he had to hang on with his legs as he turned back to face her. He extended one arm, pressing his other hand against the wall for balance, as she reached up to grab his hand, so he could pull her up.

"We aren't going to be able to do this much longer," she said to him.

"Maybe we can use the rope that Liam brought along," he suggested. "And do what with it?" she asked, "Shinny up? I'm not sure that's such a good idea."

She stole a glance at the spires, crags and rocks below her. One slip and it would all be over. She closed her eyes and tried not to think about it. By the time they had made two complete revolutions around the tower, the bars were almost out of Sean's reach. They were also only extended about a foot from the wall. There was barely enough room for him to turn around, wrap his legs around it and lower himself towards Stella.

He looked down at her and then past her to the others struggling behind. This may be the last one we can do this way, he thought to himself. He was sitting on the bar, dangling his feet over the end, looking back and down at Stella. She looked up at him with an expression of worry. It was clear to him that she didn't think she'd be able to stretch that far.

He looked back over his shoulder at the next bar. It was even further away and narrower. Let's get her up to this one, he thought, and then

217

try to figure out plan "B." He maneuvered his legs to lock them securely around the bar, and then placed his hand against the wall for balance, getting ready to reach down to Stella.

All of a sudden, his hand went through the wall, followed by most of the rest of him. He was about to pull himself out, when Stella shouted for him to stop.

"Don't move," she yelled.

He froze where he was, half of him inside the tower and the other half still clutching the iron bars with his legs outside the tower wall.

"What do you see?" Stella asked.

"Nothing," answered Sean. "It's all dark in here. And cold. It's really, really cold. Can I come out now?"

"No," she replied. "I think that if you come out, the spell will change again. That may be the way into the tower for all of us."

She turned back to the others who were climbing up behind her.

"I think Sean found the way into the tower," she called to them. "We need to stay close together – as close as we can. If Lochen and I are right, the spell will change if there's too much of a gap between us, and we'll be separated."

The others moved up the rungs of metal, pulling each other up. Wherever possible, two of them stood on a single rod, pressing close to the tower wall. When they were all as far as they could go, Stella turned back towards Sean's legs. With his arms inside the tower, there was no way he could pull her up.

"What if I squeeze past you?" suggested Liam. "I could drop the rope down for each of us to pull ourselves up and into the tower while Sean keeps whatever opening he found from closing. Do you think that would work?"

She looked at the scant amount of iron bar that remained exposed to which Sean was still clinging. She didn't think there was enough room for Liam to get a secure perch.

"Don't worry," said Liam, sensing her reluctance. "I'll push him closer to the wall once I get up there. I'll be fine."

In spite of her misgivings, she moved as close to the wall as she could to give him room to get by her. He stretched upward to the bar around which Sean's legs were wrapped. Once both his hands were holding the metal, there was no more room for him. This wasn't going to work, he realized.

But now he was stuck. His arms were extended and his body was leaning forward. He was at enough of an angle that he couldn't push himself back upright. Even if he did, he'd be standing on the end of the beam next to Stella, with nothing to hold on to.
"What's wrong?" asked Stella, when she realized he hadn't moved.

"I'm beginning to think this wasn't such a good idea," he laughed nervously. "I don't have enough room to pull myself up and I'm too far forward to stand up straight. Any ideas?"

"Climb up his back," shouted Natalie, who had moved up to the bar from which Liam had vacated.

"Are you serious?" asked Stella. "What am I supposed to do once I'm standing on his head? Grow wings and fly?"

"Uncoil the rope from around his shoulder," she explained. "Then climb over Sean's legs and into the tower. Find something to tie the rope to and we can follow you in."

219

Quest of Eight Part Four: The Race to Virkio

Richard Reda

"You make it sound so simple," mumbled Stella.

She looked up at Sean, still hanging half in and half out of the tower, the stones of the wall appearing to seal him in tightly. Then she looked at Liam, hanging from the bar with his feet on the edge of the rung on which she was sitting. This is nuts, she thought.

"Did you hear that?" Stella asked Liam.

"Yeah," he answered. "It sounds crazy, but I can't think of another solution. You better hurry, though. My arms are getting tired."

"Just what I need to hear," muttered Stella.

She reached up to grab his belt and began to pull herself up. When her feet left the metal rung, and her full weight was on Liam's back, he gave out a grunt, trying as hard as he could to stifle it. She inched her way up his back to his shoulders where she found the end of the rope and began to uncoil it.

She realized she had climbed too far up his back and had to scoot back down towards his waist to get better access to the loops that ran over his shoulder and around his ribs. When she had unwound as much as she thought she needed, she reached up to his shoulders and began to climb back up.

The stress on his arms created a cramp in his shoulders. He reacted reflexively, pulling himself up slightly to relieve the pain. He did this at the same moment Stella shifted her weight and began climbing back towards his shoulders. He could feel his feet starting to slip.

"Faster," he shouted. "Move faster."

His instructions came too late. His feet gave way and he swung forward out over the abyss. Stella fell backwards. Her arm shot out in an attempt to grab his shirt or the remaining coil of rope, but missed. She tumbled head over heels and dropped downward.

"NO!" shouted Natalie.

She thrust our her hand in a failed effort to catch Stella as she shot past her. Lochen had to grab Natalie to keep her from falling after Stella. Before he knew what happened, Liam felt the rope around his shoulder jerk sharply, almost pulling him from the beam from which he was hanging.

Stella still had the other end in her hand and managed to hold it tightly. She came to a sudden stop as the rope snapped taut. It slid through her hand, burning the skin, but came to a halt when her hand reached the knot Liam had tied at the end to keep it from fraying.

She hung from the end of the rope by one arm, swaying back and forth and spinning slowly. When she realized she had stopped plummeting, she opened her eyes, and stopped holding her breath. As her body slowly circled, she watched as the mountains rolled past her field of vision and were replaced by Quinn, who had climbed back downward.

"Are you OK?" he asked once he was at eye level with her.

"I think so," she answered.
"Can you swing towards me?"

"Can I what?"

"Grab the rope in both hands," he said to her softly and slowly. "Don't look at anything but me. Start moving your feet back and forth. Not too hard. Take it slow. Start swinging towards me."

Her predicament began to become clearer as her initial panic wore off. She realized that Liam was still hanging on by his hands several feet above him. She did as she was instructed and began to kick her feet.

Quest of Eight Part Four: The Race to Virkio

Richard Reda

At first she made small arcs back and forth, but quickly picked up momentum. Quinn reached out and just missed her.

"You're getting closer," he shouted, encouraging her. "One or two more, and I'll have you."

She made the mistake of looking down when she swung away from him, at the instant she reached the end of the arc.

"Oh, poop," she gasped.

The length of the tower plunged downward into the rocks. The view was dizzying. Her hair streamed behind her as she moved pendulum-like down and then up towards Quinn.

"Ooooohhhh, I really hate this," she shouted.

To Liam's relief, Quinn caught Stella in his arms and pulled her to safety. He took the rope from her hands and tied it to the bar immediately above him. He shouted up to Natalie and told her to try to loop the section of rope closest to her around the beam on which she was standing. She gave it a gentle tug, nearly pulling Liam off the bar, but was able to wrap it around the end of the beam.

"Liam," Quinn shouted. "I think you can let go now."

"You think?" he shouted back. "That doesn't sound very reassuring. Are you sure?"

"Yes, I'm sure," Quinn shouted back, adding under his breath, "At least I think I'm sure."

Liam let go of the bar and grabbed the remainder of the coil of rope around his shoulder. He dropped a few feet until the slack was taken up, and then he jerked to a stop and swung immediately beneath Natalie.

"Now what?" he asked.

"Pull yourself up to where Natalie is standing. Lochen, you need to move up to where Stella was to make some room."

"Certainly," Lochen answered, climbing up past Natalie.

Once Liam was back on the beam, he loosened the coil of rope and tossed the end up to Lochen. Lochen tied it around his waist and moved up to where Sean was still half in and half out of the tower.

"I'm going to climb in after Sean," he told the others. "Once inside, I'll pull Sean the rest of the way through. If our assumptions about the Alchemist's spells are correct, this rope should be sufficient to keep the current spell unchanged while the rest of you follow after us."

"And what if your assumptions are incorrect?" asked Solveig. "What if the wall seals up and we lose you completely?"

"Then I hope you cherish the memories of all the wonderful times we had together," he answered.

"I must have been asleep that day," she mumbled sarcastically.

Lochen climbed over Sean's legs and through what appeared to be the solid wall of the tower. Once inside he explained to Sean what had recently transpired and pulled him the rest of the way into the chamber. He looked around for something to secure the rope to, but could see nothing in the dim light.

"You were right," he told Sean. "It is incredibly cold in here."

"No kidding," Sean answered through chattering teeth. "What happens now?"

Quest of Eight Part Four: The Race to Virkio

Richard Reda

Lochen moved back to the part of the wall through which he passed. He expected to feel the stone, but his hand passed through it as if it were not there. He pulled his hand back in and felt along the wall until he came into contact with stone that was solid.

"We need to pull this rope as taut as possible and lean against this section of wall. It should give us support so that the others can climb in after us. Call out to them to let them know to begin once we're ready."

Sean followed the rope back to the area where it appeared to go through the stone. He got down on his hands and knees and crept forward. His head went through the wall as easily as going into water, and it popped out on the other side. He looked down towards Natalie who was staring up at him.

"Tell Quinn to untie his end of the rope. He can tie it around his waist. You need to loosen your section, too. Use it to climb up into the tower. Lochen and I will hold on to the other end. Once we're all in, we can pull Quinn up. OK?"

Natalie looked from Sean, back down to Quinn and then at the rope. There had to be an easier way, but she couldn't think of one. Finally she nodded that she understood and called back to Quinn with the instructions. Once he had tied the rope around him, she loosened the loop she had placed around her beam and waited for Lochen and Sean to pull it in.

Natalie grasped the rope in both hands and then wrapped her feet around it and began to shinny up. She was thankful she didn't have far to go. When she reached the wall, she hesitated, staring directly at what appeared to be solid stone.

"I sure hope this isn't real," she said to no one in particular.

"It's very real," she heard Lochen's voice, as clear as if he was standing right in front of her. "And at the same time, it's an illusion. I realize those appear to be contradictory concepts, but I am certain that the tower is real, and that the opening through which we have passed is the result of a very real spell. It's the spell that has created the incongruity in what our senses are telling us."

"I don't think she was really expecting an answer," she heard Sean say. "I think her question was restorable."

"I believe you mean rhetorical," replied Lochen.

"Whatever," said Sean. "I don't think she was actually talking to you."

Natalie ignored the debate and plunged ahead. She moved easily through the wall and inside the tower. Once her body was more than halfway in, she let go of the rope and crawled to her feet.

"We're over here," announced Lochen, who was standing a few feet from the entryway.

She ran over to join them, adding her weight to their end of the rope. In a few seconds Liam's head appeared, and he climbed in to join them. One by one the others followed. As Quinn climbed up the rungs of metal, those inside took up the slack in the rope, pulling it tighter.

He was the last to come through. It took all of them to counterbalance his weight. He had untied his end of the rope and hung from it down the outside wall of the tower. He pulled himself upward as the others dug in their heels and pushed backwards, dragging the rope and Quinn into the tower.

"I thought you guys said it was cold in here," he said once he was on his feet.

Quest of Eight Part Four: The Race to Virkio

Richard Reda

They looked at one another, each of them shivering in the cold, dank air.

"This is like a nice spring day," he added. "Where do we go now?"

Liam rewound the rope and put it back over his shoulder while Lochen surveyed their surroundings. They were in a large circular room – much larger than it seemed could exist inside the tower. In fact, they couldn't see the opposite side. The floor was covered in a thin mist. The mist appeared to become thicker towards the center of the hall, and rose up to the ceiling – or where they assumed the ceiling was. The vapor from their breath floated upward and blended in to the layer of fog that hid the top of the hall from view.

The only light in the room came from the center, deep inside the fog. The walls were dark gray and turned to black the higher they went, until they disappeared in the clouds above. There were archways to the right and left. Lochen walked over to the one on his left and looked in, but didn't enter. He returned the way he came and then went over to the other exit. Again, he looked in, but didn't enter.

"It's likely that the hallways those two openings lead to are simply illusions," he told the others. "Similar to the stone staircase on the outside of the tower. They probably lead nowhere and at best return to the same place they started."

"We need to do something," said Sean. "It's freezing in here."

Only Quinn, who was more acclimated to sub-zero temperatures, and Solveig, who was still wearing the cloak the old woman had given her, appeared to be tolerating the extreme cold. The others were beginning to shiver, their lips turning almost as deep a shade of blue as Solveig's skin.

"I think we should cross over to the other side," said Stella.
"Wouldn't it be safer to go around?" asked Natalie.

"I would venture a guess that if we simply walk around, close to the wall, we will find nothing different than what we already see," said Lochen.

"This whole thing is an illusion, isn't it?" suggested Liam.

"I think you're right," answered Lochen. "It's all part of the spell. It would have been interesting to see how this would change if we were to come through here again."

"Maybe on the way back, Professor," interjected Sean. "And I hope it's warmer then."

"Highly improbable," said Lochen. "But not impossible."

"Let's get this over with," said Liam as he began to walk forward into the mist.

"Wait," said Natalie. "Wouldn't it be a good idea to tie ourselves together with that rope? Just to make sure we don't get separated?"

"But what if whoever is in front falls down a pit or something?" asked Sean. "Wouldn't we all get dragged in?"

Everyone turned to look at him.

"What?" he asked. "I'm just saying."

"I think that's a great idea," said Solveig.

Liam removed the rope from his shoulder and tied one end around his waist. The others followed suit and in a few minutes they were bound to each other in a caravan of sorts. When everyone was ready, Liam continued to lead them. After only a few steps, they all began to notice the temperature dropping even further.

Quest of Eight Part Four: The Race to Virkio

Richard Reda

"Ohhh, man," said Sean. "This can't be right. It's getting even colder than it was before."

Even Quinn had to agree that the frigid air was reaching an unbearable stage. The moisture from their breath was caking on their faces. Ice crystals were forming on any skin exposed to the air. The rope had become stiff with frost.

The fog was getting thicker and thicker, the air heavier and heavier. After several more seconds, none of them could see the person who was only two feet in front of them. The air was so cold it was painful to breathe. Summer had been wrapped inside Lochen's hood until he rose it to cover his head.

"Oh, I'm sorry, Summer," he said when he flipped the hood up and flung her out.

"I hope you don't mind," she answered as she crawled back inside the hood and wiggled her way onto the top of his head, wrapping the material tightly around her.

"Are you guys still up there?" asked Quinn. "I can't see any of you, and this rope has frozen stiff. I can't feel if anyone is pulling on it."

"Yes," said Solveig. "We're here. Or at least I am. Maybe we should keep talking so we know no one got lost."

"I'd stick out my hand to touch whoever is in front of me," said Stella. "But I'm afraid it would freeze and break off."

"I can't see anything," said Liam. "Wherever this light is coming from keeps reflecting off the fog. It's like trying to see in the middle of a snowstorm. And it keeps getting colder. I didn't think that was possible. My eyes hurt, my nose hurts, I'm afraid my tongue is going to freeze. Maybe this isn't the right way."

"Keep going," Lochen and Stella both said.

"It's the right way," added Lochen. "If for no other reason than it seems like the worst..."

His words were cut off when the rope around his waist was suddenly jerked forward, knocking him off his feet. The floor beneath Liam's feet had unexpectedly disappeared and he was sliding down a tunnel or a tube of some kind that was coated with ice. There was nothing for him to grab on to in order to stop. He tried digging his heels in to the surface to slow himself down, but that did nothing.

He was careening down at a frightening speed, pulling each of the others right behind him. They had all been taken by such surprise that none of them had been able to do anything to stop their descent. They were all yelling and screaming, trying to slow down, their voices echoing off the sides of the narrow shaft. It felt like they were dropping to the very bottom of the tower.

The incline quickly leveled out, circling around several times, slowing everyone's speed. It ended at a round stone-lined opening in the side of the tower. The gray sky that blanketed the surrounding mountains rapidly came into view.

Liam kicked with all his strength to try to stop his forward movement. He expected to shoot out of the tunnel, over the edge of the tower and out into and over the chasm of rocks. Instead, he slid out onto what appeared to be the roof of the tower. It was flat and clear, and as round as the tower itself.

When he looked behind him, all of the others had skidded and swirled to a stop and the tunnel through which they had flown had disappeared. He stood up and looked around. Behind him loomed the other four towers. And near the edge of the roof, towards tower two, was another bridge.

Chapter eleven

They all walked to the edge of the tower roof towards the bridge, untying the rope as they went. It was narrower than the first bridge and made of wood. It arched from the roof of tower one to its highest point about twenty feet away, and then down another twenty feet over to an opening in the side of tower two, about fifty feet from the top. The bridge had a guardrail on both sides, but no walls under the railing as the first bridge had. The wood was old and weather-beaten. In many places it had cracked and splintered.

The floor of the bridge was covered with a solid layer of slats that appeared to have been well traveled. The centers had worn down and were thinner than the edges. Wooden pegs secured the slats to the frame underneath. In a few instances, the pegs had worked their way up and either protruded from their holes, or were missing altogether.

Quest of Eight Part Four: The Race to Virkio

Richard Reda

The wind was still blowing, but seemed somewhat abated in the areas between the towers. However, the wood could be heard to creak whenever a gust blew. Areas of the bridge looked wet – probably from the light dusting of snow that had begun to fall.

Liam coiled the rope, slung it over his shoulder once more, and then moved to the end of the bridge. He looked over the side at the truss work that supported the bridge. Heavy beams were supported by large blocks built into the sides of both towers. The beams criss-crossed in a network that appeared to be sturdy, although Liam could see that a number of the beams were showing signs of rot.

The landing at the opposite side of the bridge was hidden from view because of the bridge's arching shape. Lochen walked to one side, following the ramparts on the roof of tower one, trying to see where the bridge ended. He had little success. He could see some kind of shadow or opening, but not enough to have a clear idea of what was at the other end.

"It seems safe to cross," said Liam. "There are a few places that might not be as strong as others. Maybe we should cross one at a time."

Lochen looked at Stella.

"I don't have the sense that this bridge is under the same kinds of spells as the towers. Do you?"

"No," she said. "I can't tell why, but it doesn't feel the same."

"Then again," Lochen added, "since the most sensible thing would be to cross one at a time, that might not be the right thing to do."

"What if we tie the rope to each other again?" asked Natalie.

"I don't think that will work here. When we all passed through the wall into the first tower, we were all still in close proximity to one another. Aside from when we crossed into the tower, we were never out of each other's sight. That arch in the center of the bridge will effectively separate us, even if for only a few seconds."

"That's going to put a lot of weight on that bridge at one time," said Liam.

"I can fly across," offered Summer. "That should help."

"It's not you I was thinking of," answered Liam.

"Are you trying to suggest that some of us are overweight?" asked Solveig.

"Uh…no…that's not what I meant," stammered Liam. "It's just that all together our weight might be too much for some of those support timbers – uh…regardless of how…er…uh… petite some of us are."

"Nice save," whispered Sean.

"We need to approach this cautiously," suggested Lochen.

"What if we staggered the order and the distance as we crossed?" asked Natalie.

"Yes," said Lochen. "An excellent idea. We should try to displace the weight as much as possible."

"It might be a good idea to put the most stress on at the beginning," said Liam.

"I agree," said Lochen. "Even in staggering our approach, if we can have the amount of weight taper off towards the end, any structural weaknesses might be minimized."

"<u>Might</u> be minimized?" asked Solveig. "Can't you be more certain than that? Have you seen how high above the ground we are? Have you seen those rocks below?"

"Yes," said Lochen. "I'm sure I've been far more observant than you believe me to have been. I am well aware of our altitude and the depth of the crevasses. I am also quite confident that I can estimate our velocity and the time to impact should any one of us fall, but I don't see the point."

"Why do I bother?" Solveig mumbled. "Never mind. Let's get on with this. Who's going first?"

"Quinn," Lochen announced.

"ME?" asked Quinn, incredulously. "You want me to go first? I don't understand. I usually bring up the rear. I'm better at bringing up the rear, really, I am. I'm not good at going first. It's not that I'm scared; I'm just not very good at it. What if I make a mistake? I really think someone else should go first."

No one was paying any attention to his ranting. They all lined up in the order Lochen had proposed: Quinn, Stella, Lochen, Natalie, Liam, Solveig, and Sean. Summer would remain nestled in Lochen's hood, since the winds were still strong and unpredictable.

"Liam's really good at going first. Or maybe Sean could do it," Quinn continued to ramble. "I can go first some other time. I know we should all take turns, but I don't think it's my turn, yet. I'll be glad to go first some other time. How about next week? I could go first next week."

When everyone was ready, Quinn was still yammering, with his back towards the bridge, facing the line that was ready to move. Summer finally climbed out of Lochen's hood and flew within inches of Quinn's nose. His eyes crossed as he tried to focus on her.

Quest of Eight Part Four: The Race to Virkio

Richard Reda

"Move it!" she ordered.

He stopped talking and turned around. He bent down slightly to put a hand on each of the rails, and extended one foot forward. He tapped his toe on the bridge floor, and then looked back over his shoulder at the others. Seeing no sympathy there, he put his weight on the extended foot, closed his eyes and scrunched his face.

Nothing happened. The bridge didn't collapse. It didn't even creak. He let out his breath, looked back again at the others and smiled. Maybe this won't be so bad after all, he thought. He slid his hands forward and took another step. Again, nothing happened. He relaxed a little and continued to inch his way to the center point of the bridge.

Stella followed about ten feet behind him. She was getting irritated with his crawl, but decided against commenting. It was probably wiser to proceed slowly. Each step he took began with the extension of his foot and the tapping of his toe on the bridge.

"What are you doing?" she finally asked, unable to contain her impatience.

"I'm checking to make sure it's solid," he whispered over his shoulder.

"Why?"

"What if this bridge is like the wall of that tower?" he explained, still whispering. "I could step onto a plank that isn't really there."

She hadn't thought of that. She looked down at the wood beneath her feet and then back the way they both had come. She could see their footprints in the light layer of snow. Since his stride was so much longer than hers, she could see where the impressions of his larger feet were imprinted, compared to several more impressions that belonged to her.

What if he is right, she thought. I could have fallen through. She was no longer as impatient as she had been seconds before. She looked at the span between where she was standing and where Quinn was still tapping with his toe. In the nearly ten feet, he had taken three steps. She would take about three times that many steps to cover the same distance. Maybe his toe tapping was a clever idea.

She looked more closely at the floor of the bridge. The snow had been gradually accumulating. By now it was almost an inch deep. If there was a spell on the bridge that made parts of it an illusion through which trespassers could fall, she wondered; wouldn't the snow fall through, too? Could the Alchemist have put a spell on the snow? She didn't think so.

"I don't think you have to worry about the bridge not being real," she said. "Don't you think the snow would fall through if it wasn't really there?"

"Maybe it's there just enough to keep the snow from falling through, but not enough to keep me from falling through," he whispered back.

"Why are you whispering?" she asked, realizing that she was whispering, too.

"Why are you whispering?" she repeated in her normal voice.

"In case there's someone waiting for us in the next tower," he answered.

He was right, she concluded. He should never have gone first. Eventually, he reached the peak of the bridge's arc and could see the other end. He stopped at the top and stood up straight. Then he turned back to look at Stella. He could see that Lochen had started to follow them. Noticing that Quinn had reached the highest point of the bridge, he called to him.

Quest of Eight Part Four: The Race to Virkio

Richard Reda

"What can you see?" he asked.

"I can see you," he answered, smiling and waving.

"In the other direction," Lochen clarified. "What can you see at the other end of the bridge?"

Quinn turned back towards the tower, moved his head slowly from one side to the other, and then turned back towards Lochen. "I can see the tower," he answered. Seeing the look on Lochen's face, he quickly added, "And there's a landing exactly like the one on your end of the bridge. There's a big doorway, too, but the door's closed."

"Keep going," Lochen called. "But don't touch the door until we're all on that side of the bridge."

Quinn turned back towards tower two and continued his foot extended, toe tapping method of crossing the bridge. As soon as he took his first full step on the downward portion of the bridge, it let out a loud creak. Everyone stopped where they were and grabbed the railing. Quinn turned back and appeared as if he were planning on returning.

"Don't even think about it," shouted Stella. "Keep going."

He turned back towards the second tower and continued. After a few more steps, Stella was near the apex and Natalie had set foot on the bridge. A gust of wind blew through the space between the towers, and the bridge felt like it swayed slightly, letting out another painful groan.

"I felt that," shouted Quinn, forgetting about whether anyone was waiting on the other side. "Did you feel that? How could you not feel that? I felt that."

"Keep going," answered Stella.

Quinn picked up the pace, but he kept tapping the bridge with his toe before he stepped forward. As he approached the midway point of the descending half, the creaking of the wood became more regular. It matched his movements step for step. The wood on this side of the bridge was apparently in worse condition than on the side that Liam had been able to examine.

By now there were four of them on the bridge – five, counting Summer. Quinn fixated on the landing that was less than ten feet in front of him. Three more steps, he told himself. Only three more steps. He stuck his foot out, tapped his toe and then moved forward.

This time the bridge not only creaked loudly, it shifted. Everyone could hear the cracking sound as one of the support beams gave way. It didn't break through completely, but it splintered and broke, shifting the floor of the bridge near Quinn's left hand almost a foot downward.

He released his grip from the left hand rail and turned towards the right, grabbing that rail with both hands. He crouched over, waiting for the entire bridge to collapse. Nothing happened. From Stella's viewpoint, he looked like a downhill skier, bent at the waist and leaning forward.

"Keep moving," she told him. "The best thing you can do is get off this bridge."

"OK, OK," he answered.

He remained bent over, and stuck his left leg out sideways, tapping that foot on the floor boards. When he was certain the floor was solid, he slid his hands sideways and crab-walked to his left. The bridge dropped again. This time both sides shifted.

Stella had to control her fear and force herself to keep from running the rest of the way. She, too, was holding tightly to the railing on the right, having passed the top of the bridge. Lochen was near the top when he stopped and turned back to look at Natalie. He motioned for her to stop and told her not to move.

Quinn opened one eye and stole a glance at the end of the bridge. Two more steps he told himself. He extended his foot and tapped. He closed his eyes and slid sideways another step. Nothing happened. He repeated this once more and with that last step was only a foot or two from the end. Another gust of wind shot between the towers and the bridge creaked once more.

Without bothering to tap his toe, Quinn took a quick leap and landed on the stone balcony at the entryway to tower two. The bridge shifted with the change in the weight on it. Now the right side dropped down, leveling the bridge out sideways, but increasing the decline towards tower two.

When the bridge shifted, the sudden movement caught Stella off guard. She jerked her arms backwards to keep her balance, but the snow beneath her feet made the old wooden boards slippery. Her feet flew upward and she landed hard on her back. She slid downward and in her effort to stop, she skidded sideways.

She was moving towards the edge of the bridge, in between the floor and the railing, still several feet away from the nearest rail post. She tried digging her heels in to slow down, flailing her arms, trying to find something to hold on to. She couldn't see exactly where she was, but she saw enough to tell her that she was about to go over the side.

Quinn saw her fall and took a tentative step back onto the bridge. He was startled to a stop when he heard Lochen shout at him.

"No," he yelled. "Stay where you are."

Lochen had just started down the same half of the bridge when he felt the shift and saw Stella slip and fall. He moved cautiously forward, trying to close the gap between them as quickly as he could when he saw Quinn begin to move back onto the bridge. He shouted to him to stay put and made a diving leap down the center of the bridge path, landing flat on his stomach.

He shot across the snow-covered wood at the same instant Stella reached the edge. He kept his eyes glued to her waving arms as she tried to twist and turn to stop her motion. By now she had managed to flip over onto her stomach, but had been able to do nothing to stop her momentum. Her legs shot out over the side of the bridge and the balance of her weight was ready to take her the rest of the way when she felt something snag her hand and pull her back.

As Lochen skidded down the bridge, he reached out in the nick of time to catch Stella's hand and pull her along behind him. The two of them skimmed across the snow covered slats and crashed into the door at the landing. At the same time, the bridge creaked and shifted once again.

By this time Natalie had passed the halfway mark, Liam was approaching the apex and Solveig was at midpoint on the ascending part of the bridge. Sean, still on the landing at tower one, watched with apprehension.

"Are you all right?" Lochen asked Stella.

"Yes," she answered somewhat breathlessly. "Thanks. I thought for sure I was going to get a close up view of those rocks at the bottom."

"OH, WOW!" Quinn shouted. "That was way cool. You saved her. You just jumped into the air and slid down the bridge and grabbed her."

"Yes," said Lochen, getting up and brushing the snow from his clothing. "I was there. Remember?"

Quest of Eight Part Four: The Race to Virkio

Richard Reda

Natalie was holding both sides of the rail to make certain she didn't slip, as she moved as fast as she could. Once Liam reached the top of the bridge, he could see that Natalie had already made it all the way across. He slipped slightly taking his first steps downward, and grabbed the railing for balance. He turned back to caution Solveig.

"Hold on tight to the rail," he shouted. "It's starting to get slippery."

His voice was muffled by the wind. Solveig lifted her head to ask him to repeat what he said, and her feet went out from under her. She had been holding the railing with one hand, and consequently, fell to the side. Her legs shot out over the edge of the bridge as she wrapped her arms around the railing to keep from going any further.

"What?" she yelled back to Liam once she regained her footing.
"I said...never mind. Just be careful."

Before Solveig reached the top, Sean started to follow. Ten feet from the end, Liam hit a patch of ice. He landed hard on his back and slid the rest of the way down. The effect of now the fourth person falling hard on the bridge was that it shifted once more. This time the section attached to tower one gave way.

The movement was so significant that it tossed Solveig into the air. She landed in a heap a few feet past the highpoint and began to slide downward. Instead of fighting the movement, she managed to turn herself to face tower two, tucked her arms into her sides and glided smoothly and straight to the landing.

Sean, on the other hand fell flat on his face and skidded all the way back to the tower one landing. He jumped up and tried to get a running start. He pumped his legs to keep his feet moving as fast as he could while he held on to the railings. The pounding of his feet, though, sent tremors through the rotted sections of the framework. The bridge creaked louder than ever, groaning over the howling wind.

No one on the other side could see him. Summer had to be restrained by Lochen. She crawled out of his hood and started to fly back to see what was keeping Sean. As she launched herself off Lochen's shoulder, he reached up and caught her legs at the last second.

"No," he shouted. "You can't go back. The wind's too strong."

"I have to see what happened. Why hasn't he crossed yet? That bridge is starting to collapse."

Lochen moved to the edge of the landing, and stretched out as far as he could, but he still couldn't see past the bridge. He had no view of the opposite landing or of where Sean might be. He could see, however, that the stanchions under the far side of the bridge had cracked and were pulling away from the tower. He could also see that the bridge was beginning to shake.

He thrust out his arm in an attempt to cast a spell on the bridge. His earlier concerns about casting spells over the Alchemist's spells were quickly forgotten. He had to try to stop the bridge from coming apart long enough for Sean to get across. He could see the spell take the shape of a globule as it left his hand.

It looked more like he was flinging goo from his fingertips. The spell was a clear, quivering mass, moving in slow motion. Three feet from his hand it fizzled and dissolved into nothing. Whatever spells the Alchemist had cast easily defeated Lochen's capabilities. The trusses under the bridge continued to loosen.

Liam grabbed the railings in both hands and started back across the bridge.

"No," shouted Stella. "You might cause even more damage."

"If we don't do something, Sean might not make it," he shouted back.

"You might not make it," answered Stella. "Let me go. I weigh less."

"No one is going," inserted Quinn. "Give me your rope."

Liam did as he was asked, without any questions. Quinn took the rope, tied an extra knot in the end and began to twirl it over his head in a circle. He let out more rope, increasing the size of the circle until he ran out of room. Then he hurled it with all his might towards the top of the bridge.

His attempt missed, and the end of the rope fell off to the near side. He quickly pulled it back in and tried again. Once more, the wind caught it and carried it away from the bridge. On the other side, Sean was still scrambling up the incline. He could feel the bridge supports breaking apart beneath his feet.

He thought that his running might have weakened the supports. He slowed down and began the tedious process of pulling himself up by the rails. He heard and felt another creak. Looking back he could see that the bridge had pulled away from the landing by more than a yard. Through the gap he could see the deteriorating buttresses.

The large blocks, which supported the framework, had also broken apart. The right side of the tower one frame had come away completely and was hanging in midair, supported only by the beams on the left side. Sean turned back towards the top of the bridge. It looked very far away. He thought if he could make it that far, he could run the rest of the way if he had to.

In the meantime, Quinn had tried several times to throw the rope over the highpoint of the bridge, and each attempt had been unsuccessful.

"There's not enough weight to it," he said. "I need something to give it some heft."

"Try this," said Liam.

He took one of the larger daggers from his belt and tied it to the end of the rope.

"It's not much weight," he said, handing the dagger and the rope back to Quinn. "But if you try throwing it like a weapon, you may be able to get it farther."

Quinn once more spun the rope in a circle over his head. He could feel the added weight of the knife, but he wasn't sure it was enough. This time he let go a little earlier. All eyes watched the end of the rope sail through the air. The knife glided, cutting through the wind, staying on a straighter path than the rope had all by itself.

He had released it too early. He quickly pulled it back and tried again. This time his aim was more accurate. The knife sailed high into the air, straight for the center of the bridge. Quinn played out the rope to reduce the drag on the dagger as it started the downward arc. The blade and the end of the rope disappeared over the apex of the bridge, but came to a stop.

Quinn gave the rope a shake, but the rope didn't move. He had hoped that the knife would slide down the opposite side, taking the rope with it. This didn't happen. In fact, nothing happened. He gently pulled on the rope, but it still didn't move. What none of them could see was that the knife had landed two feet on the other side of the bridge's summit, and stuck deeply into the wood.

"It probably stuck in the wood," said Liam. "Just leave it. It's better than nothing, and you may not be able to get it any further."

Sean had been inching his way upward, and hadn't noticed the knife and the rope. It was still more than a dozen feet away. Even if he had seen it, at that distance it would be of no help. Another gust of wind surged up from below and the bridge twisted radically. Sean fought to keep his balance as he slid sideways with the motion of the bridge.

For a few seconds, the floor on which he had been standing was wrenched around perpendicular to the ground. The remaining beams still secured to tower one were twisted severely. If they hadn't been soft with rot, they would have snapped in half. As it was, the moisture that had seeped into the wood allowed it to be flexible. Once the wind subsided, the bridge swung back to its earlier position.

The twisting had also dumped all the snow off the pathway. Sean was able to get a better footing and pulled himself along the rails faster than before. A few feet ahead of him he saw the knife wedged into the floor of the bridge, with the rope still attached to it. He took short, quick, sliding steps forward, never releasing his grip on the railing.

Just as he reached the location where the knife was planted into the wood, the water that had leached into the crevices surrounding the stones that held the lone surviving support beam in tower one froze. The freezing water expanded as it turned to ice, forcing the stone from its seating. The pressure created a small crack in the side of the block. The stress of the weight of the bridge and the motion caused by the wind widened the crack until it extended from one side of the block to the other.

When that happened, the part of the stone protruding outward from the tower, and on which the support beam rested, fell away, dropping fifteen hundred feet to the ground below. The falling block was followed by the support beam, which was followed by the bridgework above it. Since the other side had already broken away from the tower, the entire end of the bridge that had previously been attached to tower one, crumbled and began to drop.

Sean felt the bridge start to give way before he heard the screeching of the wood as it tore apart. He didn't bother looking back over his shoulder to see the source of the horrendous noise. At this point he didn't really care. He knew all he had to know: something very bad was happening.

He scrambled and clawed upward as the angle of what he was climbing changed more and more radically. At the other end of the bridge, his friends heard the noise and for a few seconds had no idea where it was coming from. The bridge was breaking away on the far side and was still hidden by the arch.

Seconds after the screeching started they could see the peak of the bridge begin to drop. It was as if it was happening in slow motion. The top of the arch shuddered and began to lower on the horizon. There was little change at this point in the near end of the bridge. Then the crumbling framework came into view beneath the surface.

They all watched, as the bridge seemed to fold in half. The beams that spanned the center of the bridge cracked and then snapped, breaking at midpoint. The far half of the bridge twisted. The distant part of the structure broke away first, sending the remains in an arcing motion down and away from tower one and turning towards tower two.

One by one, the truss beams splintered, cracked and snapped like dry twigs, and all the others could do was watch in horror. The main beam that ran along the outside edge of the bridge was the last to go. For several seconds the far section dangled over the abyss, suspended in air by the last beam. The weight began to pull at the foundation attached to tower two.
Eventually, the near half of the bridge gave way as well. It started with the support on the right side – opposite the side where the dangling half was hanging. When the stanchion on the right pulled free of the tower, the entire bridge swayed towards the onlookers. They backed up, pressed against the tower wall with nowhere else to go.

In the shock of what was transpiring before their eyes, Quinn had forgotten all about the rope. He still had one end wound around his hand. As the large wooden structure finally collapsed and fell into the chasm, the rope began to pull on him – the blade still stuck somewhere in the morass cascading down the mountainside. Not wanting to lose the rope, he quickly looped his arm around the end to tie to himself even more tightly. None of the others had noticed what he was doing.

"Sean," shouted Summer, as she watched the bridge drop further and further down.

"Sean," she screamed.

She was still being held in Lochen's hand, and she pushed his fingers away, wiggling to escape his grasp. Knowing that she would fly out to see what happened, and quite possibly be swept away by the very strong and very unpredictable winds, he tightened his grip.

"Let me go," she shouted, beating her fists against his hand. "Let me go."

"Not until you promise me that you won't fly out there," Lochen said to her softly.

She was in tears. All she could think about was how she felt when Sean and Quinn disappeared down that chasm over the lava river. How long ago was that? It seemed like ages. She knew Lochen was right. Even if she wasn't in danger of being blown away, there was nothing she could do. She could sprinkle faerie dust on him, but it probably wouldn't be enough to lift him up to the landing.
In her frustration, she stopped fighting Lochen, although he still didn't release her. She wiped the tears from her eyes and turned away, somewhat embarrassed. She looked up and saw Quinn. He was leaning against the wall, tugging on the rope.

"What are you doing?" she asked. "Are you crazy? You're going to get pulled over the side."

The others all turned to look at what was happening.

"Let go of that rope," Summer shouted. "Let go before we lose you, too."

"I don't want to lose the rope," Quinn answered, grunting as the rope pulled him towards the edge of the landing. "The knife must have stuck in one of the boards. It can't have gone too deep. I'm sure it will pull free soon."

"It's not worth it," said Liam. "Let go of the rope."

"Actually," said Quinn, "I can't. It's sort of tied around my arm."

He had twisted the rope around his arm and further looped it around his hand. There was no quick or easy way to untangle him. Whatever the knife had stuck into had probably twisted and turned, as the bridge broke apart. Now it was pinched tightly around the blade and handle. Whatever piece it was attached to was pulling Quinn closer to the edge.

Lochen dropped Summer unceremoniously to the ground and ran over to add his weight to Quinn's to keep him from being pulled over the side. Solveig and Natalie crowded around to add their support. Liam pulled another knife from his belt and moved to cut the rope. In their efforts to secure Quinn, they were now blocking Liam from access to the rope.

The rope was sliding back and forth along the edge of the landing. The wreckage in which the knife was stuck was swinging at the other end, carried by the wind. Liam tried to reach over Lochen, but every time he did, the shifting weight made those holding on to Quinn move back and forth, pushing him out of the way.

"Lochen" he shouted. "Move out of the way, so I can cut the rope."

At the moment the bridge had first started breaking away from its foundation, Sean was clawing his way to the apex. When the tower one end of the bridge broke loose and the bridge broke in half, the part he was on folded downward. In a last ditch effort, he leaped upward and caught the handle of the knife, the blade of which was deeply embedded in the wood.

He was hanging from the handle as the flooring tore from left to right. What he had been climbing fell off and dropped to the bottom of the chasm. He pulled himself up and grabbed the rope right where it was tied to the knife. At the same moment, the other half of the bridge gave way.

This just keeps getting better all the time, he thought. Large pieces of the frame began to break off. The chunk in which the knife was stuck swung free and crashed into the side of the mountain at the base of tower two. Even knowing it was coming, they found the collision jarring. He nearly lost his grip. The good part was that the piece that was still attached to the knife had twisted around the rope and was tightly secured. It had also broken up even more when it crashed into the mountain.

He knew he couldn't waste any time and he began to climb up the rope. It seemed to be secured to something, but he was sure that wouldn't last. He dodged falling pieces of lumber, making the rope sway back and forth as he moved to avoid being hit.

Above him on the landing, Quinn had braced his feet against the low wall along the floor of the landing and was pressing his back against the tower wall, the rope tightly tangled around his arm and hand. Lochen had braced his feet against the same low wall and was stretched out face down, pushing against Quinn to keep him from being pulled over the edge.

On the other side Solveig, Stella, and Natalie were similarly crowded together, also trying to hold on to Quinn. Summer was jumbled up inside Lochen's hood, and Liam was leaning over Lochen's extended body, swiping at the rope, missing it by mere inches.

"Lochen" he shouted. "You need to move so I can reach the rope. If I don't cut it, we're going to lose him and anyone who's still holding on to him."

"I'm afraid if I let go," grunted Lochen, "he'll get swept over. Whatever is on the other end of this rope is incredibly heavy."

"OK," said Liam. "Let's try this. I'll count to three. As soon as I say 'three' you drop down to the floor and I'll leap across to cut the rope. We may lose a little ground, but not enough for him to fall over the side."
"Sounds good to me," grunted Lochen.

"Me, too," agreed Quinn through tightly clenched teeth.

Below them, Sean was pulling himself up the rope while being buffeted by the wind and dodging falling debris. Every time he made a little bit of progress, something would push him back down. The rope, sliding through his hands, burned the skin. He looked up and saw the last vestiges of the bridge break away from the tower foundation.

The bridge and the supporting beams twisted overhead and slowly dropped downward. He swung himself towards the wall to avoid as much as he could. He had timed his movement so that he'd be out of the way at the precise moment that largest part of the collapse would be passing him. He was only partially successful.

The bulk of the wreckage missed him, but a trailing beam struck the wood into which the knife was wedged. The vibration shook Sean nearly off the rope, but at the same time, it dislodged the knife.

At the exact same moment, Liam was counting.

"One," he said. "Two, THREE!"

At the moment he said "three," Lochen dropped to the floor and Liam dove across him, bringing his blade down towards the rope. The other end of the rope, which had been knocked free, shot up into the air with Sean still attached. Quinn fell back against the tower wall and to the floor of the landing, jerking the rope high into the air as he fell.

Lochen landed flat on his stomach in his effort to get out of Liam's way. Solveig, Stella and Natalie fell in a heap when the tension on the rope disappeared and Quinn flew backwards. The rope slid a hair's width away from Liam's slashing blade, and he dropped to the floor, landing across both Lochen and Quinn, in a pile.

All eyes followed the rope and Sean, as he soared through the air, over the landing wall and crashed into the large wooden doors that stood at the end of the bridge. He slid downward, landing in a heap on top of Quinn, Liam, and Lochen, narrowly missing Solveig, Stella and Natalie. Summer was buried in the folds of Lochen's hood and had no idea of what had just happened.

Sean pushed his hair up out of his eyes and saw that he was nose to nose with Quinn and could feel Liam and Lochen squirming beneath him. He let go of the rope he had tightly clenched in his hands, and then stood up.

"Well," he said. "That was fun. What's next?"

Chapter twelve

Everyone was staring at him in disbelief. He slowly got to his feet and dusted the snow and bits and pieces of the bridge off his clothing, as if nothing unusual had happened. One by one everyone else stood up, each waiting for someone else to say something. Silently he untied the knot around the knife and handed it back to Liam. He then handed the rope he had been holding back to Quinn. He looked up at everyone staring at him. He turned to look behind him to see if they were looking at something there. Seeing nothing unusual, he turned back to them.

"What?" he finally asked.

"We thought you fell to the rocks," said Natalie.
"We couldn't see you, and then the bridge began to collapse," said Solveig.

Quest of Eight Part Four: The Race to Virkio

Richard Reda

"We threw the rope over so you could grab it," said Quinn, "but it wasn't heavy enough, so we tied a knife to it to add some weight. It went over the top of the bridge, but then it didn't move, so we thought it got stuck someplace and you couldn't reach it."

"Quinn was getting pulled over the side. I thought I had to cut the rope. I'm sorry. I never would have tried to cut it," said Liam, apologetically, "if I knew you were climbing it. I'm really, really sorry."

"Aw, forget it," said Sean dismissively. "I was never in any danger. Did you really think that a broken old bridge would be a problem? I could have scaled the wall itself if I had to."

By now Summer had extricated herself from Lochen's hood. She was overwhelmed with relief to see him unharmed. And then she heard Sean's remark. Her rush of relief at his safe return was immediately replaced by a flush of anger at his casual dismissal of the danger they all had faced. She flew up into the air and hovered inches from his face, where she bonked him on the nose with her fist.

"Don't you dare make a joke of this," she shouted at him. "We were all – every one of us – worried about you."

"Ow," he yelled, rubbing his nose. "It was no big deal, really."

"Yes it was!" she insisted, bonking him once more on the nose. "It was a very big deal. We could have lost you. We could have lost Quinn. We could have all been lost."

"OK, OK," he answered, trying unsuccessfully to pull his head out of her reach. "Stop hitting me.

"Liam was almost about to cut the rope," she went on.

"I said I was sorry," Liam interjected.

"That's not the point," she swung her head in his direction and responded . "You should have cut the rope. Quinn almost got pulled over the side. And everyone who was holding on to him to keep him from getting dragged over could have gone with him. Including ME!"

"Then why are you mad at me?" pleaded Sean. "It seems like he's the one you should be whacking on the nose."

"I said I was sorry," Liam repeated.

"He doesn't need to apologize," Summer argued, turning back and once more bonking Sean on the nose. "He did the right thing. We thought you had fallen and Quinn was tangled in the rope. Cutting it made sense. And I'm whacking you on the nose," and she whacked him once more, "because you think this was all a joke – just fun and games."

"STOP hitting me!" he shouted. "All right, I'm sorry. It's not a joke; and getting hit is not fun and games."

"Turn around," she shouted back.

"Why?" he asked suspiciously. "You're not going to push me over, are you."

"DO IT!"

He slowly turned towards the large empty space between towers one and two, trying at the same time to keep a wary eye on her.

"Look down," she ordered.

He snuck a peek over the edge; bobbing his head forward and quickly pulling it back to check on where she was hovering. Seeing that she was hovering in the same place, and was making no movement towards her, he looked again, this time a little longer.

"Do you see that? Do you see those rocks?" she asked. "What if he had cut the rope?" she repeated. "What do you think would have happened to you?"

"I said I was sorry," whined Liam.

"Shut it," Summer said to Liam. And then to Sean she asked, "So? What if he had cut the rope? Do you really think you could have flown around all those falling pieces of wood? The last time I looked, I'm the only one who can fly. Not you. Do you really think you could have climbed up the tower wall?"

"No," Sean answered moodily. "If he had cut the rope, I admit, it would have been a real problem. I'm sorry I worried you. I'm sorry I put the rest of you in danger. OK?"

Summer's anger evaporated.

"OK," she said.

"Now, will you please stop hitting me?" he asked.

The tension in the rest of the group faded. Summer flew over and kissed him on the cheek. Liam took the rope from Quinn, re-coiled it and strung it over his shoulder. Sean was hugged and patted on the back. Sean leaned over and whispered to Liam.

"I'm sure glad you didn't cut that rope," he muttered. "I'd have been a goner."

"Me, too," Liam answered. "Glad that I didn't cut the rope, that is."

Lochen then looked up at the gray sky. The snow was coming down harder. He shifted his gaze to the landing and the low wall that enclosed it. The snow had accumulated to a couple of inches and was falling steadily.

"We need to get off this landing," he announced.

There wasn't much space on the landing. It was about two feet wider than the bridge on either side – almost eight feet wide - and extended from the tower about three feet. The wall rose less than a foot high and boxed it in on the sides as well as the front on either side of where the bridge had ended. With all of them crowded around, there was little room to move. In the center of the landing was a large door.

The door was actually a pair of doors ten feet high and four feet wide. They had large bronze studs in perfectly straight lines up and down, left to right, each one six inches from the other. There were two large bronze handles, one on either side of the center where the two doors met, but no keyhole or any other indication of a lock. The bronze had turned green with age, but still appeared to be solid.

The wood was a deep, dark gray, almost black. Lochen placed his hand on one of the doors and knocked. The sound was a dull tap. No echo could be heard.

"Did you expect someone to answer?" asked Liam.

"Not really," answered Lochen. "I wanted to see if I could gauge how thick they were."

"And could you?" Natalie asked.

"Enough to know they are very thick and very heavy. They also appear to be solid – not like the   stone in tower one that we were able to crawl through."

He ran his hands along the outer edges, reaching up as high as he could, pressing against the wood to verify what he had just said about it being solid. He was also looking for some kind of hidden latch or depression that would open the doors. He asked Quinn to give him a lift so that he could feel around the arched top. He felt carefully around the entire doorway, including along the bottom.

"It appears that the doors open inward, if they open at all," he concluded. "There are no signs of any hinges on this side, but that wouldn't be unusual."

Starting at the bottom, he pressed each of the bronze studs, again asking Quinn to lift him up so that he could push the ones near the top. Nothing happened. He then tried again, this time pressing two at a time. Still nothing happened.

"Solveig," he said after studying the doors closely. "I'd like you to press the studs in the same manner and at the same time I do. You take the left door, and I'll take the right door. When you have gone up as high as you can reach, have Sean stand on Liam's shoulders so they can lift you to the top."

Patiently and precisely, they pressed matching studs on the two doors. When that yielded no results, they tried again, this time each of them pressed two studs – four in total – at exactly the same time. Still nothing happened.

Lochen stepped back from the doors, as far as the narrow landing would allow, and studied the door, the surrounding stone doorjamb and the rest of the wall. He was deep in thought and the others waited until he spoke.

"I have to admit," he finally said, scratching his head and looking puzzled. "I'm at a loss. I can't imagine what kind of spell has been placed on these doors. It's obvious that this is the way into the tower; otherwise why would there have been a bridge from tower one to this particular point?"

Quinn was confused. He had never known Lochen not to figure out a problem. He squeezed to the front of the group and grabbed the door handles in both hands. He twisted them downward and pushed. The doors opened inward without a sound.

"I hadn't thought of doing that," said Lochen.

"It seemed like the only solution left," answered Quinn. "I thought you were looking for something else."

The doors had swung wide open and a gush of warm air blew outward. The interior was dark, but not completely black. There was a low red glow coming from somewhere deep inside. The warmth was a welcome relief from the ice cold of tower one and the snow and chilling wind they encountered in their cross over to tower two. They began to enter, all at the same time.

"Hold on. We need to be careful," Stella reminded them. "As inviting as this warmth is, it's a safe bet that there are spells cast on this tower, too."

At her words, they all stopped en masse, and looked into the cavernous room before them. They turned their heads in unison to the left, and then to the right. Not seeing or sensing any danger, as a single unit they took a few tentative steps forward into the chamber. When their eyes adjusted to the dimmer light, they could see that the walls circled around much like in tower one.

"Is it my imagination," asked Natalie, "but does the inside of this room look larger than the outside?"

"I thought the same thing about the first tower," said Solveig. "I didn't say anything because I wasn't really sure. But now that you mention it, I see the same thing."

"I'm sure it's all part of the spells cast by the Alchemist," replied Lochen. "Much of what we see is merely an illusion."

Richard Reda

The air was much warmer and the source of the light was still undetermined. It was coming from something deep in the chamber. It was difficult to see very far into the room, so the group took a few short steps, stopped, and looked around before taking another few steps and repeating the process.

Once they were a few yards inside the tower, the hall quickly darkened. It didn't go completely black. Instead, it was as if someone had turned out half of the lights. Liam, who was at the back of the group, instinctively turned around to make sure no one had snuck up behind him. That was when he saw that the doors had silently and effortlessly closed.

"I don't want to alarm anyone," he said. "But I think we've been shut in."

Everyone turned around to see the closed doors. On the inside they looked exactly like the outside. The bronze studs mirrored the ones on the other side. The only difference was that there were no handles. There was no apparent way to open the doors, not that anyone had an interest in going back outside. However, the thought of no options other than going forward filled them all with a sense of dread.

Within seconds of the shutting of the doors, some unseen force ignited a torch on the far side of the doorway. The torch slowly lowered to a low, wide wall – a trough that was filled with some kind of flammable substance. Once the torch touched this substance, a streak of fire began to flare. The streak sped through the trough, which paralleled the walls of the chamber, and then ran back and forth across the distant hall, returning to the starting point, creating some kind of pattern along the way.

Summer wiggled out of Lochen's hood and flew up into the air to gain a higher vantage point in an effort to see if the pattern gave them a clue as to where to go.

"Be careful," shouted Lochen, once he realized what she was doing. "We don't know what spells have been cast in here."

"Get back here," shouted Solveig. "We're not supposed to separate."

"I'm not going far," she answered. "I won't leave your sight."

She floated on the rising heated air towards the blackness, which cloaked whatever ceiling existed above her. The change in temperature was dramatic and severe. She immediately began to perspire.

"You're already out of our sight," called Natalie. "We can't see you. Please get back here."

She was getting uncomfortably hot within only a few seconds. She continued to climb higher in the heavy air, trying to make sense of the pattern. Then she smelled something burning. It was very close to her. She spun around to see what was behind her and saw nothing. The smell persisted and now she could hear a low sizzling sound.

"What the...?" she said. "What's burning?"

She spun around again trying to find the source of the odor and the sound. It was right behind her.

"It's me!" she shouted in realization. "I'm burning."

She immediately tucked her wings in close to her side and dropped back to the others, who, she was thankful to find, were still there. When she was several yards above them, she spread her wings to slow her descent. Instead of gliding to a stop, she flipped onto her left side and spun like a corkscrew, landing on the floor.

"Your wing!" shouted Stella. "It's been singed. The left one – the top has been burned off."

"Are you all right?" asked Sean, pushing his way to the front as everyone crowded around Summer.

"Yes," she said. "Yes, I'm fine."

She reached back to assess the damage. Her hand ran over the ragged top edge of her left wing. She could feel parts of it crumble in her hand. She looked as small particles of ash dropped to the floor.
"I don't know how that happened," she said. "I wasn't anywhere near a flame."

"How bad is the damage?" asked Liam.

"It's not too bad," she said, pulling the edge around to the front, and patting the smoldering sections with her hands, wishing, rather than believing, that the damage wasn't too severe.

"Well, it's kind of bad," she had to admit, looking more closely at the scorch marks.

"No," she finally said, dejected. "It's really bad. I can't fly like this."

"I don't expect you will need to fly, or even should try to fly, as long as we're in or around these towers," said Lochen. "The spells are too unpredictable and too dangerous."

"Was that meant to try to cheer her up?" asked Solveig.

She turned to Summer and asked, "How long will it take for the damage to repair?"

Summer gave a plaintive look at Lochen and then to Stella.

"I don't think we can help you," said Stella. "Lochen's already found out his powers don't work in here. I'm afraid to try any potions or spells of my own. I don't know how the Alchemist's spells will change whatever I cast. Sorry. It looks like you're going to have to let nature take its course on this one."

Summer let out a sigh, stroking the damaged wing as if it were an injured pet. She was more angry with herself than anything else.

"I don't know how long it will take," she said, answering Solveig's question. "All I know is that it will take TOO long."

"And you were mad at me for being reckless?" asked Sean. "I hope it was worthwhile. Did you see anything?"

"Yes," she said, still feeling miserable about her wing.

And then she recalled what she had seen and perked up.

"Yes," she repeated more emphatically. "I did. This trench goes all the way around the room, I think. I couldn't see all the way, but I'm sure it circles all the way around. And then it comes back and it outlines the same shape as the stone that I used to wear – the one I gave to Sean that fit into his armband and that he gave to Stella. The piece she's wearing in her headband – before the one that we just found: the triskelion."

Stella's hand went up reflexively to the stone in her headband.

"Interesting," said Lochen.

"What?" asked Solveig, turning towards Lochen. "Why is that interesting? Does that mean something special?"

"I don't know," answered Lochen. "I only find that it's interesting."

"Arrgh!" Solveig groaned. "Sometimes you can be such a tool. <u>Why</u> do you find it interesting?"

"Because the shape of the stone," he answered without reacting to her comment, "according to what we've learned recently, was created only after the larger stone had been broken apart. That tells me that the design of this trough occurred after the larger stone had been broken apart as well."

Everyone looked at him waiting for him to go on.

"And that is significant because…why?" she persisted when it was clear he wasn't going to provide any additional explanation.

"Because the design is, therefore, not happenstance. It was created this way for a specific reason, to emulate this particular piece of the stone."

He gestured towards Stella and asked, "May I see it, Stella?"

"Certainly," she said, removing the band from around her head and handing it to Lochen.

He turned it around in order to shed as much light on it as he could, lifting it in the air slightly above his head. He moved it back and forth, changing the way the light glanced off, and then brought it closer to his face. He seemed to focus intently on the triskelion, wiping it a number of times with his thumb.

"Have you noticed that there appears to be something inside the stone?" he asked Stella. "I hadn't seen this before. Or if I had, I didn't think much of it."

"Yes," she answered. "I've seen what looks like clouds moving. It's more evident with the additional piece. I've also noticed at certain times there's what looks like a flashing light in the center – sort of like lightning. It only comes from the triskelion, though; not from the other piece."

"When does that happen – the flashes of lightning?"

"I haven't paid much attention," she admitted. "I couldn't really tell you. I don't think it happens on a regular basis. It's probably a reaction to something. What are you thinking?"

"Interesting," he repeated.

He turned back towards the center of the chamber. He shifted his gaze from the stone to the trough of flame and back to the stone again. He rubbed his thumb across the stone and held it closer, looking for a flash of light. In a few seconds, one appeared. Stella had been right. The flash appeared only in the triskelion. It burst from the very center.

Even though the two pieces of the stone had merged into one, there was still a line of demarcation and a slightly darker coloring to the triskelion. He walked to the edge of the trough, close to the fire and followed the shape a few steps. He looked from the trough to the stone and back again. He continued walking until he came to a bend that mirrored the shape of the central piece of the stone.

He walked back to the group, all of whom were watching him in silence. He looked closer at the stone, waiting for another flash of light, shifting his gaze from the stone to some unidentified spot off in the distance. He didn't have to wait long. Another burst appeared. He immediately raised his eyes towards the center of the chamber.

"Yes," he said to no one in particular. "It could be lightning. Or fire. It could be a burst of fire."

He lifted his head and looked at the faces staring at him.

"It could be fire," he repeated.

"What could be fire?" asked Solveig. "What are you talking about?"

Quest of Eight Part Four: The Race to Virkio

Richard Reda

"We need to follow this channel of fire," he said, not having really heard her questions. "To the center. That's the key. We need to go to the center of the flames."

"Center of the flames?" shouted Quinn. "Are you nuts? Won't we get burned there?"

"Hmmm. I don't think so," Lochen responded, handing the headband back to Stella.

"Again with the 'I don't think so?'" interjected Solveig. "Can't you be more certain? It's not like we get a 'do-over' if we get something wrong."
"This is all an illusion," he said. "Yes, I know. If we make a misstep we will suffer the consequences. But remember what Stella and I said at the first tower – all is not as it seems. Trust me. We need to go to the center."

"Let's get moving, then," said Sean as he headed towards the section of the trough Lochen had previously walked over to.

"Not that way," called Lochen, pointing forward. "We need to go straight ahead. We need to keep the two legs of the triskelion nearest to us at equal distances away, as much as we can. They'll only deceive us if we follow along side of them."

"What do you mean, 'they'll only deceive us?'" asked Natalie. "You said we're supposed to follow them and now you say we shouldn't. You're not making any sense."

"Tell me about it," mumbled Solveig. "I can't make sense out of most of what he says."

"They are not the key. The center is. The trough – overall – is still part of the spell. It is likely to change if we attempt to simply follow its course. We could be following it indefinitely. I am sure it would merely continue to extend before us, never reaching the center. If you hadn't noticed, the temperature has been steadily rising. It is becoming an oven in here. We won't last much longer, especially if we're following false leads. The center is the key."

No one elected to pursue the debate. They all gathered behind him as he led the way. He bent down and scooped Summer up and placed her on his shoulder as he began.

"Until you are able to fly again," he said to her, "I would feel better if you were close by."

"Thanks," she said.

She took a position in the folds of his hood, situating herself so that she was stretched out over his shoulder and could see where they were headed. In a few seconds, she kicked the hood off of her legs, as the heat quickly climbed.

Lochen led them away from the door and the nearest leg of the triskelion. He kept turning back to look at it, gauging a spot he believed was midway between two of the legs. When they reached a point at which Lochen believed they were equidistant from the two legs of the triskelion that were on their side of the chamber, he appeared to be making some kind of mental calculations. The ends of both legs were barely visible and he had to make his best guess as to the precise starting point.

Once he was satisfied, they began walking towards the center. At first, the view ahead was in darkness. There was some light from a large fire as it merged in the middle of the room, but it was obscured by ripples of smoke and waves of heat.

After a few minutes, the two channels of fire were clearly getting closer, and the conflagration in the center of the room was becoming much clearer. Between their exertion and the climbing temperature, they were all sweating extensively. The heat was getting unbearable. Quinn appeared to be suffering the most.

"Are you sure this is the only way?" he asked.

"Don't think about the heat," Lochen instructed him. "Keep in mind that it's all an illusion. Think about something else."

"It's hard not to think about the heat," countered Quinn. "There's fire all around us; we're walking into a bigger bunch of fire; the place feels like an oven; my feet are burning from the heat of the floor; I'm sweating like a walrus in a desert; and did I mention? There's fire all around us."

"I am well aware of our surroundings," answered Lochen. "However, dwelling on them will not speed this process up, nor will it alleviate the rising temperature. You need to take your mind off the heat. Think about something cold."

Quinn closed his eyes momentarily to conjure up an image of his home. He smiled for a second and then opened his eyes again.

"It's not working," he said, swiping his arm across his brow. "I imagined a picture of my home. It was on fire."

"How much further?" asked Sean. "This is even getting too hot for me."

"We're almost half way there," answered Lochen to several groans.

"Look," he pointed to the left, "there's a bend in the leg. It matches the bend in the triskelion. We're moving along the final section."

The trough on the left had been trailing away from them before, but now was angled towards them. The one on the right was also more clearly visible and was also moving closer. The flames towards which they were walking looked more and more like a bon fire. The roaring was getting louder as the heat continued to climb.

They could feel the exposed skin on their faces and hands burning. Summer reached back and held on to her damaged wing. She had no feeling in her wings. They were like hair in that respect, but she was certain she could feel them starting to burn again. As uncomfortable as it was with the material from Lochen's hood covering her, she was driven to protect her wings, so she pulled the hood up and wrapped it around her.

"I think my hair is on fire," said Sean, as he ran his fingers across his head. "I'm sure my eyebrows burned off twenty feet back."

"How much closer do we have to get to that inferno in the middle?" asked Solveig.

"Very close," Lochen answered. "We have to go into it."
Everyone stopped. He had gone three or four more steps before he realized no one was with him, other than Summer, who had little choice. He stopped walking and turned to face them.

"We mustn't stop," he told them. "This heat will roast us if we delay. We need to keep going."

"But you said we had to go into the fire," said Natalie.

"Yes," said Lochen. "That's where the exit is. I'm fairly certain."

"You're fairly certain?" wailed Sean. "I thought you knew for sure. Somehow, 'I'm fairly certain,' doesn't fill me with the same confidence."

"All right," said Lochen. "Then I know for sure that this is the way out. Is that better?"

"Really?" asked Quinn. "You know for sure?"

"No," said Lochen. "Of course not. But if that makes you feel better and will get you all moving again, then I'll be glad to lie."

"Ooohhh, I wish you hadn't told us it was a lie," said Sean. "Now it's spoiled."

"How is it spoiled?" asked Lochen. "If it was a lie to begin with, which it was, then how does your knowing it was a lie make it any different? It's still a lie."

"Really?" Sean asked in disbelief. "How is it different? If I didn't know it was a lie, genius, then I would have thought it was the truth and I would have believed it. But now that I know it's a lie, I don't believe it."

"But you would soon know if I was lying," Lochen reasoned. "And at that point would it have still been spoiled?"

"Noooo," said Sean, "because I would have believed it until I found out it was a lie and then I wouldn't believe it but it would be too late by then."

"I'm not sure I understand," said Lochen.

"He's right," said Stella, who could no longer tolerate the inane conversation. "Lochen's right, I mean. Well, Sean's right, too, but that doesn't matter. Lochen's right about where the exit is. I can feel it. I know it for sure. Something is pulling on the stone in my headband. We need to get to the center of the fire. We'll be safe. Let's keep moving."

"Okay, then," said Quinn, with renewed excitement. "Let's keep going."

Without any further discussion, they continued. Stella gradually moved sideways and forward, keeping pace with Lochen. When she was close enough, she whispered so the others couldn't hear.

"I hope you're right," she said.

"I beg your pardon," he responded.

"I said I hope you're right – about the center of the fire being the exit."

"You mean you didn't really feel anything?" he asked in surprise.

"No," she said.

"Then why would you say such a thing?"
"Because I had enough of that stupid argument about your lying and it being spoiled by you telling them it was a lie. Really? Are the both of you nuts? Besides, you were also right that if we stayed where we were, we would be charcoal in a matter of minutes."

"Thanks," said Summer, who had overheard everything. "I didn't really want to hear all that."
Before long, they were within feet of the blaze. It was enormous. Flames licked the air, shooting up more than twenty feet. The air hurt to breathe. Everyone's clothes felt like they were on fire. It hurt to walk; it hurt to move.

"Where does all the fire and heat go?" asked Liam, looking up at the ceiling that no one could see.

"Nowhere," said Lochen. "Because all this doesn't really exist. Keep that in mind as you follow me."

Without waiting for any response or objections, he walked straight into the blaze. Knowing the potential consequences of getting separated, the others had little choice but to follow him. The heat and the light were blinding. Each one of them felt like they were being stabbed by thousands of needles.

They closed their eyes, expecting to be instantly roasted as they crossed from the stone floor into the raging fire. Their expectations were not met. No sooner did they step into the flames than they each felt a cold breeze on their faces.

When they opened their eyes they saw Lochen a few feet ahead of them, staring at another bridge. They were on the roof of tower three, completely in the open air.

Chapter thirteen

There was no evidence in the floor beneath them as to how they had been moved from the blaze in the center of the chamber inside the tower to the cold, windy air on the roof. Like the previous two towers, the roof of tower three was flat and circular, with battlements surrounding the outer edge. Also like the towers before it, this one had a bridge connecting it to an opening in the next tower.

And similar to what they faced before, this bridge was unlike the previous ones. There was no supporting structure underneath it. Instead, it was made of four lines of sturdy chains. There were two lines that extended from the tops of two of the battlements all the way to the opening in tower four. The other two lines extended from

271

the floor on which they stood, passing between the crenellation between the battlements, over to the next tower.

Spanning from one side to the other of the lower pair of chains were slats of wood. Every ten feet or so, there were additional chains that connected the top pair – the "hand rails" – to the bottom pair. The wooden slats appeared every six or eight inches, and in some places had rotted through.

"Oh, poop," said Natalie, looking down through the spaces between the slats. "This keeps getting worse, and we keep getting higher and higher up."

By now thin clouds were forming in the spaces between the towers. The ground below was still visible through the periodic breaks in the clouds – enough to remind them all exactly how high they were.

They had all moved from the center of the roof to the edge where the bridge was. The snow was falling even harder than before and had started accumulating on the roof and on the bridge's slats.

"Please," begged Quinn. "Don't tell me you want me to go first again."

"All right," said Lochen. "I won't tell you that you have to go first again."

"Thank you, thank you," Quinn answered in relief.

"But you know that you do, don't you?" asked Liam.

"I know that I do what?" he asked, certain he didn't want to hear the answer.

"Go first," inserted Sean. "What did you think?"

"But Lochen said I didn't have to," he wailed.

"Not exactly," Lochen answered. "I said I wouldn't tell you. I never said you didn't have to go first."

"But why me? I really think you need me at the back end to make sure no one sneaks up on us. Why do I have to go first?"

"Because you're the heaviest," Lochen explained. "If the stress on the bridge is going to weaken it, it's better to know that up front."

"You mean it's all right if it caves in when I'm walking across?" Quinn objected. "Thanks a lot."

"No," answered Lochen. "That's not what I meant. With all of us walking across it, any weaknesses that exist are going to be more likely to cause the bridge to collapse as more of us that add to the stress. If the greatest amount of stress is placed at the end of our crossing, it would seem more likely that any collapse would happen then. However, if we stagger the weight, as we did on the last bridge, and displace the stress as much as possible, I believe we mitigate the potential damage. Does that clear things up for you?"

"Do I still have to go first?"

"Yes."

"Then it didn't clear things up, but I'll do it," he mumbled.

Lochen turned to Sean and asked, "Are you all right going last again?"

Sean smiled and answered, "If I say no, do I still have to go last? Never mind," he added before Lochen could respond.

"At least this time we'll be able to see you," said Solveig.

"Right," answered Sean. "As I drop through the air?"

273

"That's not funny," piped Summer. "You better be careful."

They gathered near the chain bridge. The wind had picked up and was shaking the bridge, blowing it back and forth as well as up and down. The snowfall had increased as well. The flakes were much heavier and were accumulating quickly. The force of the wind and its effect on the bridge were the only things keeping the snow from piling up on the wooden slats.

Quinn grasped a chain handrail in each fist and repeated his foot extension, toe tapping method of crossing. The slats were close enough together for him to step over two or three in each stride. With his first step, once his full weight was on the bridge, the shaking diminished, but wasn't eliminated altogether.

Lochen examined the anchors, which were screwed into the stone and held the four long lines of chain, top and bottom, in place. They seemed to be well secured and in good condition.

"I don't think we need to spread ourselves out as much on this bridge," he said. "We don't have any issue with a questionable frame work from beneath."

Once Quinn was a few yards out, Lochen told Stella to follow after him, and then he followed just a few steps behind. As more of them advanced onto the bridge, the swaying motion changed. It was no longer driven by the wind, but by the weight and motion of those crossing.

It was no longer swinging side to side, but the up and down motion was getting worse and worse the farther Quinn moved across. For Stella, who was immediately behind Quinn, it wasn't quite as bad. However, by the time Solveig got on, it was like a whip being cracked.

"Quinn," Lochen shouted over the wind. "Stop for a minute so that the bridge will level out some."

Quest of Eight Part Four: The Race to Virkio

Richard Reda

Quinn stopped, but he didn't turn around. What none of them knew was that he hadn't opened his eyes since he took his first step. The wind and the cold didn't bother him, nor did the shaking of the bridge. But when he tried to look down at his foot before taking a step, all he could see were the rocks far below, catching glimpses between the slats and through the mist of clouds.

He was just past the half way point and so far all the slats had held. At least the ones on which he stepped, which were one in every three or four. Stella, on the other hand, had stepped on every one of them. One or two, she noticed, seemed to bend slightly under her foot, but she wasn't sure if the wood was soft or if she was reacting to the bouncing motion of the bridge.

Lochen trod along the edges of the slats, nearer to where they were attached to the chain. Because of this, he wasn't aware that any of the slats were weak or damaged. At the time Quinn stopped, Natalie was only about ten feet onto the bridge. So far, everything was holding.

When the undulating had been reduced as much as it was going to be, Lochen told Quinn to continue. Shortly after his first few steps, the rippling effect began again. Before anyone could call to Quinn to stop again, or before anyone could figure out a way to counter the motion, Natalie stepped out onto one of the slats that Stella thought bent slightly under her weight.

The slat was wet enough with snow that Natalie's foot skidded out from under her. To avoid losing her balance, she shifted her body and the same foot stomped downward, catching her weight. Her heel crashed into the center of the slat; her left hand flew in the air in an attempt to keep her balance.

All her weight landed on the weak slat, cracking it cleanly in half. She tried to move her weight to the other foot, bringing it down hard on the slat in front of the broken one. That one, too, broke in half, and she dropped into the space created by the two broken boards.

Quest of Eight Part Four: The Race to Virkio

Richard Reda

She lost her grip on the chain rail with her other hand. The snow had made both rails slippery. As she dropped out of sight, she managed to hook one arm around the lower rail, and she swung out to the side of the bridge, hanging by one arm underneath the wooden foot pieces.

Lochen, who was right in front of her, had been concentrating hard on his own steps. The cracking sound of the boards was lost in the howling wind. Summer was tucked deep inside his hood; glad she didn't have to watch any of the crossing. Liam, who was immediately behind her, had been looking back towards Solveig to see if she and Sean were doing all right.

As he turned back, expecting to see the back of Natalie's head, he was momentarily confused when he saw the back of Lochen's head instead. He looked left and then right, wondering where she had gone. Just as her arm was starting to slide off the cold, slippery chain, he looked down.

Without thinking, he dove onto his stomach and skidded across the intervening planks. He had jumped too hard, and began to slide over the broken boards, passing Natalie's arm. He used his toes to hook his feet into the spaces between the boards, and brought himself to a halt. He reached down into the gap where Natalie had fallen and clutched her clothing. He had a good grip on her cloak, but he had no leverage to pull her up.

"Hold on," he said to her. "We'll get you up."

"I am. I will," stammered Natalie. "Just hurry. I think I injured my arm when I fell. I can't feel anything."

She had looped her left arm around the chain and was grasping her wrist with the other hand to keep her arm from flopping loose. Liam struggled to get to his feet, but stopped when he heard the board beneath him begin cracking. He looked up and back at Solveig, who had just then noticed that Natalie had disappeared and that Liam was lying down on the path.

"What are you doing?" she shouted over the wind, not comprehending the dilemma immediately.

"Get over here," he shouted back. "I can't hold her much longer."

Solveig moved as quickly and carefully as she could, holding on to both chain rails and stepping along the outside edges of the planks in the same manner as Lochen. As soon as she was within reach, Liam motioned for her to stop.

"Be careful," he warned. "I don't know how many more of these boards are rotten. The one I'm lying on is about to go, too."

Solveig gently lowered herself to the floor, stretching out and displacing her weight as much as she could. She reached down and took hold of Natalie. However, Natalie was at such an odd angle, it was hard for Solveig to get both of her arms around Natalie's body.

"Can you switch your grip?" she asked. "Can you move over to the middle of the bridge? I can get a better grip on you there."

"No," Natalie answered. "I have no feeling in my left arm. If I let go of my wrist, I'm afraid I'll fall."

"All right; all right," said Liam, getting worried about losing her. "Let's try this."

Without letting go of her cloak, he straightened out his body so that it extended in the opposite direction of Solveig's, but spreading his weight out over several slats, as she had done. He pulled himself further out over the opening and moved his right arm behind Natalie and under her good arm.

"Solveig," he said. "Can you reach through and grab my hand? If you can, then with your other arm, pull her as close to you as you can."

Solveig reached around and under Natalie's wounded arm, feeling around for Liam's hand. At first she couldn't find it in the folds of Natalie's clothing, but eventually she did. She grabbed his wrist as tightly as she could.

By now Sean had caught up with them. He could see Solveig and Liam stretched out on either side of a break in the path and noticed that Natalie was nowhere to be seen. He got down on his hands and knees and then onto his belly. He crawled slowly up behind Solveig.
"Don't get startled," he shouted to her. "I'm going to hold onto your legs, so you don't get pulled down."

"Thanks," Solveig shouted back.

She turned her head to look at him. She could feel the accumulated ice and snow between her body and the bridge floor. She had been worried that she would have to extend too far over the opening to get a good grip on Natalie, and that in doing so, would get pulled over herself. She knew Liam would never be able to hold on to the both of them. Sean was a lifesaver.

With Liam's hand held tightly in hers, she inched her other arm around Natalie's back. She couldn't quite reach her other hand, so she hugged as firmly as she could. She could feel Sean's arms holding her legs. This was as good as it was going to get, she thought.

"Ready?" she asked Natalie.

"I suppose," Natalie responded.

"On the count of three, let go of your hand, slip it under the chain and reach up for my neck. OK?"

"Got it," Natalie answered, her voice beginning to shake.

"Liam," Solveig continued. "You keep hold of her cloak. Sean," she shouted back, "can you hear me?"

"Yes," he answered. "On three, I'll start pulling you back."

"Good. All right, then. One, two, three!"

Natalie released her own wrist and her injured arm flopped loose. She dropped a few inches as Solveig's grip around her slipped, adjusting to the shift in weight. Natalie's good arm shot up and she wrapped it around Solveig's neck. Sean pulled hard and dragged Solveig backwards a few inches – enough to get her more securely on the wooden planks.

When it was clear Solveig wasn't going to slide off, Sean got up and scrambled along the opposite edges of the slats over to the gap and helped pull Natalie up. Wincing in pain, Natalie crawled up and onto the bridge, sitting on the nearest solid board, dangling her feet over the broken slats.

"That was close," said Liam.

He looked over his shoulder and saw that the others were near the end of the bridge. They were completely unaware of what had happened.

"It looks like the rest of the bridge is solid enough," he said, getting to his feet.

"Yeah," said Natalie, "but what if we have to come back this way? What do we do then?"

"This crossing will be the least of our worries," said Sean. "The last one is gone completely. How are we going to get back to tower two?"

Quest of Eight Part Four: The Race to Virkio

Richard Reda

"There's no sense in worrying about that now," said Solveig. "We'll think of something. Lochen will think of something."

"I hope you're right," said Natalie. "I don't think I can do this again."

She got to her feet and Liam helped her over the gap. Then he turned and headed towards the others, who had reached the landing on the other side. Solveig and Sean made the crossing together, both of them stepping lightly along the outside edges of the planks.

"What happened?" asked Stella when they were all together.

"We had a little mishap," said Liam. "Everything's all right now – well almost everything. Natalie hurt her arm."
"I'm all right," insisted Natalie, although she was cradling her arm.

"If you're injured," interjected Lochen, "we need to know. It will make a difference in how we proceed."

Reluctantly, Natalie explained what happened to her arm. She had dislocated her shoulder. When she described the injury, Quinn said he could fix her.

"How?" she asked. "I didn't know you were a healer."

"I'm not," he said, "but I did that all the time when I first started sledding with a dog team. The dogs would take off and I wouldn't be ready, and the next thing I knew – POP – my shoulder would be dislocated."

"You still haven't said how you can fix it," Natalie objected.

"It's probably better if you don't know," Quinn answered. "Trust me."

He reached over and gently held the hand of her injured arm. He reached up with his other hand and softly rubbed her shoulder. This isn't too bad, Natalie thought, and she relaxed a bit. As soon as she did, Quinn jerked her arm towards him. A bolt of pain shot up through her arm as the shoulder snapped back into place.

"Yeowwww!" she yelled. "What are you doing? Are you crazy? That really hurt!"

In her anger, she reached over and punched him harmlessly in the shoulder. She failed to notice that she used her injured arm to do so. When it dawned on her, she was stunned that there was no pain, whatsoever. She moved her arm in a circle, flexing and stretching it.

"It doesn't hurt anymore," she announced. "How did you do that?"

"Magic," he said with a broad smile. "Something my grandfather taught me."
"Are you sure you're all right?" asked Lochen.

"Yes," she said. "Really. It's fine."

"Then I think we need to move on."

They turned to face the opening in the wall at the end of the chain bridge. It was the same size and shape as the ones before it, but there were no doors. It was all black. Lochen reached forward to touch it and his hand went into what felt like a thick, gooey liquid. He pulled it back almost immediately, having expected some form of resistance, but discovering none.

"Interesting," he said, looking at his hand. "I'm not sure what to make of it. The substance seems impervious to the wind and elements, but it lacks any real substance."

"And what exactly does that mean?" asked Sean. "Is something there or not?"

"Something is definitely there," Lochen answered. "And it seems that we can easily pass through."

"And that's bad, how?" asked Sean.

Lochen turned to look at him.

"Can you see what's on the other side?" he asked Sean.

"No," Sean answered. "It's all black."

"That's how it's bad," replied Lochen. "I have no idea of what we would be walking into."

"Do we have any other choice?" asked Stella. "If you see one, please share, because I don't."

"No," answered Lochen. "I see no other options, but that doesn't do anything to encourage me."

Liam suggested they all hold hands and step into the black goo together. Since they didn't know how far they would have to go or what they would or wouldn't see on the other side, at least this way they wouldn't lose each other.

"I think the idea of holding on to each other is excellent," said Lochen. "However, I think we should cross one at a time. If the first one encounters danger, the others may be forewarned."

Before anyone could volunteer or object, he announced that he would go first.

"Oh," said Quinn. "NOW you want to go first. Remember that the next time."

"I will," answered Lochen. "But you can go second. Hold my hand, and hold it as tight as you can. If the way is clear, I'll pull on it in my direction. If there's danger, I'll squeeze your hand and you pull me back as quickly as you can."

"What if there's no danger, but there's no floor?" asked Quinn. "You'll be pulling but I'll step onto the same...uh...unfloor. And it'll feel like you're pulling me in on purpose. I don't think this is such a good idea."

"No," admitted Lochen. "You're right. Then let's reverse it. If I pull you towards me, pull me back out of the tower. That will signal danger. If I squeeze your hand, then it's safe to proceed. Is that better?"

"But what if something on the other side scares you?" Quinn asked. "And you just react by squeezing my hand. I'll think it's all right to come in when it's not."

"I don't react that way if I'm startled," answered Lochen. "I think you're procrastinating. Hold my hand and let's be done with this."

"Man, what a grouch," mumbled Quinn as he grasped Lochen's hand. "Don't blame me if this goes bad."

Ignoring him, Lochen removed Summer from his hood, suggesting that Liam hold on to her. He looked to see that the others were holding one another's hands and then he turned and stepped across the threshold. He was still in the gelatin-like passage when he had gone as far as his reach would allow him. He began to pull on Quinn's arm so that he could go all the way through, but then remembered that Quinn would consider that a danger signal and pull him back. He was afraid the spell might change with such a failed attempt. Without knowing what was ahead, he squeezed Quinn's hand, signaling for him to advance.

Quest of Eight Part Four: The Race to Virkio

Richard Reda

I hope I'm right, Lochen thought to himself. When he felt Quinn entering the passage, he moved ahead, stretching out his free hand, searching for the end of the viscous material. A few steps more and he felt cool air on his hand. He tried to move faster to the open air, but felt the restraint of Quinn's hand on his other hand.

Quinn felt the tug and immediately thought Lochen was in danger. He started to retreat and pull Lochen with him. Lochen, feeling himself being yanked back, gave Quinn's hand a squeeze. Quinn felt the squeeze, stopped and then started shuffling slowly forward. Lochen had not thought he would need to hold his breath upon entering, and hadn't filled his lungs in anticipation.

His lungs began to ache, starved for air as they were. He moved ahead towards the inside edge of the goo. He moved too fast, pulling on Quinn's hand. Quinn stopped and once more began to retreat. What is wrong with him, wondered Lochen. What is wrong with him, wondered Quinn. Lochen squeezed again and Quinn inched forward.

Lochen's arm was now clear of the opening, but he was still not able to breathe and he was beginning to struggle to keep his mouth closed. Unable to tolerate it any more, he gave a quick snap of his hand to free it and leaned forward to stick his head through the mass. The slime was too thick, though, for him to shake himself free of Quinn's grip. Quinn stopped once more and began pulling Lochen back.

Lochen pulled with all his might, trying to get his head through to the fresh air. The pulling only made Quinn more resolute in trying to drag him back to what he believed was safety. All the time Lochen was squeezing Quinn's hand, signaling it was safe. He must really be confused, thought Quinn, who, by now, was also having difficulty holding his breath.

Deciding that Lochen needed rescuing of a different sort, Quinn stopped pulling him back and he took two quick, long steps through the threshold, ready to face whatever danger was terrorizing his friend. He further thought it might be safer if everyone came to Lochen's rescue. He gave a jerk and yanked the line behind him into and through the gelatin to the inside of the tower.

"What's wrong with you?" both Lochen and Quinn shouted at each other once they had caught their breath.

"I couldn't breathe," declared Lochen, his hands on his knees, gasping for air.

"I thought you were in trouble," answered Quinn.

"The only trouble I was in was you not letting me get through."

"Well, then maybe next time, someone else should go first, besides you," Quinn countered indignantly.

"My thoughts exactly," said Lochen.

As soon as the words were out of his mouth, Quinn realized what he had said.

"Oh, poop," was his only response.

While the two of them were arguing, the others were studying their surroundings. Once more they were in a large, circular chamber. The stone floor extended ten to fifteen feet into the hall to a round opening that dropped down below them like a wide, deep well. The walls rose high all around into a darkness that hid the ceiling from view.

"What was it with this Alchemist guy?" pondered Sean out loud. "Didn't he like to see ceilings?"

The cavernous interior was lit from an unidentifiable source and the sounds of the wind outside were completely cut off. All they could hear were the echoes of their voices off the walls, and the sound of rushing water.

"Where's that noise coming from?" asked Summer.

Stella walked to the edge of the floor and peered down the well. It was black below, except for a shimmer of light in the center. The light wavered. It looks like it's glowing through water, she thought. It is, she realized.

"It's water," she announced. "It's down there and it sounds like it's rising."

Sean quickly scanned the near walls. There were no signs of any openings or stairs. He moved around the circle to one side, still not seeing any way out. At the same time Liam explored the other direction. Careful not to lose sight of the others, they were able to go all the way around. There was nothing.

"I can see it now," said Stella. "That's definitely filled with water and that water is definitely rising."

In a few seconds, the water reached the top of the well and spilled over onto the floor on which they were all standing. Each was at a loss as to what to do. Lochen remained calm, looking from the water to the ceiling and then back again.
"I have to assume that this water will continue to rise," he said, "until it reaches the ceiling. At that time, we either find a way out, or we drown."

"Wonderful," said Sean. "Any other options?"

"Yes," he answered. "We could jump into the water."

"We won't have to jump before too much longer," said Solveig. "It's already over our ankles. In a few more minutes, it'll be over our heads. What good is jumping into it going to do?"

"We need to swim to the bottom," said Stella. "Remember, the worst solution is probably the right one."

"I agree," said Lochen. "And we need to do it quickly. Our escape lies at the bottom of that well, and the more the water rises, the farther away that escape gets."

The water was now up to the knees of most of them. Summer was fluttering in a lopsided manner until she came to rest on Lochen's shoulder. Stella was already waist deep. She turned to Natalie.

"Your Highness," she said. "If you would take the lead by going first, I will be the last to make sure we don't lose anyone."

"Agreed," Natalie answered.

Without any time for debate or discussion, she stepped to the edge and dove in. She swam out to the middle and poked her head above the water.

"It's a little cold at first, but it's not too bad. We need to hurry, though. I can see a light towards the bottom, but it's starting to fade."

"Go. Go," shouted Lochen, pushing the others towards the well.

Without another word, Summer leaped off his shoulder and did a perfect swan dive into the pool, quickly disappearing from sight, right behind Natalie. Quinn grabbed his knees, jumped up into the air and splashed in. One by one the others jumped in, somewhat less dramatically. Lochen turned to see Sean standing hesitantly on the edge, already waist deep.

"Water," he mumbled and grimaced. "Why does it have to be water?"

He pinched his nose shut and jumped in. Lochen immediately followed, and Stella dove in after him. Even though she had taken the lead, Natalie swam up and down, guiding and checking on the others. As sea sprites, she and Stella could hold their breath for a very long time. She knew the others couldn't, and wanted to make sure they were all safe.

When she saw they were clustered fairly close together and that Stella was herding them like a sheep dog, she went back to the front. She swam up next to Summer and motioned for her to hold on. Summer reached over and grabbed Natalie's cloak. Then Natalie shot forward like an arrow. Summer never knew anyone or anything could move so fast in water.

Natalie made a beeline for the light. It was getting much brighter now. The water was crystal clear, but it was also getting much colder. She tapped Summer's hand, motioning for her to let go, which she did. Natalie then pointed ahead, and Summer swam on by herself. Natalie went back to help move the others along. Stella started doing the same thing.

She and Stella still had plenty of air in their lungs, but the others were starting to show signs of stress. They were stroking faster and faster, which only exerted more pressure on their straining lungs. They were fighting harder and harder to swim to the bottom, when, all of a sudden, they realized they were swimming upward instead of downward.

Natalie wasn't sure exactly when that happened, but she could feel the change in the way she was swimming. She started to soar towards the top – to what was now the surface. She had to restrain herself from not getting too far ahead of everyone else.

A few seconds later, the others noticed the change. Their lungs were straining, but somehow, knowing that they were headed to the surface – whatever that may be – made the effort a bit easier. Summer once more latched onto Natalie, her tiny lungs pounding in her chest. She knew she wouldn't last much longer. None of them would.

Natalie kicked with all her strength, pushing to the surface. She looked over her shoulder to make certain that the others were still keeping up. Solveig was right behind her, swimming strongly, in spite of how long they had been submerged. Lochen was flailing his arms and kicking his feet erratically in what she assumed was an attempt at swimming, but he seemed to be doing all right.

Liam and Sean were not far behind. Sean was making such unusual faces that Natalie almost laughed. Liam was still dragging the coil of rope with him. It was weighing him down, but Sean was helping to pull him along. Quinn was struggling. Stella had grabbed his hand and was moving him forward.

She turned back to what now seemed to be the surface. The light above looked like it was getting closer, but it didn't seem any larger or any brighter. In fact, the light had a gray cast to it. As she swam harder and got closer, she could detect movement in the water. The surface was only a few yards away.

What she was heading towards looked like a narrow opening. From the other side, she assumed it looked like a small pond or pool of water. The opening also looked like it was starting to close. She was barely going to make it. At the rate the gap was shutting, she worried that the others would be left behind.

In spite of the decision for them to all stay together, she pushed ahead. Once she was near the surface, she reached back, grabbed Summer's arm and threw her up and out. She caught a glimpse of Summer breaking the surface of the water, and then getting swept aside. Hoping she had done the right thing, Natalie turned around and headed back towards the others.

She motioned to Stella, who pulled Quinn upward, kicking furiously. As she passed Lochen, she grabbed his arm in mid-flail and dragged him with her. Natalie dove further down and took Liam's and Sean's hands in hers to pull them faster.

The opening was getting smaller and smaller. She watched Stella push Lochen up and through, and then watched as Stella squeezed Quinn through. For an instant she was worried that Quinn would get stuck like a cork in a bottle and doom the rest of them. Stella gave him a very un-lady-like poke and he popped through.

Stella turned back to Natalie, who freed one hand long enough to motion to her. Keep going, she signaled, and Stella shot out of the water. Natalie gave one more strong push and shoved Liam upward, followed immediately by Sean. Just as the small gap closed shut completely, she managed to kick one last time.

She broke the surface of the water and exploded into the air. A gust of wind caught her and blew her across the roof of tower three. She skidded to a stop against the ramparts in a heap with all the others. The wind had gotten even stronger, and the snow was falling much harder.

To their surprise, as they each exited the water, they were completely dry – as if they had never been submerged. They got to their feet and looked around. Like the towers before this one, the roof looked exactly the same – flat circular stonework surrounded by crenellated battlements.

Sean walked across towards the direction of the first two towers. He looked down at the chain and wood bridge they had recently crossed. None of the planks were broken. It looked exactly as it had when they first saw it. He looked around tower two, and, although he couldn't get a complete view, he was able to see the end of the wooden bridge extending from the roof of tower one.

He hoped they would find an easier and faster way out of all this, and that they wouldn't have to cross either one of those bridges again, but he was glad to know there was at least some kind of escape route. He turned back to join the others.

They were gathered on the opposite side of the roof, facing tower four. He saw the look on some of their faces before he saw what they were staring at. They all shared a look of disappointment and defeat. He turned to see what the problem was. There was no bridge.

Chapter fourteen

Instead of a bridge, three lines of rope extended from the roof of tower three to an opening in the side of tower four, exactly like the one they had come through to tower three – an archway with no doors: just a black hole. Two of the lines of rope were parallel to each other and ran from the floor of the roof to the base of the landing on the other tower. The third line was a few feet above and centered between the two lower ones.

Every ten feet or so, the parallel lines were connected with a short piece of rope, apparently to keep them from drifting apart when being crossed. Nothing connected the top rope to the lower two.

"What are we supposed to do with this?" asked Solveig. "There's no bridge."

"That is the bridge," said Lochen.

"No way," said Quinn.

"I'm afraid so," said Stella, who was looking closely at the anchors to which the ropes were secured.

"It looks like we walk on the two lower ropes while holding on to the top rope," offered Liam.

"You say that like it's nothing," said Quinn. "It's not nothing; it's something – a really big something."

"Come on," said Sean. "This is like climbing in a bunch of vines. It's easy."

"On the contrary," said Lochen. "I'm certain that when you were climbing in a bunch of vines, you weren't nearly two thousand feet in the air, in freezing cold weather, with severe and unpredictable winds."

"Welllll, not exactly, I suppose," admitted Sean. "But, still, it's not as hard as it looks."

"Then you can go first," blurted Quinn, before Lochen could appoint him to take the lead.

"Fine," said Sean.

"Fine," said Quinn, folding his arms across his chest and looking with a mixture of defiance and pleading at Lochen.

"Fine," added Lochen after a moment's thought. "And this time, Quinn, you can go last, which should make you happy."
"I'd be happier if we didn't have to cross this thing, but going last is all right with me."

"We should get started," said Natalie. "The weather doesn't look like it's going to get any better, and it's getting dark, too. I'd rather not be doing this at night."

Without any further discussion, Sean jumped up to the ledge and planted his feet on the two bottom ropes, and grasped the top one firmly in both hands. The others lined up behind him in an order similar to how they had crossed the earlier bridges. Lochen had swooped Summer up and once again placed her inside his hood.

"This time," she said, "tell me you're going to pull your hood up before you do it."

"Then get prepared," he answered, "because I'm doing it now."

He flipped the hood up and she crawled to the top of his head. He then moved closer to the ropes, immediately behind Stella.

"We should probably keep at least ten feet or so between us," he said. "I'm worried about the strength of this rope."

Sean didn't waste any time. He deftly shuffled his feet across the lower ropes, never lifting them high enough to lose contact. He held the top rope in both hands, slightly over his head and pulled himself along. He moved quickly and efficiently across the bridge. Within seconds, he was far enough ahead for Stella to begin to follow him.

She watched how he moved and imitated what he did. She placed her feet on the two lower ropes, and reached for the top one. However, it was further over her head than it had been over Sean's head. She had to extend her arms fully to reach. His weight on the lower ropes had increased the distance for Stella between them and the top rope.

"Let him get further ahead," said Lochen, seeing how much she had to extend herself. "Allow more slack in the rope. It should be easier for you to reach, then."

She waited until Sean was almost at the halfway point and then stepped out onto the ropes again. Lochen had been right. It was easier for her to hold on. Moving in the same manner as Sean, she inched her way forward. When she was nearly halfway, Sean was already off and waiting on the landing. Then Lochen stepped onto the ropes.

The top rope was lower on him, coming just under his chin. That made pulling himself a bit awkward. He couldn't center his feet on the two ropes below, since the top rope was held either to the left of his head or the right. As a result, he began to sway back and forth.

The lower ropes began to swing with his motion. As he tried to steady himself and stop the swaying motion, the lower ropes began to bob up and down. Stella, who by now was at the midpoint, was unprepared for the sudden changes in the ropes' movements, which were exaggerated as the swinging moved from Lochen up towards where she was.

She lost her footing on the lower ropes and was hanging from the top one. It was as if the floor had moved out from under her. She looked down to see where the lower ropes went and became fixated on the rocks nearly two thousand feet below. She sucked in her breath and without knowing it, held it.

She swung her feet frantically, trying to regain her footing. Her toes stretched out, missing the ropes each time they swung by. At the same time, the top rope was bobbing up and down as it swung back and forth.

"Lochen," yelled Sean. "Stop moving."

His voice was lost in the wind. Natalie, who was next in line, had been studying Lochen's movements as she prepared to step out onto the ropes, and hadn't noticed that Stella was whipping around. She stepped forward and looked up as she grabbed the upper rope. A blur of movement far ahead of her caught her eye.

She stopped and stepped back onto the roof to lean sideways far enough to look past Lochen. She saw Stella being buffeted by the wind, swinging radically out of control, nearly making complete circles around the upper rope, holding on for dear life.

"Lochen," Natalie shouted. "LOCHEN! Stop moving."

Lochen heard his name being called and looked back to see Natalie waving her arms and pointing past him. He turned towards tower four to see Stella twisting and turning in the wind, hanging on desperately to the rope. He started to move forward to come to her rescue.

"No," shouted Summer. "You're only making it worse. You're too much taller than she is. Every time you take a step, you push her further away from the bottom ropes."

"But we have to do something," he said. "She can't hold on much longer."

Lochen was right. Stella's arms were quickly tiring. Her hands burned from the twisting and turning of the rope. She had closed her eyes because the rapid, jerking motion as her view changed from sky to rocks to tower and back, was making her dizzy. Even with her eyes closed, she was feeling light-headed.

Bolts of pain shot up her arms into her shoulders with each bounce – each time the wind lifted her into the air and then dropped her down. She tried moving her hands along the rope, but she was afraid to loosen her grip. The realization that she wasn't going to make it across quickly sunk in. Her throat tightened and she fought back tears.

She was almost to the point where her arms gave out when she felt something tighten around her waist. Her eyes popped open and she found herself face to face with Sean. He had jumped back onto the top rope, wrapped his arms and legs around it and scooted back to where she was.

"I've got you," he said once he had lowered his legs and wrapped them around her waist. "You can let go. I won't drop you."

She opened one hand and moved it from the rope to his shoulder. Then she moved the other one, and quickly clasped her hands around his chest, hugging him tightly. The rope bobbed with the change in weight, but Sean was already moving back. He never unwrapped his legs from around Stella's waist, and she didn't let go of the bear hug in which she held him.

Hand over hand he moved, pulling the two of them to the landing. With one final flip, he swung off the rope and landed on the threshold.

"You can let go now," he said.

"Thanks," she told him as she pealed herself away. "If this is the only way back, you all can leave me here."

At the other end of the rope, the others had been watching closely and mentally following each move Sean made. They all breathed more easily when he reached the end.

"Finish crossing," Natalie shouted to Lochen. "I'll wait until you reach the end before I start."

"Excellent suggestion," he shouted back. "It's probably safer that way."

Quest of Eight Part Four: The Race to Virkio

Richard Reda

He continued to cross. Without Stella's weight on the top rope, he was able to widen the space between it and the lower ones, making it somewhat easier for him to move. He was still not correctly centered and by the time he reached the midpoint, he had pulled the top rope downward and with his feet, he pushed the lower ropes upwards.

The lower ropes had risen so much that one of his feet was about eighteen inches higher in the air than the other one. He was nearly sideways himself. From Summer's vantage point, the tower towards which they were headed appeared to be tipping over.

"I don't think this is the right way to be crossing this thing," she said.

"I believe you're right," grunted Lochen.

He was struggling to hold on and to move forward at the same time. The gusts of wind only lifted him higher and soon he was facing the sky, with his back almost perfectly parallel to the ground – if the ground below had been flat instead of rocky and pointed.

His hood slid off his head and Summer nearly fell out. She bounced around in the material, and was afraid she'd be shaken loose and blown away. With all the wind and the shaking, it was hard for her to tell which way was up. Finally, she was able to straighten up and climb out.

She grabbed onto Lochen's hair as if she was climbing a rope. Periodically, a gust of wind would lift her away from his scalp and she'd be flapping in the breeze, strands of his hair wound tightly in her hands. Eventually, she resituated herself on the top of his head, twisted his hair in her fists to keep from falling, and peered over his forehead.

"Whatever you're doing," she said, "you need to find a different way of doing it.

"It looked so much easier," he replied. "I don't understand why it's so difficult."

Step by step he continued. As he neared the end, the anchored ropes forced him to straighten out. Once he was near enough, Sean reached out and took his hand and pulled him the rest of the way.

"There," exclaimed Lochen, once he was back on solid footing. "That wasn't so bad after all, was it?"

"How about next time, you ride in the hood of _my_ cloak," suggested Summer.

"You don't wear a cloak," he answered, missing the point of her comment. "And if you did, I hardly think I would fit."

Natalie had watched Lochen's bizarre method of crossing and made sure she didn't emulate it. She moved as easily and efficiently as Sean had. Crossing one at a time seemed to be the best approach.

Liam and Solveig followed in due course. Both made the passage without much difficulty, having learned from those who preceded them. Before he began, Liam had taken one more look at the condition of the ropes where they were connected to the anchors. He could see some fraying, but they looked strong enough to last.

Finally, it was Quinn's turn. He faced the same difficulty as Lochen. The top rope wasn't high enough to allow him to get perfectly balanced on the two lower ropes. He tried hunching over, ducking under the top rope and holding it behind him. That didn't work. He couldn't get a good grip and he couldn't easily move forward.

Then he tried leaning backwards to hold the top rope in front of him, but that was worse, and he quickly gave up on that idea. Instead, he raised both arms over the top rope and pressed it against his chest, holding it under his arms. He was still off balance, but he felt he had a better grip on the top rope.

As he slid across the ropes, he soon encountered the same difficulty Lochen had, and began to lean further and further backwards. His feet kept pushing the lower ropes upward. Before long, his feet were almost as high as his head. The top rope was bowed downward and starting to slip out from under his arms.

Liam jumped off the landing and onto the ropes. He grabbed onto the top line, pulling it down as far as he could as he stepped on the lower lines, mirroring Quinn's position. He arched his back and pulled harder, trying to offset Quinn. It was working. Quinn slowly began to right himself. His feet lowered enough for him to secure his grip on the top line and continue moving his feet along the lower lines.

The added weight and the amount of stress the two of them were placing on the ropes were taking a toll, however. The knots that tied the top line to its anchor started to fray. The constant pulling back and forth rubbed the rope against the metal, wearing away one thin strand after another.

Quinn was at the halfway point when he felt a jerk in the line. He stopped moving. He looked at Liam and then back at the starting point. It was too far away for him to see anything, but the odd vibration worried him. He started moving again, this time trying to go a little faster. Then he felt another jerk in the line.

Another section of the twined rope had broken. This time Liam could feel the break, too. When Quinn stopped once more in an attempt to determine what was happening, Liam turned back to the others.

"The line is breaking," he said. "It feels like the top one."

He turned to Quinn.

"Don't stop," he shouted. "I think the line is breaking. You need to move as fast as you can, and hold on to the top rope as tightly as you can."

Quinn didn't need any further encouragement. He shuffled his feet as quickly as he could. He pulled the top line tighter and wrapped it around one of his arms while dragging himself along with the other. Then he felt another snap, and then another, and then the line broke completely.

Most people would have reacted by waving their arms for balance and arching their backs to keep their center of gravity from falling backwards. In doing this, though, they would have sacrificed their footing and slipped off the lower rope, dangled from the falling upper rope, and, if they managed to hold on, would have crashed into the side of the tower with such force, their bodies would have been broken.

Quinn, however, didn't do this. He had often encountered broken lines when dog sledding over rough terrain. His reactions were driven by these experiences. He quickly pulled the top line to eliminate the slack between where he was and where it still remained anchored into the landing of tower four.

Then he shifted the weight of his feet without lifting them from the lower lines. He swung back and forth several times like the pendulum on a clock before he gained control over his motion and steadied himself. In doing so, he almost knocked Liam off at the other end. Fortunately, Liam quickly grasped what Quinn was doing and he scurried off the ropes back to the landing.

He bent slightly forward, maintaining a tight hold on the top rope, which now trailed off to one side and down towards the rocks below. He pulled himself forward, shuffling one foot after the other in short, quick steps, never allowing too much space between the ropes and his feet. He stopped whenever a gust of wind pushed him one way or the other, or attempted to lift him higher into the air.

It took a little while longer, and there was nothing the others could do but watch, but eventually he made it. As soon as he was within an arm's length from the landing, several pairs of arms reached out to him and pulled him onto the landing.

"Thanks," he said to Liam. "I was worried for a minute that I'd end up upside down. I wasn't sure how that was going to work."

"Not so much fun going last, is it?" asked Sean, who was smiling broadly.

"I don't think it makes much difference in this place," he answered. "This is NOT a nice place!"

"Fortunately, we are near the end," said Lochen. "Of course what we may face on our return remains to be seen."

"I saw that wooden bridge – the one that collapsed – it was back the way it was," said Sean. "Since we know what to expect, crossing these bridges should be easier."

"They will all be different on the way back," said Lochen.

"He's right," added Stella. "They're all part of the spells on top of spells that the Alchemist cast. Everything is an illusion and everything changes. Even what we went through inside the towers will be different."

"Wonderful," mumbled Sean.

"For now, though, we need to see about getting through tower four," said Natalie.

They all turned to look at the opening in the side of the tower. It was similar to the access they encountered at tower three. There was no door – only a smooth, black surface of some kind. Lochen stepped forward to look at it closely.

"This doesn't seem to be made of the same substance as the last one," he said.

"Good," said Solveig. "That stuff felt slimy."

Lochen reached forward to put his hand against it. He expected to feel some kind of resistance, even if soft like the goo from before. Instead, his fingertips went right through. He felt nothing. He pulled his hand back to look at his fingers.

"Interesting," he said. "There's nothing on my fingertips. I couldn't feel anything at all when I touched the surface."

"Maybe we should hold on to each other," said Stella. "Just in case."

They grabbed each other's hands and Lochen once more tentatively pushed his hand into the opening. His fingers went through, and he still couldn't feel anything. He took a step closer and moved his hand further forward. Without warning he felt his hand and arm get sucked in. At first it was a gentle tug. Before he could pull it back, he was yanked ahead. By the time he even thought about letting go of Stella's hand, it was too late.

In seconds, they were all pulled into the interior of the tower by some unseen force. They were sucked in and thrown to the center of the same kind of large circular hall as the other towers. They landed on the floor like rag dolls, and their momentum made them slide across the smooth stone floor to the center of the tower.

"Is anyone hurt?" asked Lochen. "Summer. Are you all right?"

Quest of Eight Part Four: The Race to Virkio

Richard Reda

He reached back to his hood, trying to open it enough to uncover her.

"What was <u>that</u>?" she shouted. "One second we were outside on a landing and then, bang, we ended up in here."

"Quinn," grunted Sean in a muffled voice. "Get off me. You weigh a ton."

Quinn rolled over and uncovered Sean and Solveig, who had been buried beneath him.

"I scraped my hands," said Stella, "but other than that, I'm all right."

"Me, too," added Liam and Natalie.

Some of them got to their feet and others merely sat up. They all looked around. It was like they were under a spotlight. A beam of light was shining down on them from the ceiling. It was so bright they couldn't see what the source was. The doorway through which they had been dragged was no longer visible. The walls all around the room were a turmoil of wind and rain.

"It looks like we're in the eye of a hurricane," said Lochen.

"What's that?" asked Liam.

"It's a very powerful storm," said Natalie. "I've seen these before, although mostly from beneath the surface of the sea."

"If it's a storm," asked Quinn, "why isn't it raining on us?"

"These are very large storms," explained Lochen. "They normally start far out to sea. The spiraling motion draws water from the oceans up towards the sky, and the winds become so powerful that the storms can be hundreds of miles wide. They can move so fast that they create an opening in the center where there is no wind or rain. They're very interesting."

"How does a hurricane get inside a tower?" asked Liam.

"It's an illusion," Stella and Lochen said simultaneously.

"Consider that you were pulled through that wall of water from outside the tower into the center," said Lochen. "Are your clothes wet? No. Not at all. This is really no different than the last tower where we dove into a vast pool, swam downward, and then for no apparent reason at all, began swimming upward. And if you recall, when we exited the water, our clothing was dry. This is all an illusion."

"Maybe so," said Sean. "But that illusion just pulled us into the middle of this storm. How are we getting out of here?"

They all looked around. The wall of wind and water completely surrounded them. The circle in which they had landed was less than ten feet away in any direction.

"I don't see a lot of options here," said Sean.

"Actually," said Lochen, "I see only one."

"I don't want to think what you're thinking," said Quinn. "At least I don't think I do."
"You think we have to jump into that storm, don't you?" asked Solveig.

"Oh, brother," mumbled Summer. "I'm going to need a different place to ride."

"I promise to pull my hood tightly," said Lochen. "I won't let you fall out."

"Wait a minute now," said Sean. "Let's think about this. First of all, it's water again. Second of all, this isn't like jumping into a lake; it's jumping into a storm. Third...third...I can't think of a third, but I'm sure there is one. And did I mention? It's water again. We really need to see if there's another way. Let's not rush into this."

"It's not really water," Stella tried to explain.

"Oh yes it is," Sean cut her off. "I bet if we tried to breathe we wouldn't be able to. We'd drown. You don't drown in air. You drown in water."

"OK," Natalie cut in. "It's really water. Whether we get wet or not, you're probably right. If we aren't careful, we could drown. It's a little late to worry about that now, don't you think? Do you see any other way out of here?"

Once more they all looked around at the wall of water that encompassed them and rose up and out of sight. They looked down at the floor for some kind of opening or trap door. The stone was solid and the mortar between the stones was old and hard.

"Oooooh, poop," said Sean. "All right. I give up. But I get to go last this time," he added, glaring at Quinn.

Quinn looked slightly put out and quickly turned to Lochen.
"OK, but I go next to last."

"I'll go first," offered Natalie. "As I said, I've seen these storms before – not that it means anything."

"I think we need to do more than hold each others' hands this time," inserted Liam. "We should tie ourselves together."

"I agree," said Lochen. "The force of the water and whatever is drawing it upward will be too much for us to merely hold on to one another. And, I would add, you may have to do more than merely tie the rope around our waists. We're likely to be jostled quite severely. A loop around our waist may be insufficient."

"I can do that," answered Liam.

He removed the rope from his shoulder and rigged a simple harness around Natalie. He then motioned for Lochen to be next. He moved Lochen as close to Natalie as he could and began to tie the same harness.

"This seems awfully close," said Lochen. "Not that I object, but aren't you worried that we may collide with one another?"

"That's exactly what I expect will happen," answered Liam. "We need to reduce the amount of space as much as possible. Otherwise the ropes may snap loose and we could be crashing into each other."

He continued with the harness, tying a loop that ran over both shoulders, through the legs, and around the waist. After Lochen, he secured Stella, tying her tightly.

"This could get very uncomfortable," Lochen commented, feeling how snugly the ropes ran around his body and how close he was to the others.

"Yes," agreed Liam, "but it's better than battering one another, breaking a bone or losing one of us altogether."

"Point well taken," admitted Lochen as he tried to adjust one of the knots.

Liam then tied Stella to Lochen. After that he turned to Quinn.

"Sorry, big guy, you need to go next."

"I was supposed to go next to last," he tried to argue.

"This is as close as you get: next to next to last."

Without waiting for any further debate, Liam nudged Quinn forward and continued the train of harnesses. Then he added Solveig. When he was done attaching her, he turned to Sean.

"No way," said Sean. "I'm going last."

"Unless you know how to tie this harness," Liam said, "I have to go last. I can't really tie myself in and then tie you in. And we don't have time for me to teach you how."

Grumbling under his breath, Sean moved up and allowed Liam to tie him to the others. When he was done, it was evident to Sean that there wasn't enough rope left to tie a harness on Liam.

"No. See?" said Sean. "You were just trying to trick me. There's not enough rope. That's why I should go last. I'm used to hanging on to vines and things like that."

"Not in a hurricane," replied Liam. "I'll be fine. There's enough rope left for me to make a loop, which I can tie to my hands. It's the best I can do."

When everything was done the odd looking group crab-walked closer to the wall of water.

"How should we do this?" asked Liam. "Are you going in first, Natalie? And simply pull the rest of us in?"

"No," said Stella. "We need to go in all at once."

"This ought to be interesting," said Solveig.

"I can't watch," said Summer.

She pulled the hood around her and twisted her body, wrapping herself like a cocoon, pulling the hood off Lochen's head and winding it at the base of his neck.

"Not so tight," he gasped. "You're choking me."

"You'll be fine," she shouted to him, her voice muffled by the material. "Quit being such a baby."

Liam moved the back end of the train closer to the edge of the water. Once the line was parallel to the wall, they all started sidestepping so that they could step in at the same time. However, someone was out of step with the others and feet got tangled. The whole line started losing its balance and teetering left and right. No one was able to regain balance and the entire group, except for Liam, who was only tied at his hands, began to fall.

Arms stretched out, bodies tried unsuccessfully to turn, legs were braced, and feet were stepped on. Liam tried to pull the end of the rope and straighten them all out, but it was too much for him. This was probably not a good idea, was the last thought he had as one after another, heads fell into the raging storm, pulling bodies behind them.

He reacted too slowly. He had tried to step into the wall of water at the same time as the bodies of the others made contact. However, once their heads disappeared, they were sucked en masse into the tempest. His arms were jerked so forcefully, that he thought they were being pulled off his body.

He didn't have time to take a deep breath or to close his eyes before he was submerged. He felt himself being yanked. His body extended from the rest of the train like a flag waving in the wind. He squeezed his hands around the knots he had tied around his wrists, wishing there had been about three more feet of rope.

At the other end of the line, Natalie had her eyes wide open. Sea sprites had a protective covering over their eyes so the rush of water beating against her face didn't affect her vision. The only thing was that there was nothing to see. Everything was a blur. The gray of the stone walls and the gray of the water melted together. And the light towards which they were heading got brighter and brighter, blotting out everything else.

Lochen, whose head was immediately above Natalie's, was being battered by the storm. He felt like he was being punched, and was glad that he couldn't open his eyes, even if he had wanted to. All he could think was that it was a good idea for Summer to wrap herself in his hood. He'd have lost her for sure if she hadn't.

Summer felt like someone had sat on Lochen's hood. She felt the crush of the wind and water, and was deafened by the sudden roar. What kind of storm is this, she wondered. She had heard about hurricanes from her grandparents, but she thought they were only stories to keep her from venturing too far from her village. Wow, she thought, they'd be really upset with her if they knew where she was now.

Stella was pressed between Lochen and Quinn. She felt like she was caught in a press. She tried to move her head to one side or the other to see what was happening, but Liam had tied them so tightly together she couldn't move. Even if they hadn't been tied together so closely, the water and wind, rushing past Lochen's body was slamming into her head, keeping it pinned.

Quinn, like Lochen, was being pummeled. He tried to put his head down, but the force was pushing it back. He fought to raise his arms. Once the first one rose above Stella's body, it flew back and hit him in the face. Ow, he thought, maybe that wasn't such a good idea. He

310

made do with the one arm protecting his face. He wasn't able to lower it anyway.

Solveig could feel the force pounding all around her. She was glad to be behind Quinn, since he offered the greatest amount of protection. She couldn't imagine the beating Natalie must be taking. She could feel them moving in a clockwise motion as the whirlpool swept them around the tower walls and upward. I hope we don't get thrown off the tower, she thought.

Sean's head was jerked back with the initial force of the storm. He managed to fight and bend it forward, only because of the buffering from Quinn and Solveig. Considering that there hadn't been enough rope to harness Liam, he felt guilty for a minute that he hadn't gone last, but that was soon replaced by relief, and then again by guilt. Water, he complained to himself. What's with all this stinking water?

Liam was starting to spiral. The rope leading from Sean ended in a type of noose to which he had tied his hands. However, there was nothing to provide any stability. As he was pulled through the storm, he began to corkscrew, and the rope began to tighten. It was cutting into his wrists and crushing his hands. He tried to pull his body closer so he could reach one of the blades. He had to cut the rope before it severed his hands.

Fortunately, the force of the water and wind was too much and he couldn't haul himself forward. Instead, he felt the rope begin to loosen. He felt his speed begin to decrease. His first thought was that they were coming to the end of the storm. He was able to pull on the knot enough to move his hands closer to Sean.

He extended his fingers, pulling along the end of the rope. He was pulling too much rope. The harness holding Sean wasn't there. What had happened? He was still moving at an incredible speed, but he could tell he was slowing down. He opened his eyes, but they immediately filled with water and he had to close them again.

311

He pulled more of the rope. The knots and harnesses had unraveled. How had that happened? Where was everyone else? A sense of panic filled him.

As the light got closer Natalie could feel the rope around her coming loose. She reached around her to hold the knots together, but the force pushing against her was too much. She soon felt Lochen pull away from her. What's happening, she wondered with dread.

Except for Summer, who was still tightly enveloped in Lochen's hood, each one of them felt their bonds loosening, and the person in front and behind them begin to separate. Solveig reached forward with one hand and grabbed Quinn, and back with the other to grab Sean. Her action spurred the two of them to do the same.

Quinn quickly reached for Stella, who then felt for and found Lochen's hand. He then did the same, much to Natalie's relief. Sean reached back for Liam, but couldn't find him. He tried turning around, but that was futile. He stretched further and felt for the rope to which Liam had been tied. He inched his fingers along the line until he felt Liam's hand. He grabbed hold, but noticed that Liam didn't squeeze back. He hoped this ordeal would be over soon. He was worried about his friend.

With a sudden burst, Natalie exploded through the roof of tower four, immediately followed by all the others. She found herself several feet in the air – long enough to realize that she could be thrown or blown over the edge. She quickly bent her body and forced herself to change direction for the surface of the roof. She landed in a large drift of snow, running into the battlements on the side facing tower five.

One by one the others immediately followed her. The rope had come loose but still managed to connect one to the other. They skidded and spun to a stop, plowing into the low wall that circled the roof. Fortunately, the snow had fallen so much that there was nearly a foot on the roof and large drifts against the wall.

As they had hoped, their clothing was completely dry. They got to their feet and checked with each other to make sure no one was injured. Liam's hand had fallen asleep, the circulation having been cut off by the twisting rope. Otherwise, he was all right.

Almost as an afterthought, Lochen reached back to unwind his hood. Summer fluttered out, making sure to stay out of the gusting wind and close to the others. They looked around at the snow covered roof and the mounds of drifting snow that had accumulated between the crenellations. Then they turned towards tower five.

That was when they saw the narrow, flat expanse of ice leading from the roof of tower four to the roof of tower five. What they hadn't noticed was the movement in one of the snowdrifts on the far side of the roof, when a pair of eyes opened and noticed their arrival.

Chapter fifteen

Unaware that they were being watched or that anyone but them was on the tower roof, they looked with dismay at the narrow, icy expanse that ran from where they were to where they needed to be. There were no railings, there was nothing to hold on to, and the bridge itself, if it could even be called that, was only inches wide. If that weren't enough, it was covered in ice. Actually, on closer inspection, they saw that it was made of ice.

"We're never going to be able to cross that," moaned Sean.

"I admit," said Lochen. "It does present a challenge."

314

"A challenge?" asked Solveig. "Really? We're not talking about taking a stroll across a log that's floating on a stream. That thing is solid ice and we're – what? – only about two thousand feet above the ground."

"Yes," Lochen answered calmly. "I'm well aware of our situation. I happen to believe there is always some alternative. I merely haven't discovered it, yet."

"Well give it a good thought, genius," said Sean, "because I don't see us getting over there."

"I can do it," said Quinn.

"What?" several of them asked.

"So, NOW you want to go first?" asked Sean.

"No," he answered. "Well, yes, I suppose. I mean I can cross that bridge. I can go first and take the rope with me. I can tie it off at that end and you all can follow, pulling yourselves up."

"How can you do that?" asked Natalie. "Of all of us, I would think you'd be the last one to want to try to walk on that. It's so small, and you're so big."

"Yeah," he answered, "it is kind of small, but I've crossed crevasses on narrower things than that."

"But what about the ice?" asked Stella. "How are you going to keep from slipping? Look at it. It's not only icy, it's uphill!"

"My boots," he said. "They're made of Reyther skin, remember?"

"Yes," said Natalie. "Arctic sea creatures with really rough skin. How do you get the skin from them?"

"You don't want to know," he answered.

"I remember," said Summer. "The boots, that is; not how he gets the skin. They dig into the ice and they don't wear down, do they?"

"Exactly," said Quinn. "I'll be steady as a rock. I can do this."

"That seems like a perfectly good alternative," answered Lochen, smiling out of the corner of his mouth at Solveig.

"That's it then," Quinn announced.

He took one end of the rope in his hand and started to step onto the bridge. Liam leaped forward and grabbed the tail of his coat, pulling him back.

"Not so fast," he said. "I don't care how sure-footed you think you are, let's not take any chances."

He took the rope from Quinn's hand and tied it securely around his waist. Then he tied the other end around the nearest battlement. He pulled both ends to make sure the knots were tight.

"Just in case," Liam said. "When you get to the other end, hold the line as tight as you can. I'll come across next to tie that end off. After that it should be safe enough for everyone else to follow – well, as safe as it's going to get."

Quinn turned back to the shaft of ice and adjusted the rope so that the knots were behind him. He stepped up over the edge of the wall and onto the bridge. It was narrower than he had expected, and he had to force himself to concentrate on his feet, rather than the thin layer of clouds that floated hundreds of feet below him, and on the breaks in those clouds that revealed how perilously high he was.

Now that I think of it, he said to himself, those crevasses back home weren't anywhere close to being this deep, or high, or whatever. And the more I think about it, what I was crossing them with was much wider than this bridge, and it wasn't as icy. What was I thinking?

The others watched from behind. Lochen and Liam held loosely to the rope, feeding it out as Quinn moved slowly forward. Should he not be as nimble as he claimed to be, and fell off to one side or the other, they were prepared to stop his fall as quickly as possible.

He took one slow step after the other, carefully moving his weight from his back foot to his front foot before taking the next step. His arms were extended out to his sides to help keep him balanced, and he was paying close attention to the shifting wind. He was moving painstakingly slow, but no one wanted to rush him.

All the while, one pair of eyes after another opened in the drifts behind them. The hidden hobgoblins watch silently. If all of these strangers simply fell off the bridge, their job would be much simpler. If not, then they'd cross after them and take care of business.

At the halfway point, the wind picked up and threw a flurry of snow in Quinn's face. He stopped moving and for a second closed his eyes. He took a minute to think of home, of his family, of his dogs. This is just like home, he told himself. I'm going to cross this bridge – this crevasse – and then I'll be home. I'll have something warm to eat and I'll sleep in my own bed.

He slowly opened his eyes. Home was not on the other end of the bridge, and his momentary feeling of euphoria evaporated like the snowflakes that landed on his face. The wind settled down. The snow was still falling, but it wasn't blowing in his face. Before he started again, he looked forward to the end of the bridge.

That's weird, he thought. It doesn't look like any snow fell at all on that tower. He couldn't see the roof, yet, but he could see the end of

317

the bridge and the battlements that ran around the top. There was no accumulation of snow whatsoever. He wasn't sure if that was good news or not. Nothing about this place was good.

He looked down at his feet again before continuing. He wanted to make sure of where he was walking. He noticed that while he had stopped, the burst of snow that hit him in the face had drifted into a small pile for the next several feet in front of him. He was tempted to swipe the snow off the bridge with his foot, but decided that might be unwise.

He took a deep breath, shifted his weight from his back foot to his right foot, brought the back foot around and stepped forward. The rough edges of the Reyther skin that covered the soles of his boots easily dug into ice, but they couldn't remove snow. Nearly an inch had piled up on the path.

He stepped onto the bridge, compressing the snow. The skin on the sole of his boot dug into the snow, but not through it. At first nothing happened. Then he shifted his weight from his back foot to his front foot – the one on the compacted snow. As soon as he lifted his back foot to step forward, the flattened snow slid away from the bridge below it, taking his foot with it.

He overcame his natural instinct to wave his arms to keep his balance and keep from falling. Instead, he let himself fall forward, focusing all his attention on the narrow span of ice. He reached out as it came to meet him. Falling flat on his face, he wrapped his arms around the expanse and let his legs drop to either side, quickly wrapping them around it, too.

"NO!" shouted Solveig.

"Pull!" shouted Lochen, as he and Liam quickly took up what little slack exited in the rope."

Quest of Eight Part Four: The Race to Virkio

Richard Reda

"NO," Quinn shouted back. "Don't pull the rope. I'm OK."

I'm OK, he repeated to himself. I didn't fall off. I'm OK. He could feel the hardness of the ice through his clothing. He could also feel how narrow and how thin the bridge was. I hope it didn't crack, he thought. I'll be in a real pickle if it did.

He took a few seconds to catch his breath. Then he pushed himself up with his arms. Still straddling the bridge with his legs, and holding on to it at arm's length, he considered his next move. Wonderful, he thought. I managed not to fall off, but getting back up is going to be a problem.

He started to lift himself up, first by squirming to one side so he had room to put one knee on the bridge. That didn't work. He nearly slipped over the side. Then he tried lifting his foot behind him and hooking it over the bridge. That didn't work, either. He was puzzled. How was he going to get back up?

Suddenly, he felt himself beginning to slowly slide backwards. Oh, no, he thought. I'm not going all the way back and have to start over again. He lowered his body to the bridge and wrapped his arms around it again. Then he lifted his feet high enough to dig the sides of his boots into the sides of the bridge. That did it. He stopped moving.

"That's it," he shouted out loud.

"What's it?" Natalie shouted back. "Are you giving up?"

"No," he shouted back over his shoulder. "I figured out how to keep going. That's all."

He dug the sides of his boots in as far as he could and then extended his legs, sliding up the ramp. Once he had gone as far as he was able, he hugged the bridge tightly and quickly brought his legs up as far as possible and dug his boots in again before he could slide back.

In this manner, he looked like he was shinnying up a pole. It worked. In a few minutes, he reached the end of the bridge and pushed himself over the battlements onto the floor of the roof of tower five. He made it. He quickly got up, untied the rope from his waist and wound it around one of the battlements and pulled it taut.

"OK," he signaled to Liam. "It's your turn."

Liam had never walked on ice, so he didn't know what to expect. He nervously stepped up onto the wall and grabbed the rope in both hands. Then he put one foot out onto the bridge. He seemed steady. Then he put the other foot out onto the bridge.

"So far, so good," he said, looking back at the others.

He turned back towards Quinn and took his first step. That was when he discovered how slippery ice could be. His foot slid out from under him. He overcompensated with his other foot, which resulted in both of them flying up into the air and him falling onto his back.

In reacting to the ice, he let go of the rope and thrashed his arms as if he was trying to fly. Luckily, he landed on his back – dead center – and didn't fall off the bridge. Instead, he skidded back towards where he started and somersaulted backwards onto the stone floor. It happened so fast that no one was able to immediately understand how close he came to falling off the tower completely. It was, instead, almost comical.

"Way to go, Grace," said Sean.

And then he realized what almost happened.

"Oh, I mean...I...I don't know what I mean," he sputtered. "I'm sorry. Are you all right?"

"Aside from a bruised dignity, yes, I'm all right," he answered. "And you don't have to apologize. I probably would have laughed at me, too."

"Is he OK?" Quinn shouted from the other tower.

"Yes," Lochen shouted back. "He'll soon be making an effort to improve on that last attempt. Perhaps this time he'll be a bit more successful."

"Tell him not to walk," Quinn shouted.

"How am I supposed to cross if I don't walk?" Liam asked.
"Tell him to pull himself across. Let his feet slide on the ice. It will be easier that way," Quinn explained.

"OK," said Liam, mounting the bridge once more.

He held the rope tightly in both hands, set his feet firmly and squarely under him and then pulled. He slid forward almost effortlessly. He eased his hands forward one at a time and repeated the pulling motion. He slid forward again, still keeping his balance. He started laughing.

"This is almost fun," he shouted.

"Yeah," responded Solveig. "Except for falling thousands of feet onto rocks, it's a blast."

"Well, yes," he said more soberly, "except for that part."

He dragged himself across the bridge without any further mishap and jumped off when he reached the other side. He took the rope from Quinn and pulled it as tightly as he could. Then he tied it off, double-checking the knot before he signaled to the other side that everything was ready.

"All right," said Lochen. "Who's next? Since we're crossing one at a time, and the bridge appears to be solid, I don't see the need to follow any particular order."

"I'll go," said Solveig.

She climbed up to the rampart, and grabbed the rope in the same manner as Liam had. She took a deep breath and then relaxed – as much as she could, regretting now having made the comment about the possibility of falling thousands of feet to the rocks. She focused on the far side of the bridge and began pulling herself across. It turned out to be easier than she thought, and she made it across without incident.

"All right, then," said Lochen once Solveig was across.

Natalie offered to follow. Lochen was helping her up onto the wall. Summer had climbed back into his hood and had crawled out onto his shoulder to watch. Sean stood nearby, adamant that he would go last. And Stella was standing a few feet away from the others.

Just as Natalie stepped onto the bridge, everything stopped. Stella looked around to see what had happened. Nothing was moving. Even the snowflakes had stopped in midair. The moist air that everyone exhaled was frozen in place. The wind had stopped. All sounds had stopped. It was absolutely quiet.

Natalie had one foot on the bridge, her hands on the rope and her other foot poised in the air ready to plant. Lochen was like a statue standing behind her, one hand on the wall, the other extended to help her keep her balance. Summer was perched motionless on his shoulder. Strands of her windblown hair standing out from her head – not moving. Sean was right behind Lochen, his mouth open, ready to say something.

322

Quest of Eight Part Four: The Race to Virkio

Richard Reda

What was going on, Stella wondered. Before she could say or do anything, she was surrounded by a wall of light. It was six feet high and formed a circle more than ten feet in diameter around her. The wall cut through the stone ramparts and extended briefly out over the chasm between the towers.

It was as clear as water, but quite visible. She turned completely around to see the full circle. She looked up to the sky in an effort to locate its source. That was when she realized it was coming from her. More specifically, it was coming from the stone in her headband. She reached up to remove it, but it wouldn't come off.

"Hey," she shouted. "Can you see this?"

No one answered. No one moved. Nothing happened. She stopped trying to remove the headband.

"Hey," she shouted louder. "What's happening? What is this?"

She stepped forward and reached out tentatively to touch the partition. She felt a mild electrical tingle. It didn't hurt, but she jerked her hand back in surprise. When she realized nothing had happened, she reached out again. She felt the same tingling feeling and saw the glass-like sheet surrounding her shimmer slightly at her touch.

She pushed harder, but was unable to move it. She ran her hand down the wall to the stone floor. There was no room beneath it and it was much too high for her to climb over it. She looked back to her friends and saw that they hadn't moved at all. She looked back up at the sky. The snowflakes still hung suspended above her.

"Hey!" she shouted once more, unable to think of anything else. "Who's doing this?"

Then the flashes started. A bright yellow flash burst to her right and struck the clear wall near the top. She raised her arm to shield her

323

eyes. The bright light faded away and she brought her arm down. Near the top of the wall she could see some kind of image. It wasn't very distinct — more like when a bright light temporarily burns an impression on the retina of the eye.

It was blurred and floating, but she thought it looked like some kind of geometric shape above some squiggly lines. The more she stared at it the more she thought it looked familiar. But then she thought she was only imagining it. A few seconds later another flash struck. This one was near the bottom of the clear wall and closer to the front.

The flash itself was identical to the first one — an extremely bright yellow burst of light. The image, however, that it left behind was different. The geometric shape was the same, but the lines below it were different. The first ones had been softer, more curved or wavy. These were curled.

"I've seen this before," she said out loud.

She looked back at the first image that now looked more like an etching burned into the shimmering wall. It was clear like the wall itself, but she could see it. Then the third flash struck. This time the light exploded behind her. She spun around to see the image take shape almost at the top of the wall, directly in back of her.

Once more the same geometric shape appeared over a series of lines. These lines were more stark — pointed. She looked back at the first apparition. It hadn't changed any more than before. She looked at the second one, and it, too, looked like an etching in the barrier. Then she looked back at the third burst. By now it was fading and sinking into the fabric of the wall — whatever that fabric was.

"That cave," she blurted out. "That's where I've seen these images. They were carved into the wall in that cave Quinn took us to."

324

Another flash exploded. This one was again in front of her, towards the top. As soon as the light began to dim, she recognized it. It looked like the tree symbol that was one of the markings on the wall in that Ice Kingdom cave.

"What does this mean?" she shouted into the air, hoping, but not really expecting an answer.

As the fourth image burned into the wall, a fifth flash burst, once more behind and to Stella's right. Nearly centered from the top to the bottom of the wall, she could make out a symbol similar to the small circles that Quinn believed represented the stars and the planets.

"Is this some kind of map?" Stella asked.

Another burst of light appeared – high and to her left. Another image she recognized from the Ice Kingdom. She began to get frustrated. She was certain that these images were related to the images carved on the cave wall, but couldn't unravel the meaning of why they were appearing here or what they meant.

She stepped up to the wall and beat on it with the palms of both hands. The barricade shook only slightly, moving not an inch. She pushed her shoulder against it with no different result. She felt all around, up to the stone rampart where the clear wall crossed over the gap and back again. There was no opening.

Another flash of light burned another image. This one was in the section of the wall that extended out past the rampart. She walked back to the edge and looked over the stone to see where the partition ended. It seemed to drop all the way down to the bottom of the gorge.

"This is nuts," she muttered.

Quest of Eight Part Four: The Race to Virkio

Richard Reda

Her initial anxiety was quickly turning to rage. She kicked at the bottom of the field, even though she knew it wouldn't have any effect. She jumped up to swipe at the snowflakes that still hung immobile in the air. Her hand passed through them.

"What the...?" she muttered, suddenly shocked.

She hadn't touched or felt or moved the snowflakes in the least.

"That's not possible," she said.

She jumped again and swung her arm. She was certain she had leaped high enough to hit them. She looked down at the snow accumulated at her feet. None of it had moved. There were no footprints other than those that were made before the wall appeared. Why didn't I notice this before, she asked herself.

She kicked at the snow. Her foot passed through without making contact. She bent down to scoop it in her hands. They slid through with no effect.

"Am I dead?" she said.

"Am I dead?" she shouted at the sky.
Another flash of light hit the wall. Another image made its mark.

"Answer me!" she screamed. "What's going on?"

One final blast of light added one last image to the other seven that were scattered in no discernable pattern on the clear circular field. It was then that Stella remembered the other place she had seen these symbols.

"The band," she said. "They were on that band in the citadel where Ena Ray was imprisoned."

The band that Summer had snuck away from him. The band that Stella and the others grasped to escape the citadel and placed on the door to the portal that confined the gargoyles. As this revelation was dawning on her, more lines began to appear on the wall. It was, indeed, a map.

Stella stared at the symbols and the various markers and terrain features that surrounded each of them. Soon she felt her eyes begin to ache. She closed them and rubbed them with her fingertips. Before she opened them again, she saw an exact replica of the wall outlined in her vision.

At first she thought it was the effect of the bright light. She kept her eyes closed, waiting for the markings to disappear. Instead, they became sharper. She found she could look from one symbol to the next and then back again. She opened her eyes. The wall was still there, but the markings were fading.

She closed her eyes once more. The images were as vivid as before. She shifted her internal gaze from the first one – the geometric shape, which she now understood was a triangle, and the waving lines, which, as Quinn had indicated, represented air. She could see distinct indications of landmarks and other guides that gave hints to a specific location.

"What does all this mean?" she shouted.
She could see mountains begin to form in the images seared into her mind's eye. She could see rivers, oceans, shorelines, and lakes. She could see open expanses that might have been deserts or fields – it was hard to tell. She could see areas that looked like they were forests. She opened her eyes once more. The wall was still shimmering around her, but the markings were disappearing.

She closed her eyes again. The map, or whatever it was, was still very plain. She tried to study every inch of it, every marking, every location, every feature. She didn't know what any of it meant, but thought it might be one more of the Alchemist's spells, and she was afraid the images would disappear from her internal vision.

"I don't understand any of this," she wailed.

"Any of what?" asked Sean. "It seems pretty simple to me. We pull ourselves across the bridge to get to the top of tower five and start looking for another piece of that stone. Isn't that what this has all been about?"

Her eyes popped open. Natalie had one foot on the bridge, her hands on the rope and her other foot poised in the air ready to plant. She turned to look back at Stella, wondering why she would ask such an odd question.

Lochen had his arms raised, helping Natalie keep her balance as she stepped out onto the edge of the wall and placed one foot on the bridge. He stopped what he was doing and turned back towards Stella. He nearly bumped his nose into Summer, who was perched on his shoulder, the wind whipping her hair.

"Oops," he said to her. "Sorry about that. I forgot you were there."

"That's all right," said Summer. "I'll get back into the hood."

"I beg your pardon," he said to Stella. "I'm not sure what you're referring to. What don't you understand?"

Stella stared at them blankly, and then looked up to see the snow falling on her face. She spun around looking for any signs of the wall that had surrounded her seconds ago. She moved to the edge of the roof and peered over the side, then turned back again.

"Didn't you see that?" she asked.

"See what?" they all asked.

"That partition, that...that...wall, or whatever it was. It was all around me. You were all motionless. There were flashes of light. They burned images into the wall and those images were the same ones on the wall in the cave in the Ice Kingdom and on the band Summer stole from Ena Ray. Didn't you see any of it?"

"Are you all right?" asked Lochen as he moved away from Natalie and over to where Stella was standing.

"Yes," she snapped. "I'm fine. Of course you didn't see it. Did you? You didn't see anything? Right?'

"When did you see all this?" asked Sean.

"Just now," she answered. "For the last twenty minutes, maybe more. It was right here!"

"For the last twenty minutes, we've been crossing this hunk of ice," Natalie answered. "What are you talking about?"

"Hey," shouted Liam from the other side. "Is anything wrong?"

"Just a minute," Natalie answered. Then she turned back to Stella. "What happened? Explain it to us."

Stella took a few minutes to give them a shortened version of what she saw. As she was describing it, she reached up and touched the stone in her headband. As soon as she did, she stopped talking and a strange look fell across her face.
"What is it?" asked Natalie. "What just happened?"

"It's not there," she answered. "The stone. It's not there. Someone has already taken it."

"Who?" asked Lochen. "How?"

"I don't know," she said. "I only know that it's gone."

"So, what now?" asked Sean. "We did all this for nothing? Are we supposed to go back with...what? And where do we go back to?"

"No," said Lochen. "We keep going. This may be part of the spells. We can't know for certain."

"It's not part of the spells," said Stella. "But you're right. We need to keep going. There may be some clue over there that will tell us what to do next. But I _do_ know for certain. The stone is gone."

Lochen was not convinced she was right, but even if she was, there may also be a clue as to who took it and where he, she or they went with it. He turned back to Natalie and motioned for her to start crossing.

"Regardless of whether the stone is gone or not," he said, "there's nothing for us here. We need to join the others. We can still look around."

He looked back over his shoulder at Stella and continued.

"I'm sure you're right, but we can't afford to take that chance."

"No need to make excuses," she told him. "I'd do the same thing if I were you. And you're right. We shouldn't be separated from each other for too long. Besides, we may find a simpler way back once we're on that tower."

Lochen doubted that very much. He didn't think there would be any easy way back, but he kept his thoughts to himself. He turned back to Natalie.

"Be careful, Your Highness," he said. "Hold on tightly."

Natalie took one more uncertain look at Stella, and then began to make her way across the bridge to the other side. She stopped several times as gusts of wind shook the rope and made her passage even more slippery. In the end, she made it without any mishap, allowing Liam and Quinn to help her down.

Lochen motioned for Stella to go next. She didn't need any encouragement. He helped her up onto the wall and watched as she slid up the slender ramp, pulling the rope, to the other end. Once she was safely across, he turned to Sean.

"There's no need for you to go last," he said. "I'm more than happy to go after you."

"Thanks," answered Sean, "but I kind of like being the tail end of the parade. Go ahead."

Lochen nodded, and then stepped up onto the wall. He was about to begin his crossing, when Sean shouted a question to him.

"Should I untie the rope," he asked, "and bring it with me when I come? Or should I just leave it here?"

Lochen looked back towards Quinn and the others, trying to decide. The rope had turned out to be very useful. If they left the rope in place, and found another way down, either someone would have to go back to untie it, or they'd have to leave it behind. On the other hand, if Sean untied it and brought it with him, and there was no other way back, Quinn would have to make his way down the thin bridge with no support at all.

Weighing the options, and considering his own suspicions that there would be no easy way back, other than returning across this bridge, he decided it was better to leave it in place.

"Leave it tied," he called to Sean. "Just in case."

"OK," Sean replied.

He watched as Lochen pulled himself along the rope and up the slope. Even something this simple he managed to make look complicated. Several times he pulled his feet well ahead of the rest of his body, ending up leaning backwards in a precarious position. Then he somehow managed to twist himself nearly completely around.

It took him almost twice as long to cross as it did everyone else. In the end, he had lowered himself to the bridge, straddling it and facing back towards Sean. How is that even possible, wondered Sean. The others were close enough to grab him and pull him onto the roof. Then it was time for Sean to cross.

As he stepped up onto the rampart, he had an eerie feeling of being watched. He turned back to the tower four roof and looked around. The snow was coming down heavily and his vision was somewhat obscured, but he could see clearly enough that there wasn't any place to hide – or so he thought.

He didn't see any movement or any shapes other than the snow that had drifted up against the rampart along the top of the tower. You must be imagining things, he told himself. This whole place is way too spooky. He was going to be glad when they all got out of there. He turned back to tower five and quickly scampered across the thin track of ice to the other side.

A few seconds after he arrived on tower five, some of the piles of snow furthest away from the bridge began to break apart. The hobgoblins hidden there shook the snow off and slowly stood up. They moved around the parapet, alerting the others that the time had come. More than a dozen, who had been left behind, gathered in the center of the roof. The one who had been designated as their leader crept over to the bridge.

He studied the rope and saw that it was still secured to the opposite side. He motioned for the others to join him. They crowded around, surveying their targets.

"How nice of them to leave us a rope," said one of them. "We can all cross at once."

"It should be a simple job," another said. "A quick toss over the side and we're done."

Chapter sixteen

*T*he snow that had been falling relentlessly over the other towers seemed to stop at the end of the ice bridge. The roof of tower five was completely clear. The sky above was a deep gray, heavy with cloud cover, making visibility limited. Once Sean arrived, everyone was clustered together, unsure of what to do next.

"What exactly are we looking for?" asked Quinn.

"A piece of stone," answered Stella. "Like the one in my headband – maybe smaller. I'm not sure exactly."

She didn't see any point in voicing her belief that the stone was no longer here. In spite of Lochen's opinion that she could be wrong, she knew she wasn't. Still, there may be clues as to where the other pieces might be, or, she hoped, an easier way down from here.

There was little light by which to see. Everyone took tentative steps away from the end of the bridge, not sure of where to go or look. Stella, convinced the stone was gone, walked idly towards the left, along the wall, looking over the side more than anywhere else. Natalie, sensing something was bothering her, followed close behind.

Lochen went in the opposite direction, staying close to the wall that ran around the outer edge of the roof. He noticed some large containers spaced at regular intervals. He thought this was too obvious a place to secure the missing stone, but was intrigued by the containers. He walked towards the closest one, as the night soon began to obscure the others. Summer, still covered in the folds of his hood, was, more or less, a captive audience.

Solveig walked towards the center of the roof, and Liam, Quinn and Sean, at a loss for where else to look, followed her in a clump. The top of tower five was a circle, like all the others. This one was the largest – about fifty feet across. The opposite side was too far away to be seen clearly in the dimming light. Night was falling, and the darkness was settling over the roof of the tower like a blanket.

As Solveig and her followers moved further towards the center, they began to spread out slightly. It was so dark that none of them wanted to venture too far from the others. One of them was looking at the stone floor; one was looking around the roof, his vision sweeping left and right, searching for any signs of danger' and the third was looking up at the sky, marveling at the lack of snowfall on this tower.

Stella stopped walking after a few seconds and gazed out into the darkness. Natalie came up next to her. She turned back towards the others and couldn't see anything more than ten feet away. When she was sure there was no one close by, she spoke to Stella in a hushed voice.

Quest of Eight Part Four: The Race to Virkio

Richard Reda

"You're convinced the stone is gone, aren't you?"

"Yes," Stella replied.

"Did you see something? You were acting pretty strange back there."

"Stranger than normal, you mean?" Stella asked with a smirk.

"You know what I mean," answered Natalie, refusing to be baited.

"No," said Stella. "In answer to your question. I didn't see anything about the stone itself. It's just that I could feel the pull of it all the way to these towers. That feeling faded once we were inside the first one. I just thought it was because of the spells."

"When did you become certain?"

"I guess it was when you were crossing the ice bridge and that...whatever it was, appeared. I knew then that the sensation I no longer had wasn't because of the spells. It was because someone else got here first."

"You're sure it was here in the first place?"

Natalie reached over and took Stella's arms in her hands, turning her to look into her eyes.

"Yes," Stella answered without hesitation. "I'm more certain than ever. It was here and now it's not."

"Is there another piece, or was the one that was here all that was left?"

Stella thought for a few seconds before answering.

"Yes," she said with conviction. "There is another piece; but I have no idea where it is."

"What about that vision or map – whatever you saw before we crossed over here?"

"No," Stella said, shaking her head. "I still don't understand what that was all about, but I know it had nothing to do with either piece of the stone."

"Do you remember exactly what you saw?"

"Yes. It's as clear as crystal – burned in my memory. If I close my eyes, I can see every detail, as if the images were right in front of me. I just don't know what they mean."

"It seems to me that it's information of some kind that we may need later on."

"When?" Stella said in frustration. "We need a clue of some kind now!"

"What we need now is to gather as much information as we can and get out of here. I have a bad feeling about this place."

"Me, too," said Stella, relieved that she wasn't the only one with the sense of foreboding.

While Stella and Natalie were deep in their conversation, Lochen had wandered over to the nearest container. It was tall, coming up to just below his chest, and round – about a foot or so across. The container seemed to be made of stone, looking like a large vase – narrow at the bottom, widening out higher up, and then tapering in at the top.

As he approached the urn he saw it was filled with some kind of liquid that came up to about three or four inches from the rim. It was a pale blue in color, and iridescent. He carefully lowered his head towards the top. He felt Summer crawl forward on his shoulder.

"I would suggest that you keep back," he said to her. "I am uncertain as to the properties of this substance. I am aware of some potions that have particularly potent and damaging aromas. It might be best to exercise some caution."

Wordlessly, she wiggled backwards and lowered her head to his shoulder, peeking forward to see what he was doing. He waved one hand across the top of the vase, pulling the air towards him. He took a careful sniff.

"Interesting," he said.

"What's interesting?" asked Summer.

"It has an unusual odor. I smell a distinct presence of sulfur, but it seems to be tinged with a faint air of copper. Most unusual. And something else I can't quite identify."

He waved his hand again, sniffing the wisp of air that he moved towards his nose. He straightened up, lost in thought. After a few seconds of silence, he bent forward again, this time a little closer and waved the air over the vat towards him once more.

"Definitely copper," he said. "And something else. I've smelled this before, but where?"

While Lochen was trying to discern the substance in the container, Solveig had moved further towards the center of the roof. Her foot brushed up against something and she heard it skitter across the stone a few feet in front of her. She bent over to see what it was. Hunched over, she stepped from left to right, scanning the floor. Then she saw what she had kicked.

It was a long, curved object. It appeared to be broken at one end and pointed at the other. It glistened with a color like a rare and beautiful pearl – milky white with a subtle blue hue. She reached down and her hand hesitated for a second before she picked it up. It was silky smooth to the touch.

She raised it in the air to see it better, holding it like a knife with the pointed end down. In fact it looked exactly like a knife, she thought. It was about nine inches long, and she could see that the point was very sharp. She turned to show it to whomever was closest to her.

She saw Sean a few feet away from her and she heard alarms ringing in her head. A sudden sense of danger flared up inside her. Without knowing why, she looked down at his feet. Immediately in front of him was a pool of an odd looking silver substance.

"Beware the blood of the dragon," she heard the old woman's voice as clearly as if she were standing next to her.

"Stop," she shouted to Sean. "Don't step in that."

Sean jerked to a stop, startled by the sudden noise. He looked down in front of him and saw the edge of the puddle of silver. Forgetting the object in her hand, she subconsciously stuffed it into one of the pockets in her cloak.

"Why?" he asked. "What is it?"

"I don't know," Solveig answered, "but I think it's dragon's blood."

"Dragon's blood?" repeated Quinn. "I thought dragons were only imaginary. Are you playing a trick on us?"

"Beware the blood of the dragon," she could hear the old woman say.

"No," she answered. "I'm not playing a trick, and no, they're not imaginary."

Liam walked over to where Sean was standing and squatted down next to the edge of the pool. He studied the liquid for a second or two. Then he looked back at the others.

"I don't know about dragon's blood, but the blood of some creatures can be more dangerous than the creature itself. There are some things in the Swamp that could...well, I'll just say, it's better to avoid them at all costs."

He pulled a knife from his belt and scraped the tip of the blade through the fluid. The point began to crackle and crystallize. The frost crept up the blade to the handle and kept moving. Liam quickly dropped the knife before the freezing reaction reached his fingers. The knife froze, turned to crystal and shattered in seconds.

"Oh, poop," was all Quinn – or any of them – could say.

"Where did this stuff come from?" asked Sean.

He followed the edge of the puddle back towards its source. The area of the pool widened out and then narrowed again. All four of them were following it. A few yards away they saw the neck and then the body of the dragon.

"Oh, poop," Quinn repeated.

"Oh, poop is right," echoed Solveig.

At the same moment that Solveig and her entourage discovered the body of the slain dragon, Lochen was putting the pieces of his puzzle together. He had waved the aroma of the liquid in the urn towards himself several times, but hadn't been able to identify the other scents. Finally, against his better judgment, he bent his head closer, mere inches from the liquid, and sniffed.

"Was that a good idea?" asked Summer, who had to hold on tight to his cloak to keep from being dropped into the canister. "Next time give me a little warning."

"Sorry," he responded absentmindedly. "It's difficult to get past the aroma of the sulfur and the copper. I should know what this is, but I can't identify...yes...I knew it! It's potassium nitrate and mercury! Of course there are some other ingredients that can't be produced by people. That's what makes it unique."

"That's what makes what unique?" asked Summer.

"I knew I had come across this before," he continued, reveling in the fact that he had finally figured out what was in the urns.
"Wonderful," said Summer in a voice tinged with sarcasm. "I'm happy for you. Really. What does this have to do with finding the stone? I thought that's what we were here for; not to smell some stinky blue stuff."

"I suppose it doesn't have anything to do with finding the stone," said Lochen defensively. "But it is really a rather unusual discovery."

"I can hardly contain myself," mumbled Summer. "So, what is it?"

Her question focused him on what he had discovered. Her question also made him realize the danger of what he had discovered. This realization descended over him like a cloud. He looked at the urn, and then back towards where the others were last seen.

"We need to get out of here!" both he and Solveig shouted at the same instant.

The sudden shouts startled Stella and Natalie. They turned towards the voices, unable to see anyone else through the thickening darkness. Stella turned towards Solveig's voice which was coming from the center of the roof. Natalie turned towards Lochen's voice, which was coming from somewhere along the wall.

"Follow the wall," Natalie shouted.

She grabbed Stella's hand to keep from getting separated. The two of them walked in quick strides, keeping close to the wall, heading back towards the bridge.

"What is that thing?" shouted Sean.

He was too startled by Solveig's sudden shout to have heard Lochen. His eyes were fixated on the corpse in front of him.

"What is that thing?" he repeated.

"It's a dragon," Solveig whisper-shouted at him. "We need to get out of here."

She jerked his arm to get him to stop staring at the body. Then she noticed that Liam and Quinn were zeroed in on it, too. She reached over and pulled on both of them as well, trying to get them all to turn away and head back to the bridge.

"Stop staring at it," she whisper-shouted again. "We have to move."

"If it's dead," said Liam, "why do we have to leave? And why are you whispering? I don't think it can hear you, and it won't matter if it can."

"Because its mother may be nearby," snapped Solveig pulling and pushing each of them.

"Its mother?" shouted Quinn in disbelief. "You mean there may be something bigger than that around?"

342

"Yes," shouted Solveig, now giving up all efforts at being quiet.

Not being able to see exactly where they were, they moved in the wrong direction, heading away from Lochen and Summer, and in the complete opposite direction of Stella and Natalie.

"Watch out for that blood," warned Sean.

"Oh, poop," shouted Quinn.

He immediately veered off in a different direction, oblivious of whether or not he was running towards or away from the pool of dragon's blood. He was out of sight before Solveig could stop him. She grabbed Sean and Liam before they could get away and held them in place.

"Wait a minute," she ordered, holding their sleeves tightly. "Lochen, where are you?"
Lochen heard Solveig's voice and started to walk towards her, but then stopped.

"I'm here," he answered. "We should stay where we are," he added to Summer.

"But you just said we had to get out of here," she argued. "What is that stuff? Why do we need to get out of here? What's going on?" The panic in her voice rising.

"Lochen" shouted Natalie. "We're following the wall back to the bridge."

"As will I," he answered. "Solveig, did you hear that?"

"Yes," she answered. "I have Sean and Liam with me, but Quinn wandered off."

"No I didn't," he shouted back. "I'm here. Only, I don't know where here is."

He was walking with his arms outstretched, moving in circles, trying to find his way back. Natalie and Stella found the wall where the rope was tied across the bridge and stopped. In a few seconds Lochen and Summer returned.

"What's going on?" Natalie asked. "What happened?"

"We're not safe here," Lochen answered. "I found a large vat filled with a blue liquid. Solveig," he shouted again. "Where are you?"

In a few seconds Solveig, Sean and Liam emerged through the darkness. Quinn was still nowhere in sight.

"Will somebody please tell me what's going on?" demanded Summer.

"There was a body back there," stammered Sean.

"A body?" shouted Summer. "Who was it?"

"Not who," corrected Liam. "What! It was the body of a dragon."

"Lochen!" shouted Summer. "How did you know there was a dragon's body   out   there?"

"I didn't," he answered.

"Then what frightened you?"

"It was the substance in the vat," he answered.

"That blue stuff?" asked Stella.

"You saw it, too?" asked Lochen.

"Yes," she answered. "I saw a number of them lined up along the wall. I assumed they went all the way around the roof. Why? What's in them?"

"Beware the dragon's breath," Solveig could hear the old woman's voice.

"Dragon's breath," she and Lochen said at the same time.

Lochen looked at her, surprised.

"Yes," he said. "How did you know?"

"It's a long story," she answered. "But I don't know what it means."

"What's dragon's breath?" asked Liam.

"It's an extremely volatile substance," said Lochen. "I don't know anyone who has actually made it or used it. I remember seeing a very small sample years ago when I was first learning the sorcerer's craft. It's quite remarkable, actually."
"What's so remarkable about it?" asked Sean. "Does it smell bad or something?"

"Well," said Lochen, "it has a very distinctive odor, predominantly sulfur with a mix of copper, but it's not the aroma that makes it remarkable. It burns."

"Big deal," said Sean. "So it burns."

"But the natural reaction to the fire it ignites," explained Lochen, "is to throw water on it. Water only makes it burn stronger. Water won't put it out."

They all looked skyward. Even in the darkness, they could feel the moisture in the air. The snow that had been falling heavily throughout

345

most of their journey was only inches away, on the other side of the wall surrounding the tower.

"We need to find Quinn and get out of here," announced Solveig. "I'll go look for him. The rest of you start going back across the bridge."

"Do you think it's wise for us to separate?" asked Natalie.

"We're already separated," Solveig answered. "Quinn's out there somewhere. Look. This roof isn't all that big. If he hasn't stepped into the pool of dragon's blood, he should be all right."

"Dragon's blood?" exclaimed Summer. "There's a dragon bleeding somewhere?"

"No," answered Liam. "It's dead. At least we assume it's dead. Its head was cut off."

"What?" shouted Natalie.

"There's a dead dragon somewhere near the middle of the roof," said Sean. "As long as you don't step in the blood, it's all right."

"You're right," Stella said to Lochen. "We need to get out of here and quickly."

"Yes," he said. Turning to Solveig, he added, "Please be careful. Find Quinn as quickly as you can. I'll see that the others begin to cross back to the other tower, but I won't leave without you."

"I'll do what I can," she answered. "But if I'm not back in ten or fifteen minutes, you have to go without me. Is that clear?"

"Yes," he answered. "It's clear, but I won't agree to it. We can argue later. Go find Quinn."

Solveig wanted to finish the argument, but instead turned around and slowly made her way into the darkness, calling out Quinn's name. Lochen gathered everyone else together and herded them to the bridge.

"Sean," he said. "I would be grateful if you would go first. You are the most agile. Clear the snow off the bridge as you cross to make it as safe as possible for the rest of us."

"You've got it," Sean responded.

He jumped up onto the ledge and was about to grab the rope, when he noticed it was moving. At first he thought it was merely the wind, but the movement seemed too regular. He put his hand out and touched it without putting any pressure on it. The vibrations were regular – too regular to be the wind.

He looked down the bridge. By now the night had settled and the darkness was all encompassing. He could only see about fifteen feet in front of him. He gently grasped the rope and slowly and carefully eased his way forward. He heard them before he saw them.

He could make out heavy breathing as the hobgoblins pulled themselves up from tower four. Then the first one broke through the darkness. Fortunately, he was busy watching his feet as he slid up the bridge. Sean backed away and leaned against the rampart. He turned back towards the others and motioned for them to keep quiet.

He inched ahead again, squatting down to make himself as small as possible. At that moment, there was a break in the clouds and a narrow ray of moonlight burst through, lighting up the bridge. Sean nearly fell over. He could see a line of hobgoblins pulling themselves up the bridge. The line disappeared into the black of the night. He jumped off the bridge.

Richard Reda

"We've got company," he announced to the others. "And I don't think they're welcome company."

Lochen and Liam ran to the edge of the wall. By now they could see the line of hobgoblins as they approached closer and closer. They were carrying crossbows, swords, and axes. Sean was right. This was not a welcome sight.

"Can you cut the rope?" Lochen asked Liam.

"Yes, but I don't think that will stop them," he answered.

In spite of this, he leaned forward to cut the rope. A crossbow arrow whizzed past his head, narrowly missing him. He backed away quickly.

"That was close," he said.

"Cutting it might not be useful anyway," said Lochen. "They're probably the ones who killed the dragon and they didn't have a rope to get up here then."

"Good point," Liam responded, glad to have an excuse not to try again. "We have to think of something else. Sean. Can you take them out with your slingshot?"

"I could if I had any stones," he replied. "I don't have anything to shoot at them."

"We better act fast," said Stella. "They're only a few feet away."

Lochen didn't waste any further time debating with himself the potential ramifications. He ran over to the nearest vat of dragon's breath.

"Help me move this," he said. "And be very careful."

Liam ran over and the two of them began to gently roll and slide the urn. The liquid inside sloshed close to the top, but they managed to keep any from spilling. They moved it to the opening at the end of the bridge. With one single, fluid motion, they lifted the bottom and poured the contents down the bridge.

It didn't disperse like normal liquids. It slowly seeped down the ice, flowing over the sides and adhering to the bottom. Nothing dripped off. Instead, it seemed to be absorbed into the ice itself. They waited, watching as the last of the mixture oozed out of the vat and down the bridge.

"Why isn't it igniting?" Sean asked, no longer whispering.

The lead hobgoblin was only a few feet away. He heard Sean's voice and looked up to see five faces staring at him. No, he said to himself. There were six. One of them was a faerie, perched on the shoulder of one of the others. He smiled widely, but it was anything but a friendly smile.

"I don't know," said Lochen. "I don't remember what we did with it in sorcerer's class."

Liam pushed his way to the front, pulling another knife from a sheath attached to this leg.

"Don't be foolish," Stella said, pulling his arm. "You can't fight them."

"I'm not planning on fighting them," he said.

He swung the blade of the knife downward, scraping it against the stone wall, bringing it down immediately in front of the bridge. A spark flew from the edge of the blade and jumped onto the trailing line of the blue liquid. The initial burst of flame was so powerful that it blew Liam back several feet and singed his eyebrows.

It also consumed the lead hobgoblin. It happened so fast, he didn't know what hit him and he dropped over the side in a ball of flame. The second one in line began pushing backwards down the bridge, but the others couldn't move fast enough, and number two was quickly engulfed in the blaze. Those at the end of the line could see what was happening and jumped back to the safety of the roof of tower four. Most of them escaped the fire as it roared down the bridge. As the heat melted the ice, the blaze intensified. Soon, the sky itself was on fire, as the dragon's breath was fueled by the giant flakes of snow falling from the clouds.

The inferno grew and grew, reaching higher and higher into the sky, changing the darkness to near daylight. It took on the form of a hungry animal, devouring the bridge and leaping to the massive drifts of snow on the roof of tower four.

Within seconds, the entire tower resembled a giant torch. The top of the torch was lost in the rampaging fire that was lighting up the sky. Those on the roof of tower five watched in shock and amazement. The fire was sucked down into the tower and burst up again, renewed by some unseen fuel. Then it would disappear deep into the tower once again, only to rise like a Phoenix bird from its own ashes, soaring into the sky, igniting a fresh supply of snowflakes.

The six spectators watched, mesmerized, as the scene repeated itself several more times before finally coming to completion. When it was over, the heat that rose into the air dissipated many of the clouds, opening up the sky to the moonlight. Beacons of light shown on the remains of tower four.

The roof appeared to be gone completely. Much of the battlement surrounding the roof had broken away and fallen to the bottom of the ravine. All that could be seen were charred stones on the far side that disappeared into the depths of the hollowed out shell.

Quest of Eight Part Four: The Race to Virkio

Richard Reda

The bridge from tower four to tower five was gone. Barely more than the landing at the top where it connected to tower five remained. The rope that Liam had carried for so long had evaporated. Little was left beyond the knot that tied it to the top of the tower.

"I guess we won't be going back that way," said Sean.

"How astute," replied Lochen.

He stared at the damage, actually hoping that the tower and the bridge would somehow magically reappear. It made sense to him. This was all an illusion, he reasoned. Sean had told them that the wooden bridge had reappeared, and that the broken slats in the chain bridge seemed to regenerate. Why not this one?

"So, how exactly are we getting back?" asked Summer.

"I don't know," Lochen replied. "I'm sure there must be some kind of access through the roof. At least I hope so."

As the fire had been raging, it had provided some additional light for Solveig as she searched for Quinn. She had made her way back to the body of the dead dragon, although she wasn't sure how she did that. She hadn't realized in the dark how enormous the dragon had been. She hoped there wasn't another one nearby.

When the flames burst up behind her, she initially turned around and thought about heading back. She caught herself realizing that there probably wasn't anything she could do, and continued her search for Quinn. At least the light helped her to see where she was going and, if nothing else, to avoid stepping in the spilled dragon's blood. She hoped Quinn had managed to steer clear of it.

A few minutes later, she found him. He was on his hands and knees, near the far side of the tower roof, up against the wall. It looked like he had dropped something and was searching for it. He seemed oblivious to her approach.

"Are you all right," she called to him.

He jerked his head up, but didn't get to his feet.

"Yeah," he answered. "I'm fine."

"What are you looking for?" she asked.

"Stella was right," he said. "The stone is gone. I think it was here somewhere. I can't tell for sure, but I get this really weird feeling. Come here. Feel for yourself."

She walked to where he was and even before she got down on the floor, she could sense something powerful. A tingling sensation rose up through her feet and through her body. Not only could she feel that the stone had been here, she knew, as well as Stella – and now Quinn – that it was gone: taken by someone else.

The firelight was beginning to fade. She reached down and pulled Quinn to his feet.

"We need to get moving. We aren't going to have much light left from whatever is burning. I don't want to get stuck here in the pitch dark."

"OK," he responded. "What was that, anyway? It looked like some kind of explosion."

She thought about telling him of the dragon's breath, but noticed several other urns along the walls. They appeared every ten feet. This whole place is a potential bon fire, she thought.

"I don't know," she answered. "But knowing Lochen, I'm sure he had something to do with it."

As the light continued to fade away, she tried to fix in her mind where the fire was so that when it disappeared altogether, she'd be headed in the right direction. As they neared the carcass of the dragon, she made sure to side step the puddle of blood. In the last glimmers of the firelight, she was certain she could see some kind of movement reflected in the surface of the pool.

She slowed down as they were walking past it. The top layer looked like it was quivering. She was watching it closely. The combination of the dying embers of the fire, the moonlight falling behind the clouds that were reshaping in the sky, and the motion of the wind seemed to make the substance almost radiate. The silver color sparkled. She stopped and looked more intently.

"Uh, what are you doing?" asked Quinn. "I don't think we should stop, do you?"

She was certain she could see something moving in the reflection in the blood. And then she felt a rush of wind coming from above her, and she heard a deep, low flapping noise. She looked up and instead of seeing the black of the sky, she saw a blue-white image grow and grow and grow.

"We need to get moving," said Quinn, pulling her hand.

He stared up at the image that soon blotted out the sky. He slowly backed away, unaware that Solveig wasn't moving with him. In seconds, the image took shape. It was the largest beast he had ever seen: a giant, blue-white dragon. When the dragon was still several yards above the tower roof, it let out an ear-piercing screech. Quinn covered his ears in pain.

The others, who had been staring at the remains of tower four heard the same screech, and spun around, startled not only by the noise but also by the apparent pain communicated in the screech. They realized that Solveig and Quinn were in the direction of that horrible noise. They began moving towards it to find their friends.

Solveig was frozen in place, watching the dragon lower itself towards the tower roof. Its wings spread wide, extending from one side of the tower to the other. As its body descended, enormous talons reached out from its powerful hind legs preparing to land. Its front legs with equally treacherous talons were poised to attack or defend.

She stared in awe as the creature focused its gaze on her, pinpointing her position. The dragon screeched again. The others covered their ears as Quinn had, trying to block out the painful sound. All Solveig heard, instead of a screech as the beast dropped to the ground immediately in front of her, was a plaintive cry, "What have you done to my child?"

Chapter seventeen

B'nair had started running through the brush at the base of the mountain range at the same time Lochen had reached out to pull Summer back from the gust of wind that blew her nearly off the stone bridge leading to tower one. The small group of hobgoblins that made it out of Virkio was running with him. He had decided he had seen enough of underground passages, and preferred to be above ground.

After several hours they stopped to rest. He clutched the stone in his hand and could sense not only the location of the remaining lost piece, but also the location of the other portion, still worn in Stella's headband. He knew whatever power that was attached to this small gem would not be enough to combat or defeat whoever was in possession of the other pieces. He would deal with that after he found the part he was now in search of.

He was becoming frustrated by the time it was taking them. He wondered if he had been too rash in his decision to travel above ground. The terrain was becoming more difficult to cross. There was no path to follow and they had been blocked by rocks and impenetrable areas of thick brush.

"This is taking too long," he muttered angrily.

"There's another way," suggested the hobgoblin closest to him.

B'nair stopped and looked over at him.

"What's your name?" he demanded.

"Vardelos," the hobgoblin answered without hesitation.

"Show me," B'nair ordered.

He was led a short distance back the way they had come. Before B'nair could object, Vardelos turned towards the right and around a large rock outcropping. There was a narrow gap in the mountainside. He turned back to B'nair.

"In here," he said. "It will take us to another series of tunnels, but there won't be any obstacles in the way."

B'nair grumbled at the thought of going back underground, but welcomed the opportunity to make faster time. He didn't know if the team that had been left behind would be successful in disposing of whomever was following him and he was concerned that they would not only catch up, but would get ahead of him.

At first the tunnel was dark. A few feet in, though, Vardelos struck a flint and lit a torch that had been left behind by the original tunnelers. He began running, and B'nair and the others kept right behind him. About two miles into the tunnels, Vardelos was able to douse the fire from the torch. At first the sudden change in light startled B'nair.

"What are you doing?" he demanded. "We won't be able to see."

"Give your eyes a few seconds," Vardelos answered him. "They will adjust to the light within the passageway."

He was right. In a matter of a second or two, B'nair could see clearly. The light wasn't bright, but it was enough to allow him to see. He looked around the walls and ceiling for the source, expecting a single point of illumination. Instead, he saw thin veins that lined the rock walls. These veins were glowing. He had seen this before, but he couldn't recall where.

"What is this?" he asked in a less demanding tone.

"We don't know," Vardelos answered. "It seems to glow from within. But be careful not to touch it."

"Why?"

"When these tunnels were first excavated by our ancestors, there are stories of many of them disappearing without explanation. We first thought the mountains under which they were digging were cursed, but then it seemed that it was these lines that lit the darkness."

He looked back at B'nair and saw a look of skepticism on his face.

"That's the belief they had and handed down the generations. I don't know of anyone who actually believes it, but no one has had the courage or daring to test it. Long ago, there's a story of some who did, and they disappeared, too. Only one ever returned, and he couldn't explain what had happened to him."

That was when B'nair remembered where he had seen this stone before. There were larger pieces of it in the caves where he had overseen the mining the Trepans were doing before the disaster that cost him his hand and eye. Like a recurring bad dream, his memory of chasing that Dozor across a bridge that looked like this material, came rushing back to him.

He stopped running, a look of confusion on his face. The hobgoblins behind him stopped immediately, and Vardelos, turned back to join them.

"What's wrong?" he asked.

B'nair didn't answer immediately. He was trying to recall all the details of that incident. Too many pieces were missing. He couldn't remember why this stone was relevant.

"This one who returned," he said to Vardelos. "What did he say happened to him?"

"It's only a tale," he said, trying to deflect any importance from the story. "If it really happened at all, it happened a very long time ago."

B'nair fought to keep his impatience from controlling him. He tried to relax.

"I understand," he said as congenially as he could. "But tell me what you remember – anything might be helpful."

"Of course," answered Vardelos, still not completely comfortable. "He said he and a few others had been exploring these old passages. They saw the glowing stone and remembered the warnings about it. He said he made some off-hand comment about where the earlier miners had disappeared. He had stopped. The others with him were several feet ahead.

"He said he looked at the stone, and reached out to touch it. As he did this, he said he mumbled something to the effect that those miners probably hadn't disappeared; that they were probably sitting in a bar in Nohkmar Cambin. As he said this, he claimed he saw a flash of light and the next thing he knew, he was in a bar in Nohkmar Cambin."

"That's thousands of miles away," said B'nair.

"Yes, I know. I'm only telling you what he said. No one believed him. He claimed it was true and that it had taken him several months to get back. He was ordered to tell the truth. He swore he was. Eventually, he was arrested and tortured. He never changed his story."

"I need to think," B'nair told him.

He moved off by himself and sat on the floor of the tunnel. He looked at his burned hand, welded to the axe handle. Think, he told himself. What happened? He tried to recreate every step of the way. He had chased the Dozor. The Dozor shot stones at him, and eventually knocked him off the bridge.

He cracked his whip and snagged the Dozor's leg. He fell to one side of the stone bridge and the Dozor fell to the other. At that moment one of the Dozor's friends dived onto the bridge and kept him from being pulled over. B'nair remembered the feeling of the bridge's footing breaking loose. Something cut the whip and he fell.

He remembered looking up and seeing the stone slab with the Dozor and the other person on it falling after him. Then there was a flash of light and they were gone. No. There was something before that. The other person said something about wishing he was home. Then came the flash.

He stood up abruptly. He had heard of this substance. It could transport people great distances instantly. The question was, though, if these glowing veins were from the same substance. And, if it was, did only one person have to direct it to a location? The Dozor was held in the grasp of the other one.

"Grab hold of one another," he shouted.

The hobgoblins looked at him in confusion. Instead of doing as they had been ordered, they merely looked from one to the other; each waiting for someone else to make a decision.

"Do it," B'nair shouted even louder, pushing them towards each other. They fell into a rough line and held each other by the arm. Vardelos reached out and took the arm of the closest hobgoblin. B'nair then extended the arm that held the axe and motioned for Vardelos to take it. He looked back to the line to make sure everyone was tightly connected.

"Don't let go," he ordered.

He looked at Vardelos, sternly at first, and then he smiled.

"Do you trust me?" he asked.

"Yes," Vardelos answered after only a moment's hesitation.

B'nair smiled broadly. His smile had always been reptilian and far from endearing. The scarring on his face did nothing to improve this. A wave of fear crept through Vardelos. B'nair squeezed tightly and moved closer to the wall where one of the thicker veins of stone stood out. He shifted his gaze between the vein and the faces of the hobgoblins. Then he reached out with his free hand and placed it on the stone.

Quest of Eight Part Four: The Race to Virkio

Richard Reda

At the instant he did that, he closed his eyes and focused his thoughts on the image he had burned into the mind of Budala – a long deserted stronghold, far away and overgrown with vines and thorns. There was a flash of light, and a clap of thunder, and then they were all gone. The tunnel was empty.

Before any of them could react, their surroundings had changed instantaneously. They stood on the edge of a forest. In front of them was a huge wall. The wall extended in both directions and seemed to encompass several buildings of various sizes. The walls were covered with dead vines.

The vines were thick at the base and covered with very long and seemingly very sharp thorns. The vines had grown over the top of the wall and appeared to cascade down the other side. Between them and the wall was an old dirt road. The road led across a dried out moat, which was also filled with the dead vines.

A wide, wooden bridge spanned halfway across the moat. A large drawbridge had been lowered sometime in the distant past, to connect the bridge to the only break in the wall – the entryway to the village that the wall surrounded. Over time, the chains that raised and lowered the drawbridge had rusted and fallen away.

It was evident to the small group gathered not far away, that the drawbridge was no longer needed to keep everyone out. They could see inside that the entire village was overgrown with the same thorny vines that had climbed up over the wall and down inside. It was all dead; black and ominous. The ground around the outside of the wall, as well as what they could see leading into the stronghold, was nothing but blackened dust.

"Even the earth is dead," whispered one of the hobgoblins.

"Where are we?" asked another, not really expecting an answer.

Quest of Eight Part Four: The Race to Virkio

Richard Reda

B'nair tore his gaze away from the structure and looked at Vardelos.

"You can let go now," he said. "We're here."

"Yes," he answered, embarrassed as he released his grip on B'nair's arm. "But where is 'here?'"

More than five hundred years after the Alchemist found the piece of the pendant that he hid in the towers of Virkio, he discovered a second piece. Little is known of where and how he found it, but find it he did. He knew that he couldn't hide this one in the same place as the first. Even with all the spells and hexes he had placed in and around Virkio, in time they could be broken or bypassed. Whoever was able to do that would eventually find the stone hidden there.

The Alchemist knew he couldn't prevent it from falling into the wrong hands, and, therefore, he knew he couldn't afford to allow such hands to possess two pieces of the pendant. He realized he had to find a different and distant place to protect his second find. He gave this much thought.

He remembered that long before there had been a village that had suffered a devastating plague. The leaders of the village had closed their doors to the local people and had planted poisonous bushes around the outer wall to keep them away. The plague swept through the area, and many of the local people died. Those inside the walls of the fortress did nothing to help.

In the end, the plants they had nurtured to keep away those infected with the plague destroyed the land, the food, and the water supply of the village. In the end, all the steps they took to save themselves failed. In the end, they destroyed themselves.

He had come across this place at the beginning of the plague. He had worked long and hard to save the people who had been locked out of the stronghold – away from food, water, and medicines. He had begged the village leaders to open their doors. They refused. When the plague finally passed, most of the people exiled survived. No one inside the walls did.

Now that he was in need of a place to hide another piece of the pendant, he thought this offered an ideal location. He traveled through the forest until he came to the ruins of the fortress. It was locked up as tightly as it had been centuries before when he was last here. He thrust his arm forward, and the giant drawbridge lowered on its rusted chains. It slammed to the ground, snapping one of them. Not long after he left, the other chain eroded and broke away.

He looked in through the entryway and saw the desolation on the inside. The dead had long ago turned to dust and were now intermingled with the poisoned soil. Banners that once hung brightly and gaily from homes and shops now drooped – aged and rotted: markers of the death and destruction that this citadel now represented.

He stepped onto the bridge and peered through the nettles. He saw the perfect location at the end of the main road. He knew he wouldn't be able to make his way to this location without cutting away the dead brush, but he needed that brush to help conceal the stone.

He waved his arm, circling it around his body and raising it above his head. Dark green smoke engulfed him and he changed his form. As the smoke dissipated, he was transformed into a large dark green snake, covered in scales of steel. The scales would protect him from the thorns. Even though the brush was dead, the thorns were still filled with poison and a scratch could be fatal.

The piece of the pendant was held in the serpent's mouth as it slithered along the ground. Centuries of dust rose into the air, stirred by his passing. He wove in and out, not disturbing any parts of the venomous barrier until he reached his destination. Once there, he transformed himself into his original form, removed the stone from his mouth, and hid it in plain sight.

When he was satisfied, he returned to his serpent form and left the fortress. After he was back on the outside and back to being the Alchemist, he started to raise the drawbridge, securing the stronghold to its original condition, but then changed his mind. He thought the deception more complete if it appeared there was nothing within to hide. And then he was gone.

Close to fifteen hundred years later, someone had discovered the hiding place. B'nair and his team of hobgoblins stood on the bridge looking into the morass of vines and thorns and the decaying buildings inside the fortress.

"It's in there," announced B'nair.

"What is?" asked Vardelos.

"A stone like this one," he answered.

He pulled the remnant from a pocket inside his vest and opened his hand. The fragment was flat on his palm; the colors were more vibrant and the haze deep inside the stone was moving more noticeably. He closed his hand and could feel the presence of the missing piece.

"What do they do?" Vardelos asked.

B'nair turned to look at him, wondering why he wanted to know. He studied the hobgoblin's face, looking for some sign of treachery. Can he be trusted, B'nair asked himself. He decided to find out.

"They bestow a certain power on the holder," he answered. "But that's not why I'm searching for them."

Vardelos showed no sign that he was a threat to B'nair's leadership. He waited for B'nair to explain.

"They will release an even greater power, and that's what we are seeking, and why we need these stones."

"Then we should hurry," said Vardelos.

He began to cross the bridge until B'nair reached out and pulled him back.

"I'm sorry," he said.

He stepped back and motioned for B'nair to take the lead.

"I didn't mean to presume," he tried to explain.

"That's not why I stopped you," B'nair answered. "Look closely at those brambles. They may look dead. They may even be dead, but the thorns still carry a lethal poison. We need to proceed with caution."

He turned to the others and made sure they understood. Then he crossed the bridge and entered the stronghold. He swung his axe, cutting away a passage through the brush. He cut it widely, moving down the central road. As he hacked through the vines, he could feel the pull of the hidden stone get stronger and stronger.

After more than an hour, they had only gone about a third of the way into the fortress. B'nair swung his axe back and forth, lopping branches. Broken bits flew through the air. One such piece ricocheted off a nearby post and shot back towards the band of hobgoblins. The one standing behind Vardelos felt a mild sting as the splinter made a small cut across his cheek.

Quest of Eight Part Four: The Race to Virkio

Richard Reda

He thought nothing of it, merely brushing his face. B'nair kept cutting. He was relentless. He looked up and saw an old, dilapidated shop at the end of the road. It seemed an unlikely place to secure an item of such power, but the pull of the stone was unmistakable.

Another hour went by. B'nair was slowing down, but not by much. Some of the others pulled swords and axes and widened the opening he had been creating. The one with the scratch on his cheek began to feel hot and lightheaded. His legs were beginning to tire. Twice he had to sit on the ground to catch his breath and regain his strength. No one paid much attention to him.

By the time they reached the end of the road, and had cleared away enough of the brush to gain access to the shop, the scratch on the hobgoblin's face had turned black. His face was bathed in sweat. His eyes were red, his skin had a gray color, and he felt waves of blazing heat followed by fits of cold gripping his body.

When B'nair turned to his followers before entering the shop, he was struck by the cadaverous look on this one member. The others turned to look at what had caused him to appear shocked. Their comrade was a vision of death. He was shaking uncontrollably. His eyes rolled back in his head and a thick black foam spilled from his mouth as he fell to the ground.

"Back away from him," shouted Vardelos. "He's been infected."

"What has killed him will not pass to you," said B'nair. "He's been poisoned by these brambles. Let it be a caution to all of you. Stay clear of them."

He turned back to the shop, ordering them all to stay outside. He pushed the ancient door aside. It was eaten through with age and infested by parasites, nearly crumbling at his touch. The shop had belonged to a glass blower. Inside the shop were shelves filled with glasses, bowls, vases, and figurines.

B'nair stepped into the shop and carefully walked past the displays. The floor creaked beneath his feet, but held his weight. Dust covered everything; cobwebs filled every corner. Tools hung from the ceiling, and a large forge sat cold and idle at the back.

He walked to the ancient kiln and could still smell the ash from fires long dead. He looked to either side of the kiln and saw the glass blowing tools of the shop owner. Next to the tools were a number of barrels. Inside the barrels were bits and pieces of glass – discarded scraps and supplies for items that were never made.

The pieces varied in size, shape and color. In one of the barrels, at the top and along the side, sat one piece that would normally go unnoticed. This one, however, unlike the others around it, glimmered in the dim light. It looked as if there were a small cloud inside it, moving and flashing. B'nair smiled and then reached into the barrel to pick it up.

How clever, he thought, to hide it in plain sight. He put the piece on the top of a work bench and then reached inside his vest for the matching piece. He put it down on the bench a few inches away from the one he retrieved from the barrel. The two stones began to vibrate and then slid across the workbench towards one another.

With a bright red flash they collided and sealed themselves to each other. B'nair reached down and picked up one end. Where they joined together was very narrow. The gap between them looked jagged and widened as it extended from the point of contact. It looked to B'nair as if another piece would fit in this space. He immediately thought of those he believed were following him back at Virkio.

His thoughts were disrupted when he felt a change in the air. He didn't see anything immediately, but he could sense something was different. He looked outside, through the doorway. He saw Vardelos and the other hobgoblins. They were just standing there. Nothing looked out of the ordinary until he realized they were not moving at all.

"What's happening out there?" he shouted.

No one reacted. No one changed expression or position. What's going on, he wondered. He was about to go back out and teach them some respect, when he was suddenly surrounded by a wall of light. He jerked to a stop, looking right and left and then behind him. The wall rose from the floor to the ceiling and formed a circle around him more than ten feet in diameter.

It was a clear wall, identical to the one that had encompassed Stella. Although neither one of them knew it, this event was occurring at exactly the same time for both. B'nair studied the wall and then looked in his hand at the joined pieces of the pendant. This seemed to be the source of what he was seeing.

He tried to put the gem back down on the workbench, but he could not let go of the stone. It didn't feel like he was clutching the stone all that tightly, but he was unable to open his fingers and release it.

"Vardelos," he shouted. "Come here."

Nothing happened. The hobgoblin didn't move. B'nair grew angry and stepped forward, but his way was blocked by the shimmering wall. He felt a slight electrical charge and backed away.

"Vardelos," he again shouted, this time even louder.

Nothing happened. No one responded. In fact, no one moved at all. He looked more closely at the ones who were immediately outside of the shop. They looked to be frozen in mid-conversation. What's happening, he wondered.

"Answer me," he commanded. "What's going on? I know you can hear me."

He moved his axe towards the wall. He could feel the resistance and the same tingling sensation. He lifted his axe and swung. The blade sliced through the apparition as if it wasn't there. He felt a stronger surge of energy pass through his deadened hand and up his arm. It was uncomfortable, but not painful.

The path through the clear wall made by the axe disappeared in the same manner as if the axe had passed through water. He looked at the floor, and could see no space between it and the wall. He looked at the ceiling and could see no gap there, either. Then the flashes started.

The first one took him by such surprise that he nearly fell over in his effort to step away from it. A bright yellow burst of light struck the wall near the top and to his right. As the light faded away, he saw an image begin to take shape.

One by one the same markings that appeared to Stella were burned or etched into the barrier surrounding B'nair. The symbols that appeared initially meant nothing to him. They burst onto the barricade in a random order all around him.

"What does this mean?" he shouted. "What is doing this?"

In his frustration, he swiped the blade of his axe through one of the images. As before, the axe easily sliced through, meeting no resistance at all, and the image remained unmarked. B'nair reached forward with his other hand, the stone still clenched in his fingers. He pushed with all his strength. The wall gave only slightly, but he was unable to pass through.

Once the eight icons had been burned into the surface, other markings began to appear. These emerged without the flashes of light that had scored the symbols into the wall. Instead, they simply appeared to take shape. He started to see what looked like rivers and shore lines. For most of his life he had traveled to distant places. He was familiar enough with charts and maps to recognize the images and terrain features that gradually became evident.

His anger and frustration melted away and were replaced by fascination and curiosity. He could see mountains begin to form. He was unaware at the time that the images were slowly being burned into his mind's eye. He could see rivers, oceans, shorelines, and lakes. He could see open expanses that might have been deserts or fields. Some of the areas he was certain he had visited before.

His eye was starting to ache. He closed it for a second and could see the impressions that were now marking his retinas – not just the one that was still alive, but he was certain he could see the images in the one that was blind.

Stunned, he lifted the patch that covered his dead eye. Keeping the other one closed, he hoped he would find his vision returned. It had not. The only impressions visible to that eye were false. He lowered the patch and opened the other eye. The wall was still shimmering around him, but the markings were disappearing.

He closed his eye again. The image was as clear as it had been on the wall. When the images and markings were being etched into the barrier, he had been more focused on what was happening rather than what the markings meant. Now that they had disappeared and could be seen only in his mind, he wondered what they meant.

He kept his eye closed and took a minute to study the map. He didn't have to do anything other than think of another area for the chart to move. Something stirred in his memory. He recalled Ercon telling him of the stories of the hobgoblin ancestors; about the Enchantress and the Alchemist; about the wars with the Kelpies.

He began to put pieces of the stories and the histories together. The witch and the Alchemist had fought the Kelpies – separating them from one another and hexing them. B'nair played that thought over and over in his mind. Hexes and spells; not death or destruction. The legends always talked about hexes and spells.

"They're not dead," he said aloud.

"Who's not dead," a voice said, startling him out of his reverie.

B'nair's one good eye popped open to see Vardelos standing in the doorway to the shop. He spun around, looking at the workbench, the forge, the tables and shelves and the barrels of scraps. There was no indication of the wall or the lights or the images.

"What did you say?" he demanded.

Vardelos took a hesitant step backwards. His leader had entered the shop, looked around for a second, then closed his eye and uttered the words, "They're not dead." He had assumed B'nair was speaking to him, but he had no idea to whom he was referring.

"You said, 'they're not dead,'" he stammered. "I only asked you, 'who's not dead.'"

"How long have you been standing there?"

"I don't understand," Vardelos answered.

"You and the others," continued B'nair. "You were all standing outside the shop, waiting. I saw you. How long have you been standing inside this building? How much time has gone by?"

"We were following right behind you," he responded. "You walked in and looked around. You reached into one of those barrels. This all happened in seconds."

371

Quest of Eight Part Four: The Race to Virkio

Richard Reda

B'nair stared at him. How could all that he saw have taken place in mere seconds, he wondered. More hexes and spells, he decided. Vardelos continued to wait in silence. B'nair had learned long ago to trust no one. Although he didn't trust Vardelos, he sensed nothing that indicated the hobgoblin was lying.

"It's time to leave," he announced. "I have what we came for."

He brushed past Vardelos and exited the shop. He moved quickly past the others who had been standing outside. They all fell in line behind as B'nair led them through the path he had minutes before cut through the thicket. He moved silently with a sense of purpose unknown to his followers.

He marched them all out of the village, and out of the fortress. He stood for a few seconds on the bridge and looked around, seemingly getting his bearings. He heard a growling noise coming from the shadows in the forest just beyond the end of the bridge.

"We need to go," he said.

"But what of the others?" asked Vardelos. "The ones you sent Budala to gather. Will they know where we are going?"

B'nair had forgotten about them. He had instructed Budala to bring another fifty hobgoblins to join them. He could leave one of his company behind to wait for the new arrivals, he thought. Then he heard another growl. He didn't need to see the source. He recognized it: a jackal. Where there was one, there was sure to be a pack. Anyone he left behind would soon fall prey to them. Leaving one behind would be nothing more than a death sentence.

The transporter stone had greatly reduced their travel time. It would be days before Budala and the others would arrive. B'nair could not, and would not, wait that long. However, he was torn between leaving with such a small band of fighters and waiting for who knew how long for a greater force.

"It can't be helped," B'nair declared once he had decided.

If the legends of the Kelpies were only half true, finding and releasing only one would more than make up for his not waiting for the strength of an army of fifty hobgoblins. Besides, he reasoned; he wasn't sure that Budala would convince anyone to come with him, or that he'd find this place if he did. B'nair could be waiting forever. That wasn't going to happen.

"If need be, we can return for them," he added, knowing it was a lie.

Whether Vardelos knew it was a lie or not, he kept silent. He knew better than to challenge a Rebbercand with an axe. And more than that, he, too, had heard the growling, and recognized the sounds of jackals. He would do as he was ordered.

"As you wish," he finally answered. "Where are we going, if I may ask?"

B'nair allowed the edges of a smile to creep across his face. He wasn't really surprised to find he would encounter no resistance to his commands. He surveyed the others who were waiting for their instructions. There were about a dozen. He had no idea what he would encounter along the way.

He knew there were others searching for the stones he had found. They may come after him to steal them away. He recalled how his workforce in the mines of the Trepans was devastated by an unseen army. That workforce was comprised of battle-tested Rebbercands. Now all he had was a handful of hobgoblins whose battle skills were unknown to him.

Quest of Eight Part Four: The Race to Virkio

Richard Reda

He squeezed his hand around the gem and placed it inside the pocket of his vest. Something about it told him that, at this point in time, he had the upper hand. He knew where he had to go next, which was something that was probably still a mystery to whomever was following him. He also knew that where he was headed, he would be increasing his power.

"We're going to the Venomous Swamp," he finally answered.

"The Swamp?" Vardelos asked. "Are you certain? That place is very inhospitable, even for hobgoblins."

"Yes," B'nair said. "I am quite certain. It's the closest place."

"The closest place for what?" Vardelos asked nervously.

B'nair looked closely at Vardelos, his one eye roaming up and down the hobgoblin, and a smile once again creeping into his face. He wondered if the tremor he detected in the question was because of the location that had been identified, or what they may find there.

"To find a Kelpie," he answered.

Without waiting for any questions, he led his small band around the fortress to the opposite side of where the sounds of the jackals were coming. They ran off the bridge, around the dried out moat and away. The jackals howled at their departure.

At the sound of the word "Kelpie," a very large creature who had been tucked away, napping under the bridge came wide awake. The sounds of the jackals were something he had long become accustomed to, and no longer paid any mind. The reference to the Kelpies, however, startled him awake.

He remained motionless, hidden in the darkness under the bridge – his home for all his life. His large, deep green eyes were partially covered by his thick, heavy brows. He moved his head only enough to peer up through the cracks and gaps between the beams of the bridge to see who would dare to voice the names of those dreaded and evil sorcerers.

He heard their footsteps as they ran off his bridge and faded away. The jackals gave one last long moan, bidding the intruders farewell. The creature thought about what he heard and decided he would wait to see who came after them. This time, he would be alert. He would be ready for them.

Chapter eighteen

Solveig stayed where she was. Her heart was pounding in her chest. She had never seen anything so big before, and she had never seen a dragon before. She didn't know they really existed. She also wasn't sure what had just happened. She knew Quinn had backed away as the giant dragon descended. She was about to run, herself, although now that she could see more clearly how large this beast was, she realized there was no place she could go to escape it.

Her throat was tight with fear, squeezing off her voice. She tried swallowing, but found her mouth felt like it was filled with cotton. She was so frightened that all her senses were on high alert. She was aware of the minutest details. She could see, hear, smell and feel everything that was happening as if it were happening in slow motion. The dragon's wings had blown the wind in swirls around her as it dropped to the floor of the tower roof. Its hind legs came down slowly, the talons scraping against the stone.

At the same time its front legs touched down, it folded its wings against its side. She was mesmerized by the color. Parts of it were a deep, rich blue. But when it moved, and the moonlight broke through the clouds, the blue shifted to a pale color, almost an iridescent white. In spite of the terror that filled her, she was captivated by the beauty of the large scales that covered its body.

A very long and very thick neck extended from the long lean body. Large bristles rose in parallel lines up its neck to the top of its large head. The bristles at the top swept back from the dragon's face and had several extremely sharp looking barbs on the ends. Centered in its head were two large, piercing eyes.

The eyes were all blue with milky white centers. Beneath the eyes was a long, large mouth, nostrils flaring at the top, clouds of mist billowing from them. She watched as plumes of smoke rose into the air. No, she thought, it wasn't smoke. She could see tiny crystals in the clouds the dragon breathed. It's frost, she realized. I thought dragons breathed fire, she said to herself. Could this one breathe ice?

Once more the dragon bellowed. Quinn was knocked to the ground by the vibrations of the sound waves; covering his ears as the screeching pierced deep into his head. The others on the far side of the tower could see the beast and hear its roar. They, too, covered their ears. Solveig heard no screech. She heard the same cry as before.

"What have you done to my child?"

Suddenly Solveig realized that the cry was coming from the dragon. And then it dawned on her that this was the mother of the slain dragon they had discovered when they arrived on the roof. And with that dawning came one more: she thinks we killed her child, she thought. No, she corrected herself. She thinks I killed her child.

She raised her hands in protest, oblivious to the fact that she would be unable to stop anything this creature wanted to do by the mere raising of her hands. As she did, she once more saw the blue coloring to her skin. It seemed even deeper than before. When she moved them, something else caught her eye. In the reflection of the moonlight breaking through the clouds, the blue shifted to a pale color, almost an iridescent white. Her eyes shot from her hands to the dragon and back.

"What the...?" she said out loud.

The dragon cocked its head and then lowered it. Solveig was still looking at her hands and their shifting color. When she looked up she saw that the dragon's face was only a few feet in front of her. Reflexively, she took a step backwards.

"We...we...I...I...didn't...your child...we," she stammered.

The dragon sniffed at Solveig, looking every inch of her over with her penetrating eyes. The two enormous fangs that hung from the top jaw were almost as tall as Solveig was. She could suck me in and swallow me whole, she thought. She wouldn't even have to chew.

The dragon raised its head and then turned to the carcass. She looked from the body and then back to Solveig.

"Who did this, if not you?" it asked.

Only Solveig heard the words. To everyone else the sound was an indecipherable, ear-piercing screech. Solveig couldn't answer that question, but knew that the explosion of fire that had occurred behind her meant someone else was here. She thought it was probably whoever had found the stone before they arrived.

"Others," she answered. "They came for the stone. The same one that we came here to find."

She knew she couldn't hide the fact that she and her friends were here for the same thing. Then she thought of something else that might save her.

"We also seek the Alchemist," she added.

This wasn't exactly true, but it was also not exactly a lie. If these towers and the spells were actually the handiwork of the Alchemist, maybe the dragon was, too. She hoped, but didn't really believe, that Lochen was right, and that all this was just an illusion.

The dragon did not react to this statement, but studied Solveig more closely. It moved its head to one side of her and then to the other. Solveig stood motionless, trying not to exhibit any fear, which was getting harder and harder to do. And then she saw the dragon's head jerk up. It reared its head back, ready to strike.

Solveig was so fixed on the dragon's head, that she didn't see what had caused the reaction. Instead, she saw the clouds that had blanketed the sky fade away and were replaced by thousands of stars twinkling in the black sky. All at once, a sense of peace fell over her. Her fear evaporated and she smiled. The air was cold and she could see her breath as the vapor floated up towards the stars.

"It's so beautiful," she said out loud, unaware that she was doing so. "Lochen would love this."

"I do love it," he answered. He was standing right next to her.

"Where did you come from?" she asked him.

"I've never left you," he replied.

She sensed that she had had this conversation with him before. But when, she asked herself. His appearance, she realized, was what the dragon reacted to.

Quest of Eight Part Four: The Race to Virkio

Richard Reda

"What are you doing? Don't you know what kind of danger you're in?" she whispered to him, keeping her eyes on the dragon, who was peering down at the both of them.

"I could never leave you to face danger alone," he answered, quite matter-of-factly.

"Neither could we," muttered Summer, as she crawled out from under his hood.

Solveig turned to look at her, and then looked behind her to see the others had followed Lochen to join her. The dragon lowered its head to look more closely at each one of them. In that instant, a flood of information filled Solveig's thoughts. She stepped forward, closer to the dragon.

"You are Uzradzi, the Guardian of Virkio," she announced. "And friend to the Alchemist."

The dragon reacted only for a second, taken aback by the statement.

"We have searched for a long time for the Alchemist to seek his help," she continued. "We are searching for answers. Others who came here before us did this to your child. They came here to find the stone of the Enchantress."

She motioned to Stella.

"Our Enchantress has another part of that stone. Now the ones who stole the stone and killed your child plan to cause more harm. Please help us."

The dragon looked at the lifeless body at her feet, and then back to this person who was as blue as she was.

"And you are Solveig, princess of the mountain people," the dragon answered in a voice only Solveig could understand. "I was told of your arrival."

Before Solveig could ask any questions, the dragon lowered its head and met Solveig's gaze, eye to eye. Then she extended one of her wings.
"Get on my back. All of you," the dragon said. "And hold on tightly."

Solveig told the others what to do. She took the lead, stepping on the edge of the wing carefully. She could see the hardened scales and expected the surface to be slippery. She was surprised to find the scales were as course as sand and that she could easily climb up the wing and onto the dragon's back.

She made her way up the dragon's neck, using the spikes that ran in parallel lines down the spine as a ladder. The others did not wait for an invitation, following her immediately. When they were all situated, the dragon raised its head and Solveig felt her breath escape by being suddenly lifted high into the sky.

The dragon began flapping its wings and at the same time moved to the edge of the tower and jumped off. At first she dropped downward towards the rocks. Once the rush of wind racing upward filled her wings, the dragon quickly changed direction and swooped up and around tower five.

She rose higher and higher, circling as she climbed. Natalie recalled the last time she rode this high on the back of a beast, and a shiver ran up her spine. Without any warning, the dragon changed direction and dived down towards the towers. As she soared over the tops of each of the towers, she roared.

A blast of flame surged from her gigantic jaws. But instead of yellow and red fire, the dragon breathed streams of blue and white that crystallized everything in her path. She breathed frost and ice, rather than fire. In two quick passes, the towers were coated with a thick layer of ice.

The dragon made one more pass. This time she headed right for the roof of tower five. In a quick, tight circling motion, her tail flicked the several canisters that were assembled around the battlements. The contents spilled out onto the roof and over the sides, oozing down the tower wall.

In a final movement, the dragon flicked her tail, swiping it like a match head across the stone floor. The scales and barbs on the end of her tail sparked and ignited the dragon's breath. The first flames to catch were little more than small tongues of fire. As the ice the dragon had breathed over the surface began to melt, the fire was fueled.

In seconds, the dragon was climbing straight up into the sky and the towers – all five of them – covered in ice exploded into flame. One after the other, the towers were bathed in a blazing inferno. As high as they were, they could all hear the roaring firestorm.

"I guess we won't have to go back the way we came," shouted Sean over the noise.

The dragon made one more large circle high above the fire, watching as her child's body was consumed until it disappeared. She let out a final screech into the night sky and then turned to the east, flying on a steady and deliberate course.

"Where are we going?" Quinn asked.

"I don't know," said Solveig. "I only hope she lets us off someplace safe."

Some of them tried to look over the side and down to the ground below, but they saw nothing recognizable. Even Liam had no idea where they were or where they were headed, other than east.

"How did you know the dragon's name?" Lochen asked Solveig after a while.

"You told me," she answered.

"I most certainly did not," he said. "I had no idea that dragons actually existed. How would I know what one is called?"

"You told me in a dream," she answered, smiling.

"I suppose I can't argue with that," Lochen said after thinking this over for a few seconds.

They flew for hours, past the dawn and well into the day. They had crossed over a mountain range, a forest, and a field. They were so high they couldn't see signs of civilization below them, so they had no idea if they were passing over any towns.

By early afternoon, the dragon seemed to have changed direction slightly and was beginning to descend. Liam stuck his head out over the side of the dragon's neck to get a better look at the terrain. It was a partially wooded area, but mostly open fields and patches of marshland. Nothing looked familiar, and at the same time, it all looked familiar. Maybe it was seeing things from this angle, although he had a sense of where his home was from here – a few hundred miles south, he believed.

The dragon dropped even further towards the ground. They were over a large clearing in the middle of a pleasant looking forest. The ground was hilly and there were large patches of trees scattered all about. The dragon circled once, apparently looking for something, and then quickly and suddenly landed.

"You may get off here," she announced.

Quest of Eight Part Four: The Race to Virkio

Richard Reda

As before, only Solveig heard words. The others only heard a high-pitched screeching sound. By now they were getting used to it, and it wasn't as painful to hear, but it still wasn't a pleasant sound, nor anything any of them could understand.

"Where is 'here?'" asked Solveig.

"This is as far as I can take you," the dragon responded.

"What happens now?" asked Solveig.

"There is a path through the woods not far from here. Take that path to the end. Do not stop and do not deviate. You will have enough time to reach it before nightfall, but do not delay."

"Thanks," Solveig replied. "But where are we and where are we supposed to go?"

"Down the path," answered the dragon. "Without delay."

She said no more and quickly rose into the sky, flying back the way she had come. The others had merely watched and listened, understanding only Solveig's side of the conversation. It meant even less to them.

"How is it you speak dragon?" asked Sean.

"I don't know," said Solveig. "Maybe it has something to do with me being blue; or maybe it was something in the tea that old woman gave me; or maybe it is something with this cloak. Next time some old woman drags me into her cottage under an old tree and gives me some tea that turns me blue, I'll ask her!"

"Geez," grumbled Sean. "I was only asking."

"So," said Quinn, trying not to ask something that would make anyone angry with him. "Where do we go from here?"

Solveig snapped her head around and glared at him. When she realized he was being serious, she relaxed slightly.

"She told me that we have to find a path in the woods and take it to the end."

"She?" asked Natalie. "The dragon was a 'she?'"

"Yes," answered Solveig. "And the dead one was her child."

"It was a wonder we all weren't dealt the same fate," added Lochen. "Thank you for intervening for us."

Not sure if he was serious, Solveig let the comment go without a remark. She turned in a circle, looking for something that resembled a path. Not finding anything, she looked to Liam.

"Do you see a path?" she asked. "That's what we're supposed to follow, but I don't see anything."

Liam took a deep breath and surveyed the area. He saw the same thing Solveig did – no sign of a path.

"This way," said Stella, pointing towards the southeast.

"How do you know..." started Sean, but he stopped as suddenly as he started. "Looks good to me," he finished.

"It's part of the map," Stella tried to explain. "The one that I saw on the roof of the tower. The one that none of you saw. The one that appeared...that the light...it came out of...never mind. It's too hard to explain. We have to go this way."

Not waiting for any questions, discussion or argument, she pushed passed them and headed into the woods. At first she seemed to be walking aimlessly in no particular pattern. And then, just as quickly, they found themselves on a path – a well-worn passage through a gently wooded area.

"This is really weird," said Summer. "That path wasn't there a minute ago."

After landing, she had climbed out of Lochen's hood and was fluttering along on her own power. She rose a little higher in the air and looked back the way they had come. The path was in plain sight behind them, as if they had been walking on it all along.

"Weird," she repeated.
They walked for several hours until they heard a growling sound. It seemed to come from off to their right. At the time they heard the sound, they came upon an opening to their left – not a path so much as a break in the trees.

"Ignore it," said Stella. "We need to keep walking."

A few minutes later, they heard another growl. This one came from behind them. It was shortly followed by a rustling of the bushes and one more growl from their right.

"I know that sound," said Quinn.

"Me, too," said Lochen and Sean at the same time.

"They're jackals," the three of them said.

A shiver ran down Solveig's spine. She recalled the sound, too. It was the same noise that she had heard when she had gotten lost in the woods – before she discovered the old woman. Or had the old woman discovered her?

"We need to find some place we can mount a defensive," said Liam.

"No," said Solveig. "We need to keep going. We can't delay. The dragon said not to delay."

"Did the dragon know that we'd be followed by jackals?" asked Sean.

Two more growls were heard. By now any hope of escaping to the left through the clearing was gone. The sounds were coming from that direction. The group tightened up, moving closer to one another. Summer flew higher and started to circle back to see where the predators were.

"No," said Solveig again. "We need to stay together."

"Why can't she fly back a little to see where they are?" asked Natalie. "We can't delay," insisted Solveig. "We don't know how much further we have to go. We need to get there before dark."

"Get where?" asked Liam. "You don't know where we're going. Maybe we were led into a trap."

"The dragon said not to delay and not to deviate," said Solveig.

"And it's not reasonable to believe the dragon would send us into a trap," inserted Lochen. "If the dragon wanted to do us any harm, she could have done that back on the tower. In fact, all she had to do was leave us on the tower. She didn't really have to do anything."

"But what if the dragon didn't know there were jackals around?" asked Quinn. "Maybe the dragon didn't know we'd have to protect ourselves."

As the debate raged no one had stopped walking, each of them trying to keep up with Stella, who was marching forward at a strong pace. Natalie was close behind her, with Solveig and Lochen keeping up.

Quest of Eight Part Four: The Race to Virkio

Richard Reda

Summer fluttered back and forth, still feeling the need to do some kind of reconnaissance.

Liam, Sean and Quinn were reluctantly following along, torn between putting some distance between themselves and the jackals, and finding a suitable defense. At least one of them was ready to ignore the rest and turn to attack. The appearance of three jackals and the sounds of several others changed that dramatically.

"We're surrounded," shouted Sean.

"There's nothing in front of us," Stella called back. "We need to keep going forward."

Sean bent down and picked up a few small stones from the dirt as he began to close the gap between him and the others ahead of him. Liam drew a long sharp blade from a scabbard behind his back. Lochen pushed back his sleeves, getting ready to cast a spell. Solveig looked over at him.

"I don't think that's going to work, but be my guest," she said to him.

By now about seven jackals had made their presence known by moving out from behind the foliage. They were enormous. Their fangs glistened as they bared their teeth. Two were running alongside the group on the right; two more were on the left. The other three were spread out behind.

"They're herding us," said Sean. "They're trying to box us in and move us straight ahead."

"Good," said Solveig. "Because that's the way we want to go."

"No, it isn't" shouted Liam. "They're moving us into a trap. Can't you see that?"

"Then let's give them something to think about," said Lochen.

He stopped in his tracks and spun around to face the three that had closed in on them from behind. He raised his arm and thrust it forward. A bolt of lightning shot from his hand and a large glass-like bubble quickly expanded to a circle fifteen feet in diameter, heading right for the jackal in the center. It was widening as it went, growing larger and larger to encompass all three of the beasts.

The jackals moved through it as if it wasn't there. The surge of energy pushed against the trees, bending them under the power and shaking the leaves. It was clear that the spell Lochen had cast was powerful. However, it didn't have any effect on the jackals.

"Whoa," shouted Quinn. "That's not good."

Sean loaded his slingshot and fired. The stone snapped free of the shot and sailed through the air, directly at a spot between the eyes of the center jackal. At the last second, it veered upward and over the jackal's head, missing it completely.

"That never happens," muttered Sean. "I never miss. How did that happen?"

"We should probably move faster," suggested Quinn.

He was silently wishing the wolf he had saved – how long ago? – was here now to get him out of this dilemma. Stella and Solveig were still walking quickly, not moving a step off the path, but not running, either.

Sean fired two more shots in quick succession, one at the jackal on the right of the one he missed and the other at the one on the left. The shots either ricocheted off of nothing he could see, or they stopped short of their target and fell to the ground. Neither one struck the jackal it was intended for. Instead, it only seemed to anger them.

Quest of Eight Part Four: The Race to Virkio

Richard Reda

The growling became barking and howling. The quick walking of the predators became more of a trot. The seven they initially saw doubled in number, but the narrow path ahead still remained clear of them.

"It might be time to run," Stella suggested to Solveig.

"Do you think that will do any good?" she asked.

"Probably not, but at least we won't be delaying."

"Right," said Solveig. "Run," she shouted.

Summer flew up into the air and back towards the jackals. She tried sprinkling faerie dust over them, but quickly learned that was a mistake. She thought it would lift them up off the ground enough to stop them from being able to run. All it did was to elevate them as they jumped and snapped at her.

She narrowly missed being impaled on the razor sharp fangs of one of them, and then saw that the others she had sprinkled were now leaping – covering twice as much ground as before. She flipped over and sped away, returning to the others who were clustered together, running ahead.

The jackals were much closer. In fact, they were close enough to attack but had not yet done so. They were growling, their jaws were snapping, and they had moved to within a few feet of their apparent prey, but had not attacked.

For Solveig, this was reliving the nightmare before she ran into the old woman. What is it with these forests, and jackals, she wondered. She had fixed her focus far down the path instead of on the dangers that surrounded her. Off in the distance she could make out something that looked like a cabin.

"Look," she shouted. "Up ahead. I think we can make it."

All eyes shifted forward. They all saw the same thing. The path they were on seemed to end rather suddenly. Out in the middle of no place and at the end of the path was a very strange looking cabin. It was narrow – only about four feet wide - and seemed to be made of the same wood as the surrounding trees; so much so, that it blended in almost to the point of being invisible.

It seemed to lean precariously to the left, but was only about four feet high, topped with an irregularly shaped roof that was covered with pieces of bark. There was a single opening: a door on the left side of the front, and no windows. It was not the cabin, though, that had attracted Solveig's attention. It was the person in front of it.

There was what appeared to be a porch on the front of the cabin. It looked like a large, flat root, more than an actual porch. It was as wide as the structure itself, and only large enough for one person. That one person seemed to be sitting in a chair, watching them run and smiling at them. Solveig had a sudden realization. She only hoped she was right.
"Stop running," she said as she gradually slowed down.

"But what about the jackals?" wailed Quinn. "I don't want to be dinner for some jackals."

"They won't hurt us," she said.

"Are you sure?" asked Lochen as he followed her lead and slowed down to a walk.

She looked at him out of the corner of her eye and smirked.

"Reasonably sure," she answered.

"Ah," was Lochen's only response.

She slowed down to an almost casual walk. In spite of the apparent danger, the others did as she told them and stopped running. They clustered more tightly together, following her lead. The jackals approached even closer, still growling fiercely and snapping their jaws within inches of whomever was closest to them.

"Ignore them," Solveig said. "Just keep walking. We're going to that cabin."

The person sitting on the porch in front of the cabin watched them intently. As the group got closer they could see him more clearly. He stood up and stepped off the porch. Actually, it was more like a hop than a step. He waddled like a penguin for a couple of steps and then stopped.

He was a short, very round man with a very round head. He had no hair to speak of – only a thin fringe of white around the sides and back of his head that draped in wisps over his ears, which were small and round. He had faint, white eyebrows that looked like small, pointed tents over each eye.

He was very pale; almost ashen, except for rosy cheeks. His eyes were as round as the rest of him and as brown as his clothes. His small, round hands ended in short, stubby fingers that were extended and pressed together, fingertip to fingertip, over his large, round belly.

He was dressed in what looked like leather. It was dark brown, soft-looking and wrinkled. His pants came just below his knees and his lower legs were covered in stockings. His small feet were in shoes with the toes completely squared off, and had a large buckle on the instep. He wore an old vest over a baggy long sleeved shirt – all of which was the same dark brown as his pants and stockings.

He was bobbing back and forth, as if waiting for their arrival. The jackals had slowed down, matching the walk of the small group they surrounded. They continued to growl and snap, but went no further.

The little man took another waddling step forward and flung out one of his hands.

"Go away," he ordered, with a dismissive wave, immediately returning his hand to its original position – tented over his belly.

The jackals dispersed immediately, silently disappearing back into the woods. The man looked up at the new arrivals and smiled broadly.

"Hello. It's good to see you. I'm Sarnanok," he announced in a frail, whispering voice. "I've been expecting you."

Chapter nineteen

It took a few seconds for everything to sink in. They had heard the name before, but few of them could remember where. Lochen was more familiar, as was Stella, but neither of them were certain they had heard him correctly. The person they knew as Sarnanok had lived centuries ago. This person happened to have the same name, was named after the original one, or was a descendant.

"What an interesting name," said Lochen. "There was a potion master by that name who lived a long time ago."

"Yes," the little man answered, smiling broadly – obviously impressed. "I know. That's me."

"That's impossible," said Stella. "You'd have to be almost two thousand years old."

"Uh, yes," he said. "That would be about right. In fact, I believe I'm two thousand, one hundred and sixty-five – or at least I will be on my next birthday. Although," he added under his breath, "I'm not likely to see that day come."

They were too astonished to have grasped the import of his last comment. Sean and Liam were pre-occupied with the sudden disappearance of the jackals. Quinn was studying the tiny cabin that blended neatly into the surrounding woods.

"Oh," he added, brightening up even further, "I'm not a potion master, though."

"I see," said Lochen. "Perhaps I'm thinking of someone else."

"Well," answered Sarnanok, "I don't know who you might be thinking of, but I have been known to mix potions...and other things. I'm actually an apothecary. That is, I _was_ an apothecary. In fact, I..."

He was interrupted when he turned to look more closely at Solveig. His expression quickly changed to one of mild shock.

"Oh, my word," he said.

He took a few tentative steps closer to Solveig. He was at least a head shorter than she, and cocked his head, peering up at her.

"I see you've met Beebee," he said.

"Beebee?" asked Solveig.

"Yes," he said. "She had a penchant for turning people blue. She's a little..."

Quest of Eight Part Four: The Race to Virkio

Richard Reda

He circled an ear with the index finger of one hand, indicating that Beebee was a little nutty.

"You know," he continued. "Or maybe you don't. Judging by the deep blue color and the iridescent nature, I have to think she gave you some awful tasting tea that, for some reason unknown to you, you couldn't stop drinking and the cup kept filling all on its own. Am I right?"

"Yes," replied Solveig, astonished at how accurate he was.

"Hmmph," he muttered. "A mixture of rodent tails, decayed fungus, and monkey sweat. I don't use the stuff myself."

"Oh, yuk!" groaned Solveig. "I didn't really need to know that."

"It's the fish bile that gives it the pungent taste," he continued.

"Enough," she pleaded, raising her hand motioning him to stop. "Please. I really don't want to know."

"Regardless, though," he persisted as if she hadn't spoken. "It was necessary, since I'm also guessing you ran into Uzradzi."

"The dragon?" asked Lochen. "What do you know of the dragon?"

"She's very close to the Alchemist," he said.

"She's his pet?" asked Quinn, incredulously.

"Oh, no," answered the little apothecary. "No one has a dragon as a pet. She's more like a friend. And a wonderful friend to have, I might add. It's not good to have a dragon as an enemy, especially not one as powerful as Uzradzi. When Beebee turned you blue, that was a signal to Uzradzi that you were a friend and to be given safe passage. The potion also enabled you to speak to the dragon. Oh, and the dragon's child as well. How is the little one doing, by the way? I assume you saw him, too."

Solveig felt her throat tighten and her eyes well up with tears. She turned to the others, not sure how to explain.

"It was..." interjected Lochen, "he was...killed."

A look of shock and pain replaced the smile on Sarnanok's face. His knees weakened and he reached out his hand to keep from falling. Natalie and Liam quickly stepped forward to catch him and helped him back to the porch and into his chair.

"How awful," he finally said, shaking his head in dismay. "What happened?"

"We don't know," said Natalie.

"There were others who arrived before us," said Stella. "Hobgoblins by the look of the ones we saw."

"Someone, maybe one of them..." Solveig began, "...they must have...he was beheaded."

"Oh, NO!" wailed Sarnanok. "Are you certain?"

"We saw the body," said Quinn, "But there wasn't a head on it, so I guess we're certain."

"Can we get you some water, or something else to drink?" asked Summer.

The ancient apothecary had become even paler than before. The rosy coloring in his cheeks faded and his face sagged. He had looked robust when they first saw him, but now he looked frail. He raised his head and looked towards Summer, unsure of what her question had been. Then he seemed to understand.

"No, thank you," he said. "I'm all right. It was a shock, that's all. His mother must be distraught. I'm sorry. Where are my manners? Please. Come inside."

They all looked at one another and then to the tiny doorway and the tiny cabin into which it led.

"I don't think we'll all fit," said Sean.

Sarnanok looked back at his cabin and then at all of them, especially at Quinn.

"He may have a tight fit," he said, pointing to Quinn. "But I'm sure we'll manage."

He rose from the chair with an assist from Natalie. He waddled to the door, pulled it open and went inside. The others looked at one another and followed. Quinn not only had to duck, but he had to turn sideways and wiggle through the small entryway.

Once inside they were confronted with a large room and a high ceiling. Sean scanned the interior and then stuck his head back out the door and gave the outside the once-over. The same illusion of size that they encountered with the towers occurred here: the inside was considerably larger than the outside. How do they do that, he wondered.

"Oh," said Sarnanok.

He stopped abruptly in the center of the main room and turned toward Solveig.

"Before I forget," he continued. "Would you like to stay blue, or would you like to be turned back?"

"That depends," she said warily. "What do I have to drink?"

"Nothing," he answered, smiling at her.
"Then, yes," she said. "As attractive as this may be, I'd prefer looking a bit more normal."

"I understand completely," he replied.

"Wait," said Lochen. "Do you anticipate that we may need for her to remain looking like that? This Beebee person expected it would be necessary, and you appear to have confirmed that. If we're to encounter another dragon or some other situation where her coloring would put us at an advantage or serve to save us, maybe it would be better for her to remain this way."

"I can't say for sure," answered Sarnanok. "I don't know where you're going or what you may encounter. I also don't know what other powers she has, or how they are affected by this spell. The problem with potions like the one Beebee used is the long-term effects. Leaving her as she is for an indefinite time could render the spell permanent. On the other hand..."

"Excuse me," interrupted Solveig. "I'm right here! It's me you're talking about. And I'd prefer NOT to be blue, if that's all right with everybody else."

"Of course, of course," replied the apothecary. "I can take care of that right here and now."

He went up and stood right before her. He reached up and placed his index finger in the center of her forehead and began rubbing it in a small clockwise circular motion. Solveig looked up, cross-eyed, at his hand, waiting expectantly.

Quest of Eight Part Four: The Race to Virkio

Richard Reda

Everyone's eyes were glued, watching the little man's finger swirl on her forehead. Gradually, the blue hue began to fade. He turned back to see everyone looking and he smiled broadly, proud of how easily he was able to reverse the effects of the spell. Then he noticed a change on the faces of the onlookers.

Their expressions went from wonder to frowns, to near disgust. He continued to rub his finger in the circle on Solveig's forehead, but the sudden change made him falter. He turned back toward Solveig to see what had caused their dismay. He removed his finger and stepped back to look. As he did so, Solveig raised her hands.

"Green!" she shouted. "You turned me green. I'm not green. I never have been green. This is worse. I'd rather be blue."

"Oops. Sorry," he apologized. "I was going the wrong way."

He quickly stepped back, placed his finger on her forehead and started rubbing in a counter clockwise motion. He rubbed vigorously and could see the green fading. He looked back at the others and watched as their expressions changed from concern to smiles. Satisfied, he stopped rubbing and backed away.

"That should be better," he said.

"Yes," answered Solveig, looking at her hands. "Thank you. This is much better."

He was looking up at her and smiling. After a few seconds, his face sagged and the smile was replaced by a look of sadness. His thoughts had drifted back to the news he had received about the death of the dragon. He didn't need to explain, and no one had to ask. They all immediately understood the sorrow he was feeling.

Quest of Eight Part Four: The Race to Virkio

Richard Reda

"We're sorry to have had such bad news to share," said Lochen in an effort to get back to the reason they were here. "It was the dragon that brought us here, but we're not sure why. Can you tell us?"

Sarnanok motioned to some chairs and they all sat down. When they were settled, he began. He told them some of what they already knew. There had been an uprising of a number of sorcerers – the Kelpies. They were abusing their power and destroying anyone who opposed them. The Alchemist and an Enchantress named Meri Hocto were the only ones who had the courage and the ability to confront them. They plotted and planned, waiting until they could isolate the Kelpies and defeat them one by one.

They were able to cast spells and put each one of them into a deep sleep, hidden in the far reaches of the world. At the same time, two sorcerers that Meri was training in the hopes of joining forces with the Alchemist and her rebelled. She managed to banish them. Sarnanok was aware that his audience had recent encounters with these two sorcerers, but didn't explain how he knew.

At the time Meri banished them, the pendant that was a source of her power was destroyed – broken into four pieces and scattered to reaches as far and remote as the locations to which the sorcerers had been banished. The band that held the stone also disappeared, as did the Enchantress.

"I can see that you've found two of the pieces of the pendant," he said, looking at Stella.

"Someone else has found the others," she replied.

"I know," responded Sarnanok with an even graver look on his face.

He continued his tale. The spells on the Kelpies would last a long time, but not forever, and if the pieces of the pendant fell into the wrong hands, as it appears some of them had, the Kelpies could be released.

"But how would anyone know where to look?" asked Natalie.

"I know," said Stella.

"And so does the person who has the other pieces of the pendant," said Sarnanok.

"How?" asked Liam.

"That wall I was trying to tell you about," Stella tried to explain.

"When the Alchemist and the Enchantress hid the dormant Kelpies," continued Sarnanok, "the locations were imbedded into parts of the pendant. When those parts were reunited, the map manifested itself."

"But two pieces were reunited before now," said Summer. "Why didn't the map appear then?"

"Because one of those pieces," said Sarnanok, pointing to the pieces in Stella's headband, "is the center. It's the heart of the pendant, and it has considerable power, but it contained no information about the Kelpies."

"So," said Stella. "If the map appeared to me, it also appeared to whomever has the rest of the pendant."

"That's correct," said Sarnanok. "And it's safe to assume that this person is searching for the nearest hiding place."

"How do you know all this?" asked Lochen.

"Once the Enchantress disappeared," he explained, "the Alchemist knew that a time would come when the forces of evil would rise again. He believed that at the same time the forces of good would also rise to challenge them, and he needed to put certain things in place for when that time came."

"And you think we're the forces of good?" asked Quinn.

"Of course," answered Sarnanok. "The Alchemist knew that you would come together to challenge the growing threat. He told us about you."

"How could he – or anyone – know that?" asked Liam. "It was pure chance that we even met one another. We're all from different parts of the world, from different people."

"Chance?" repeated Sarnanok. "I think you're mistaken, but that's an argument for another time."

"But how could he know that we'd find each other and that we'd be able to overcome this force of evil?" asked Natalie.

"Nature must have a balance, or it won't survive," he said.

"Wait a minute," interjected Summer, before he could explain any further. "Go back to that part about him telling you about us. What did he say, exactly?"

"Well, he didn't provide any names or descriptions," said Sarnanok. "He only revealed enough to prepare us for your arrival and to enable us to assist you. He identified several of us as sentinels – guideposts, if you will, in your journey. Each of us has a different purpose."

"How many sentinels are there?" Stella asked.

"I don't know. None of us do. And before you ask, no, we don't know where they are, either. He was careful not to give any of us too much information. He was concerned about the danger if any of us were captured by the Kelpies or their henchmen, and anyone of us knew too much."

"And all of you volunteered to do this at the same time?" asked Lochen. "Two thousand years ago?"

"Volunteered?" commented Sarnanok. "An interesting thought. No, we were selected. And yes, we are all more than two thousand years old. The Alchemist cast a spell on all of us that slowed down our aging process. Our sole purpose is to provide you with something you need. Once we've done that, we'll be finished. But enough of all this. Your enemy has too much of a lead as it is."

"Where is he going?" asked Liam. "If we know, maybe we can head him off."

"I have no idea," said Sarnanok. "I can only tell you that you must proceed to where the stone had been hidden."

"But why?" asked Stella. "If it's already been taken, what is the point of our going there?"

"I don't know that, either," answered Sarnanok. "But I've taken you as far as I can. My time will soon be over."

"All right," said Natalie. "If we have to go to where the stone was hidden, then let's just do it. Maybe we'll find something there that will tell us where to go next. Where was the stone hidden?"

"Another question I'm afraid I can't answer," replied the apothecary. "However, I believe she knows."

He motioned to Stella, and all eyes turned towards her. She was startled and began to object – to claim that he was wrong; she had no clue. But then a dawning came over her face.

"I do!" she said, surprised by her own knowledge. "It's a deserted fortress on the edge of a forest. It's falling apart and overgrown with brambles."

"The fortress of the Thumpers!" said Liam with a gasp. "We can't go there. It's too dangerous."

"Worse than what you've already faced?" asked Sarnanok. "And overcome?"

"No," he eventually admitted. "I guess not."

"Then we should make haste," announced Lochen. "There is still sufficient daylight. We should go now."

"I agree," said Sarnanok with a sigh. "Although I will be very sorry to see you leave."

"If you will tell us what we are supposed to obtain from you," said Lochen, "we can depart."

"I've already given it to you."

"What was it?" asked Sean. "Did I miss something? Did the rest of you get something, and I didn't?"

"I provided you with the reason for your quest," answered Sarnanok. "It is all I have."

Solveig had been noticing that the apothecary seemed to get weaker and weaker as he spoke. His cheeks were no longer the rosy color they had been when they first met him. At first she thought he was only getting tired. Then she recalled some of his comments. He's dying, she realized.

"Can we stay a while longer?" she asked. "Do we really have to leave now?"

Her eyes started to mist. The little man looked up at her and could see that her question was not prompted by a fear of what they were to face, but her understanding that his time was almost at an end. It had been centuries since anyone had cared so much for him. A tear formed in the corner of one of his eyes. He felt deeply touched and deeply ashamed at the same time. He did not deserve her compassion.

"Yes," he said; his voice little more than a whisper. "It's time, and you have very important work to do. I will see you out."

He rose to his feet slowly and with difficulty. Solveig went to his side and held his arm. He patted her hand and smiled. Without any further words, he led them to the tiny door and out to the tiny porch.

"This way," said Liam.

While he didn't know exactly where they were, he knew where they had to go. No farewells were exchanged. The others followed behind Liam as he led them through a thicket. In seconds, the cabin was lost from sight, and so was Sarnanok. Solveig wiped a tear from her check, but didn't look back.

They walked for several hours. There was no sign or other indication of the jackals. Sean maintained a lookout at the back of the line as it wound through the woods and over hills. It was eerily normal. There was little conversation. Each of them seemed to be lost in their own thoughts.

Late in the afternoon they crested another in a long series of hills and exited the forest. The line of trees extended far to their right, and a short way away from the edge they could see the ruins of the stronghold they were seeking. Liam gave an involuntary shudder at the sight.

Less than an hour later, they were approaching the bridge that crossed the dried up moat when they heard the familiar growling of several jackals. The sounds were coming from the woods opposite the bridge and the fortress. Sean spun around, slingshot at the ready, but couldn't see the source of the noise.

"They must have been following us the whole time," he said.

"I don't think so," said Liam. "If it was the same pack, they would have had several better opportunities to attack. Why would they wait until now?"

"You mean this is a different pack?" asked Quinn. "What is it with this place? It's full of these lousy jackals."

They were all huddled close together at the foot of the bridge, stepping slowly and carefully backwards onto the wooden timbers. They were so focused on the invisible threat hidden in the woods that they didn't see the creature emerge from under the bridge and stand slightly behind them in the dusty culvert.
"They won't bother you," it said.

The voice was booming. It was so deep and so loud it made everyone's eardrums vibrate. It was also very gravelly. It sounded like a swarm of bees buzzing inside a large, hollow, metal drum. As a single unit, they all spun around to face the sudden intrusion.

They came face-to-face with a giant troll. He was at least nine feet tall and completely green. His head was the size of a horse and covered with scraggly green hair down to his large green shoulders. His eyes were a deeper green, set underneath a large brow. He had a wide mouth with thick lips covering uneven teeth that were large and square and green.

Quest of Eight Part Four: The Race to Virkio

Richard Reda

His body was very broad and muscular, his chest and arms – as green as the rest of him – were bare, except for being covered with tattoos, which appeared to move. His hands were as large as his head; his fingers thick and strong with nails that were cracked and broken. His legs were beneath the level of the bridge, but no one was interested in seeing what these looked like.

"Who are you?" shouted Liam, spreading his arms as if to protect the others as he tried to back away.

"I am Sooli Vahn," rumbled the troll. "Are you them?"

"Uh...maybe," said Liam. "It depends."

"Depends on what?" asked the troll, puzzled by the response.

"On whether whoever you were expecting you plan on eating," piped up Sean.

The troll lowered his head as if embarrassed, and shook it slowly from side to side.

"I don't do that anymore," he said. "I won't hurt you. I just don't know if I'm supposed to help you."
Everyone had forgotten about the jackals. In fact, there were no more sounds coming from the forest. It was as if they had disappeared. Everyone's focus now was on the strange creature in front of them.

"Are you a sentinel?" asked Natalie, peeking over Liam's shoulder.

The troll's head jerked up. What might have passed for a smile – or possibly a grimace – spread across his face.

"Yes," he roared. "I am. I mean, really I'm a troll, but I'm a sentinel, too."

A smile, they all decided. It was supposed to be a smile.

"I thought there was no such thing as trolls," said Summer.

"There aren't; not anymore," Sooli Vahn replied, shaking his head slowly. "I'm the last one."

"How long have you been here?" Summer asked.

He extended his right arm and looked at the shifting images. He looked from his wrist up the arm to his shoulder and then over to his left arm from his shoulder down to his other wrist.

"Since right after the Kelpie wars," he said.

No one needed to ask what he meant. He had been here for two thousand years. The markings on his body appeared to provide a history or some kind of accounting of his past. Quinn was more captivated by the tattoos than he was afraid of the creature. He stepped closer to look at the markings. He saw images near the top of the troll's right shoulder. It appeared to be a troll tossing someone or something into its mouth and eating it. There was a cloaked figure in the distance behind the figure of the troll.

"What's that?" he asked, pointing to the moving images.

Embarrassed, the troll once again dropped his head and mumbled, "I don't do that anymore."

"Excuse me," said Lochen. "Can you tell us if there have been any others here before us – recently that is."

He had noticed the brambles that had been cut through and the passage that led into the fortress. Stella had been right. Others had gotten here first. The stone was probably gone. They needed now to learn how long ago and where those individuals had gone. The troll perked up at the question.

"Yes," he said. "I can."

"And...were there?" Lochen continued when he realized that the troll had only indicated that he could answer the question, not that he had indicated what that answer was.

"Yes," he said. "See?"

He motioned to his chest. Everyone moved closer. They saw tattoos of what looked like hobgoblins being led by a one-eyed Rebbercand with an axe. They went into the fortress. The images moved in a stop motion effect, changing one after the other. Then they saw the same group coming out of the fortress and standing on the bridge. Finally, they moved across his chest and faded away. Summer flew around to look at his back.

"These markings are all different," she said. "There's nothing more that tells where they went."

"No," said the troll. "The drawings only show what I see or what I do."

"This doesn't help us at all," said Solveig. "We already knew someone had gotten here first."

The troll dropped his head again and shook it sadly.

"I'm sorry," he mumbled. "The Alchemist's spell only made drawings of what I've seen or what I've done; not of anything beyond that."

"What now?" asked Natalie.

"I don't know," said Lochen. "Without knowing where they were going, we would be proceeding blindly. I suppose Stella could make a guess from her map."

"Oh," said Sooli Vahn proudly. "I know where they're going!'

"You do?" asked Summer.

"Yes," he said.

"And that would be...?" asked Lochen when it was again clear the troll was only answering the specific questions he was being asked.

"They're going to the Venomous Swamp," he said.

"What for?" asked Liam with a sense of heightened concern.

"Because it's the closest place to find a Kelpie," answered the troll, yawning widely as he spoke. "All this thinking has made me really tired."

"In the Swamp?" asked Liam, not really expecting an answer. "There's a Kelpie hidden in the Swamp?"

"Do you have any idea where that might be?" asked Lochen.

Liam thought for a few seconds, considering some options. In the mean time the troll's color seemed to fade. The deep green of his skin took on a grayish cast. He was having difficulty keeping his eyes open. Solveig could see immediately what was happening.

"We need to go," she said. "We can figure the rest of this out on the way."
The troll yawned widely once again. He held onto the bridge tightly with both of his enormous hands to keep himself from falling over.

"I'm sorry I couldn't help you more," he said, his speech becoming slurred. "I'm so tired. If it's all right with you, I'm going to crawl back under my bridge and take a nap."

He didn't wait for an answer. He also didn't make it back under the bridge. His legs gave out and he tumbled gently to the ground. The dust in the dried out moat rose high into the air as his bulk settled down onto the bottom of the ditch. By now he was more gray than green in color, and his hair had thinned out considerably, turning nearly white.

A sense of sadness gripped all of them as they watched in silence. He had fallen asleep before he hit the ground. Soon afterward it was clear that he was not breathing and that his body was rapidly decaying. In minutes, the giant had passed from this life and had turned to a much larger, but essentially the same, pile of dust they had found in the cottage where Beebee had lived.

Their task complete, the long watch of the sentinels was over and they were released from whatever spell the Alchemist had cast.

"What do we do now?" asked Summer.

"It's time to finish this quest," said Lochen.

And so the end began.

Quest of Eight Part Four: The Race to Virkio

Richard Reda

ABOUT THE AUTHOR

Richard Reda spent most of his life working for various agencies and Departments in the Federal Government. He believes this gave him a solid foundation for writing fantasy and fiction, so much so that he was encouraged to return after retirement to write some more. He lives with his wife in Manassas, Virginia, where he retired – the first time.

The *Quest of Eight* series originated as bed time stories for his grandchildren. As the grandchildren got older and the bed time stories got longer, it was suggested to him that he write them down. So he did. One, however, was not enough. Follow the continuing saga in the next chapter - *Part Five: Release of the Demons.*

www.ingramcontent.com/pod-product-compliance
Lightning Source LLC
Chambersburg PA
CBHW071149250626
47159CB00001B/34